Hannah, her green eyes flashing with indignation, thrust the door open so quickly it crashed loudly into the wall behind. 'How dare you!' The switch of red hair shivered between her shoulder blades. She pushed herself at George Bunting, glaring rebelliously up into his eyes which were as dark as coal and at least twelve inches above her own. 'I wouldn't marry you if you were the last man alive.' She flicked her gaze insolently down the length of him, from the neatly cropped waves of his thick, black hair, over the navy blue jacket and grey breeches, right down to the highly polished black leather boots.

'I'm a wealthy man,' he persisted. 'The Tor needs a woman's touch. I want a woman who will give me more sons – strong sons. You'd have the finest home around these parts.' He passed a derisory glance over the little stone cottage and untidy yard. 'What can you make out of a place this size?'

Hannah's chest heaved with anger. 'I'll be no skivvy at Bunting's *Claw*!' She emphasized the derogatory name and felt pleasure when the dark eyes flinched. His square-cut jaw tightened noticeably. 'You'd do well to think on it,' he said stiffly, then strode across the farmyard to the large, grey stallion tethered to the broken five-barred-gate. Grasping the saddle he thrust his booted foot into the stirrup, swung his long leg over the horse's back, and, reining the horse round, he galloped out of the yard without a backward glance.

PROUD HARVEST

Janet Haslam

CORGI BOOKS

PROUD HARVEST
A CORGI BOOK : 0 552 14138 0

PRINTING HISTORY
Corgi edition published 1994

First publication in Great Britain

Set in 10pt Linotype New Baskerville by
Phoenix Typesetting, Ilkley, West Yorkshire.

Corgi Books are published by Transworld Publishers Ltd,
61–63 Uxbridge Road, Ealing, London W5 5SA,
in Australia by Transworld Publishers (Australia) Pty Ltd,
15–25 Helles Avenue, Moorebank, NSW 2170,
and New Zealand by Transworld Publishers (NZ) Ltd,
3 William Pickering Drive, Albany, Auckland.

Reproduced, printed and bound in Great Britain by
Cox & Wyman Ltd, Reading, Berks.

PART ONE

Sins of the Father

Chapter One

1960

'Never!' Fred Critchlow blazed, raising his voice to a pitch
Hannah was not accustomed to hearing from her placid
father. 'I've told you before and I'll keep on telling you.
You're old enough to be her father. I wouldn't agree to
my daughter marrying one of your sons. But you . . .
never!' He gave a disgusted snort.

Hannah's long, red hair, tied in a pony-tail, flicked
from side to side like that of an angry cat. George Bunting
wanted to marry her! This was the first time she had
heard of it, and it did not please her. She had come
upon the conversation by accident. While out collect-
ing the eggs the handle of her basket had broken and
she had been returning to the pantry to get another.
It was so unlike her mild-mannered father to raise his
voice, that when she had heard the angry voices she had
immediately stopped to listen.

She did not have to wait long to know what the
argument was all about. The first few sentences told
her plainly what George Bunting's visit was for. Disbelief
stiffened her short form and the basket and the eggs were
forgotten.

The passage where she stood, between the cottage and
the pantry, was covered over. But one end was open to the
elements and the wind's icy blast rattled down, tangling
her old brown skirt around her legs and adding more mo-
mentum to her irritably dancing pony-tail. She wrapped
her arms around herself, more an act of preservation
than merely from the cold. George Bunting continued

his arrogant assumption that she would think him a good catch. An old man! He must be every day of forty-five, she thought mutinously. And she wasn't even eighteen yet. It was revolting! It was obscene! The very idea made the hairs on the back of her neck stand on end.

'I'm a wealthy man,' her suitor persisted. 'She'll not get a better offer.'

Not get a better offer! Anger boiled in her veins and her long red pony-tail began the agitated twitching again.

Her father gave a sarcastic laugh. 'My Hannah will get the pick of the bunch – when *she* decides she is ready! She's still a child. And even if she wasn't, I'd never agree to her becoming tainted by *your hands*!'

He laid particular emphasis on the last and behind the door Hannah gave a nod of approval. It was not like her father to use hurtful words. But the occasion called for it and he had her full backing.

'That had nothing to do with me!' George Bunting's voice rose in anger. 'It was that silly bitch I took for my first wife. It was her line that was tainted. The Buntings have no bad blood in their veins.'

No bad blood! Hannah gave a snort of disgust. No, he thought his blood was blue! They were an arrogant lot, the Buntings. Upstarts, the residents of Aldale called them. Thought he was the lord of the manor, did this one. His great, great grandfather had built the first house at the top of the Tor, the highest hill in the vicinity. The Tor had then become known as Bunting's Tor. That first building had been small, but over the years each new generation of Buntings had increased its size, until the present house had the scale and bearing of a manor house – and George Bunting got up everyone's nose by conducting himself as if he really was the squire of the district.

It had been that attitude that had been his downfall. Thinking himself too good for the local women, he had gone far afield to find a lady suitable to be his bride. He found one in Sheffield. Her family were very wealthy and he had taken great pleasure in making the fact known to all the locals. It was not until his second son, Sam, was born, that he was to realize taking a bride from a family he knew so little about had been a bad decision. Although closely resembling his first son, Jed, Sam had been born with a deformed hand. The thumb was thicker than normal and the first and second fingers were fused together in one thick digit that ended in a strange point. The other fingers were missing altogether. The hand resembled the claw of a lobster or crab and the local community, only too ready to find fault with George Bunting, had taken great pleasure in changing the name of Bunting's Tor to the derogatory term, Bunting's Claw.

Her father gave another sarcastic bark. 'You can call your dead wife names and you still expect me to hand my daughter over to you? You're despicable . . . ! And mad. You must be to think a young girl would want you.'

'Hannah might be young in years but she has a good head on her shoulders,' George Bunting stated baldly.

'Aye, too good to consider you,' her father scoffed.

'She knows how to run a farm and I've seen the way she works.' George Bunting continued as if her father had not spoken. 'She isn't frightened of getting stuck in or getting her hands mucky. She's just what I need. The Tor needs a woman's touch. And I'm not that old. I want a woman who will give me more sons – strong sons. I'll not make the same mistake twice. I know your Hannah comes from good stock. She'll bear no weaklings.'

A gasp flew from Hannah's lips and her arms tightened instinctively around herself. Not frightened of getting mucky! Good stock! He was looking for a servant and a cow.

It was the final straw. Her large green eyes flashing with indignation, she thrust the door open so quickly it crashed loudly into the wall behind. 'You've got a nerve!' she blazed, and stormed into the kitchen, arms rigid and fists clenched tightly with her fury.

'Hannah!' her father gasped, his face turning white with horror. Then he was reduced to stuttering and stumbling, as he tried to stop her and his words became lost in the awful realization that she had overheard their conversation.

But it did not matter that her father was struck dumb. Hannah had enough words for both of them and she would not be halted. 'How dare you!' The switch of red hair shivered between her shoulder blades. She pushed herself at George Bunting, glaring rebelliously into his eyes, as dark as coal and at least twelve inches above her own. 'I wouldn't marry you if you were the last man alive.' She flicked her gaze insolently down the length of him, from the neatly cropped waves of his thick, black hair, over the navy blue jacket and grey breeches, right down to the highly polished black leather boots. He was in the full riding gear that was his usual mode of dress. Fitting for the lord of the manor, she thought sarcastically. 'I'll be no skivvy at Bunting's *Claw*!' She emphasized the derogatory name and felt pleasure when the dark eyes flinched.

His discomfort did not last long. 'You'd have the finest home around these parts,' he countered sharply, the well-known arrogance returning to his eyes with a flash.

'Oh, you think so, do you?' She placed her hands on the rounded curve of her hips and narrowed her eyes into icy slits. 'Well, I don't share that opinion. I already live in the finest home around these parts.' Her chest heaved with the force of her anger, thrusting her well-developed breasts upwards and outwards.

George Bunting did not miss the action. The dark eyes dropped to her chest and the corner of his mouth twitched.

Neither did her father miss anything. 'Get out of my house,' he blazed, thrusting himself in front of his daughter and stretching his spine so he was almost nose to nose with the taller man. He was well aware his daughter already had a body that could turn men's heads. She was the image of her mother, and Cissie had been one of the most beautiful women around Aldale. It had always worried him – watching Hannah turning into a replica of the woman he had loved so dearly. He could not count the sleepless nights he had endured, seeing the trouble it could get her into, knowing he had a job before him to protect her from the less honourable members of his own sex. He was only thankful she had inherited her mother's fighting spirit along with her looks. It was in the red hair, he had always teased the both of them. But he hoped it was a character that would prevent his daughter being easily led astray. 'And get yourself off to Patty Swain's,' he ground spitefully. 'You'll find her more your age!'

Hannah gave a disbelieving snort. 'I think Patty is more particular than that!' she put in drily. Both men's heads turned sharply to her. 'At least I should have thought she was,' she added without concern, tilting her nose in a manner that closely resembled George Bunting's normal expression. She did not care if she was not supposed to know, let alone speak of the trade Patty Swain conducted from her little cottage in the village and on the many jaunts she took into Derby. Everybody in the village knew about it and Patty showed no shame for the way she earned her living, so Hannah had never been able to understand why it was a forbidden subject. 'But I do know there's nobody here that wants you,' she added pointedly. 'So take my dad's advice and get yourself off!'

'Aye.' Fred Critchlow turned back to his opponent. 'And don't come back. If I live to be a hundred the answer will still be the same.'

George Bunting looked about to protest, then changed his mind. He was at the front door, Hannah and her father close behind, before he spoke again.

'Don't dismiss it so easily, Hannah.' His dark eyes settled pointedly on her face; it could have been his hands, from the shudder that ran through her flesh. 'It would make you a very wealthy woman. You'd want for nothing. I'd get a cleaner in to see to the housework – if that was what you wanted.'

He was changing his tune, she thought sarcastically. Only minutes before he had wanted her because she was good, strong stock! She tossed her head and gave a bark of disbelieving laughter. 'Where from?' she questioned sceptically. He was so hated in the village that the only help he could get was from the silly young girls who thought taking a job up there would get them closer to his eldest son. They never stopped to consider the fact that Jed had not only inherited his father's dark good-looks, but also his lordly arrogance, and his physical allure never kept them there for more than the few weeks it took to find out. She gave another laugh. 'Not if you had an army of cleaners, cooks and bottle-washers!' she declared, her lip curling with distaste.

George Bunting's square-cut jaw tightened noticeably. He turned to her father and received a stony glare in return. 'You'd both do well to think on it,' he said stiffly. Then he spun round and marched across the frost-hardened mud of the little farmyard, to the large, grey stallion tethered to the broken five-barred-gate which hung drunkenly on its rusty hinges.

Grasping the saddle he thrust his booted foot into the stirrup and swung his long leg over the horse's back. Reining the horse round, he paused and passed a derisory glance over the little, stone cottage and untidy yard. 'What can you make out of a place this size?' He directed his scornful gaze at Fred Critchlow. 'You must be like chickens pecking in the dust!'

Hannah's mouth tightened against the insult. But before she could get her angry retort from her lips, her father snapped back, 'We make enough!'

George Bunting gave a sneer. 'Enough!' he mocked. 'To keep a dozen cows and a handful of hens and ducks, and let your daughter live in a ramshackle place like this.

If you thought anything of her you'd be only too happy to let her come to a fine house.'

'Why . . . !' her father began, but never got the time to complete his sentence. The old broom Hannah used to keep the muddy yard in some kind of order was propped against the cottage wall. In an instant it was in her hands. Wielding it in the air, she charged across the yard. Before George Bunting could react, she gave the stallion a hefty thwack on its rump. The grey gave a startled neigh, reared on its hind legs, its front hooves feverishly pawing the air. Then it bolted out of the yard and down the lane, George Bunting swearing volubly as he fought to regain control.

'Oh Hannah!' Fred Critchlow cast his daughter a look of despair. Then he turned to watch the horse and rider hurtling down the lane. Before they reached the bend and were out of sight, the horse slowed and it was obvious George Bunting was back in control. But her father still shook his head at her. 'He could have been killed!' he rebuked.

She glanced him a grim smile. The unexpected anger that had fired him for the past minutes, was gone. He was once more the Fred Critchlow everybody loved: kind and gentle and ready to give a helping hand. 'He's far too good a rider,' she said, excusing her actions to her father, but not to herself. She felt no guilt for what she had done. 'Don't go all soft on me,' she teased affectionately, as she propped the broom up against the wall and followed him inside. 'For a minute there you had me thinking I might have got some of my red-hot temper from my dear old dad, after all!'

'Not so much of the old, if you don't mind. And I've never been known to not stick up for my own,' he pointed out.

'Go on,' she taunted. 'You're as soft as butter.'

'Oh yes!' He cast her a sternly warning glance. 'And butter can be rock hard – when there's a good frost.

And you might just be about to find that out, young lady. Making comments about Patty Swain! How do you know what she gets up to?'

'Eeh, Dad!' She shook her head. 'I'm not daft.'

'No,' he agreed. 'But it isn't very sensible to have such talk in front of other people.'

'I'm not frightened of George Bunting,' she asserted, laying her hands on her hips in the way she had done to Bunting not minutes before.

Her father shook his head, but had to smile at the picture she made. She looked so much like her mother. He had never found a word to explain the colour of the hair his wife and daughter had both been blessed with. It was not ginger and it was not auburn, but a mixture of both. No matter how she turned, what light she was in, a part of it shone and gleamed; sometimes like flames, at others with the sheen of a chestnut colt, even, on occasions, with a redness that was almost scarlet.

'What are you grinning at, Fred Critchlow?' she asked, knowing the thoughts in his head, using the words and manner of her mother to make his smile broaden. She could see he was uneasy about George Bunting and she wanted to make him forget the man and relax.

'Nothing, Cissie,' he replied, rising to the teasing, the way he always did when she was telling him off.

'Then take the smirk off your face and get on with something!'

He lifted his hand to his silver hair and doffed an imaginary hat. 'Yes, yer ladyship,' he said.

But, as Hannah laughed, he fell serious once more. 'You should be careful of George Bunting,' he said, concern deepening the lines on his wrinkled, weatherbeaten face. 'You shouldn't go anywhere near his place.'

'I won't, Dad,' she assured, and reached on tiptoe to plant an affectionate kiss on his cheek. She stood back, her hands resting on his shoulders and her gaze pinned pointedly to his. 'Now, are you going to get those cows in or am I? Because if one of us doesn't do it soon, their udders are going to burst.'

He glanced at the clock on the mantel. 'Aye, you're right – as usual!' He took hold of her hands and stared at the work-roughened skin, and felt his heart dip. If only he could have found a good home for her, he thought. One where she would not have to do man's work. But not with the likes of George Bunting.

'Promise me one thing first,' he said, looking up into her eyes with fatherly concern. 'If he ever comes back when I'm not here, don't let him get over the doorstep.'

She tossed her head, on a laugh affected for her father's peace of mind. 'I'll keep the broom handy,' she replied unconcernedly. She did not want him fretting about it. 'And I wouldn't have any hesitation in using it on him, either!'

He gave a nod. He knew she would not hesitate to use it. In a way it pleased him. But getting a man like George Bunting riled could be playing right into his hands. There was nothing he liked better than a good fight and showing his opponent he could master them. It was a frightening thought. 'I'll go and get the cows in,' he said flatly, took his cap from the hook by the door, placed it on his head, stuck his feet into his wellington boots and went out.

As he crossed the back garden to take the shortest route to the field, he hoped the next few years would fly by. His worst fears were coming true far earlier than he had anticipated. He wanted to see his daughter settled down with a man of her own choosing – when she was old enough to make a wise and proper choice. Until that day he would feel uneasy. Especially with men like George Bunting sniffing around, still of the opinion they were in the dark ages when a wife was something you bartered for. The man had not offered any money for Hannah . . . not yet! But he was not stupid enough to think Bunting would not get around to it, when all else failed. He was too hard-nosed to take refusals and rejections.

Cocking his leg over the wall, Fred Critchlow dropped down into the long, damp grass edging the field. A family of rooks took noisily to the air, disturbed by his intrusion. He looked up, watching their black bodies soaring higher and higher, and wished he could endow his daughter with the same ability to flee from danger at a moment.

'Come up! Come up!' he shouted, swinging his arm high in the air to beckon the two straggling cows still at the bottom of the field to come and join the others, already clustered around the gate. He wanted to get on with the milking, hoping the activity would ease the burdens of his mind. But the cows required no assistance in being led home. As he opened the gate the first one began to meander slowly down the dirt-track leading to the farmyard, followed by the rest of the herd. He walked behind, knowing he was an unnecessary part until they reached the shed, and all he could think of was Hannah and her safety. He did not know what to do, how to persuade George Bunting to leave her alone. But he did know that until he had succeeded he must be extra vigilant in his care for her. It was going to be difficult, but he must make every attempt to always be there with her. He must never leave the path open for George Bunting to sneak in. He must never leave her alone!

Chapter Two

On the day before Christmas Eve, Hannah took the farm collie, Sal, for their usual walk on the hills. It happened every Sunday afternoon. It was the day Aunt Renee made her trip from Derby and Hannah always liked to make herself scarce for the event.

Renee was her father's sister and Hannah had never been able to understand how someone as caring and considerate as he, could be so closely related to someone so selfish and grasping. Renee only made the weekly visits to get a free supply of eggs and vegetables from the plot Hannah and her father cultivated next to the cottage. She had to catch a bus from Derby into the village, then walk all the way up the lane to the farm, there being no transport coming that way. But the long walk never put her off. Rain, snow or shine, she always turned up, red-faced and grumbling.

It made Hannah's blood boil to see her father handing over the stock he had worked so hard to produce and which he could ill afford to give away. But he was too soft to refuse and his sister was too brass-nosed to care that she might be robbing him of his income.

Picking up a stick lying in the grass, Hannah tossed it away. 'Fetch!' she called, and Sal came bounding down the hillside, black and white fur streaked back as she raced into the wind. She quickly retrieved the stick and returned to drop it at Hannah's feet, to be thrown again.

Hannah dutifully obeyed. The stick flew through the air and Sal went streaking after it. Hannah laughed and wrapped her thick, grey duffel coat more tightly around herself. The wind was bitingly cold and had soon put a healthy glow on her cheeks and given the tip of her nose the appearance of a cherry. It whipped her blue skirt tightly round her legs and attempted to lift it up in the air. Fortunately, the straight fitting coat reached almost to her knees and stopped her skirt lifting too high and becoming indecent.

Sal returned the stick, just as the wind pulled the right side of Hannah's hair from beneath the confines of her coat. She had left it hanging loose today, stuffing it inside the coat to control it. Struggling to get the hair out of her eyes, she tossed the stick once more. Sal raced in hot pursuit.

The wind was getting stronger as they got nearer to the top and so Hannah stopped where she was, having no wish to get her head blown off. Sal continued to return the stick and she continued to throw it. While she waited for each return, Hannah gazed out over the countryside she loved so much. The softly undulating hills had always fascinated her. She never tired of looking at the sea of green. Even at this time of year, with the tree branches bare of leaves, the predominant colour was the green of the fields. It was broken only by the higgledy-piggledy criss-crossing of dry stone walls and bushy hedges, which turned the hillsides into a crazy patchwork of unconforming shapes. In the bottom of the valley lay the village, built on either side of the banks of the River Derwent. But the grey-slate tiled roofs of the first houses were all she could see. Over on the far hillside were two small farms, much like her father's. To the north was the Tor and Bunting's Claw, perched on high like the home of some great bird of prey, atop the highest hill around. She smiled at the comparison; not even thoughts of the vulture-like George Bunting were going to spoil her day. It was Christmas and she loved the season which allowed her to add a touch of colour to the cottage and put extra food on the table without having to consider the cost. There was only her father and herself, but they still celebrated in true style. She glanced at her watch. Renee would be gone shortly and she could go home and get on with making the mince pies.

Sal returned the stick and Hannah crouched down and scratched the soft fur on her head. 'You miss the sheep, don't you?' she said. Sal gave a bark, as if she understood. Hannah laughed and tossed the stick away again. Sal was a trained sheepdog and she missed having to do her real job. So did her father, Hannah thought on a sigh, and hoped the winter would not be a hard one. If the bad weather was short they would not have to dip too deep into the money put aside to replace the sheep they had lost in the bad winter of 1955.

Five years and he had not yet been able to replace their little flock, she thought sadly. She comforted herself with the knowledge that spring was not that far away. When it arrived the cattle would not need so much feed and they could re-plant the vegetable patch. At the moment all they had left were a few winter cabbage and the remains of the potatoes. All the brussels and turnips and parsnips had gone, and so had the fruit from the orchard. The months from Christmas to March were always the leanest ones. Winter on the hills never failed to be tough; but they got by.

The wind lifted her hair again and she held it fast and turned to look up at Bunting's Tor. George Bunting's castle! It wasn't fair, she thought bitterly. If her father managed to get some more sheep it would mean he had to rent grazing off the lord and master; their own single field was only just big enough for their dozen cows. Her vision misted and she had to screw her eyes up against the tears the wind caused, as she stared into its blast and across the hills to their nearest neighbour. Her father had scraped and saved all his life. And the likes of George Bunting had been born to all that!

But she would not have swapped. Not for all his money.

It had never made him happy. She turned away, fastening her gaze on the little farmyard nestled on the hillside, the two great oak trees standing at the corner of the cottage walls. 'Home!' she whispered feelingly, and when Sal returned the stick she threw it down the hill and began to retrace her steps. By now Renee would have got her weekly supplies, given her father an ear-bashing for his lack of produce, and be on her way back to the village to catch the bus into Derby, where she lived with her long-suffering husband and daughter.

It was as Hannah reached the bottom of the dirt track the cows used and turned out onto the lane to walk the last few yards home, that she saw the big, grey stallion coming towards her. Sal had run on in front, but now she returned to walk at Hannah's heels, as if she sensed her sudden unease.

'Good afternoon, Hannah.' George Bunting reined the horse to a sudden halt, causing the animal's hooves to skid on the hard surface.

'Afternoon, Mr Bunting.' She made no attempt to keep the stiffness out of her voice. She had no wish to speak to him and she was not afraid of him knowing that. She fixed him with a cool glare, letting her silence speak for her. If he made any move to dismount she would set Sal snapping at the stallion's fetlocks, making it rear as she had done the day he came to the farm. And she did not care if he got hurt.

Fortunately, for him, he made no move to leave the saddle. 'Been for a walk?' he asked, pleasantly enough, but she did not miss the way his dark eyes stripped her of the bulky duffel coat.

'No law against it, is there?' she returned impertinently.

He laughed with an amusement that, although softening his face, could not rid it of the pompous affectation. 'None whatsoever. You're a woman after my own heart, Hannah. Rain, shine or blizzard, I love these hills. They mean everything to me. We have a lot in common.'

'I don't think so, Mr Bunting,' she said, with a bitterness in her voice that matched the wind, her anger accentuated that he dared to presume she was anything like himself. The wind whipped the loose strand of hair across her face. His eyes followed it, lingering on the long richly coloured tress.

'A touch of sunshine in an otherwise gloomy day,' he said, and leaned forward in the saddle, as if about to reach over and remove the strand of hair for her.

Before he had time to touch her, she swiped angrily at her hair, shoving it forcefully back into the collar of her coat. Then she turned quickly away and hurried on, Sal keeping close by her side.

Her father was in the cowshed, perched on a three-legged stool, already begun on the milking.

'I presume she's gone,' she said, as she walked past the row of shiny churns and breathed in the warm animal smell. Stopping by her father, she peered over his shoulder as he studied the cow's udder.

'Aye, she's gone,' he replied drily. He gave a sigh. 'Camomile's got mastitis.'

'Rosemary,' she corrected. She gave all their cows a proper name. Just to give them a number was unfriendly, she told him. But, no matter how hard he tried, he always got them wrong. Buttercup became Daisy, Geranium turned into Poppy. 'It's a good job we don't have a herd of hundreds,' she teased, and went to the cupboard by the door to get the ointment.

'I'll see to it,' she said, after hanging her coat on a nail stuck in the wall for that purpose. 'You get on with the others.'

Her father moved to the next cow in the row and Hannah took up position on the stool and began gently massaging Rosemary's teats with the soothing ointment. She did not tell her father she had bumped into George Bunting. She was relieved he had been in the cowshed and not in a position to have witnessed the meeting. The matter was causing him far more concern than it was causing her and he had tried to put a stop to her Sunday walks altogether, fearing that she might bump into the man. If he knew she had done just that, he would chain her to the table. She smiled fondly at his concern. He was only thinking of her welfare, but she would not let George Bunting frighten her into becoming a prisoner in her own home.

'What had Renee got to say for herself?' she asked, turning her mind to another topic – if not necessarily a more pleasant one.

'The usual.'

She gave an understanding nod and continued to massage the tender udder. She knew exactly what her Aunt's usual was: moaning about the long trek up the hills; suggesting he should deliver to her in their battered old pick-up; telling him the walk up the hill would kill her one of these days. 'She can always go to a shop and save her strength,' she remarked drily. It was only her own insistence that if Renee wanted her vegetables for free, she had to come and fetch them, that had stopped him giving in and taking her a regular supply.

'She is my sister!' He stopped milking and cast her a reproving glance.

'Yes,' she returned knowledgeably. 'And you're soft, Fred Critchlow.' She straightened herself upright, Rosemary's treatment completed. 'And if she wants them bad enough, she'll make the journey.' She returned the ointment to the cupboard, then moved on to begin milking Delphinium. She did not blame her father for being too kind for his own good, it just made her hopping mad when she saw his good nature being taken for granted. If Renee had done anything in return she would never have spoken a word on the matter. But with Renee it was a one-way street. She took all, expecting it as her right, yet never gave anything in return.

'I suppose you're right,' her father reluctantly agreed. Then the matter was dropped while the milking was completed.

'It's blowing up a good one.' Fred Critchlow bent his head back to stare at the darkening sky. He gave a grimace. Then he turned to fasten the shed door, closing the cows in safely for the night.

Hannah looked up, as she slipped her arms into her coat again. It had been blowing all day, but the force had increased greatly since she had come down from the hills. The clouds were now skittering across the sky with alarming haste and the boughs of the nearest oak tree were bending to bounce against the slates of the cottage roof. 'We'll not get much sleep tonight unless that stops,' she said pointedly, recalling the last high winds, when the branches had kept up a continual thumping on the roof for the entire night.

Her father gave a sigh. 'I was going to lop them off.'

'Yes – you were!' She fixed him with a telling stare. But she could not place all the blame on his shoulders. He always needed badgering into doing anything out of the normal routine but, after two days of nagging to get the ladder and the saw out, she had given up.

'It's too late now. I'll do it first thing in the morning.'

Yes, you will, she thought, determined to get the ladder out for him and push him up it. But if she told him of her plans he would only start fretting about having enough time to get everything done, so she changed the subject. 'We'd better get the birds shut in,' she said, and began to round the hens and ducks up and get them into the coops.

As the evening wore on the wind got stronger. The overhanging oak branch battered relentlessly on the roof and the window-panes shuddered with each enormous gust.

Hannah made the mince pies. Then she got the small Christmas cake out of the cupboard, it was already covered

23

in marzipan and she added a layer of white icing.

'That will have to do,' she said, as she stood back to survey the one forlorn robin and a much-used sprig of paper holly. She had intended getting some new decorations for the cake, but had forgotten.

Her father did not reply. He was sleeping soundly in a chair in front of the fire. Hannah shook her head in disbelief, wondering how anyone could sleep with such a racket going on. She looked around the room, at the little Christmas tree perched on top of the dresser. She had remembered to get some new shiny balls for that. And they had plenty of holly around the room and a huge bunch of mistletoe hanging from the ceiling. It was only the cake that was lacking and once she had tied a big, red ribbon around it that did not look so bad.

When there was nothing further she could do in preparation for Christmas Day, she threw a shovelful of coal on the fire and got out the sewing-box and a pile of mending that had been awaiting her attention for several weeks. She hated sewing but needed something to keep her mind occupied and away from the worrying imaginations of what was going on outside.

She had just finished sewing the torn sleeve of one of her father's shirts, when the light began to flicker. Her gaze leapt anxiously to the pink glass globe. 'Don't you dare go off!' she warned, but nevertheless put the sewing down and went to get a supply of candles out ready . . . just in case.

When she picked up the sewing again she had three candles standing on the table. A fourth candle, along with a box of matches, was standing on the mantelpiece by the side of a brass-framed photograph of her mother and father; within arms reach should they suddenly be plunged into darkness. She glanced at her father in the chair opposite: eyes closed, mouth open and snoring gently, yet his pipe somehow managing to remain stuck to his bottom lip. Sal was curled into a tight ball at his feet.

An extra strong gust hit the cottage. The window rattled and the walls seemed to shudder under the attack, and the oak tree sounded as if it was battering a hole right through the slates. Hannah gave a gasp, her eyes pivoted to the ceiling and she begged for the gale to diminish. Strong winds always disturbed her, making her fear for the safety of the stock. The cowshed was so old and battered that it looked as if a breeze would flatten it. And this was far from being a breeze.

She was forcing herself to work the needle, when her father began to rouse himself.

'What time is it?' He scraped his fingers through his hair, making it stand up in silver spikes on the top of his head, and screwed his bleary eyes up to focus on the clock.

'Quarter-past-ten,' she replied.

'I think I'm off.'

She looked askance. 'You don't expect to sleep up there?' She lifted her gaze to the ceiling, just as another terrific gust sent the oak tree dancing with renewed zeal. There was an ominous slithering sound, followed by the crash of a roof slate hitting the ground. She lowered her eyes slowly to her father's face. 'It would be impossible,' she said, adding a sigh of resignation when he ignored her and stood up. The noise would keep her up all night and she would have preferred to have his company.

He gave a shrug. 'I'll sleep,' he replied confidently. 'You're always telling me I could drop off on a clothes line.' He gave her a grin that put a smile on her face.

'I'll stay here and finish this lot,' she looked down bleakly at the pile of mending, but was grateful it was there to give her something to help pass what she knew was going to be a very long night. 'If the lights don't go out first,' she added, as the light-bulb faded, flickered several times, then managed to find the strength to return to full brightness.

'Don't wear yourself out.'

'I won't,' she promised.

'Night, love,' he said, and made for the stairfoot door.

'Night, Dad.' She smiled as he opened the door and Sal bounded up the stairs before him, ready to take up her usual sleeping place, curled between his legs.

The lights continued to flicker, but did not go out. At times she began to think the wind was abating, then it would suddenly roar to life again, twice as bad as before. Her ears were pricked to the sound with each stitch she worked. It was almost midnight before she put the last of the sewing down with a grateful sigh. Her eyes felt like lead and her eyelids were fighting her desire to stay awake. Pushing the sewing-box aside she went over to the sofa, pulled up the crocheted blanket that covered the old, worn leather, and lay down, throwing the blanket over her. The light was left on. She had no intention of going to sleep. She only wanted to rest. She did not want to be so worn out that she was useless when daylight finally came, was her last thought.

She was in a cave. There was a strange noise and darkness surrounded her. Her mouth was filled with a bad taste – dry, like dust. She struggled, fighting off a great spider's web that had closed around her. Her fingers tangled in the holes as she tore frantically at the restricting mesh that trapped her arms and legs. It fell on her face and she gave a startled cry and pushed harder to get it away from her. It took several attempts before her face was clear and she felt safe to pause to collect her breath. It was then that reality returned. The fire had burnt low, but the smouldering coals still emitted enough glow to let her see where she was – lying on the sofa, the spider's web nothing more than the crocheted blanket.

Giving a gasp of relief, she sat up. The noise was only the continuing wind and it was dark because the electricity had finally failed. Telling herself she had nothing to fear, she pushed herself up off the sofa. But her heart was still thumping in her chest, as she made her way to the candle standing on the mantelpiece. It was as her trembling hand struck the match, that she realized the moaning, buffeting of the wind was now accompanied by another noise: a strange creaking, as if something was under great strain. And the taste in her mouth, the dust, was still there. It filled her nostrils and tickled the back of her throat.

Holding the match high, she turned around. The pale glow radiated round the room and her heart stilled. The floor was littered with crockery that had previously been on the dresser. Her father's pipe-stand lay on the floor, his collection of pipes scattered around. So was all the holly, and the mistletoe was rocking drunkenly over the back of the chair her father had been sitting in.

'Dad!' she suddenly said, her voice, trapped in fear, little more than a whisper. She quickly turned back to the candle, set light to the wick and tossed the match into the fire just as it burnt her finger. 'Dad!' she cried, grabbed the candle and hurriedly picked her way over the debris to the stairfoot door.

Her heart was thumping like an express train as she took the first stair. It was not until she was halfway up and had turned the corner in the narrow winding staircase, that she saw the truth.

'Dad! Dad!' she screamed, over and over again, her voice rising with dread as her terrified eyes stared at the sight before her. She could not get up the stairs. The way was barred. The narrow landing above her head was filled with twisted branches that seemed to move and grow in the flickering yellow light from the candle, as it shook with the tremor that ran through her entire body. Above the branches was the blackness of the night sky. The oak tree had fallen, taking the roof off the cottage.

'Dad!' she screamed, not knowing what else to do.

There was no reply and tears blinded her eyes and the invading branches looked more grotesque through her misted vision. She sank down, sitting on the stairs and clinging to the candle with both hands. Emotion tore through her in great waves as intense as the wind that still gusted above her head, its moaning noise now seeming to take on a cackling laugh that mocked her distress.

'Dad! Please, Dad!' she begged. But she knew it was useless. If he could have come to her, he would have. It was several minutes before she regained enough control to think she should be doing something. He might be hurt, she realized. He could be trapped. She did not stop to question why he had not called out. In an instant she was clawing at the branches, forcing a way through. The gnarled, dry, old wood tore at her flesh and tangled in her hair, as she scrambled through, heaving herself upwards towards the great trunk. The wind continued to come in shuddering gusts and the tree and the cottage trembled. But she had no thought for her own safety. Getting to her father was the only thing on her mind and she was spurred by an inner anger that she had wasted so much time doing nothing.

It took an eternity to get herself on to the trunk. When she finally made it, she paused, catching her breath and taking in the full extent of the damage. Her heart sank. The tree filled the landing and blocked the space that had previously been her father's bedroom door. She reached for the candle she had lodged with difficulty in the branches. Her hair knotted to a branch and she yanked it free, leaving a huge clump attached. Clasping the candlestick tightly in one hand, she forced herself onwards, inching along the rough trunk. Her skirt tore as it, too, fell foul of sharp, clutching branches. The candle's flame flickered and almost extinguished several times, as the wind tore past the open hole above her head.

'Don't go out!' she begged, and wished she had thought to bring the box of matches with her. To be closed in darkness with all this was too horrible to contemplate. But she had gone too far to go back. Her father always kept a torch by the bed, she told herself, clutched the candle more tightly in her hand and carried on.

She had reached what would have been the bedroom door, when there was a mighty crack behind her, followed by an ominous crunching and crumbling. The whole framework of the cottage rocked, so did the tree.

She gave a startled cry and had to grasp the trunk with both hands to stop herself falling. The candle fell from her grip. 'No!' she begged, as she stared fearfully at the flickering flame, balancing precariously in the lower branches. She wanted to grab it back, but for several seconds was too stunned. The after-effects of shock trembled violently through her limbs. A sharp point on the trunk pierced her palm, but she could not lift her hand away to free it of the pain.

It was only seeing the candle's flame was about to set the tree alight, that spurred her back to life. She reached for it, having to lean so far down that she almost fell. With a sigh of relief she righted herself, the candle once more in her grip. She held it high and looked around. The walls to either side were still intact. But the tree had now forced her own bedroom door off its hinges. Through the opening she could see the outside wall of her bedroom had collapsed.

The place was falling around her ears, she thought. But the fear for her own safety was overcome by the need to get to her father. Without another thought for the tumbling masonry, she resumed the slow crawl forward.

She was well into the remains of the bedroom before she could see clearly. Holding the candle up above her head to cast its glow and give a better view, she froze.

The tree had fallen across the bottom half of the bed. The bed's legs had given under the impact and the bed was crushed. The huge trunk was lying right where her father's legs would have been and the top half of the bed was obliterated by a pile of roof slates and broken wooden rafters. The only indication that anyone was there was a small area of blue-and-white-striped pyjama in the region of her father's thigh, and protruding from beneath the great weight of the trunk was a furry, black and white tail.

The candle rocked unsteadily in her hand and tears swelled in her eyes. Before they had time to run down her cheeks, she was scrabbling down the rest of the trunk. She left part of her skirt on the bottom-most branch, but did not notice. Her father was buried and she had to get him out.

She had to get to the far side of the bed before she could reach the tiny area between it and the corner of the wall that was oddly clear of debris. The rough bark took the skin off the back of her thighs, as she slid quickly to the floor. But she hardly noticed the pain. Putting the candle down by her feet, she began tearing feverishly at the debris covering her father.

'Dad! Dad!' she screamed, flinging roof slates and broken wood aside with no consideration about where they were going. Tears gushed from her eyes. Before she had cleared the rubble from his face she knew he was dead. Even when she could see him and knew it was futile, she continued to remove the broken slates; though her actions slowed and she cleared the remainder away with a reverence that was filled with the love she had for him.

When the last bit of debris was removed, she gazed despairingly at the trunk which lay over his crushed legs, at the pathetic little tail that stuck out from beneath.

'Oh, Dad!' she said, placing her hands against the trunk and giving a mighty shove. It did not move. The wind could make it tremble, but all her strength was useless against the great weight.

Feeling a fresh flood of tears welling in her eyes, she sank to the floor. Her Dad was gone, and so was Sal. It was right, she thought, looking from the tail that strangely had got away without any damage, to her father's face. Sal, who had never left his side except for the Sunday afternoon walk with her, had gone with him. It gave her a little consolation to think they were still together.

I hope there are sheep where they have gone, she thought. Then, with no regard for the wind whistling over her head and chilling her flesh, she wrapped her arms round her legs, dropped her head on to her knees, and gave herself up to despair.

Chapter Three

Hannah had no recollection of the passing of time. She did not notice the moment the candle finally gutted. Dawn broke and she looked up to find the sky lightened to a dirty grey and the wind, though still blowing strongly, no longer of the strength of the night-time gale. When she looked down at the candle it was to find it extinguished, the cold hardness of the melted wax indicating it had been that way for some time.

She also found she was too numb to move. She had been sitting so long exposed to the cold elements that her limbs had frozen, ceasing to function. Realizing she needed to get help, she forced her arms to uncurl from her legs. It took several minutes. She could almost hear her joints creaking. Her legs proved more difficult. There was not enough room to stretch them out fully in the confined space and she could not rid them of the numbness and regain the strength to stand up. When she attempted to use her arms to pull herself up onto the bed, they also lacked the strength. She fell back with a groan of despair, and one of pain, as she landed on the hard, metal candlestick.

Comforting herself with the knowledge that she was still aware enough to feel pain, she sat back to wait, praying that someone would come by and see what had happened. But it was Christmas Eve. Everyone would be busy with their preparations. It was not a reassuring thought. The lane running past the farm only led to Bunting's Tor. After that it diminished to nothing more than a footpath across the Tor and down the other side. It was not the season to see a constant flow of hikers passing by. And with the present weather she could not imagine any of the villagers taking a leisurely stroll.

No-one would come – until it was too late – she told herself, just as a loud, disgruntled 'moo' came from the cowshed.

They needed feeding. They needed milking. The ducks and hens would be going berserk still shut in their coops. She tried again to push herself up, again she fell back with a thud. Her head began to spin and she had to rest it on her knees for several seconds before her senses returned to normal.

'Please, someone, come!' she begged.

'Fred! Hannah!'

At first she thought she was dreaming. The voice, seeming to be in answer to her plea, could only have been drummed up by her imagination.

'Fred! Are you there? Hannah! Answer me!'

'Yes,' she called, but her voice was weak, the sound little more than a whisper.

'Fred!' The voice came louder, more insistent. 'Hannah! Where the blazes are you?'

'Christ, Dad! I can't get up the stairs. The bloody tree is blocking the way.' It was a second voice and now she recognized them: George and Jed Bunting. She knew it was Jed and not Sam from the coarseness of the words. Sam would not have resorted to such harsh language. For the briefest moment she pictured the darkly handsome Jed, who was the image of his father, in both looks and arrogance. But it did not matter who had come to get her out – just so long as someone had come. 'Here,' she called, her voice still letting her down. They did not hear.

'Get out of my way. Let me see.' It was the first voice again: George Bunting angrily pushing his son aside. 'Christ Almighty!' There was a moment's silence. Then, 'Hannah! Hannah!'

'Here,' she called again. 'I'm here.' Her voice gained strength, but still not enough to be heard above the wind. She reached behind and found the candlestick. The cold metal felt icy to touch but she wrapped her fingers round it and knocked it against a broken roof slate. The sound was little more than a tap, could have been any one of a hundred branches blowing in the wind. And she had thought her arms could lift her up; she gave a groan of self-reproach.

'Hannah!' George Bunting called again.

She lifted the candlestick again, gathered all her strength and threw it against the slate. 'Here!' she called, her voice coming so suddenly loud and clear that it actually startled her. 'Here!' she repeated, feeling gratitude to the unknown force that had returned her voice, swell up inside her and threaten to close her throat. Quickly swallowing it back, she called again.

They heard. She heard Jed say so. His father abruptly shut him up, then called, 'Hannah, is that you?'

'Yes,' she returned feebly, feeling her strength ebbing now she had made her presence known.

'Where's your father?'

She looked to the bed and felt emotion clog her throat and could not reply.

The silence was enough for George Bunting to get the message. 'Don't worry, we'll get you out,' he called.

The confidence in his voice made tears flow from her eyes. She was going to be saved. It was as if the realization had sunk in only at that moment. Her head flopped against her knees, in the position she had spent the night, and she began to sob, only this time her tears were those of gratitude.

'Are you at the front or the back?' The insistence of his voice told her it had not been the first time he had asked the question.

She lifted her head, brushing her untimely emotion aside. 'Back,' she called.

'Are you trapped by the tree?'

'No,' she returned flatly. Not me, she thought, and

looked once more at her father's body, then at Sal's sad tail.

He did not reply. She heard him hurriedly instruct Jed to get round the back. They were there in seconds. She heard George Bunting declaring it was the only way; Jed telling him it was stupid. In the next moment she heard the sound of boots scraping against the bark.

Praying that the precariously positioned trunk would remain firm and what was left of the cottage walls keep standing long enough for him to reach her, she listened with bated breath to each laboured step.

It did not take him long. There were no branches on the bottom half and the rough bark provided a reasonable footing. He slipped twice: each occasion celebrated by a flow of explicit oaths from himself, and a hastily indrawn breath from Hannah, as she pictured the fancy riding boots getting scratched and the spotless breeches and jacket getting soiled.

She had been right about the boots. The rest had been exchanged for plain, black trousers and a thick, woollen sweater of olive-green. But when his dark head finally appeared round the remains of the wall, it did not matter what he was wearing. She just felt like crying all over again. 'Christ Almighty!' He stopped, poised on the trunk like a frog about to leap. He looked at Fred Critchlow's body lying on the bed. Then to the bedraggled figure hunched in the corner: broken twigs tangled in her hair; clothes all torn; no part of her visible flesh free from cuts, bruises and the stain of dried blood.

'Are you hurt?' It seemed a ridiculous question to ask. He could see she was in a bad way, but had meant did she have any broken bones or the like.

She shook her head and he gave a great sigh of relief. Then he let himself down carefully into the small space she was occupying. He reached his hand down to her. 'Come on,' he urged, when she hesitated. He was eager to get her away from her father's body.

She shook her head again. His mouth tightened.

'No,' she quickly put in, understanding he thought she was reluctant to touch him because of who he was. 'I don't know if I can move,' she explained, attempting a smile that came out all lopsided. She lifted her arm and placed her hand in his and tried to push herself up. Nothing happened. Her legs were still locked in the bent position. 'See . . . !' She grimaced at her own inability. 'My legs won't move.'

The last had been unnecessary. He could now see that her fingers were blue from the cold. 'Christ! You're frozen.' He began to rub her hand between both of his own. 'When did it happen? How long have you been here?'

'In the night,' was her only reply. She had no knowledge of what time she had woken up, how long she had slept.

He emitted several voluble curses, then hoisted her up and threw her over his shoulder. Taking no notice of the gasps of pain coming from behind his back, he climbed on to the tree trunk once more and began the downward journey. Going down proved far trickier than coming up. His boots slipped on the bark, and with his hands holding tight to Hannah he was having to rely on his legs for balance. On several occasions she visualized them both landing in a heap amongst the winter cabbage, which lay below them. When he finally reached a point where he could hand her down into Jed's arms, she felt giddy with relief.

'What shall we do with her?' Jed asked.

'Get her into the car. She needs to be got warm. Fred's gone. There's nothing to do for him that can't wait until later. We'll take her home first.'

Hannah's mind immediately revolted against being taken to Bunting's Tor. Her head jolted upright. 'No,' she began to protest. But the suddenness of the action made her head reel. Her eyes seemed to be rolling around inside her brain, knocking her thoughts away before they were fully formed. She felt her body go limp like a rag doll and her head lolled backwards, as if her neck had turned to jelly. Her vision settled hazily on the cowshed. 'The milking,' she said, hearing her own voice as if coming from a distance, not sure if she had actually spoken out the words.

'We'll see to all that,' she heard George Bunting reply, from an even greater distance. The next moment a grey wave came along and washed her into oblivion.

*   *   *

Hannah opened her eyes on to a vision. The biggest fire she had ever seen, roared up the chimney of a large marble fireplace. She was cocooned in a soft blanket, in a bed that was strange to her, in a room that was unknown. It was not a bedroom, but a large sitting room filled with furniture of a quality she had only dreamed of.

'Where was she?' she asked herself, and despite the fire's heat, shivered.

Pushing herself up on her elbows, she took a good look around. There was a large three-piece-suite of green velvet and the curtains were matched to the same shade. There were two leather, high-backed chairs which showed none of the scuffing of the old worn sofa at home. On the mantelpiece stood an array of Crown Derby china and a pair of flamboyant silver candelabra. And the floor was covered in a thick pile carpet a couple of shades darker than the curtains and suite.

'Where was she?' she questioned again. She looked down at the bed. The pink satin eiderdown was as strange to her as everything else. And . . . !

She pushed the blanket away and gazed bewilderedly at the white broderie anglaise nightdress she was wearing. It was not her own nightdress. She was sure she had never seen it before. But why was she wearing it? And why was she there – wherever *there* might be?

She was still puzzling over the dilemma when the door opened.

'Hannah! You're awake.' Sam Bunting showed his clear pleasure at the unexpected development.

'Sam?' She gazed at him blankly. It was several seconds before a frown creased her brow. She looked round the room once more: Bunting's Claw! She should have known. There could not be another house around these parts that was so extravagant. But why . . . ?

'How are you feeling?' Sam closed the door behind him and came into the room, his deformed left hand hidden inside the pocket of blue denim jeans. He was halfway across the floor when the veil slowly lifted from Hannah's mind.

Clutching the blanket back, she pulled it up to her chin. The previous night, the gale, the fallen tree, all came back to her. She could see her father lying covered by the fallen roof, Sal's little tail, her body squashed beneath the great oak tree. She could feel the cold, icy air wrapping around her as it swept through the roofless cottage and the pain of her stiff legs as George Bunting hoisted her over his back. And with the memories came the realization that her father had gone and, worse still, what being at Bunting's Tor could mean for her.

'Where's your dad?' Her voice shook as she asked the question. Her own father was dead and his death had put her in the very position he would have done everything to avoid.

'He's down at your place.' Concern shadowed Sam's dark eyes. He raked the fingers of his right hand through the black hair that was so like his father's. 'Jed is with him . . . and men from the village. They're trying to move the tree.' He paused and sucked his bottom lip. 'They got your dad out earlier,' he added gently.

She gave a nod. Emotion rose from the pit of her

stomach. It clogged her lungs, building up a pressure inside her chest that made her breathing become laboured. She clutched at her throat, suddenly sweating and gasping for breath.

'It's all right, Hannah.' Sam quickly bent over her, resting his hands on her shoulders. 'It's all over now. You're going to be fine. Just relax. Let yourself relax.' He pushed her gently back against the pillow and continued to speak soft words of reassurance.

It took a while, but she finally managed to calm her rapid breathing. Then she lay staring up into Sam's anxious face. All she could think was that her father was dead and she was at the mercy of George Bunting. When he had appeared up the oak trunk she had been so grateful to him for saving her life. Now she wished she had been killed along with her father and Sal, gone to a place where George Bunting could not get his hands on her.

'All right now?' Sam peered anxiously into her eyes and she gave a nod. 'The doctor will be back to see you this evening.' When she frowned, he said, 'The doctor has been once already, but you weren't aware of it.'

She frowned again. What else had happened to her that she had not been aware of? She thought of the nightdress. She was naked beneath. Who had put her in it?

'He said to give you warm drinks and soup . . . if you woke up,' Sam continued, with little concern for the distressing thoughts going through her head. 'I've got some chicken broth ready-made. Shall I get you a bowl?'

She shook her head. How could he expect her to eat? It would choke her. 'Don't leave me,' she begged. The words slipped from her lips and she was not sure where they had come from.

He smiled. 'I won't be far away. I'll leave the door open if you like. You'll be able to see through to the kitchen from here.' He paused. 'You should eat something. Get some warmth inside you.'

She felt tears pressing at her eyes. Sam did not understand. He thought she was afraid of being alone. It was his father she was afraid of. But she could not tell him that.

'I want to go home,' she said feebly, knowing it was a futile request. If her memory served her correctly she had no home to go to. And even if she had, she could not see George Bunting allowing her to go, now he had got her in his clutches.

Sam shook his head. 'You can't go home,' he said. Then, as if reading her mind, added, 'If they can move the tree there won't be much of the cottage left. But I don't hold much hope of them getting it moved. Besides, you need looking after for the time being.'

'But I can't stay here. What about the animals? They need feeding. The cows need milking!'

'Dad is sorting all that out. So you've no need to go worrying. Now, I'm going to get that broth.' He stood upright and took his hands from her shoulders.

As he moved away Hannah's eyes dropped to his left hand. She had not intended to do it, it just happened. Her gaze fastened on to the claw like pincers and followed them as he drew back. It was not until the hand was hastily stuck inside his pocket, that she looked up to meet his gaze and knew exactly what she had done.

His head fell forward, his neck seeming to diminish into his shoulders. 'I'm sorry,' he said, unable to look her in the eyes.

'I . . .' she began. But he spun on his heels and hurried from the room, giving her no time to complete her apology.

She pressed her head into the pillow and stared at the ceiling and hated herself. He had been so nice, only showing consideration for her well-being. The hand had been touching her for ages and she had not noticed, had not felt anything different from the other, normal one. She gave a groan of contempt, aimed at herself. In the space of a second she had hurt him as surely and swiftly as if she had given a slap to his face. She had asked him not to leave her because she felt she had found a friend: one who would help protect her. Now she had alienated him, making him think she was no better than the villagers who shunned him and made loud comments about being touched with the devil's mark.

'Oh, Dad!' she whispered. 'What am I going to do?' But she knew her father could not help her now. She was on her own, had to make her own decisions.

What decisions? she wondered bleakly. She had no money to repair the cottage – if it could be repaired. So she had nowhere to go, nowhere she could insist George Bunting immediately take her.

She turned bleakly to the fire. The flames were roaring up the chimney and its heat still filled the large room, but she shivered. Fear, she told herself. It was impossible to be cold in such a warm room. She hesitated uncertainly. Oh no! she begged. She was not ill, she insisted, could not be ill, not here! Her legs ached but that was only because she had sat so still and stupidly waited until George Bunting could come and be a knight on a white charger – when she should have been getting herself out and going to the village to get help.

She was still berating herself for not having the sense she was born with, when Sam returned.

He was carrying a tray containing a bowl of broth. He smiled at her, but she could see the uncertainty from her thoughtless reaction was still in his eyes. Although she ordered herself not to look at his left hand, she did not miss the tea-towel that was draped purposely around it – hiding it from view.

Her heart turned inside her chest, but she felt that to make any comment would only have added to his shame. So she remained silent and watched him cross the room and her mind's eye was filled with the sad, little boy who used to stand alone in the school playground.

'Sit yourself up.' It was an order, but not with harshness, only a gentle demand for her own good.

The thought of food was still unpalatable to her. But she could see he would not allow her to refuse, so pushed herself slowly up the bed, pulling the blanket with her and tucking the edge tightly under her chin.

It was as he placed the tray across her lap that she gave another shiver. 'Are you cold?' He glanced at the leaping flames of the fire, then frowned into her face.

'Not really.' It was only a half-lie – half of the time she was cold – the other half she was burning hot. 'The room is plenty warm enough. It's just . . .' she hesitated unsurely.

'Just that you got frozen stiff as a board,' he put in. 'So get some of this inside you. It's just what you need. Nothing sticks to the ribs better than a good bowl of broth.'

She gave a little laugh, then found herself fighting tears. It had been one of her father's favourite sayings for good hot food, 'It'll stick to your ribs.' Now she would never hear him say it again. On a little gasp she dropped her head and let the tears fall: for her father who was gone; for herself, because she did not know what she was going to do.

'There now!' Sam lifted the tray from her shaking legs and placed it aside on a small table. Then he rested his good hand on her shoulder and spoke comfortingly to her, as he had done before. But his left hand remained hidden beneath the tea-towel.

She bit her lip but her tears would not subside. Sam's concern only made them worse. Minutes before she had made obvious her revulsion for his hand. She had hurt him, yet he could push that hurt aside and still be nice to her. 'I'm . . . I'm sorry . . .' she stammered, brushed her tears aside and looked up into his face with remorse.

His smile was so gentle that a fresh spurt of tears rolled down her cheeks. 'It's only natural,' he said, giving her shoulder a little squeeze with his right hand. 'You've lost your dad. It's all been a big shock. You're bound to feel a bit low.'

She gave a watery smile. A bit low was not how she would have explained it. She felt in the depths of despair, totally lost and very frightened. She did not know what to expect when George Bunting came home, which would happen sooner or later. She did not like to admit it, but he had saved her life and, it seemed, was now seeing to her farm for her. She was beholden to him. It was a harrowing thought. With a great sigh, she sank down the bed once more. 'I can't eat anything,' she said, suddenly wanting Sam to be gone, to be alone to try and think and work out what she was going to do.

But Sam had other ideas. 'Yes you can!' he insisted, quickly returned the tray to her lap, sat down on the edge of the bed and began to spoon-feed her, all the time keeping his deformed hand concealed by the tea-towel.

When he was satisfied he could not scrape another spoonful out of the bowl, he left her to rest.

The hot food had helped. She felt warmer inside, a bit more like her old self, and the shivering bouts appeared to have come to an end. It was not many minutes before she fell to sleep.

It was the noise of dogs barking that woke her. Rousing herself, she rested on her elbows and looked through the window. She could see the large, stone, stable-block across the yard, but no signs of life. Then she heard an engine. In the next moment George Bunting's dark green Jaguar went slowly past the window, followed by a cow, then another.

Rosemary! Camomile! Poppy! Her father's cows! All of them; followed by Jed in the Land Rover with a cacophony of clucks and quacks coming from the back.

What was he doing? She felt something heavy sink low in her stomach. He had brought all their stock up to the Tor. He obviously thought she was there to stay.

43

It was too much! If he thought he could claim all her stock . . . as well as her!

She was halfway out of bed when Sam came back. This time his left hand was stuffed into his pocket.

'What's going on?' she demanded. 'I've just seen all *my* cows go past the window!'

'That is what I was coming to tell you.' He rushed forward, grabbing her arm before she could get both feet to the ground. 'Dad has brought them up here so they can be properly looked after. Get back in bed,' he added insistently. 'You should not be getting up yet.'

'I'm fine.' She brushed angrily at his hand but he refused to let go. 'I want to know what he thinks he is playing at!' She glared furiously into Sam's face, her mother's fighting spirit brought back with force, more by the realization that George Bunting had arrived, than any real concern for her stock. Whatever else he might be, the man was a master when it came to tending animals and she knew hers would be safe with him. It was herself she was not so sure about.

'Hannah! Hannah! Calm yourself. We're not trying to steal them. They couldn't be left down there without anyone to tend them . . . now could they?' He looked at her with a pained expression.

She stared at him for a long moment, unwilling to concede, then finally realized she had to agree with him. 'But he should have asked me first,' she added pointedly, not prepared to totally back down. George Bunting was presuming too much. He might have saved her life but that did not mean he could take liberties.

In the next moment the cause of her distress appeared at the door.

'What's going on?' he demanded. His dark eyes filled with suspicion as they rested on his son's hand, fastened to her arm, and she hovering half-in and half-out of bed.

'Hannah was of the opinion you had taken up cattle rustling. She was on her way to sort you out. *I* am trying

44

to get her back into bed,' Sam explained pointedly, and let go of her arm and squared round to his father. 'The doctor said she was to stay in bed until he had seen her again.'

George Bunting gave a grunt and came into the room. Hannah was not sure if the sound had been one of approval or disapproval. But she did know his eyes were assessing her with far too much familiarity. The cotton nightdress suddenly seemed very thin. She leapt back into bed, pulling the blanket close to her chin.

'How are you feeling now?' He pulled off his brown leather gloves and tossed them on a chair. Then he removed his battered old Barbour jacket and handed it to Sam.

Hannah watched each movement carefully, unable to take her eyes off him. He was still wearing the olive-green jumper. But now it was accompanied by a pair of old, brown, cord trousers and a pair of black wellington boots that were much too dirty to have come inside the house. She had seldom seen him wearing ordinary clothes and he looked so different, almost normal.

He came over to the bed. 'Are the legs painful?'

'No. I'm fine now.' She folded her arms, even with Sam in the room she felt she needed protection. 'How's the farm?' The cottage, her home, was of more importance than her own indisposition.

He hesitated, stuck his hands in his pockets and studied her for a long moment.

'Is it that bad?' Sam took the words right out of her mouth.

She sat up straight, clutching the blanket to her, knowing the answer before he spoke.

He gave a nod. 'I'm afraid so.'

She gave a groan, her fingers tightening round the satin edging of the blanket. 'What . . . ?' she began, then fell silent. Did she really want to know the depressing details?

45

George Bunting obviously thought so, for he continued, 'We had to get a crane to lift the tree to get your dad out.'

'And Sal?' They could not have left Sal. She could not bear it if they had. Her eyes pivoted to his face, begging the right reply.

He gave another nod and she visibly shrank with relief. 'We got them both out,' he said. He did not tell her there had been sweet little left of Sal for them to remove. The collie had taken the full force and apart from the tail the only evidence of the dog's presence was a flattened patch of black and white fur. But, as if he had known it was what she would have wanted, he had forced himself to pick it up and place it on the stretcher at Fred's feet, giving the order that it was to be buried with him.

'After we'd got them out we tried to lift the tree away.' He paused, his large shoulders lifted on an eloquent shrug. Hannah bit hard on her lip. 'The walls had gone,' he continued slowly. 'As soon as the tree lifted, the whole of the back wall collapsed. Most of the rest followed like a pack of cards.'

She gave a little whimper and bit harder on her lip. Everything was gone: her home; its contents; even her clothes. She had nothing . . . nothing at all!

'Go and make some tea,' George Bunting snapped at his son. 'Go on!' he insisted, when Sam hesitated long enough to pick the gloves up from the chair and take them out along with the wax jacket.

As if he was the servant, Hannah thought, wondering why his father was so desperate for a cup of tea. Or was it that he wanted to get her on her own? Pulling the blanket more tightly round her, she glared at him coolly. If he thought she was easy pickings, he was in for a shock.

'I'm not going to hurt you.'

She found no reassurance in his words. 'What are you going to do with *my* stock?' she enquired pointedly.

'They will stay here until you are able to make other arrangements.'

She almost smiled. Did he really expect her to believe him? He knew she had nowhere to take them to, knew there was little chance of her taking them back. So he could be free with his generous suggestions.

'I'll have to think of something.' She stiffened her shoulders. 'I'll get it sorted out *in a few days*!' She laid emphasis on the last, but it made little effect on him. 'Is the cottage really not fit to live in?'

'There is nothing left of it – only a pile of rubble and one front corner.'

She nodded her head in slow understanding, but at the same time felt defeated.

'You can stay here for as long as you want,' he said. 'You know that, Hannah.' His dark gaze fixed her pointedly.

Oh yes, she knew that. But on what terms? 'I can't stay here!' she declared fiercely.

'You can . . . if you want to!' He reached out, laying his hand on her shoulder.

She recoiled as if from a flame. 'No I can't,' she snapped. He drew his hand back with a sigh. 'What would people say if I stayed here . . . ? With three men!'

'What does it matter what *people* say?' The superiority was back in his voice, the attitude that he was always right. It made her happier. She was more accustomed to the arrogant George Bunting than the man who had been before her for the past minutes. 'Besides . . .' he continued, his gaze resting meaningfully on her own, '. . . there is a way around it!'

'Oh no there is not!' She knew exactly what he was meaning: that she should marry him! 'Just as soon as the doctor has been I shall be up and away from here. There's no reason for me to stay,' she pointed out, as she watched his jaw stiffen. 'I thank you for what you have done for me, but I shall trouble you no longer than is necessary.'

'Oh, Hannah!' Sam exclaimed, as he returned with

three mugs of tea and overheard her. 'You can't go yet. You're not fit.' He placed the three mugs down on the table and immediately stuck his left hand in his pocket.

She gave an inward sigh. Hiding the hand had obviously been done for her benefit. Her presence was making him act the way he did when he left the privacy of his home. It made her doubly aware that she had to get away from there, for Sam's benefit as well as her own.

'Where will you go?' George Bunting voiced the question uppermost in her mind. 'You can't just walk out of here without knowing where you're going.'

'I'll go to my Aunt's.' She knew Renee would not want her, but the words slipped out before thought.

He gave a bark of laughter. 'Renee!' His voice was filled with sarcasm. 'And be used as her servant!'

It would be preferable to being used as your servant . . . and worse! she thought. She gave a sigh. She had forgotten he knew Renee as well as she did. In their younger days Renee had set her cap at him, making a real fool of herself by putting on airs and graces to try and persuade him she was lady enough to be his wife. Even when they were both married she had never stopped trying. She gave a grim smile. As soon as her Aunt found out where she was she would be up there like a whippet, not out of any consideration for her niece's well-being, but to try and get her hands on George Bunting.

'Well, I can't stay here!' she stated baldly. Although there was a small, perverse part of her mind that said it would have been fun to hang around and watch him put Renee in her place, her own welfare was more important than watching her Aunt squirm, she reminded herself. 'I'll find somewhere. Renee will have to take me in for a short while.' And it would be short – only as long as it took her to find a job and a better place to live.

George Bunting looked about to object, changed his mind and gave a sigh of exasperation. He turned to his son. 'You try and talk some sense into her. I'm going to help Jed get the more reasonable members of the Critchlow household settled in.'

As soon as he had gone, she turned to Sam. 'I'm not staying!' She favoured him with a glare as forceful as the one his father had received.

'Then where will you go?' He picked up a mug of tea with his right hand and handed it to her. 'You can't really be serious about going to Renee's. And you can't expect us to let you just walk out of here without knowing you're going to be safe.'

She dropped her gaze and stared bleakly at the thick brown liquid in the mug. He made her feel so ungrateful, and she was not ungrateful, only frightened.

'What will you do for money? Do you have any?'

She shook her head and toyed nervously with the pink satin eiderdown. 'I'll have to get a job,' she replied flatly.

'Doing what?'

Again she shook her head. Even in her school days she had come home and helped on the farm. She had never considered any other occupation. Her father had needed her help and it had been a natural progression from part-time to full-time farm-hand. It was all she knew. That and housework. 'I could be a cleaner,' she suddenly said. 'People always need cleaners.'

'Oh Hannah! You can't be a cleaner. You're too good for that.'

His faith in her ability put a tiny smile on her face. 'There's nothing wrong with cleaning. It's an honest job.'

'But you're good with animals. You know how to run a farm.'

She frowned, reminded of his father's words: not frightened of getting her hands mucky; good stock!

'There might be a farm looking for somebody. If you really don't feel you can stay here.'

She shook her head. She could not stay there. Neither could she see herself getting taken on by anyone else. 'They would not consider me strong enough for the job.'

She ran her gaze sadly down her short form concealed beneath the bedding. If she had been built like an Amazon she might have stood a chance. But no-one would look at her and see a body capable of handling a cantankerous beast, or tossing a bale of hay over her shoulders.

Sam picked up his tea, took a swallow, and thought for a long moment. 'I can understand you not wanting to stay here while you're like this. I know you'd feel better if there was a woman around to look after you.' Forgetting himself, his deformed hand came out of his pocket and made a sweeping gesture over the bed. She gave a little smile, happy that he had relaxed in her company once more, and made a mental note not to be so silly in the future. 'We need some extra help: in the house, but out there as well.' His left hand swept towards the window and the farmyard, then returned to his side, but did not go into his pocket. 'It wouldn't just be housework you'd be doing. And it wouldn't be charity. You'd be working for your living.' He set her with a meaningful stare.

She shook her head. 'No, Sam. I'm not staying here.'

His face fell and his hand suddenly went into his pocket.

'It's nothing to do with you,' she quickly said. He thought she was being like the rest of the village, she realized sadly. Refusing to stay because of him and his hand. Fearing that if he touched them some of it would rub off. 'It would not be right, me living up here with three men.' It sounded a lame excuse, even to herself, and she could see he was of the same opinion.

He dropped his head and stared at the floor. 'Yes, you're right,' he said, without any conviction in his voice.

She gave a sigh, knowing she had hurt him all over again. 'I don't think I want to carry on farming. Not without dad.' Another lame excuse. If he knew anything of her, he was well aware of how much the hills and the countryside meant to her.

Proving her last thought correct, he lifted his head

and shook it. 'You're not a town mouse, Hannah. You wouldn't be happy without fresh air.' He paused, settling his gaze on her face. 'Don't make any decisions yet. You're not thinking straight. Get yourself right and things will look clearer.'

She did not reply, could not. She knew only too well that her brain was only functioning on half-power. But it was not so dulled that she did not understand the danger of staying around his father.

Taking her silence as refusal, he dropped his head again. 'Get some rest now,' he said. Then without lifting his eyes to look where he was going, hurried from the room.

She stared down at the mug of tea for several moments, then put it away on the table. She could not drink. It would choke her before it got past her throat. She had made Sam feel he was the reason why she would not stay there.

At that moment she hated herself. But how could she tell him the truth? How could she explain to the son, exactly why she was afraid of his father?

Chapter Four

Hannah forgot it was Christmas. Apparently so had the Buntings. There was not one decoration in the house: at least not in the part she had seen, which amounted to kitchen, bathroom, and the sitting-room that had become her own room. There was no grand dinner of turkey and plum pudding. Christmas Day went by just like all the rest and it was the day after Boxing Day before she remembered it should have been the festive season.

Not that she was feeling festive. The doctor had forbidden her to do anything except give her legs a bit of exercise by walking round . . . inside the house! She had to be kept warm at all times, he ordered. She was not even allowed to get dressed. A thick woollen dressing gown, which she hated because George Bunting had gone out and bought specially for her, had become her everyday attire. It was bright red, a colour she would never have chosen for herself. It clashed violently with her hair. She also begrudged wearing it because she felt certain that not allowing her to dress was only the doctor's way of making sure she was kept there. She had made her feelings on that very plain to him, but he had refused to listen, saying for the time being she had to rest and not fill her head with silly notions.

'That is ridiculous! I feel fine!' She glared at Dr Hallam. She had been at the Tor for four days and she was perfectly all right now. She refused to be made to stay against her will.

The doctor shook his head and the long flick of silver hair that he swept loosely to the side, fell down to hang between his concerned eyes, as they peered over the top of his spectacles. 'In body you might feel fine. Fortunately the freezing you received has left no permanent damage. But you are still suffering from shock and are in no way fit to go finding elsewhere to live.' He folded his stethoscope in half and put it away in a black leather Gladstone bag that had seen better days. He clicked the bag shut and stood with his hands resting on the top and stared at her. For twenty minutes he had watched her erratic mood swings: from fierce determination to silent resignation. It was only to be expected, after what she had gone through. And he could understand why she did not want to stay at the house that was the butt of jokes for the entire community thereabouts. But he would be lacking in his professional judgement if he allowed her to go. Besides, he wanted her where he could keep an eye on her. Not just to watch over her health, but because he felt he owed it to her father to make sure she was safe. She was far too young to go out into the world and live alone.

'If you knew where you were going to . . . well . . . !' He lifted his hands explicitly, then returned them to the bag. 'But you don't. So, for the time being you must stay here. Mr Bunting is quite happy to keep you and you should be thankful for that.'

She did not miss the note of rebuke in the last. She stared at him blankly, feeling, as she did after all his visits, that her hands were tied. She did not suggest she would go to her aunt. She had done so at the beginning. But Renee had not made the expected visit, and she took that to mean her aunt's fear of getting lumbered with her was greater than her need to get near to George Bunting.

'When will I be fit?' she asked, studying the fallen lock of hair hanging between his bushy, grey eyebrows. With the tweed jacket and plus-fours he always went around in, he reminded her of a mad professor. Fortunately, he was too good at his job for anyone not to respect him. Had he not been, she had the feeling his appearance would have made it difficult to take him seriously.

'Soon,' he replied, refusing to commit himself.

She gave a sigh. He did know what he was talking about, she reminded herself. The sensible action would be to take his advice and not do anything that would put her back. She would need to be in full health to get anyone to give her a job. And when she could convince him she was back to full strength, he would have no argument. She gave another sigh. 'But I keep thinking my dad would not have wanted me to be here.' She stared at her fingers as they toyed with the edge of the satin eiderdown – the way they had done so many times since waking up to find herself in George Bunting's home.

The doctor nodded his head. The flick of wayward hair poked in his eye and he finally brushed it back to its proper position. 'I know what you mean,' he said. He didn't, she thought. 'But circumstances have changed. Your father would want to know you were being looked after. He would be grateful someone had taken you under their wing.'

Not George Bunting's wing! She kept the thought to herself. If she told the doctor of the proposals of marriage he would laugh it off as part of her condition, thinking the wind had chilled her brain and affected her reason. He would consider it just one more 'silly notion' that had crept into her head. Nobody would believe someone as old as George Bunting would expect a young girl to marry him. Reluctantly accepting that fate had taken her life out of her hands, she gave a nod of agreement.

'Good!' the doctor expressed with feeling. He picked up the Gladstone bag with both hands. 'You can get up for longer now. Keep giving your legs gentle exercise, but you can sit in a chair the rest of the time instead of staying in bed. Only inside the house, mind! You're not to go outside yet. You must not risk getting a chill.' His head inclined sternly towards her, as if he considered she would not obey his orders.

'I'll behave myself,' she assured, but there was the

54

flatness of resignation in her voice. For now, at least, she thought. But not for a moment longer than she had to!

'Good!' he repeated. 'I'll be up to see you again in a day or two,' was his parting comment.

She heard him talking to George Bunting in the kitchen, but could not catch what he was saying. It could not have been much, it was only a matter of seconds before the back door closed behind him. As his shooting brake went past the window on its way out of the yard, George Bunting came through the door.

He never knocked before entering, neither did Sam. It annoyed her that they did not respect her privacy. Then what else should she expect, she asked herself, looking up into his arrogant face and tugging the blanket up round her chin?

He did not miss the action and one corner of his mouth lifted in the suggestion of a smile.

It was an annoying little quirk that she had come to know so well over the past days. It gave her the impression he believed he had got her right where he wanted her. As if he was saying: go on, play your prudish little games, my time will come.

'The doctor said you can get up.' He came to a stand-still right by her side and hovered over her, giving her a crick in the neck from having to look upwards and backwards at the same time.

'I need my clothes,' she said, refusing to give in to the pain in her neck and staring at him pointedly. It had been bad enough having to parade in front of him in nightwear for the limited periods of exercise. She had no intention of spending the entire day looking as if she was ready for bed.

'They were badly torn and not worth keeping. I . . .' He did not get time to finish.

'You threw them away!' she snapped angrily. They might have been torn but they were all she had. Did have, she corrected. Now she had nothing: no father; no home; and now no clothes, either. What did he expect her to do? Walk around naked! 'Well, you'll have to find me some!' she demanded.

He gave a weary sigh. 'I was going to say that. *If* you had given me the chance! I'll get you some of my wife's old things to be going on with. She was taller than you.' He let his gaze run down the bed to her feet then back up to her face. 'But the rest is about the same,' he added.

Colour flew to her face, from both the intimate appraisal and the fact that he intended to dress her in his wife's clothes. But she bit back her objections. The alternative, having him buy her new clothes, was even more abhorrent, would put her more in his debt. 'Only until I get some of my own,' she said meekly.

He gave a nod. 'Whatever you please.' It was spoken in a manner that suggested he was giving her everything she desired.

Not everything, she thought, hardening her gaze on his face. 'I mean I shall buy them myself!' she pointed out firmly.

His mouth twisted in the irritating little quirk. 'Do you have any money?'

She gave an incredulous snort. Back to normal, she thought, not unhappy with the change. When he was being unusually nice it made her forget herself. She must remember how easy it was to return him to the arrogant man she disliked so much. 'I have the farm and the stock,' she blurted out before thinking.

His eyebrows lifted as if in surprise.

She dropped her head and toyed with the eiderdown. 'At least, I have the stock,' she amended, before he had a chance to point out that her farm consisted of one field and a pile of broken down stones . . . which was surrounded on all sides by *his* land. No-one would consider buying it. No-one but him, that is! At least it was something she had to give, in payment for his assistance. She would not call it kindness because she knew he was doing it all for his own gain.

She looked up at him uncertainly. 'I do still have the stock?' she questioned. 'Or have you already added them to your own ledger?' Her voice was bitter on the last. She would put nothing past him.

'What do you think I am?'

She thought it best not to answer that one.

His hand flapped towards the window. 'Your stock is out there until *you* tell me what to do with it! Just give me the word and they can go to market. Or I'm happy to keep them here – if that is what you want.'

It was there again: the conciliatory tone of letting her have everything she wanted. Well, it would not work. She would not be made to feel beholden to him. 'What do you want with my herd? You've got a field full of pedigree Friesians out there.' Forgetting herself, she tossed the covers back, knelt up on the bed and jabbed her finger at the window. 'Aren't you frightened my dozen cows might taint your pure stock? I'm surprised you haven't already wrung the hens' necks to make sure they don't bring fowl pest to your precious land.'

In a moment he had hold of her arms. His eyes blazed into hers and at first it seemed he was going to shake her. Then his gaze softened, dropped to her angrily pouting lips, then down to her breasts as they lifted and fell with the force of her anger, each movement pressing them to the flimsy cotton of the nightdress. His own chest rose on a deeply indrawn breath.

'Stop it!' she cried, seeing the stupidity of her anger, too late. She tried to lift her hands and cover her breasts. He held her arms fast, forcing them close to her side as he pulled her forward, pressing her body right up close to his own. She could have moved her head, but she froze. As his mouth came down on hers, her only defence was a whimper.

She was lying flat on the bed and his hand was fondling

57

her breast, before her sense returned enough to tell her her arms were now free.

She pushed at his shoulders and tore her mouth away from his. 'Stop it! Stop it! Sam!' she screamed.

He gave a laugh. 'Sam is right down in the bottom meadow.' He curled his hand into a length of her hair, using it to force her head into the position he wanted. 'And Jed, as usual, is missing. So don't waste your breath shouting for him.' His hand tightened on her breast and he brought his head down to kiss her again. This time she was ready. Parting her teeth she sank them deep into his bottom lip. He gave a groan of agony followed by a string of expressive curses. The taste of his blood filled her mouth, but a mouth full of blood was preferable to what he had in mind and not until her fingers were fastened tightly in his hair did she release her teeth. Then she yanked his head viciously backwards, stretching his throat to its limits. 'Now get your hands off me,' she warned threateningly.

He gave a derisory snort and proved how inadequate her strength was by bringing his head slowly forward. She gave another yank at his hair, but this time his head was braced in preparation and she had little effect.

His eyes narrowing purposefully he returned his hand to her breast, squeezing with a possessiveness that filled her with revulsion. 'You're mine, Hannah. I won't let anyone else have you.' He gave a grimace, and looked disparagingly at the nightdress that was spoiling his pleasure. 'This is getting in the way,' he said, and sat back to lift the hem and pull it up over her body.

It was a fatal error. As he lifted his weight away from her she saw her chance. In an instant her leg came up, her foot landing a glancing blow to his temple. He gave a groan, clasped his swimming head and tottered as if about to fall off the bed. He did not fall. But his moment's insensibility gave her enough time to be off the bed and away from him.

She flew to the fireplace, grabbed one of the silver candelabra from the mantel, and turned on him. 'Now come and try it!' she warned, even before he had regained enough sense to know what was happening.

He shook his head and stretched his eyes to regain his vision. He turned slowly to her, a murderous glare contorting his features. Her hands tightened around the cool metal. She leant forward, wielding the candlestick like a cudgel, ready to strike if he came within distance. She was too intent on protecting herself from him to see that bending forward had pushed the hem of her nightdress dangerously close to the roaring fire.

In an instant his expression changed to one of horror. He thrust his arm out, calling her name in warning, just as she felt the heat against her leg. Her head spun round to see the bottom of the nightdress beginning to burn. As her eyes widened in a horror equal to his own, the flames took hold, leaping and reaching their burning fingers up the side of the nightdress. She screamed.

The candlestick flew from her hands. She did not know if it was by her own doing, or if he had knocked it from her hands. The nightdress was suddenly being torn violently from her. The fabric cut painfully into the back of her neck and she screamed again. The noxious smell of burning filled her nostrils and all she could think was that it was from her own flesh.

It took several moments for her spinning brain to know it was all over. Suddenly she found herself staring at the remains of the nightdress burning on the fire. She was trembling from head to foot, but was not cold. She wrapped her arms around herself, but the trembling would not stop. Not until she was lifted up and put into bed did she become aware she was naked.

'No!' she protested, her mind spinning back to the minutes before the fire.

'It's all right,' a voice assured.

It was too gentle for George Bunting, she told herself,

yet it was his face she was looking up at. Pale and grey, as if all the blood had been sucked from it, but definitely his face.

She lifted her arms to hold him off. But when the weight came down on her it was only the bed covers. Then her arms were taken one at a time and placed beneath the sheets.

'You're not burnt.'

She gave a nod, thankful for the reassurance. She felt no pain, but was not sure if her body was too numb to know it was there.

'Will you be all right if I leave you?' He hovered over the bed looking down at her. 'I want to go and try and get the doctor back. I think he should take a look at you.'

She did not respond straight away. The expression in his dark eyes was confusing her. It looked like guilt, but she could not believe he held himself to blame. Suddenly realizing she was keeping him there when all she wanted was to be rid of him, she gave a nod. 'Yes,' she said simply, thinking she would be all right if she was left alone.

But as he walked out of the room, she found herself wanting Sam to be with her.

*   *   *

George Bunting's version of the story was that he raced in and saved her when he heard her scream. The bruise on his temple and the mark on his lip were where she had unknowingly hit him as she thrashed around in panic with the candlestick in her hand. She went along with it, seeing no reason to speak the truth and make her life more unbearable for the short time she was going to be there.

Dr Hallam found the lie plausible, so did Jed, but then Jed was never around that often to have much thought about anything that happened on the farm: his own social life was far more important. Only Sam showed any doubts and found it necessary to repeatedly question why she had been so close to the fire without the dressing gown . . . which he seemed to be aware she never left the bed without putting on. He finally stopped probing her. But she had the feeling he sensed she was holding something back and he began to spend more time in the house, never letting her be alone with his father for too long. It made her feel safer, knowing he was close at hand. She found her strength returning and when the day of her father's funeral finally came, she felt fully returned to her old self.

*   *   *

Hannah gazed around at the crowd squashed into the small back room of The Lamb. Perhaps she should have had the church hall, after all, she thought. So many people had come to pay their last respects to her father. It pleased her. He had been a good man and she was warmed to see his many acts of kindness had not been forgotten. Softness! she thought fondly, recalling the many times she had levelled the charge at him, thinking he was being taken for granted.

I'm sorry, Dad, she said silently. I'm sorry for having to have it here, as well. She was not sure it was fitting to have a funeral in a pub. George Bunting had offered to have it at the Tor. But, knowing the villagers' aversion to the place, she had worried that no-one would come. Fortunately, he seemed to be of the same mind and when she suggested finding somewhere in the village, he agreed it might be best. So she had had to make the choice between the church hall or the back room of The Lamb, it being the only public house in the village. Thinking the number of people she expected to turn up would look lost in the large church hall, she had chosen The Lamb. Now almost the entire village was crowded into the too-small back room.

One more thing I got wrong, Dad. She turned to the window, her smile touched with sadness. She seemed to have done nothing but get it wrong since his death. At least his 'send off' had been a good one. But that was more George Bunting's doing than her own. He had organized it all for her, as well as paid for it! She wondered if he would have been so obliging if she had not kept her mouth shut about the incident that led to her almost burning to death.

It was not the time for such thoughts, she told herself, and looked up at the sky. The weather had been kind to them. She was thankful there had been no wind to remind her, and the sun had managed to peep through the grey clouds long enough to bless the occasion. 'Goodbye, Dad,' she whispered, gazing out onto the hillside that stretched up to the ruins of her old home and then on to Bunting's Tor. She pictured her father there, Sal running round the flock as they gathered the sheep in. Her mother was there too, standing holding the gate open. Strangely they were younger: her father's face how she had known it before the wrinkles of time had left their mark and no silver in his hair; her mother, like a young girl, could have been herself.

'That is a very profound expression, Hannah.' The vicar came up to her side. He was holding a half-empty sherry glass and his plump, rosy cheeks were redder than normal and looked to be a shocking contrast to his mop of white hair. His head looked rather comical on top of his black cassock.

She gave him a thin smile. 'I was just wondering if there really is a heaven,' she said, turning back to the hills and finding them now empty. She gave a sigh and turned back to the vicar. 'Can we really expect something better? Or is it a good story to soften the blow?'

'Of course we can expect better. God is a very good shepherd. He takes great care of His flock and rounds them all in – when the time comes.'

She smiled at the analogy, as if he had also seen the picture in her mind. 'And then what?' she asked.

'For eternal life. For the promise that He gave to us all, the day He allowed His own son to die on the cross.'

She gave a little shrug. It all seemed too perfect for her mind to accept without condition.

'And we also live on in the hearts of the loved ones we leave behind.' His smile was touched with a knowingness that made her blush slightly. She hoped he did not think the service he had just given her father had meant nothing to her. 'There is always someone left to carry the memory,' he added.

'Yes,' she said simply. She could understand that far easier than the religious theory of heaven. To her mind, if there was such a place as heaven, it must be so crowded by now that she could not imagine it being very pleasant. 'But where is it . . . this promised land?'

'In the heart, Hannah. Wherever you want it to be.' He lifted his glass and drained it. Then his rosy cheeks dimpled as his smile broadened and his eyes twinkled so mischievously, that she wondered if the reply belonged to the vicar, or to the ordinary man beneath the long, black frock.

She nodded and smiled. She liked that explanation best. Seeing her father and mother roaming the hill with Sal, tending their sheep and cows for eternity in a land that was forever summer, was a happy contemplation. 'Thank you,' she said, with feeling.

'Any time, Hannah. The vicarage doors are always open . . . if you wish to continue the conversation.' He inclined his head meaningfully. 'And the church doors, also. A few minutes quiet contemplation can be a great help.'

She had the hills for that. But she did not say so. He had been too kind and had not tried to shame her by making reference to her lack of attendance at the Sunday Services.

'I am always there if you need me.' He placed his glass on the window ledge and glanced at his watch. 'Now,

I am afraid I must leave you. I have another service to conduct in forty-five minutes.'

'Thank you . . . for everything,' she said, and smiled as his well-rounded form hurried out of the door, his long skirt flapping round his short legs. He was off to conduct a wedding and she hoped the bride and groom would not object to the sherry-flushed cheeks. Most of the mourners would be following him shortly, back to the church to witness the nuptials. From sadness to happiness! It did not concern her because she knew it would not have concerned her father. He would have laughed about it, happy they had something to turn their minds to more pleasant things. She smiled to herself, contemplating the condition of most of them by the end of the day. Like the size of the room, she had badly miscalculated on the catering. But no-one seemed to be bothered with the food and there were still plenty of sandwiches left on the table. Still, the sherry and whisky had gone well. She had noticed George Bunting replenish the dwindling stocks on more than one occasion. She was contemplating the need to go and thank him, when Sam came up to her. His dark-grey suit made him look so different. A real country gentleman, she had teased when she first set eyes on him. A smile came to her lips, but faded when she noticed the way his left hand was stuck inside his pocket. Oh Sam! she thought sadly.

'Are you all right?' he enquired, with a concern that put a smile on her face. He was worried that the day was going to prove too much for her. He had seen her health improve greatly over the past couple of days but she still had a paleness about her skin.

'I'm fine,' she assured.

'Was he giving you a lecture?' He had seen the vicar speaking to her and wanted to come to her aid, but had held back thinking it might be personal.

'No.' She shook her head then fell silent. Somehow having Sam close to her was enough. It was a strange feeling and she could not recall when she had first felt it. But his presence seemed to calm her, make her feel whole, wipe away the fears and insecurities that had plagued her. She gave a little sigh, wishing his father could have been like him.

Sam did not miss the sigh and for several seconds he closely studied her face. 'Is something wrong?' he finally asked. His face crinkled into a frown and he inclined his head and peered into her eyes. 'Why won't you tell me?'

She gave an exaggerated shake of her head. 'Nothing is wrong.' She hoped she sounded sincere. 'The vicar was very nice to me and just trying to help.' She knew the question had not been directed at the vicar, but hoped he would be happy with her assumed misunderstanding. His father had never tried to apologize for attacking her. Neither had he attempted to lay the blame on her own lack of co-operation. He never brought the matter into conversation, but she had the feeling it had frightened him. He kept his distance now, as if he knew she would not hesitate to shout out the truth if he ever tried anything on again. It was a weapon she held over him. It might not be strong enough to last for long but she was confident it would last for the length of time she would be living in his house. And, if she kept her mouth shut, when she was gone it could all be forgotten. But if she told Sam it would stay behind and cause trouble. It was Sam she was doing it for. She had no concern for preserving his father's reputation.

'Will you do something for me?' she suddenly asked, turning her mind to more open topics.

'What is it?'

'Find out how much the funeral and everything else has cost your father and let me know. I want to pay him back for everything. Looking after my stock. My own keep.'

'Eeh, Hannah. There's no need. You'll need your money yourself.'

'I mean it, Sam. I want to know . . . every penny!' She

had no intention of being indebted to George Bunting; at least not financially. He had saved her life once. She did not count the second time because she had only been at risk through his doing. She would always be in his debt for coming to her rescue after the gale. But the fire . . . no! And not for anything else, either. She would pay back every penny he had spent on her . . . if it took till her fiftieth birthday! 'Everything!' she repeated, and glanced down at the black suit and white blouse she was wearing. Yesterday morning he had caught her rummaging through the two boxes of his late wife's old clothes. He had not commented at the time. But in the afternoon Sam, ignoring her protests, had driven her into town to buy the new outfit, plus two pairs of shoes and a pair of wellingtons.

It took several attempts before Sam finally agreed to her demands. 'Yes, all right. I'll make out a bill if it will make you feel happier.' He had no intention of doing so. His father could afford it and Hannah could not. And, as far as he was concerned, that was all there was to it. It was about time his father learned how to give instead of always expecting to be on the receiving end.

The crowd began to dwindle away and Hannah glanced at George Bunting, trapped in the corner by Renee. She smiled to herself. Her aunt had excelled herself for the occasion. She had taken off the black coat worn for the church, and was now wearing a black dress with a full skirt and a large white collar which dwarfed her thin shoulders and made her short form appear even smaller. Even the dangerously high-heeled shoes and the frizzy, over-permed and over-bleached blond hair, piled on top of her head, did nothing to add to her height. 'Do you think someone should go and rescue him?' she asked.

'No, let him suffer.'

Sam's smile brought her own smile into the open. Then it vanished. She had to approach her aunt and get her to take her in and the way Renee had ignored her throughout the entire ceremony did not look very promising. At the church she had forced herself on to the pew next to George Bunting. During the burial she clung to his arm, affecting a state of collapse. Since reaching the pub she had followed him around like the lamb of its name. Not one word had she spoken to her niece.

'I have to talk to her.' She grimaced at Sam. Pleasing or not, it had to be done – if she wanted to get away from George Bunting.

'Do you want any help?'

'No . . . thank you.' She glanced a fond smile at him and walked away. His generosity never failed to warm her. She just hoped Renee might possess one tenth of the same concern for her.

'Hello, Aunt Renee.' Hannah came up by her side and smiled to herself at the look of relief that swept across George Bunting's face. 'Can I have a word with you?'

Annoyance flashed across Renee's garishly painted face, as she turned to see who had dared to intrude. It was gone in a moment. 'Oh, luvvy, luvvy!' She threw her arms around Hannah, suffocating her in a rib-crushing bear hug. 'What are we going to do now? What are we going to do now?' She began to cry noisily against her niece's shoulder.

You are going to have to buy your own vegetables, she thought bitterly. The crocodile tears and false affection did not fool her. Renee was a star when it came to playing before an audience. The caring aunt routine was all for George Bunting's benefit. She bit her lip against asking why her uncle and cousin had not come to her father's funeral. She felt it was rude of them not to attend. But she knew it would have been Renee's doing: having a husband and daughter around would have got in the way of her possession of George Bunting – and that would never have done!

'It's too late for tears, now. They won't help Dad . . .

or me.' She unfolded herself from the woman's clutches and pushed her away to a safer distance.

'But it's criminal, criminal!' Renee pulled a lace handkerchief from her pocket and dabbed ineffectually at her eyes. 'He was such a good man. It's always the good that die young.'

Hannah gave a sigh. Yes, she thought, and get taken for granted. She stared at her aunt. The emotional outburst had done nothing for her appearance. The dark-tan Pan-stik, caked on her thin face, now had black and white channels running through it, where her forced tears had washed it away and dribbled mascara from her violently blue-painted eyes. The pillar-box red lipstick turned her misery-twisted mouth into something that resembled a gargoyle. For an unchivalrous moment Hannah wished she had a mirror and could show Renee what George Bunting was seeing. That would not help her own cause, she reminded herself. This was one occasion when she really must bite her lip and keep sweet.

'We'll get over it,' she said, forcing herself to place a comforting arm around her aunt's scrawny shoulders.

Renee patted her free arm. 'Oh luv, you're a brave girl!' She glanced mournfully at George Bunting. 'She's a brave little luv, isn't she?' she said, trying to draw him into the conversation. He gave an unconvincing nod. 'She always was brave,' she continued. 'She always was a good girl.'

Hannah had the feeling if this continued for much longer she would be sick. 'It's all over now. We've got to get on with life again. And that is what I want to talk to you about. I need somewhere to live.'

Renee's head shot back in shock.

'I can't stay where I am for much longer.' She hurried on, before Renee could get her objections out. 'I'm not looking for a permanent place. Just somewhere to stay until I can get myself fixed up. I'll need to find a job first.'

'But what can you do . . . except farming?' The old Renee was back, the familiar hardness returned to her voice. 'George has already told me he's happy for you to stay with him. It's where you belong . . . on a farm.'

Hannah gave a sigh and pulled her arm away, wondering how she could ever have expected help from her aunt. Asking her to give something was asking her to change a lifetime's habit of selfishness. 'I don't belong there. Mr Bunting has already done enough for me. To ask more of him would be taking his kindness for granted.' It almost choked her to speak the words. 'I'm not asking much, only that you help me out for a short while.'

'Oh, George! You try and talk some sense into her.' Renee gave him a beseeching smile that made her tear-stained face appear more hideous.

'She knows she can stay with us – if that is what she wants!' he added pointedly, as Hannah's green eyes pivoted to his face, daring him to say more.

'It isn't right, me staying in a house with three men.' She fastened an insistent gaze on Renee. 'You are my only relation, *my father's sister* !' she stressed meaningfully. 'Surely you can see your way to putting me up for a few days.'

'Oh, luvvy.' The whining returned to her voice. 'I don't have the room.'

Hannah's lips tightened, knowing it for a lie. Renee's house had three bedrooms. The third only a poky box-room, but big enough for her to manage in.

'Besides, from what George has been telling me you're not in any fit state to go thinking what you're going to do. You should wait until you've got over everything.'

'I am perfectly capable of making my own decisions.' She flashed George Bunting a stony glare. She bet he had not told her aunt *how* she had nearly set herself on fire. 'And my brain has not been addled. I do know what I am doing!'

'Stop it, Hannah,' Renee rebuked in a wheedling manner. 'George is listening to all this and you're being very rude to him – refusing his offer. You'll be perfectly all right with him. And I'll pop up to see you every week, just like I did with you and your dad.'

'Oh!' She could not stop herself giving the gasp of despair. It was all clear now. Renee wanted her at Bunting's Tor so she had a valid reason to come visiting – and it wasn't her weekly groceries she was after! Had she not been so angry she would have laughed at the horrific displeasure that settled on George Bunting's face. As it was she inclined her head at him in a manner that said, serves you right. Then she turned on Renee, seeing no reason to hold her true feelings back any longer. 'Well, thank you for sparing the time to come to your brother's funeral! I'm sure Dad would have been pleased to know you had the good grace to show a little gratitude for all he did for you. But your dues are paid now. There is no need to trouble yourself with *my* welfare. Besides, Mr Bunting does not grow vegetables, and I can assure you there is no chance of him sawing the leg off one of his precious Friesians for your Sunday dinner!'

'Why you . . . !' Renee began. But Hannah wheeled round and hurried away. She had no interest in what her aunt thought about her.

She did not stop to see the surprised expressions Sam and Alf Marshall, the landlord, gave her as she made for the door. Flinging it open she rushed outside, only to career right into Jed. His hands were stuffed into the pockets of a silver-grey suit that would have looked more fitting for a wedding than the present funeral, but they were soon pulled out and held wide as she flew at him.

'Hey up!' he said, making the most of it by wrapping his arms around her and holding her tightly. 'Who's chasing you?' His grin stretched from ear to ear.

She glared into his face. The fact that he was the image of his father, and his reputation as a waster and woman-izer was as well known to her as it was to the rest of the village, made it easy for her to hate him, even though she had had little contact with him during her stay at the Tor.

'Get your hands off me!' She thumped her balled fists against his broad shoulders.

He tossed his dark head back on a laugh and tightened his hold on her.

'*Do as she says!*'

Jed's laughter came to an abrupt end, but his grin did not diminish, neither did the strength of his hold.

Hannah twisted her head round to see Sam standing in the doorway. A look of murder was on his face. His arms hung stiffly by his side. His right hand was balled into a fist and his left was curled into as much of the same as it could manage. It was the first time she had seen his left hand leave his pocket since they had reached the church. But she wished there could have been a better reason for it to do so.

'It's all right, Sam. He'll let me go,' she assured, not wanting to cause friction between the brothers. Besides, she knew it was true. Jed was just an opportunist. Under normal circumstances he would not have looked at her twice. She was much too self-possessed for his taste. His palate only ran to the brainless type he could bend to his own will.

'Too damned right he will,' Sam growled, stepping forward purposefully.

He had reached them before Jed suddenly let her go. He held his arms wide. 'All right, brother dearest. She is all yours.' He stepped back, giving her space. 'I did not realize I was treading on your toes.' His arms made a sweeping gesture that was as sarcastic as his voice.

'Have you got no shame? This is her father's funeral.' Sam advanced on Jed, pushing his nose into his face, the quiet fury in his voice far more potent than any loud bawling.

She had never seen him this way before. His manner was so unlike his usual placidity that she could only look on in astonishment.

71

'It was only a joke.' Jed's lips twisted in a bitter smile. 'I forgot you never saw the funny side of life.'

'This isn't the time for jokes. Anybody with an ounce of common sense would have known that.'

'Leave it, Sam,' she insisted, suddenly jumping to life and grabbing his arm and pulling him back. 'There is no harm done. I should have been looking where I was going.'

The grin returned to Jed's face. 'Don't worry on my account. I can sort him out any day.'

'There'll be no sorting out on *my account*!' she countered fiercely. It was a well known fact that Jed usually resorted to his fists to win any argument. 'Come on, Sam.' She gave another tug on his arm. 'The funeral is over. I want to go and wait in the car.'

'You'd better do as she says!' Jed put in, mocking the angry order that had begun all this.

Sam glared at him. He jabbed his finger hard into Jed's chest, keeping it there, as he spat, 'You keep your filthy hands off her!' Then he turned away, finally allowing Hannah to pull him towards the car.

But Jed could not resist having a final stab. 'It might be your left arm she's got hold of, but I notice she isn't letting her hand get anywhere near yours!'

Sam's steps hesitated, his body stiffening in offence.

'No, Sam,' she begged, keeping a tight hold on his arm, breathing a sigh of relief when he moved forward again. But he did not speak and his shoulders were stiff and there was a tightness in his expression that made him appear unapproachable.

As she sank into the leather upholstery in the back of George Bunting's Jaguar, Hannah hated Jed. Sam was his brother, he should have had some feeling for him. He should have been there to support him against all the slurs, not throwing them at him along with the rest of the population.

'I'm sorry,' she said, as he threw himself into the front

passenger seat. She felt to blame. It would not have happened if she had not lost her temper with Renee, had not stormed out too angry to look where she was going. She would never have willingly allowed herself to get close to Jed – his reputation was too well known.

'Forget it,' he snapped angrily, without turning to face her. 'There's no love lost between us.'

'But he's your brother!'

He twisted round in the seat. His eyes fixed coolly to hers and he lifted his left hand. 'Try telling him he's related to this and see what reaction you get.'

'It's only a hand . . .' she began.

'A hand,' he scoffed bitterly. 'You call that a hand.' He pushed it into her face, snapping the thumb and thickened digit together, so it took on the appearance of a lobster clawing for her nose.

'Stop it!' She knocked the hand away, disgusted that he could act in a way that mocked himself and give fuel to all the slurs. 'If you don't think any better of yourself how do you expect others to take you seriously?'

'Oh, they take me seriously! You should see the *serious* fear that enters their eyes when they think it's going to get near them – like your own just then,' he added bitterly.

'The only disgust I was feeling was for your own stupidity! I should have thought you would have known that for yourself.'

'Aye, the same as it was my stupidity that made you feel sick the day I put it on your shoulder.'

'No,' she blazed. 'That was *my* stupidity and I apologize for what I did.' She had no excuse. She would never forgive herself for her silly reaction the first day at Bunting's Tor.

He fell silent, turning his back on her and staring fixedly through the windscreen.

'Stop believing everything, Sam. It doesn't matter what anybody says, it's only true if you allow it to be true.'

He gave a disgusted snort. He did not turn to look at

her, but his left hand came up above his shoulder, so she could see it. 'This is not real. It's just a figment of my imagination.'

'That is not what I meant and you . . .' She pulled herself up short. She was wasting her breath. She gave a sigh. 'Oh, stop feeling sorry for yourself!' she added, frustratedly. 'It could be your legs. You could be stuck in a wheelchair and not able to do anything.'

'And I'd be better for it! Shut away where the world would not have to suffer the sight of me.'

The cold certainty of his voice drew her anger from her. She sank back into the seat, a great wave of sadness washing over her. He was so convinced he was worthless that he would not listen to reason.

Reason! she thought incredulously. There had been no reason in the way she had railed at him. She gave a sigh. All the frustration and anger left over from her spat with Renee had been flung at him . . . the very last person she should have been getting at. 'I'm sorry. Don't let *us* argue. I don't want to fall out with you!' He turned to her then. The anger in his eyes had softened, to be replaced by a bleakness she found confusing.

'But, George! The Land Rover is too bouncy for my back. You know I have trouble with it.'

At the sound of the whining voice, Sam turned back to the front and Hannah was never to know what he might have said.

'Besides, I really think I should come back with you. Hannah might need a woman to talk to.'

Hannah gave a gasp of disbelief. Could her anger have been so easily forgotten? No! *She* was not the reason why her aunt was trying to get herself back to the Tor. 'He won't let her come back, will he?' she asked anxiously.

Sam shook his head. 'I shouldn't think so.'

'I don't think there is any need,' George Bunting insisted soberly.

Renee chose to ignore him and hurried over to the

74

car. 'You'd like me to come back with you, wouldn't you, luvvy?' she said, peering through the window next to Hannah, a cajoling smile on her face, anger forgotten.

'Stop calling me luvvy!' Hannah grated, turning her head away in disgust. She had always known Renee had a skin as thick as a rhinoceros, but today she was excelling herself.

'You need someone to talk to,' Renee persisted, though the hardness of impatience was noticeably creeping back into her voice. 'You shouldn't keep it all inside. And talking to a man isn't the same as having another woman to talk to.'

Hannah's disbelieving gaze pivoted to her aunt's face. She wound the window down and stuck her head through. 'I don't need anything from you!' she hissed. 'Now, please, leave me alone. You've made it quite clear that I am of little concern to you, so I'll not take any more of your time.' She turned to George Bunting. 'I would like to go!' she said pointedly. 'Are you coming with us? Or can Sam drive me back?' If he wanted to hang around with Renee it was fine by her. But she never wanted to set eyes on the woman again. Her aunt, her only living blood relation, and she could not find it in her heart to help her when she really needed it. As her aunt's face turned puce, she wound up the window, sat back in the seat and kept her eyes forward.

'What would your father think . . . ?' Renee began, but got no further. George Bunting grabbed her arm and dragged her over to the Land Rover.

But still Renee would not give up. She laid a proprietary hand on his arm. 'I'll pop up in a day or two to see how she is,' she said. 'Whether she knows it or not, she is still suffering from shock.' On the last she inclined her head close to his, as if giving him a confidence, even though her voice was loud enough to deafen him and let everyone around know what she was saying.

'That will please him,' Sam said drily.

And me, Hannah thought, her depression deepening, as she wondered just what she had to do to get rid of the woman.

'It's pleasing somebody else, as well.' Sam gave a laugh and inclined his head to The Lamb's back door, where Jed had stood looking on with a knowing grin plastered on his face.

Hannah turned to look. George Bunting had bundled Renee into the Land Rover and was heading back to the car, and the realization that he was the one who was taking Renee home, had wiped the smile clean from Jed's mouth. But it put one on Hannah's.

Chapter Five

The day after the funeral Hannah was determined to be an invalid no longer. She got up early and chose a pair of brown corduroy slacks and a jumper of the same colour, both from two boxes of the late Mrs Bunting's stock which George Bunting had put in her room for her. The woman had been much taller and the trouser bottoms needed rolling up several times. She also needed the addition of a belt to hold the waist snug, but otherwise the clothes were fine.

She was no clearer about what she was going to do to get herself away from George Bunting. After the funeral she had been too angry with Renee to think straight and had wasted the rest of the day on bitterness and self-pity.

She was completely alone, she told herself, as she tugged a comb through her hair. There was no-one to lend a helping hand, and whatever she did had to be done by herself. The thought of all the vegetables and eggs Renee had taken from her father, made her hand pull angrily at the knots. She dropped the comb on to the little table and gave a sigh. A comb was no good, she needed a brush. And railing against Renee was serving no purpose, she told herself angrily. At least now she knew where she stood.

Shoving her fiery hair into a rubber band, she tossed it over her shoulder to hang in a long pony-tail. She gave herself a brief inspection in the large ornate mirror, then hurried out of the door. It was going to take time to find herself a job and somewhere more appropriate to live. For the time being she had to stay where she was. But she would not be a leech, like her aunt. She would work for her living. By the time she left Bunting's Tor she would owe George Bunting very little.

Sam was in the kitchen preparing breakfast. He looked round in surprise when Hannah walked in. 'What are you doing up at this time?'

'I do know what time work begins on a farm.' She stopped in the middle of the floor and looked around. She was definitely better, she told herself. It was not the first time she had seen the kitchen and she had realized the room was in need of a woman's touch. But now she saw it for what it really was – a pigsty! Everything – the walls, the floor, the sink cluttered with unwashed pots and pans, was filthy. Had she seen it in its true colours before she would never have eaten anything. It was a wonder they were not all dead from food-poisoning. Resting her hands on her hips she gave a sigh. 'This place is not fit for swine!'

Sam gave an embarrassed shrug. 'I try my best.' His gaze travelled bleakly round the kitchen. 'But there isn't the time. We're all needed in the yard. We could do with help – but you know what the chances are of *us* getting anyone!'

She gave a nod. The men from the village would starve rather than work for George Bunting.

'Anyway, what *are* you doing up and dressed? It's only seven o'clock.'

'You need help.' She held her arms wide. 'You've got it.'

'Oh no!' He shook his head, as he cracked an egg into a frying pan, then turned to her. 'The doctor said you had to rest and rest you will – until he says otherwise.'

'I'm perfectly fit.' She went across to him. 'Let me do that.' She peered at the egg sizzling in the pan, then at the second pan, filled with bacon. 'How long will they be?' She knew George Bunting and Jed would be out doing the first milking and he would be preparing breakfast to have it ready for when they had finished.

'Go and sit down!' He took hold of her arms and pushed her over to the table and on to a chair. 'You're not doing anything,' he said, peering sternly into her eyes. 'Now just stay there!' He raised a warning finger at her, then went back to the gas stove.

She stared at his back, as he began to crack more eggs into the frying pan. 'Why don't you get a housekeeper to live in?' she asked. 'Surely you could find someone from Derby. Or somewhere far enough away to have never heard of your father.' It was only locally and in the farming community that he was hated. 'The house is big enough. You've got the room to have someone living here.'

Sam glanced her a telling grimace. 'We've tried it.' He left the frying pans, took a handful of cutlery from a drawer and began to lay the table. 'It never works out.'

'Why not?'

For a moment he hesitated. Then her baffled stare made him break into a smile. 'The older ones take a shine to Dad, the younger ones to Jed. None of them have come here to actually work.'

She gave a tight-lipped smile. He had not said the younger ones were after *himself* and Jed. Just Jed. He was by far the nicer person of the two, yet they ignored him. It did not seem right. But she could not condemn others because, in the past, she had been as guilty as they.

He returned to the stove and she dropped her head and toyed with the knife and fork he had put before her. Her mind whirred back to schooldays, when Sam had been a lonely little boy, shunned by all the other pupils . . . herself included. She had always felt sorry for him. But, fearing what the other children would say, she had never been brave enough to go up to him and speak. The only person she had known not to shun Sam had been her father. He had been too kind to hurt anyone.

You never know what's round the corner, he had always

told her. Trouble can strike anyone . . . and it only takes a minute!

Now she knew the truth of those words. Oh how she knew the truth! And she wished she had taken a leaf out of her father's book and been kinder to Sam in the past. If she had shown him he had a friend then, he might not consider himself so worthless now.

She was still remonstrating with herself, when George Bunting came in through the back door.

'What are you doing up?' He hesitated, looking her up and down as she sat in the chair.

Her spine stiffened beneath the feel of his eyes on her. 'Why does the Bunting household find it so odd that I should get out of bed along with everyone else? I've already had to tell your son that I am perfectly fit and capable of doing something.'

'And I've already told you you're doing nothing till the doctor gives the OK,' Sam put in warningly.

George Bunting grinned. 'You're getting better,' he pronounced knowingly.

So why don't you believe me, she thought. Then relaxed back into the chair, as he took his eyes away from her and went to the sink. He made no attempt to remove his muddy wellington boots and she grimaced as they left a damp trail across the quarry-tiled floor. She imagined the floor should be red, but looked brown with the addition of a layer of mud. Pigs, she thought again, and almost laughed out loud when he turned on the tap, washed his hands without removing the clutter of pots and pans from the sink, then dried them by wiping them down his jumper. Lord of the Manor, she thought sarcastically! It was no wonder he was a laughing stock in the village. The few village girls who had attempted to work there must have gone back with plenty of stories about his *real* way of life.

'Are you really feeling back to normal?' He pulled out the chair opposite to her and sat down, resting his elbows on the table. His clasped fingers made a resting place for his chin and he gave her another assessing gaze.

'Yes,' she replied firmly. 'I feel fit as a flea and am quite capable of working for my living.'

'Oh no!' Sam got in before his father had a chance. 'I'll not listen to any talk of paying debts or working them off.'

She flashed him a glare. What she had asked him to do regarding the funeral expenses was between him and herself. She did not want his father to be made aware of it; not until she had gathered the money to pay him back. If he found out, she would not put it past him to do something that would get in her way and keep her in his debt. Having her under his roof put her right where he wanted her to be. And she was not stupid enough to believe he would let her go without a fight.

'How are *my* animals?' She laid emphasis on the owner-ship as she changed the subject, making it clear she still considered them to be only temporary visitors to the Tor.

'They're fine.' He reached for a huge chunk of bread from a plate Sam placed on the table, tore a piece off, waggled it in the air, and asked, 'Have you decided what you want doing with them yet?' He stuck the bread into his mouth and began to chew slowly, and waited her reply.

She hesitated uncertainly. Market was the only answer she could see. Yet she hated the thought of sending them to the slaughterhouse. They were all good milkers, but it was doubtful they would all find homes with other dairy herds. She dropped her head into her hands. 'I don't like to think of them being split up,' she said, defeatedly. She began to think it might be best to tell him he could have them. At least that way they would continue in milk production – and be cared for by someone who knew what he was doing!

'There's a chap moved into Ike Betterton's old place.

81

He's starting from scratch and I've heard he wants to set up a small dairy herd. He might be interested. I don't suppose he could afford top price, but I'd see you got a fair deal.'

She looked up, immediately interested. 'Do you think he'd take them all?'

He gave a shrug. 'I can ask him for you. If you want?'

'I do want.' Having her cows going together, staying together, would be the answer to her prayers. Her eagerness suddenly subsided. 'Does he know what he's doing? Will he know how to look after them?'

George Bunting laughed. 'Don't worry. He's worked on farms all his life. He'll know to give them each a blanket at bedtime.'

She ignored the sarcasm. 'How old is he? Does he have many years' experience? Have you met him? What's he like?' She paused. 'If he's only been a hand how has he got the money to buy Ike's place?' Farm labourers never got paid much. She wanted to know the man was reputable, before handing her herd over to him.

'Christ! Do you want to see his pedigree?' His eyebrows gave an ironic tilt. 'No, I have not met him!' he stressed, slowly and deliberately, as if speaking to a dolt. 'Apparently his wife has been left a legacy by one of her relatives . . . I didn't ask the exact figure!'

'You can mock all you like,' she snapped. 'I won't let them go to someone who doesn't know what he's doing!' A quick death at the slaughterhouse would be preferable to sending them to a life of cruelty.

He gave a weary sigh. 'For the last fifteen years the man has worked on a farm over in Leicestershire. I'm sure he knows which end of a cow is which.' His voice softened. 'Arthur Fretwell told me about him. I should see him at market. I can ask him if he knows any more, if you like?'

She hesitated. Market was not until Friday, three days away. The man could have got himself set up elsewhere by then. Or even at market, if George Bunting did not find him soon enough. She bit her lip pensively. If she took too long about it she could miss the chance of her cows all staying together.

'Why don't you let me and dad go and see the man for ourselves?' Sam took the words right out of her mouth, as he placed a plate of eggs and bacon in front of both her and his father, then went back to the stove to get his own. 'We could sound him out.' He returned to the table and sat down. 'We should be able to make a good judgement from talking to him and taking a look at what he's doing with Ike's place.'

She gave a nod. 'All right,' she agreed. She had no trust of George Bunting the man. But the farmer in him was faultless and would see through any charlatan at a glance. And he was too proud of his own reputation to send any animal to a poor home.

They began to discuss the duties of the day then. Hannah fell silent, listening as she nibbled at the bacon. Her plate was as full as the mens' and she knew she would not be able to eat it all. But she was determined to make a good attempt, wanting to show them she was no longer an invalid who needed to be fed on soup and broth.

It was not many minutes before Jed came in. He took one look at Hannah and lifted his dark eyebrows in surprise. It had been the briefest of glances, but she felt colour running up her cheeks, and hated herself for it. The last thing she needed was for the *wonderful* Jed to think his power had the same affect on her as it had on the silly village girls.

Berating herself for a fool, she watched out of the corner of her eye as, like his father, he went to the sink, washed his hands, then wiped them down his black sweater. That he also had the manners of a pig restored her composure completely and there was no sign of any embarrassment in the gaze she pinned confidently to his face, when he came over to the table and sat down.

'If I'd known you were going to choose today to return

to the land of the living, I would have left those pesky fowls to you,' he said, picking up a piece of bread and beginning to chew, unknowingly copying every detail of his father's actions of only minutes before.

'Hannah is not doing any work, yet!' Sam glared coolly at his brother.

Jed grinned knowingly and Sam's glare hardened.

'I'll be able to see to them tomorrow,' Hannah quickly put in, attempting to defuse the situation.

'You will not!' It was George Bunting this time.

'Well, if she isn't doing them, then one of you can.' Jed held his arms out over the table. The sleeves of his jumper were pushed up to the elbows, displaying muscular arms covered with red marks. 'I'm sick of getting pecked to bits.'

'They're obviously used to the gentle touch,' Sam sneered.

'So am I,' Jed returned cockily. 'And I'm very particular about who I allow to sink their teeth into me.'

'Not from what I've heard!'

'Enough!' their father blazed, swinging a warning glare several times between his two sons. 'Hannah does not want to listen to your constant bickerings!'

'Do you think the new man at Ike's place will want some hens and ducks, as well?' she quickly asked, changing the subject to a less volatile one. She was suddenly nervous that Jed might begin to goad Sam with his overprotection of her as they left The Lamb the day before. She knew there was nothing in it. Sam had only been angry because he thought Jed was acting out-of-hand at a serious occasion. But Jed would make it sound as if there was something more to it and she was not sure how their father would take it. Besides, she did not want to be the cause of anger between the brothers.

George Bunting gave a shrug. 'I've become rather partial to fresh-laid eggs and the birds seem to have settled in all right. They can stay here.'

She was not sure what to say. She did not like to ask if he intended to pay her for them.

'You needn't expect me to look after them,' Jed put in angrily, his face darkening . . .

'You'll do as you're damned well told!' his father blazed, favouring him with a glare that was hard enough to crack glass.

Hannah dropped her head and busied herself with her breakfast, and waited for Jed to come back at his father and a full-scale war break out. Strangely he did not. Until the end of the meal, the only sound was that of knives and forks scraping against the plates.

*   *   *

It was early afternoon before Hannah got the chance to put her plans for repaying George Bunting fully into practice. Jed, along with his father's Jaguar, had departed soon after breakfast without telling anyone he was going, or where he was going to. His father vanished into the yard, spitting blood and threats of what he was going to do to him when he returned. But Sam spent all morning flitting from the yard to the house like a bluebottle and she soon began to understand the constant visits were only to check up on her: making sure she was behaving herself and not getting stuck into scrubbing floors, or the like.

Fortunately they had so many dogs in the yard that no-one could come or go without a welcome chorus. The dogs provided a warning signal. Each time they began to bark, Hannah sat down and pretended to be reading the newspaper. Sam never noticed she was up to anything until it was too late. During his absences she went through the cupboards, heaving a sigh of relief when she found one containing soap and scrubbing brushes; she had begun to fear the Buntings might not have been aware they had been invented.

Men! she thought, as she cleared the filthy clutter of

pots and greasy pans from the sink. They could keep a muddy farmyard in order, but follow them inside and you found a mire.

By the time Sam returned to get the dinner ready for his father to come in to, the sink had been scrubbed, the washing up all done, and the smell of stew and dumplings filled the kitchen. She had not made the stew herself. She found it standing in a large bowl in the pantry and had assumed it had been prepared in advance; so Sam only had to warm it up.

For her troubles she received a very strong lecture on her health. Then another, before he left with his father to make the visit to the man who might be interested in her little herd.

Once they were out of the way she began in earnest. First she took the curtains down. They were full of dust. It got up her nose and clung to her hands. She would need a bath herself, after this, she told herself, as she studied the washing-machine with doubt. Her father had never been able to afford such luxuries and she was more accustomed to a dolly tub. It took her half-an-hour to get the thing going.

She was about to give up and stick the curtains in the sink, when suddenly it began to agitate and left her free to continue. The walls were next. She turned the dingy fawn back into a cream which, though obviously not its original colour, at least gave the impression of being clean. Before beginning on the floor, she took the curtains from the washing machine. She rinsed them in the sink, deciding that would be quicker than working out how to get the thing to empty itself of the murky grey water. But she mastered its mangle and quite approved of not having to wear her arm out by having to swing a handle by hand. The curtains were blowing in the wind on the washing-line and she was halfway through scrubbing the floor, before she heard the Land Rover's engine coming into the yard.

When the door opened she was ready. 'Get those boots off!' she demanded, looking up to see two pairs of muddy wellingtons about to invade her hard work.

The first pair came up short, the second pair careered into them.

'Christ Almighty!' George Bunting's mouth fell open. He looked round in amazement. 'What the hell do you think you're doing?' he demanded, and took a step forward; only to be brought up short again.

'Get out! Don't you dare come any further in those boots.' She sat back on her heels, rested her wet hands against her hips and glared at him. 'It's about time you learned this is not a pigsty.'

'Yes . . . but . . . !' Words failed him.

'You shouldn't be doing this!' Sam, who had stood gaping behind his father, suddenly found his voice. 'You'll get your legs frozen again.' His gaze dropped to where her legs were folded beneath her. 'And your feet are bare.'

'Never mind my legs!' She had not worked her fingers to the bone to have all her efforts ruined in five minutes. 'I've got plenty of padding under my knees.' She was kneeling on a mat of four folded towels. 'Now get those boots off and leave them by the door. And from now on that is where they'll always be left!'

'Why?' Sam frowned. 'Are you staying with us?'

She hesitated. It had never occurred to her that she might be giving the impression of doing it for herself, because she was going to become a permanent resident. 'No!' she suddenly replied, very forcefully. 'But by the time I go I will have knocked some sense into your heads. If you didn't get the place so filthy in the first place, it wouldn't take so long to clean.' She flapped her hand at them. 'Go on,' she insisted. 'Get them off!'

Sam moved first. He pulled his wellingtons off, then stood holding them uncertainly. 'Where shall I put them?'

'By the door.' She returned to scrubbing, as George

Bunting meekly followed, removing his wellingtons and placing them next to Sam's. Then he removed his coat before going to the sink to wash his hands.

Out of the corner of her eye she watched his every movement. She did not speak until she saw his wet hands going to his jumper. 'There's a towel!' she pointed out, without looking up. Then smiled to herself, as the blue and grey socks on his bootless feet made a couple of uncertain turns, before finding the towel hanging on the hook by the side of the sink – where it should have been.

'How did it go?' She wiped dry the patch of floor she had just scrubbed and looked up as she wrung the cloth in the bucket. 'Does he seem all right?' She mentally crossed her fingers, hoping they had come back finding a home for her cows.

'Yes . . .' George Bunting sank into a chair at the table. 'Put the kettle on, Sam? We'd better take a bowl of hot water outside with us before we look at the tractor. We hadn't better come in here with oily hands.'

Hannah scowled at him, but refused to be drawn into making any comment.

Sam hovered uncertainly by her side. 'I wish you'd stop doing that,' he said, anxiety creasing his brow.

'I can't leave it half-finished.' She returned to the floor, dismissing his concern as a touch of softness. Like her father. It was a strange thought: considering one of the Buntings to be anything like her mild-mannered father; the man she had loved so much. 'So what is the new man like?' She went back to the previous subject, and the scrubbing brush once more began to scratch noisily at the hard tiles.

'He's perfect for your cows,' Sam said, finally realizing he was wasting his breath trying to get her to stop. He went to a drawer and began pulling out an assortment of tools needed for attending to the tractor.

'Do you really think so?' She paused and looked up at him expectantly.

'Perfect,' his father replied, drawing her attention to him. 'He's been used to looking after the best. For the past eight years he's been tending Jerseys and Guernseys. Dairy and breeding. There isn't much he doesn't know about cattle.'

Her face fell. 'Is he interested in my cows then?' Her voice was flat. She did not think there was much hope. They were nothing special.

'More than interested. He's fetching them tomorrow.'

'Oh!' Her stomach lurched. It was what she wanted, her cows to stay together. But it was so sudden, so final.

Only when she had the feeling of wetness against her skin, did she become aware she was clutching the dripping scrubbing brush to her unsteady stomach. She put the brush away from her, too quickly. As it dropped with a splash into the bucket, her head rocked and she had to drop her hands to the floor to steady herself.

'Are you all right?' Dropping a wrench, Sam rushed to her side and grasped her arm. Her face had gone pale and she stared at him woodenly.

'Yes . . . yes, I'm fine.' She attempted a smile, but it was thin and unconvincing.

'Can you stand up?' Taking both her arms, he helped her to her feet.

She gave a nod of the head and took a deep breath. 'I don't know what came over me. It was just . . . well . . . the cows going.'

'Get her over here.' His father pulled a chair out and Sam guided her to it. 'Get some tea mashed. And make her a good strong one, with plenty of sugar.'

Sam hesitated. She looked firm in the chair but he was not sure he should let her go. Lifting her arm, he rested her elbow on the table and positioned her hand to support her head. Then, seeing the wisdom of his father's words, hurried to the stove and put the kettle on.

Hannah smiled, not because he had considered her incapable of making her own movements, but because

89

he had been using both hands. For that moment he had forgotten his deformed hand enough to touch her with it. Maybe only because his concern for her had made him forget himself . . . but it was a beginning. The second strange thought in the space of a few minutes, she told herself. But, as she began to wonder what she thought it was the beginning of, George Bunting began to speak.

'It was a damned fool thing to do – all this!' His hands swept wide around the room.

It reminded her the floor was not finished. 'I'll do it after my cup of tea.'

'No you won't!' Sam put in. 'If it's bothering you that much *I'll* do it!'

'You've got enough to do.' She felt suddenly guilty. The farm was big enough to keep four men in work and it was obvious they had to do most of it between the two of them. From what she'd seen of Jed he didn't exactly pull his weight and help to ease the load. 'I'll finish it tomorrow.' She knew there was little chance of them leaving her alone long enough to get it done now. And she did not want Sam having to do it. 'Perhaps it was foolish to try and do it all in one go.'

'Too damned right it was.' George Bunting scraped another chair from beneath the table and sat down, leaving the one he had pulled out previously to clutter the room.

She gave an inward sigh, despairing that she would ever get them to be tidy. But if she could get them to see the wisdom of cleanliness it would be a big improvement, she told herself, as Sam handed her a large mug of thick brown liquid that looked more like Brown Windsor soup than tea. She screwed her nose up, as the first taste proved he had followed his father's instructions to the letter: it tasted as if he had poured a whole bag of sugar into it. But she considered she had caused enough trouble for one day, so forced herself to drink it right down to the dregs.

She had been right in thinking they would not leave her on her own to get on with any more work. George Bunting went alone to mend the faulty tractor and Sam stayed in the house, completed scrubbing the floor, and doubled her guilt.

Chapter Six

When the cattle truck pulled into the farmyard Hannah had a terrible sinking feeling in her stomach. It was as if the final part of her past life was leaving her. Ivan Cauldwell was the new man's name and she was comforted to find he was all George Bunting had said. He herded her cows easily into the truck, without once having to resort to force. And he had brought his young son along with him. The nine-year-old immediately went to her heart by asking if the cows had names. She quickly found a piece of paper and wrote each name down, along with some distinguishing mark that would make it easy for him to pick them out.

Sam was extra nice to her for the rest of the day. He tried to get her to sit down and rest. But, as if sensing she needed some occupation to keep her mind busy, he did not push too hard.

She continued to busy herself with getting the house spick and span for the rest of the week, although she had learned her lesson of the first day and paced herself better, taking it a bit at a time instead of trying to get everything done at once. The house was large. As well as the kitchen and the large sitting-room it had another, smaller sitting-room, a very grand dining-room and an office with a large, oak desk and three old, green leather, winged chairs. Even when he was not doing the firm's accounts, George Bunting seemed to spend his evenings in the office. On several occasions she found him sitting in one of the chairs, gazing out of the window, in deep thought.

Upstairs was the bathroom and five bedrooms. The

bathroom alone was a luxury to Hannah, who was accustomed to having to drag a tin bath into the kitchen. But nothing could have prepared her for the very grand master-bedroom with an enormous bed. The cover was of the same blue and silver fabric of the curtains. On the floor was an intricately patterned carpet of the same colouring. She imagined it to be foreign. It reminded her of a flying carpet she had seen pictured in a book called *The Arabian Nights*, borrowed from the school library.

All the grandeur only increased her sense of not belonging. When the house had been cleaned from top to bottom, she decided it was time to begin thinking of herself.

'Have you got a warm coat I can borrow?' she asked Sam. They had finished eating dinner and the men were preparing to go back outside for the afternoon. 'I want to go for a walk,' she explained, when he looked up in surprise. 'The doctor says I can go out now.'

'Are you sure you feel ready to go walking? Where will you go?'

'She can go and tend to those cussed fowl,' Jed put in with feeling. For all his complaining, his father had made him take responsibility for the hens and ducks and he was sick of the blessed things.

Sam glared at his brother. 'I think we'd better start breeding rabbits. They're about all you can handle.'

'Have you got a coat?' she repeated, trying to return calm to the situation, which she found herself doing on most occasions Jed was at home. If they had not looked so alike, she would have found it difficult to believe Sam and Jed were brothers. They were always at one another's throats and their father was not a great help. He bellowed at Jed more than at Sam, yet she sensed that underneath he favoured Jed, allowing him to get away with things she was sure he would not have condoned in his younger son. 'I won't go far, if I don't feel up to it.'

Sam remained doubtful. She turned her attention

pointedly to George Bunting. 'Have you got anything?'

'Of course I've got a coat!' Sam put in irritably. 'It's just . . . well . . . I don't want you doing too much. Your legs might not be up to walking far . . . they might let you down, get you stuck. And it's cold out there. I know the doctor said you could go out now. But I don't think he was meaning a route march.'

'My legs are fine now!' she insisted. 'I've had no trouble walking round the house and cleaning up. Which coat can I borrow?' She had no intention of prolonging the conversation. She was going out and no-one was going to stop her.

'I'll get one,' George Bunting announced, while his son was still deliberating, and went out of the kitchen and up the stairs without speaking another word.

She had imagined the two boxes of women's clothes put by her bed, to be all that was left of the late Mrs Bunting's wardrobe. There had been no coat amongst them.

She had been wrong. He returned with a full length camel coat and handed it to her. 'Don't go far,' he added warningly.

As she was about to leave, Sam repeated the warning. Jed remained silent.

The coat was far too long, came down to her ankles. But it was lovely and warm and when she stepped out into the chilly air she was grateful for it, as well as the thick woollen gloves Sam had thrust on her. She was also grateful he had insisted on buying her the pair of wellingtons the day he took her to buy the suit and shoes for her father's funeral. There was no snow but the ground was icy and she would have been lost without boots.

She took to the fields, preferring the soft grass to the hard lane. She knew exactly where she was going. She paused briefly to stand and stare at the ruins of her old home. But she did not want to waste time and was soon on her way again. She would take time later to reflect on what she had lost.

When she reached the village, she made straight for the row of tall cottages that banked the far side of the river. There were five in all. Lifting the highly polished brass lion's-head knocker, she rapped loudly on the door of the middle one.

Old Madge Cresswell was very deaf, but she answered the first knock. 'Hello, me ducks. What you wanting?'

'I'm looking for lodgings.' Hannah got straight to the point. Madge was wearing her hearing-aid – which meant she must be going out somewhere special. About her daily business she always expected people to yell at her. 'I was wondering if you could take me in?' She knew Madge had a room she rented out in summer, to people who wanted to spend a week or two walking the hills. 'I know you don't usually do it in winter, but I am desperate. If you could just manage it for a few weeks . . . until I could find somewhere else.' She hoped she could persuade Madge to take her permanently, but anything would be better than nothing.

'Eeh, luv, you're ter late,' Madge exclaimed, lifting her work-worn hands and slapping them down against her thin thighs. 'I've got meself a gentleman, only this last week. He's an artist. Paints lovely pictures. You should see some of 'em.'

Hannah gave a sigh. If only she had listened to her own head, instead of letting herself be swayed by feelings of guilt and the need to repay George Bunting. 'Is he staying long?' Her voice was flat.

'He's paid me three months in advance. Said I'd better have it while he'd got it. But he might want to stay longer. Says it depends on if he sells much of what he paints.'

Hannah gave a bleak nod. Her first line of attack had been wiped away. Feeling sure Madge would not have anyone at this time of year, her mind had not contemplated a second move. 'Is there anyone else who might take me in?'

Madge scratched her bony fingers in her thin grey hair.

'You can try Bella Bower. She sometimes takes the odd one . . . in summer, mind. I'm not saying she'd want to take somebody perm'nent.'

'Well, thank you.' Hannah gave a thin smile. 'I can at least give her a try.'

'You had enough of Bunting's Claw then?' Madge asked, stopping Hannah as she was turning away.

'Bunting's Tor!' she insisted, the words out before she could stop them. Colour flooded into her cheeks. She was not sure why she had felt the sudden rush of anger on hearing the derogatory name. 'It isn't Sam's fault he was born the way he was.' A note of contrition entered her voice and she dropped her gaze embarrassedly to the ground. The last thing she had wanted to do was upset Madge: she might still want to fall back on her when her artist gentleman was gone.

'P'rhaps not,' Madge agreed. 'But the sins of the father!' She inclined her head meaningfully.

Hannah gave a nod. It would take more than a few angry words to change the way people thought about the Buntings. Jed did not concern her. He was everything his father was, and more. At least his father was not afraid of a day's work; Jed was just an idler. But now she had got to know a little of Sam it seemed so unfair to label him the same. Worse in fact, for the name might be aimed at his father, but it pointed at Sam's deformity.

Bella Bower lived back on the other side of the river. Hannah reversed her path, crossed the old wooden footbridge for the second time, past the market-place where the lane leading to the Tor came into the village, and made her way down the long row of terraced grey stone houses to the next to last one.

As she walked through the gate into the pocket-handkerchief-sized garden and knocked on the door, she was not hopeful. Bella Bower had a husband and three huge sons, all miners, and the house was not of great proportions.

'Hey up, Hannah!' It was Derek, the youngest of the sons, who opened the door. He was one day older than Hannah and, because of it, had always felt close to her, as if they shared something in common.

'Is your mum in?' Her voice was shaky and she felt her limbs begin to tremble, as his eyes gleamed at her in his familiar fashion. What was she doing? She suddenly began to question her common sense. Was she jumping from the fat to the frying pan? Derek had always teased her and Ralph, the middle brother, at one time had taken to hanging round the cottage. Her father had sent him packing on several occasions. But their mother would be here. She would not be the only woman in the house. Finding courage in the last thought, when Bella Bower's huge form appeared at the door, she hurriedly said, 'I'm looking for somewhere to live. If you could just put me up for a week or two, I'd appreciate it.'

Bella's fat face dimpled into a frown of disbelief, her colourless eyes becoming piercing dots, as they moved quickly up and down the length of Hannah. 'You might not be bigger than twopenn'oth of coppers, but where do you think I've got room to put you – with my great lumping lads?'

Hannah gave a shrug, feeling stupid and not knowing what to say. She thought better than to point out Madge Cresswell had told her Bella sometimes took people in.

'We can find a corner for her,' Derek put in over his mother's shoulder.

Before Hannah could object, his mother turned on him. 'Aye, and I know what corner you'd pick, you dirty young bugger!' Her large hand cracked him a hefty swipe on the side of his head.

'Hey, Mam!' He raised his arm in protection and Hannah had to fight hard to conceal a smile. He, like his father and brothers, was built like a prize Hereford bull and despite his mother's size dwarfed her by several inches. But she was still master of them all, leading them

97

along as if they really were bulls she had by the nose. 'We could take Hannah in,' he continued to protest.

His mother ignored him. She turned back to Hannah, folding huge muscular arms that any miner would have been proud of. 'I can't take you. You can see what it would be like.' She jerked her head at her son. 'With the three of them you'd never get any peace. I'd have to be with you day and night and I don't want that responsibility on me shoulders.'

Her truthfulness was not needed. Hannah had already decided that knocking on their door had been a big mistake. She quickly thanked them politely and hurried away, berating herself for a fool. She tried three more houses: two belonging to widows who lived alone; the third belonging to two sisters who had never married. The answer was the same at all of them: they did not want anyone sharing their home. By the time she got back to the market place, she knew she had to go further afield. She was not going to find anywhere to live in the village. It made her unhappy to consider leaving the hills, the countryside she loved, but there was no other solution. As she turned up the lane leading back to the Tor, she was planning how to get George Bunting to agree to take her into Derby on Friday, when he made his usual trip to market.

By the time she reached the cottage it had begun to drizzle. The wind got up, whipping the rain into her face and making her wish she had tied her hair in a pony-tail, instead of leaving it loose. It blew all over her face and it took her several attempts before she had gathered it up to stuff inside the collar of the camel coat. Then she stood staring at the crumbled stones of her old home. Nothing had changed. It was the same heart-rending sight that it had been on the way down. All that was left was one precariously balanced front corner, the rest was just a heap of rubble with one oak tree lying by its side and another remaining firm like a sentinel standing guard over the decay. She found it ironical that the old wooden cowshed was still standing: for years it had looked as if a heavy breath would have blown it down.

'Oh Dad!' Tears filled her eyes, to compete with the rain. The afternoon was drawing on and the light would soon be fading. She should get back, she told herself, but did not move. The long coat flapped at her legs and the sting of tears pressed stronger at her eyes. For several minutes she stood there, transfixed by her loss, numbed by a feeling of isolation and emptiness that reached right to her soul. She had nothing. It was not a new realization. But seeing it all with her own eyes hammered the reality home with the force of a mallet.

When finally she moved, it was not towards the Tor but into the ruins of her life. The stones were rocky and uneven. Some she pushed aside, some she crawled over on all fours. The long coat got in the way, but did not stop her. The rain came faster but she carried on. There had to be something, no matter how small, that was still whole, still the same as she remembered. Stone after stone she pushed aside, digging a hole deeper and deeper into the debris. Suddenly there was a gap. Beneath it was a patch of the rag rug that had sat in front of the kitchen hearth. Her movements became faster, speeding up with the realization that she was getting there, reaching something solid that was part of her past. The next stones were flung away with renewed zeal.

She stopped, her breath catching in her throat. Slowly she reached down, her fingers closing round the cold brass frame. It was more than she had hoped for. For several moments she could only stare at the photograph of her mother and father that had stood on the mantelpiece. The glass was cracked and one corner of the frame was broken off. But the photograph was unmarked, whole. Her mother and father smiled out at her in the way they had always done.

Tears suddenly gushed from her eyes and her head

bent low, almost bumping against the stones, as wracking sobs took her breath away. 'I don't want to leave here,' she said, sitting back on her heels and composing herself. She wiped her tears away on Sam's woollen gloves and looked bleakly round the darkening countryside. It was where she belonged, where her mother and father were. It was almost as if she could feel them around her, comforting her.

A barn owl swooped low overhead, came to rest in the bare branches of the upright oak tree and gave a loud hoot, as if telling her to go, she was on his property, she no longer belonged there.

She nodded her head. Yes, she thought, accepting that she should leave, the night-time creature making her aware of the diminishing light. It would be fully dark by the time she got back to the Tor. She had been gone for three hours and she had promised she would not be long.

She tucked the treasured photograph deep into the coat's pocket and crawled back over the stones until she was free of all the debris and could stand upright. She began to walk along the lane, but when she reached the first gate she climbed over. The route back to the Tor was much shorter across the fields and she had no fear of the darkness, she knew the hills like the back of her hand.

'Where the hell have you been?' George Bunting demanded, the moment she stepped through the door.

'For a walk . . . you know that,' she replied flatly, too drained of emotion to raise her voice.

'I didn't expect you to stay out this long!'

'Sorry,' she returned lamely, feeling the anger of his eyes stabbing her as she pulled her wellington boots off and dropped them wearily by the door.

He hesitated expectantly, until realizing she was not going to say more. 'Sam's out looking for you!' he snapped. 'Haven't you passed him?'

'Sorry,' she repeated, taking the photograph out and laying it on the table while she took the coat off.

He stared at the photograph, his eyes widening. 'Christ Almighty! You've never been all the way down there?'

And some, she thought. But she would not tell him she had been all the way down to the village. He would want to know why . . . and she was not telling him anything, until it was all sorted out and he could not stop her.

'It was too far . . . for your first time out!'

'I'm perfectly all right.' In body, it was true. It was her mind that was dulled, adding the flatness to her voice and the bleakness to her eyes. Seeing what remained of her old life had been a stunning experience that even finding the photograph had not eased. She felt empty, so very, very empty.

'It was damned stupid not to get back before dark! Anything could have happened to you!'

She gave a grim smile. What could happen out there that could not happen here? She fixed him with a pointed gaze.

'Your legs could have given out!'

It was almost as if he had read her mind, answered her unspoken question. Feeling suddenly vulnerable, she turned away and hurried to the pantry. 'Do you want pork chops or a slice of gammon?' She felt it was time to change the subject and prove to him that his concern was not only unwanted, but also unnecessary. 'I can have either done quickly,' she prompted, when he remained silent. 'Is Jed in?' She kept her voice calm, even though it had only just occurred to her that she might be alone with him.

'Is he hell!' He scraped a chair from beneath the table and flopped on to it with a weary sigh. 'Leave the blasted food alone!'

That he had sat down pleased her. She felt, if he had been about to use the opportunity to make a grab for her, he would have remained standing. 'I can have it ready for when Sam gets back.' She ignored his protest, gave up waiting for his decision, and picked up the pork chops. 'Do you think he'll be long? When did he go out?'

'About twenty minutes ago. He's in the car. I don't know how you missed him.'

She took the potato knife from the drawer to begin peeling and wondered how she had missed the car's headlights moving down the lane. Too lost in your own thoughts, she told herself. 'I came up the fields,' she said.

'Christ! You bloody little fool!'

The knife hit the sink with a clatter. Pressing her hands into her hips she turned on him. 'My father never found it necessary to swear after every breath and I'd thank you to learn some more intelligent language!'

His mouth dropped open, for a moment words failed him. 'Now . . . listen here . . . madam!' he spluttered, his face turning a furious pink. 'This is my house and I'll do what I da . . .' She wanted to laugh when he checked himself, before concluding meekly, 'Do what I please in it.'

'You make that perfectly obvious . . . to me and everybody else! If you learned how to be more like the gentleman you try to make out you are, you might find life a bit better.'

His eyes narrowed questioningly. 'Are you trying to tell me that if I stopped swearing you might judge me in a better light?'

'No,' she replied, quickly turning back to peel the potatoes, realizing her quick tongue had got her into trouble again. 'I was meaning you'd be more respected if you learnt how to respect others. You'd be less of a joke, not looked on as a laughing stock.'

He gave a bark of laughter. 'They only mock because they're jealous of all I've got.'

'All you've got!' She turned back to him in disbelief. 'What have you got? A fine house that looked like a pigsty before I got hold of it. And counting your money doesn't keep you warm at night.'

'It keeps me a damned sight warmer than your father must have been in that little hovel!'

'Don't you speak of my father!' Her anger boiled that he should dare to deride the man she loved so much. 'He was ten times as rich as you. He had love, because he knew how to give it!'

He stood up, his jaw tightening and his gaze fixing her purposefully, as he moved towards her.

Only then did she understand the error of provoking him. She turned quickly back to the sink and picked up the knife. 'Where can Sam have got to?' she asked, more for something to say than from any real concern. He knew the hills as well as she did and would never get lost.

'He's looking for you!' he reminded her harshly, so close to her that she felt the brush of his breath in her hair.

A tremor of fear trickled down her spine. 'Well, I'm here!' she pointed out, not daring to look at him. 'So maybe you should go out and let him know that fact. If he thought I would stick to the road he could be in the village by now. He could be gone for hours.' Anything to get him out of the kitchen, she thought, just as a pair of headlights lit up the farmyard. 'He's back,' she said, unable to conceal her relief that they were no longer alone.

But her relief was short-lived. The vehicle came to a standstill by the side of the stables. 'It's the Land Rover,' she said. She looked up at him. 'You did say Sam was in the car?'

He leaned over her to see out of the window. She took a hasty sidestep out of his way. 'It's Jed,' he announced unnecessarily, as Jed got out of the cab and came over to the door. His unsteady gait indicated he had been indulging in his usual pastime: drinking.

'Where's Sam?' his father demanded impatiently, as Jed came through the door.

'How should I know?' he returned belligerently, his

alcohol-reddened face looking from one to the other.

'Haven't you passed him?' George Bunting took the words from Hannah's lips.

'No.' Jed reeled across to the table and almost fell into a chair. 'What's wrong?' he finally asked.

Hannah's gaze pivoted anxiously to George Bunting. There was only one road to the Tor and she did not really believe her earlier suggestion that he would have gone into the village. Jed should have passed him . . . somewhere. The lane was so narrow that you had to stop if there was anything to pass. Even in his present condition Jed could not have missed the car. She felt herself go cold inside. 'Where . . .' she began.

But George Bunting was not waiting for questions. He was across the kitchen and thrusting his feet into his boots.

'Come on, Jed,' he ordered, as he grabbed his battered wax jacket. Jed did not move. '*I said come on!*' He flew across the room, grabbed Jed by the arm and dragged him off the chair and across the room to the door.

Everything happened so quickly that they had crossed the yard, before Hannah woke up to what was happening. 'Wait!' she called, not wanting to be left alone to worry about Sam. 'Let me come!'

'No,' George Bunting returned firmly, as he bundled Jed into the passenger seat. Then, having to leap over and around the pack of excited dogs, raced round to the driver's seat and flung the door open. 'You stay here in case he comes back before us,' he ordered, as he swung himself into the cab.

'How can he come back without passing you?'

If he heard he ignored her. The Land Rover's engine blazed into life and it hurtled out of the yard, sending dogs in all directions.

She gave a sigh. Oh Sam! please be all right. If he was hurt. Oh no! She clamped her hand to her mouth and closed her eyes tightly. She was to blame. If she had not stayed out so long he would not have had to go out looking for her. If he was hurt it was her fault!

As if sensing her distress, Seth, the oldest of the dogs, came sniffing up to her. They were all collies, all working dogs. Seth was black and white and reminded her of Sal. She crouched down, fondling his head as he nuzzled up to her neck. 'What's happened to him?' she asked, seeking comfort in the warmth of the soft furry body. 'Could Jed really have been too drunk to see the car?'

Seth gave a whine.

'Oh Seth.' She dropped her forehead against his neck, wishing he could have talked to her. She felt so alone. That seemed to be the order of the day, she reminded herself. First the useless trip to the village. Then scrabbling through the remains of her home. She had not thought that to be useless . . . but was finding the photograph worth Sam getting hurt?

She pushed herself up and stood staring down at Seth's enquiringly upturned head. 'No,' she said flatly. Her mother's and father's images were indelibly printed on her mind. With or without the photograph she would never forget them. But if something had happened to Sam because she had spent the time searching for it . . . !

No, she ordered herself. She did not know anything had happened to Sam. There was probably a perfectly reasonable explanation. 'Wait,' she told Seth, and hurried into the kitchen to fetch a handful of dog biscuits.

By the time she got back to the door the word had gone out. All eight dogs were standing clustered round the step. She gave each a biscuit. 'I don't care if he does think I'm spoiling you.' George Bunting was very particular that no-one fed *his* dogs. They were working stock, he insisted. Not to be turned into overweight lap-dogs. But for all his bluster she knew he regularly went around with a pocket full of biscuits. She had seen him slip them one . . . when he thought no-one was looking. She shook her head. He was a strange man.

The dinner was all prepared ready to be cooked and the table laid. Hannah glanced at the large wooden clock standing on the mantel. It was half an hour since they left. They should be back soon, she told herself, wishing she could have enough faith in her own reckoning to light the gas under the saucepans and have everything cooked and ready to put on the table when they walked in.

The sudden barking of dogs made her jump. She rushed to the window, expecting the canine chorus to be a greeting. There was no sight of the Land Rover or the Jaguar. There was no searching beam of headlights reaching up into the darkness of the sky, indicating a vehicle was coming up the steep hill before coming through the gates. The noise had been nothing more than a couple of dogs having a scrap. It was soon over. The yapping came to an end and her heart sank.

Realizing her loneliness was not about to come to an end, she turned disconsolately to the table, straightened a knife and fork that was already straight and almost knocked the milk jug over. Leave well alone, she told herself, lifting her hand carefully away. She gave a sigh. The longer it went on the worse her fears were becoming.

In the next moment she had her wellingtons on and was hurrying from the house. From the gate she had a good view down the hills and could see every inch of the lane until it turned the tight bend that took it into the village.

But the hills were cloaked in darkness. There was no bright illumination of a vehicle's headlights, no dark silhouette moving towards her. Anxiety turned to panic. They had all vanished now. Her eyes frantically traced the invisible route of the blacked-out lane and she wished she had thought to come out there when the Land Rover left. Then she could have watched where they went.

She suddenly jumped, startled by something soft brushing against her leg. She looked down to find the dogs all clustered round her feet. At least she was not completely alone. 'Where's your master gone?' she asked.

With the perfection of timing that could have belonged to a team of ballroom dancers, eight pairs of ears pricked up, their heads turned, noses pointing down the lane, alert eyes staring into the darkness.

'I know that,' she said. 'But thanks all the same.' She was just considering that getting her canine helpers another biscuit would be more useful than standing there, when a pair of headlights came round the bend out of the village. She held her breath until it had passed the lane that led off to Northgate Farm and she knew it was coming to the Tor.

It was the Land Rover. As it pulled into the yard she raced by its side, having the door open before George Bunting had brought it to a halt. 'Where is he? Have you found him? Is he all right?'

'No he isn't bloody all right!' He yanked the brake on and pushed her aside to give himself room to jump out of the cab.

'Why? What's happened? Where is he?' She raced beside him as he strode purposefully across the yard to the house. 'Tell me?' she begged, when he only favoured her with a withering glance.

'He's at the Infirmary.'

Her stomach lurched and she was sure her heart stopped beating as her breath caught on a loud gasp. 'Why? Oh, please, tell me!' She grabbed his arm when he reached the door.

He shook her off and hurried inside.

She chased after him. 'I'm sorry. I know it is all my fault. But tell me how he is? What has he done? Has he had an accident? Is the car damaged?' Her voice flattened out on the last. She imagined damage to his precious car would be higher on his list of concerns than Sam would be.

'No, the car is not damaged.' Reaching the table he pressed his fists into the top and leaned heavily on arms that shook with his fury. 'But Sam is . . . !' He turned on her slowly. Had she not already accepted that she was to blame, she would have done so then. His eyes were filled with a cold accusation that spiked across the distance of the room, and filled her own with more dread than she had felt all evening.

She shook her head. Not wanting to believe what her mind was telling her.

'He went down to your old place, thinking that is where he would find you.' His voice ground through her head like the rumble of distant thunder and she felt beads of perspiration break out on her lip and forehead. She must have missed him by minutes, seconds even. 'He pulled the car into the yard and left the headlights full on, to give himself some light while he searched for you. He was in the cowshed when the battery gave out and he was thrust into darkness. He thought he was skirting the rubble as he made his way back to the lane. But he fell, landing in the heap of stones. He's broken his wrist. They're putting it in plaster and I've to fetch him in a couple of hours.'

'Broken his wrist!' She was not sure if she had spoken or not. From the look in his eyes she had imagined Sam to be dead. A great wave of relief flooded through her. She could hear it roaring in her ears, feel it wobbling in her head. It reached her eyes and George Bunting blurred. Then she had the feeling someone was bending her knees for her and she was sinking to the floor.

The next thing she knew, she was sitting slumped against the table. George Bunting was cursing profusely as he hovered over her and Jed was sitting at the opposite side of the table, grinning at her.

'I asked you to stop swearing,' she reminded him, rubbing her head and wondering what had happened.

'And I could ask you to stop fainting all the time.' He glared at her accusingly.

'I do not faint all the time!' she snapped, insulted by the charge. But her head rocked giddily, as she attempted to stress the point by staring coolly at him. She dropped her gaze quickly to the table top, not speaking until she was sure she had full control again. 'It's only because I've been ill. I don't make a habit of it.'

He gave a disgusted snort. 'But I thought you were well again!' he blazed meaningfully. 'At least you were supposed to be when you insisted on being damned fool enough to go out on your own!'

'I'm sorry.' It was all she could say. She did not need him to tell her who was responsible for all this mess. 'But he's only got a broken wrist,' she added lamely.

'Only a broken wrist! It will keep him out of work for weeks. How the blazes do you think I'm going to run this place without him?'

She gave a grim smile. It was only his precious farm he was thinking of. And for a moment there he had had her thinking he was concerned for Sam.

She cocked her thumb at Jed. 'He'll have to get his hands mucky,' she said, casting him a disparaging glance.

'I already do!' He scowled mutinously. 'I do my bit.'

Only when your father puts his boot behind you, she thought bitterly.

'It takes three to run this place,' his father pointed out.

She looked up into his face. 'Then you'll have to find yourself a farm-hand. I'm sure if you pay over the odds you'll find someone who can stick you for a few weeks.'

'I've already got one.' His eyes gleamed purposefully into hers. 'You know how to work a farm – and you owe me!' he added pointedly, as the objection rose to her lips. 'Nobody else would have taken you in like I've done – without asking for a penny off you.'

She dropped her head and toyed with the knife in front of her. He was wrong, she thought bitterly. Nobody would take her in full stop. This afternoon she had been willing to pay yet they had all turned her away. Before he could open his mouth she began to nod her head.

'All right,' she agreed flatly, preferring to hear herself accepting rather than hear him ordering her to stay. 'You've got yourself a farm-hand.'

She was not doing it for him, she told herself, as she got up to set a match to the grill, then to the gas rings under the waiting saucepans. She wanted to be there for Sam. He would need someone to nurse him if he was incapacitated. It was only right that she should repay him for all he had done for her.

And it was only for a few weeks.

Chapter Seven

'I need you in the byre!'

Hannah looked round with a sigh. She was in the middle of baking and had flour and dough up to her elbows. The last thing she needed was being called out to clear up one of Jed's messes. 'What is it now?' She fixed him with an irritated glare, as he hovered in the doorway.

'I think one of the new batch is about to calve.'

She stared at him blankly. He *thought*! He'd lived on a farm all his life and he didn't know!

'You're imagining it.' Sam glanced Hannah a knowing look. His brother only knew one end of a cow from the other because food went in the top and the muck came out of the bottom.

'You'd better come and have a look.'

Hannah gave another sigh, resigned herself to the bread being spoiled, and washed her hands. It was three weeks since Sam had broken his wrist and today was the first day his father had left the three of them alone.

Although the snow had so far come only in dribs and drabs, it was not safe to risk getting too low on stores of feed and he had gone to market to replenish their dwindling stock. 'There was nothing they could not handle!' Or so he had said before leaving.

'You must be wrong.' Hannah wiped her hands dry and looked to Sam, seeking reassurance. 'They aren't due for another week . . . nine days, in fact.'

'I'll go.' Sam pushed himself up from the table.

'You stay where you are!' She hurried to the door and Jed. 'If we need you I'll come and tell you.' Keeping Sam out of action had been worse than putting half-a-dozen children in a sweet shop and telling them they could not eat anything. She knew if he got out there and there really was a problem, he would need chaining to keep him out of it. And the doctor had been very insistent that he must not put any pressure on his wrist until it was fully healed.

'Come on!' She shoved Jed out of the door, closing it very firmly on Sam.

When they reached the byre, her heart sank. The cow was stretched out on her side. Her eyes were only half-open and her rib cage heaved as if she had been chased around a field.

She glared at Jed. This had not suddenly happened. 'How long has she been like this?' Her voice rippled with anger. He was useless. The vet should have been fetched long before now.

He gave a shrug. 'I came in around eleven o'clock and she was a bit agitated. I didn't come in again till just now.'

She gave yet another sigh. It was almost two o'clock. He had left her for three hours!

The cow suddenly let out a heart-rending bellow. Her body stiffened in a violent contraction which subsided into shivering waves.

Something had to be done – and quickly.

She looked at Jed. His face had gone white and he looked about to faint. 'Go and get the vet. If he's out go and find him. Don't come back without him!'

He did not need telling twice. He was at the door, as she called, 'And tell Sam to come over.'

Trust George Bunting to pick today, she thought, as she hurried to the tap outside and filled the bucket! He could have sent Jed to get the new stocks . . . He was capable of that without getting in a mess.

Beneath her jumper she was only wearing a bra and vest. But it was no time to consider propriety and when she returned to the cow, she pulled her jumper off and tossed it on to the floor. She was scrubbing her hands and arms with the large block of carbolic soap, always left in the byre for such occasions, when Sam came rushing in.

'What is it?' He came up short. 'What are you doing?'

She met his astonishment with blank resignation. 'I don't know,' she admitted. She had watched her father perform the task on many occasions when a calf was finding its way into the world difficult. But she had never done anything so personal herself. 'That's why I want you here!' She stood up, fixing him pointedly and shaking her head. 'You're not doing it!' If it meant the cow was going to die, she was not letting him do anything that would prejudice his recovery. 'You can tell me what to do.'

'Can't it wait for the vet?'

She shook her head and turned her gaze bleakly to the inert cow.

He took one look. 'Bloody hell! The old man will kill him!'

Yes, she thought. If nothing else, when George Bunting found out how his animal had been neglected, Jed would feel his wrath. She gave a grimace. Knowing him he would squirm out of it, pushing some of the blame on to them.

'So come on . . . tell me what to do?' She knelt down behind the cow and looked at him expectantly.

He shook his head. 'You can't do it. I'll have a go with my left hand.'

'Not likely!' He could put his left hand inside the cow but he would have to push against its rump with his injured hand to get any force behind him. Before he could continue to object, she gritted her teeth against the indignity of what she was about to do, and inserted her hand gently inside the cow.

Sam rushed forward. She warded him off with her free hand. 'Don't get in the way. This is difficult enough.'

He backed off, looking less than convinced that he was right to do so.

She pushed her hand further inside. 'I can feel the legs,' she said, closing her fingers round two tiny cloven feet squashed closely together.

Sam hesitated, finally he said, 'Move up the legs until you feel the head.'

It seemed she was reaching forever. Her arm was deep inside before, with a sigh of relief, her fingers touched something else. She felt around. Her heart sank. 'It's the throat. The head is back.' She did not need Sam to tell her what that meant. Before the calf could be born the head needed turning, bringing down so that it would fit into the birth canal.

The cow gave another sudden bellow, its body contracted around her arm. It felt as if her bones were being crushed and she gave a gasp of pain.

'Come out. Let me take over,' Sam insisted.

The contraction eased and the blood returned to her arm. 'No . . . I can do it.' She forced herself to sound calm and in control. But in her mind she was wanting to tell him to go and get the shotgun and put the poor creature out of her misery, before she caused it more distress. It was only knowing that Sam would never have resorted to the gun before having a go himself, that made her continue. 'Tell me what to do!' she insisted urgently.

He looked about to protest, then changed his mind. 'All right,' he reluctantly agreed. 'You've got to get the head down.' He hurried across the byre and came back with a rope. 'Can you get this tied round the legs?'

'How do I tie a knot with one hand?'

With great difficulty! He did not voice the thought. The chances of her getting it secure were very remote. He just prayed the vet would be in when Jed got there and they would both be back soon. A job like this needed at least two strong men. 'Make a noose before you put it in,' he said, doing it for her. 'Pull it tight when it's round the legs.'

He made it sound so easy. Not wanting to disillusion him, she pulled her arm out, took the rope from him, and returned to the cow without uttering one word.

The noose went round the legs easily enough. She pulled gently on the rope. By some miracle it tightened. 'I've got it!' Jubilation filled her voice.

Had it not frightened the cow, Sam would have let out a whoop of joy. 'Right,' he said, quickly gathering himself and grabbing hold of the loose end of the rope. 'Now you've got to get your arm further down. Push the calf back and try to free its head at the same time.'

She grimaced. 'Push it back?'

'Yes. It should release the head.' If we're lucky. They had been lucky so far and he prayed it would last out a bit longer – just a bit longer!

As she pushed forward the cow contracted again. She gave a yelp. Then was reduced to quick panting breaths as the pain subsided and the use came back to her arm. 'I feel as if I'm having this calf myself,' she gasped.

'You're doing fine.'

It made her smile. He could have been urging her on in her own labour.

'Can you get behind the head?'

'I don't know. Oh . . . !'

'What is it?' he demanded, his impotence getting the better of him.

'It moved. I think it moved!'

He closed his eyes and thanked heaven. It seemed to be alive. In these situations it would have been more than likely to have suffocated. He knew how she would feel if, after all this, she did not have a healthy mother and baby on her hands. 'Let's get it out quickly then.' Time was against them. And he wanted it born alive – for Hannah's sake. 'Is anything happening?'

She found the shoulder and pushed hard. The calf slipped backwards and she fastened her hand around its neck. The mother's contractions forced it forward again and she had to rest. 'I've got the neck.' She was breathing hard. Oh, please don't let me damage it, she begged. Then suddenly remembering how she had felt her parents to be around her when she was sitting in the ruins of the cottage, she began to speak to her father. If you're near me, please make me do the right thing, she silently begged, biting her lip as she gave the calf another push backwards. Suddenly the head was down, she could feel an ear touching her arm. 'It's there.'

'Where? Is it lying on the legs?'

'Yes . . . yes.' Excitement vibrated in her voice.

'Get hold of the legs and pull when I tell you.'

She fastened her fingers round the rope's noose, fearing it might come off when Sam pulled.

'Now,' he called, and as the cow strained they both pulled together.

'Is it all right?' Hannah stared anxiously at the little animal lying motionless in the straw.

Sam immediately cleared the mucus from its mouth. Then he lifted it up and placed it by its mother's head. The cow looked past caring and Hannah bit her lip. But suddenly the mother lifted her head, nuzzled at the calf, then began licking it clean. Within seconds the calf was wriggling and kicking and very much alive.

Thank you, Dad. Hannah was sure he had been there to guide her hand. She turned to Sam. 'Now tell me I can't do it.' A teasing light filled her eyes.

He shook his head. 'I wish you were my brother.'

She began to laugh, then suddenly stopped. Inside her head was a little voice that told her the last thing she wanted to be was his brother. Not because she did not want to be classed with the useless Jed, but because being his brother would not allow her to be close to him in the way she suddenly knew she wanted to be close to him. It was strange and unexpected. But when she looked at him, she suddenly saw how like her father he was. Not in looks, in manner. Though his appearance was definitely Bunting, his manner was soft and gentle and totally alien to his father and brother.

Her face must have relayed something of her thoughts. For several seconds he watched her oddly. It was not until he said, 'You'd better get your jumper back on,' that she remembered her state of undress. Blushing furiously, she grabbed the discarded woolly from the floor and hurriedly pulled it over her head.

'I'd better go and get cleaned up.' Feeling suddenly embarrassed with him she hurried from the byre. Although she was not sure if her discomfort was from him seeing her in her underwear, or from the new-found feelings she had just discovered. The vest had belonged to his mother, was far thicker than anything she would have chosen for herself, and would not have given him any sight of her bra beneath. Even so, she was grateful to get away from him – and even more grateful that his father had not come back and caught her wearing it.

*   *   *

Jed had to drag Bill Stenson, the vet, away from treating a horse's badly torn fetlock. The calf was half an hour old when he finally arrived. He tended to the cow and pronounced mother and baby fine. Then he patted Hannah on the back and quickly returned to the horse with the torn fetlock.

George Bunting was not so understanding, or complimentary. He did not return until early evening, with a scowl on his face to match the angry black clouds that filled the sky and obliterated any sign of a star or moon.

'What the hell's been going off here?' The back door slammed behind him and he positioned himself just inside the kitchen, hands pressed to his hips, blazing eyes leaping erratically between Sam's and Hannah's astonished faces. Jed had taken it upon himself to vanish soon after the vet, and had not been seen since.

'You've got a new bull,' Sam announced, from the table where he had been reading the evening paper.

'I know that. I've seen Bill Stenson. How did it happen? What the blazes were you playing at?'

Sam gave a sigh, dropped the newspaper on the table and stood up, rounding on his father. 'It happened because number one son was being his usual hopeless self! He was supposed to be keeping an eye on them. Well he did. At eleven o'clock, then at two o'clock. It's him you should be getting at. As soon as Hannah saw what was happening, she got stuck in. You should be thanking her. If it wasn't for her you wouldn't have any new bull . . . and you'd be a cow short, as well.'

'Couldn't you have gone and looked at them?' The suggestion of gratitude had been lost on him.

'No he couldn't.' Hannah's hands went to her own hips, matching his stance as she glared at him. 'He's supposed to be resting. And it never occurred to us that we had to check up on Jed.'

'We thought even he was capable of coming and telling us if there was any trouble,' Sam put in drily.

His father's lips tightened. 'What were *you* doing?' His gaze fixed Hannah meaningfully.

'S'truth!' Sam wheeled his head away, then back to his father, his eyes blazing. 'You'll never learn . . . will you? You won't hear any bad said about your precious, *perfect* son. He's a nowter, nothing, useless. Hannah fed and watered the cows, sheep, horses, hens and ducks. He didn't lift a finger to help. Then she started in the house. All he had to do was walk round and make sure everything was in order . . . and he couldn't even do that properly!' His left hand swept through the air, the thickened digits stabbing towards Hannah. 'She's worth twelve of him. And all you can do is blame her for not doing his work as well as her own.'

His father remained unmoved. 'It shouldn't have happened!' he blazed. 'You must have had some idea of what he was and wasn't doing. You knew I wasn't around.' The condemnation of his glare fixed Hannah once more. 'The house could have waited. You should have known the farm was more important.'

'You're pathetic, George Bunting,' she snarled bitterly. Sam's comment about the *perfect* son had gone deep. She knew it was true. Jed could get away with murder, because his father saw him as whole and unblemished. He was not tainted; while the deformity of his second son he looked upon as a curse and a slur against himself and his so-called superior standing in the community. George Bunting was too pompous and self-righteous to believe the slurs were aimed at him. 'Sam's right, you can't see what's in front of your own nose. Well, don't think I did anything for you this afternoon! It was the cow I was thinking of. I'd have done it for anybody's.'

'You ungrateful little bitch!' He rushed at her, would have had his hands on her, if Sam had not got in front of him first.

'Leave her alone!' Pulling his injured arm free of the sling, he pushed the plaster cast into his father's chest.

'Your wrist! Stop it, you'll damage it!' She grabbed Sam's arm and tried to pull him back but he thrust her away, sending her bumping against the table. His father's fist came back. She clutched tightly at the tablecloth and gave a frightened gasp. 'No!' she called. But he still swung at his son.

Sam ducked and the punch hit empty air. His father swore, pushed him out of the way and advanced on Hannah. 'It's about time you learned to show a bit of respect!' His finger made threatening stabs at her. 'Who was it paid for your father's funeral? Who's been keeping you these last weeks?'

'You'll get every penny back!' She glared at him with hate, regretting that she had not immediately paid him something out of the money she had earned on the sale of the cows. But she knew it would not have been enough to pay everything she owed him and, until she knew where she was going and how much it was going to cost her, she had wanted to hang on to it.

He gave a bark of disbelief.

In the next moment Sam's clawed hand fastened to his father's throat. 'It's about time *you* learned to show a bit of respect.' He echoed his father's words, and shook him like a rabbit. 'Hannah's more than paid you back for anything you might have done for her.'

His father gave a growl, lifted his balled fist. Sam was faster. The plastered hand crunched into his father's chin, sending his head back with a jolt.

Sam groaned and clutched his injured hand to him.

George Bunting reeled backwards, but soon righted himself and was stepping towards his son, his expression thunderous.

'Stop it!' Hannah screamed, rushing at him and tugging at his arm. 'He's hurt! You can see he's hurt!'

'Get off me!' He shook her off so roughly she was sent sprawling to the floor. He lunged at Sam, grabbed him by his injured arm and spun him round by it. Sam gave a shriek of pain as he tottered unsteadily, trying to gain his balance and hold his arm at the same time. It was obvious he was in no condition to retaliate. But still his father swung back his arm, sending his fist crashing up against his chin with such violence that Sam was lifted several inches off the floor.

His knees buckled and he sank to the floor in an ominous silence. His father advanced on him and Hannah screamed. Then she was scrabbling to her feet. He was mad, she thought, and flung herself bodily at his back. 'Stop it! Stop it!' Her legs went round his hips, her heels digging into the front of his thighs. She coiled her arms tightly round his neck and forced his chin upwards. But she made little impression.

He was like an enraged bull, would not be tethered. He bucked and spiralled, trying to throw her off. 'Get off me you stupid bitch!'

'Not until you calm down!' Sam appeared to be only semi-conscious and she would have preferred to go to his aid, but she would not risk releasing his father until she was sure he would not attack him again.

'*Get off me!*' Bellowing like a tormented animal he reeled backwards, sending them both crashing into the wall. She gave a gasp, feeling his weight crushing her to the plaster.

Her legs tightened around his waist, the hard edge of her heels pushed deep into his stomach. He cursed wildly. She grabbed for his hair. One hand found it and her fingers pulled it harshly against the roots. The other hand found his ear, grasped it tightly and gave it a sharp pull. His cursing became louder and more volatile. 'You're not right in the head,' she hissed in the stretched ear. 'Look at him!' She forced his head round to face Sam's inert form. 'Look what you've done!'

'He hit me first.' He lunged away from the wall and spun several, very fast full circles.

She clung on tighter. 'And that makes it all right? He's got a broken wrist. You're supposed to be his father.'

He gave a snort of disgust. But before Hannah could continue, a chuckle of amusement came from the door.

'That's a new one, Dad,' Jed stated drily, standing in the doorway, arms folded, surveying the scene with great interest. 'You'll have to teach it to me sometime.'

That Jed, who had been the cause of it all, found it so amusing, inflamed Hannah. She pulled harder on his father's ear, twisting until blood trickled down his neck.

'Christ Almighty! Get this bloody cat off me!'

Jed chuckled and moved forward. 'You're getting old. You'd never have got yourself into this mess before . . .'

'Come one step closer and he's going to be in serious trouble.' Hannah glared at Jed, the threat of her words blazing wildly from her eyes. She gave the ear another twist and the blood ran more freely, meeting the neck of his black sweater and vanishing beneath.

'Christ!' George Bunting grabbed her legs and tried to prise them apart. She yanked at his hair. 'Stop it, unless you want to end up bald.' She was not quite sure how she had got herself into this mess. A verbal argument with him was asking for trouble – but allowing it to become physical was insane. She glared at Jed and jerked her head in the direction of Sam. 'I'm not moving from here until I'm sure he's not going to hit him again.'

'He struck first.'

'Oh shut up!' She gave his ear another twist. 'You were going to hit him. Don't try and push the blame away from yourself.' She turned her attention to Jed, who was standing staring at his brother's crumpled body. 'Well . . . !' she snapped. 'Are you going to do anything? Or just be your useless self?'

He flashed her a scowl.

She glared back at him, jerked her head at her mutinous mount. 'He's been swinging him round by his broken wrist. It must be broken again. *He needs attention!*'

The message finally sank in. Jed looked at his father, then at Hannah. 'Get off him. He won't hit him again,' he added drily, and to her relief went over to Sam.

She wanted to leap down and also hurry to Sam's aid. But she held back, slipping slowly to the ground, all the time carefully watching her opponent. He might not hit Sam again, but she was not so sure she would be spared.

Glaring at her he touched his ear, then held his blood-stained fingers out to her. 'Look what you've done,' he growled.

'You'll live,' she bit back. He was still angry, but she sensed the fight had gone out of him, for the moment, at least. She was in no doubt that he would make her pay for what she had dared to do. But that would be later, when Sam had been attended to.

'Sam!' She dropped to her knees and grasped his hand. He gave no response and he looked paler and more lifeless than he had done from the other side of the room. Feeling something trembling close to her heart, she repeated his name several times. But there was nothing: no sound, no flickering eyelid. She looked up bleakly into Jed's anxious face and was grateful that he, at least, appeared to have grasped the enormity of what their father had done. 'He'll have to go to hospital,' she said, unnecessarily.

'I'll go and get the truck up to the door.' Jed immediately stood up. 'Get something to wrap him in,' he ordered, as he rushed out.

I'm sorry, Sam, she said silently, looking down into the stillness of his face. It was all her fault. If she had not attempted to pull his father back, increasing his wrath, he might not have administered that final thump, or swung him round on his broken wrist. Laying his hand gently down by his side, she ducked round the dark presence hovering over her shoulder, and hurried from the room and up the stairs to get the blankets to wrap him in.

She got back to the kitchen at the same time as Jed was coming in through the door. 'Lay one in the back of the truck,' he instructed, as he took another blanket from her and spread it out on the floor, then got his father to help him lift Sam on to it.

Once he was wrapped up, they had him in the back of the Land Rover in seconds. Hannah had spread the blanket over the thick layer of clean straw Jed had put on the floor, making a soft bed for him to lie on. She placed a third blanket over the top of him, then stood staring at his face, so white against the pale straw. She was oblivious to the dogs leaping and yapping round her legs.

'You drive,' George Bunting instructed Jed, and to Hannah's surprise pushed her out of the way and climbed into the back with Sam.

'Can I come?' She knew the answer before he replied.

She was the last person he would want with him.

He shook his head. 'If we have to stay I'll telephone and let you know.' He settled himself in the straw and completely stunned her by lifting Sam's head and resting it in his lap. Then he called to Jed to get going.

As they went through the large stone gateposts, she could only shake her head. He was the strangest man, she thought. In the space of minutes he had been like two different people: one who was capable of such anger he could physically set about his already injured son; the other a caring parent, cradling his son's head so it was not shaken about too much by the ride.

Caring seemed an odd word to use in connection with George Bunting, especially after seeing the way he usually treated Sam: which amounted to like something the dog had dragged in. She gave a sigh, suddenly recalling the day she had gone to the village and been late back. The moment he had realized Sam was missing, he had rushed out to search for him.

Maybe there was some good in him, after all, she told herself, and turned to push her way through the canine bodyguard which had settled around her feet. All noses were lifted to the point where the Land Rover had vanished and they were oddly silent, as if the severity of the moment had finally sunk in.

'Come on,' she urged, shoving them aside. She had a long time to wait and she would rather be doing something than counting the minutes.

Putting on her wellingtons and an old green windcheater that had been Sam's, but now seemed to have become her own, she went out into the yard. It being winter all the animals were in their sheds and needed to be constantly supplied with fresh food and water. So she had plenty to do to keep her mind from dwelling on all the awful things that could have happened to Sam.

It was almost midnight and there had been no telephone call. Hannah had run out of things to do and was sitting at the kitchen table, hands clenched as if in prayer. As the hours had ticked by her frantic imaginings had diminished, but they had left behind a dull certainty that only the very worst could have happened. When she finally heard the Land Rover coming into the yard she rushed outside. She had hold of the door and was running along with it before George Bunting had brought it to a stop.

'How is he?' Her gaze went frantically to the back of the truck. 'Where is he?' The back was empty. Jed was the only passenger. She stared mutely at George Bunting.

'They're keeping him in for tonight, at least. Maybe a couple of days. He's got concussion and his wrist has had to be reset.' He pushed her out of the way to get out of the cab. 'It had snapped again,' he added unnecessarily, and made his way across the yard to the house.

She felt anger twisting inside her like a knife. For all the emotion he displayed he could be just back from market with the latest cattle feed prices. 'So he will be out of action for even longer?' She followed him into the kitchen, stopped just inside the door and fixed him pointedly. 'Did they ask how it had happened?'

He threw himself on to a chair and gave a twisted grimace. 'Yes! And I told them!' Pulling the tall, black leather riding boots from his feet, he leaned them against the table. 'Is there anything to eat?'

Only he could think of his stomach at a time like this, she thought, but had only reached the pantry door when she was proved wrong.

Jed came in after putting the Land Rover away for the night. 'I'm ravenous!' he announced.

Biting her lip against speaking the sarcastic comment that leaped to her mind, she placed a loaf of bread and a large wedge of cheese on the table. 'Was he conscious when you left?' she asked, cutting two thick slices of bread, topping them with a slice of cheese and pushing one at each of the two men.

'He came round on the journey there.'

'He was all right!' Jed asserted, as if he knew exactly what he was talking about.

Hannah scowled at him. 'I hope you're right! It was your fault it happened. It was *your* lack of animal husbandry that caused it all.'

'You know I'm no good with that sort of thing,' he retaliated, with a lack of concern that doubled her anger.

She turned on his father. 'How can you have sired anything so useless?' she spat.

'I do my bit.' Jed squared round to her, his dark eyes flashing with the fury she had previously only experienced from his father's.

'And a bit is all it is!' Pressing her hands into her hips, she stretched her short form to its limits, returning the animosity of his glare in full measure. 'You leave it all to Sam. You expect him to do everything. All you're capable of is fetching and carrying. And that only because it lets you get your hands on the car or truck and gets you away from here, so you can find some bar to prop up.'

Jed thrust his finger into her shoulder. '*You* should remember who you're talking to,' he grated, continually jabbing the finger harder and harder into her collar bone. She had to grit her teeth to stop her pain from becoming evident. 'If it wasn't for us you'd be out on the streets. A bit of gratitude wouldn't go amiss.'

She tossed her head back and gave a bark of sarcastic laughter. It could have been his father speaking, the words echoing so closely the very ones that had started the earlier argument. Her gratitude should have been overflowing! Once, maybe. But now the tables had turned. Sam was out of action for several more weeks and *they* could not do without her. 'Well, if my appreciation does not come up to the expected level, then perhaps I should leave.' She lifted her own finger and stabbed it into Jed's chest. 'But if I do *you'll* have to learn how to get your hands mucky.' She did not want to leave, but was confident her taunts would not lead to that. Not so long ago she had yearned for the moment she would be able to walk out of the door and say goodbye to George Bunting and his grand house. But now she wanted to stay and to be near Sam, not just because he was hurt, but because she had the feeling that being close to Sam was where she would always want to be.

'There's nobody going anywhere.' George Bunting thrust his son's hand and assaulting finger away from Hannah. Then he grabbed the neck of his shirt, forcing him round so that their noses, which were of identical heights, were pressed closely together. 'She's staying here! So you had better get used to it,' he ground meaningfully.

Hannah bit her lip, seeing another fight brewing. She pushed her arm between them. 'Don't you think there's been enough of that for one day.' She fixed a pointed glare at George Bunting's face. 'Let him go,' she insisted. 'You've proved your point.'

He hesitated, then finally thrust Jed away from him.

'I don't need you to fight *my* battles,' Jed stressed forcefully.

She gave a grimace, knowing it was Sam he was getting at. 'I don't doubt that. But I would have thought with your brother lying in hospital you'd have a bit more sense.' She turned her stony glare on his father. 'I'd have thought you'd both have had a bit more sense!' she stressed. Then feeling suddenly that she had had enough, she wheeled away. 'Oh, go on, fight,' she insisted impatiently, and hurried for the door. 'If you don't understand any other language but your fists,' she shouted angrily, as she vanished into the sitting room that had become her bedroom, closing the door very noisily behind her.

Within minutes there was a knock at the door. 'Can I come in?' George Bunting called.

She grimaced, wondering why he was suddenly bothering to ask. 'No. I'm in bed.' She was sitting in one of the large armchairs, fully dressed. But she had no wish to see him. She glanced at the two chairs pushed up against the door. She knew they would not keep him out, but had put them there in case he decided to visit in the night when she was asleep. The clatter of them falling would wake her up.

The chairs remained still, the door remained closed.

Several moments of silence passed. She was beginning to think he had given up and gone away, when he said, 'You're not serious about leaving?'

'No,' she replied without hesitation. If you can't frighten me away, Jed certainly doesn't have the power. She smiled to herself in the flickering glow of the dying fire. It seemed rather unchivalrous, but she had to admit to a certain relief that Sam's new indisposition took away any remaining ideas about leaving – for several more weeks, at least.

'Good night then,' he called.

She sensed, from the flatness of his voice and the hesitant silence before his feet finally moved off down the hall, that he had wanted to say more.

Good night, she replied silently, and sank back into the chair and listened to his footsteps going up the stairs. A shiver ran over her flesh. She brushed her hand over her arm, where the tiny hairs were suddenly standing on end. As she heard the bedroom door above close behind him, she got up and walked to the window. She was staying for Sam, yet Sam had given her no indication that he wanted her to stay, or that he reciprocated the feelings she had for him. She was not even sure she understood those feelings herself. They were strange and confusing. She knew she liked Sam, but maybe anything deeper was only her own insecurity. With a heartfelt sigh she gazed out into the blackness. Had it not been such a dark night, the high stone wall at the entrance to the farm would still have obliterated any view of the hills. But she knew them so well that her mind's eye could see clearly every green sweep and curve, tree and wall and bare winter hedge, and even the craggy Tor whose ominous starkness held the Bunting mansion aloft on its western side. It was all there. Yet even the picture of the countryside that she loved so much, could not persuade her that she had been right to tell George Bunting she had no intention of leaving.

Chapter Eight

When they reached the far end of the Tor, Delilah stopped, bent her head and began to nibble at the grass. They came that way every day and the chestnut roan knew Hannah always liked to pause a while at the point where the flat plateau came to an end, before it swept down to the valley on the opposite side of the hill to the farm. George Bunting's mare's daily exercise had become one of Hannah's duties. Samson, the large, grey stallion, was his property, and his alone. He never let anyone get their hands on Samson – not that anyone was eager to take control of the great brute who was as cantankerous as his owner.

It was a bright, sunny day; grey, woolly blobs of sheep dotted the Tor and the descending hillside. The green of the hedgerows was peppered with the white and pink of may blossom. Far down below was the row of five, tiny cottages where the footpath which crossed the Tor turned once more into a narrow lane. Hannah breathed deeply, drawing the sweet, warm air into her lungs. Until coming to live at the Tor, this side of the hill had not been so well known to her as the other side, where she had spent her childhood. But it was just as beautiful. She never tired of looking on the green openness of it all.

'Come on.' She pulled gently on the rein, lifting Delilah's head and turning her slowly away. In the most bitterly cold weather their daily rides were always a pleasure. On days such as this, with the sun warm on their backs and the gentlest of breezes blowing, it was tempting to stay out for hours, but she had work waiting to be done.

Even so, she was in no hurry and set Delilah at a gentle

walk along the sheep track that ran close to the edge of the steep precipice. She smiled, as she saw Sam way down below, walking up the fields after taking the cows down to the bottom pasture, his long legs striding purposefully through the thick grass. She had not regretted making the decision to stay at the Tor. The hills were where she belonged. Now she had come to terms with the loss of her father and her old life, she knew she could never be happy in more urban surroundings. Putting up with George Bunting's irritability was a small price to pay. Fortunately, he seemed to have learned his lesson and had stopped pestering her: physically, at least. He still made it quite clear that she only had to say the word and he would have a wedding ring on her finger. But he had never tried to touch her again and his manner had become noticeably less threatening, which made the verbal suggestions easy to ward off.

Her only regret was Sam. She reined Delilah in and sat watching him, as he took a short cut and jumped the wall. Her smile deepened. He was still the same: kind and gentle; leaping to her aid if he thought she was tackling some job that was too heavy for her small frame; siding with her when his father was at his most irascible; protecting her from Jed's continuing taunts. But it was all done with the concern of a brother caring for a little sister. It was not that she did not want him to care for her. But she now knew for certain that what she felt for him was not sisterly affection. It was something she had never experienced before, something that made him the last thing she thought about before falling to sleep at night, and the first thing she remembered when she woke up each morning. If that was not love, then she did not know what was.

Sam was in the top field before she urged Delilah on once more. When they reached the farmyard, to be greeted by a canine chorus, he was just vaulting over the gate at the bottom of the yard.

'Everything all right?' he called, as he came towards her.

She gave a nod and slipped out of the saddle into the middle of the excited dogs. It was Sam's usual question when she returned from the Tor: regarding the sheep, not herself. She gave her own usual joking reply, 'They're as happy as Larry.'

His dark eyes twinkled, his face creasing into a smile that seemed to set a butterfly twitching in her stomach. She felt her cheeks warming and hurriedly turned away and began to unbuckle Delilah's saddle. 'Then it would be difficult for them not to be happy on a day like this,' she added, needing something to say to cover the embarrassment she found herself experiencing more and more in his company.

'I wish that could be said for everybody.'

She looked up, her moment's discomfort swept away by his sombre tone. 'What's wrong now?' She knew he must be referring to his father.

'Jed's vanished.'

'So what's new?' She returned her attention to the saddle and lifted it off Delilah's back. In her opinion Jed's absence was something to be thankful for. He was more of a liability than a help. It was far better to know he was out of the way and not causing any damage, than wondering just what he *was* doing.

'So has the Jaguar!' he added pointedly.

'Oh!' She paused, the saddle in her hands. His car was almost as sacrosanct to George Bunting as his horse. He did allow Jed to drive it . . . but only with his permission. She could well imagine the fury its disappearance would have caused. She gave a groan, suddenly seeing the reason for Sam's concern. Being the only people around they were going to get the brunt of that fury.

'Where is he?' She looked round the empty yard, hoping Bunting might have gone off somewhere himself. The back-end of the Land Rover poked out of the barn. She gave a sigh. It had been too much to hope for.

'In the house. If I was you I'd steer clear of it for some time.'

She gave a nod, of understanding more than agreement. Having George Bunting storming around the yard was bad enough. If he was lurking in the kitchen it meant he was too angry to work and was waiting for someone to appear so he had a target for the full blast of his wrath. But it was almost dinner-time. If he wasn't fed on time it would only give him more to complain about. 'Why put off what you can enjoy immediately?' She gave a grimace of resignation. 'Besides, if we get it out of the way dinner will be more enjoyable.'

Sam gave a snort. 'It would serve him right if we went down to The Lamb and got Alf to make us some sandwiches.'

'Don't tempt me. Here . . . take this.' She handed him the saddle. As he took it his left hand accidentally brushed against her hand. He recoiled as if burnt and the saddle almost fell to the ground.

'Oops! Butterfingers,' he joked, grabbing the front of the saddle – where there was no danger of touching her again. Then he hurriedly carried it into the stable, his eyes unable to meet hers.

Why? Hannah asked herself, staring after him and feeling a heaviness closing round her heart. There were times when he forgot his hand and let it touch her freely. Then there were times such as now, when it happened by accident and he reacted with guilt and shame. As if she had shown disgust, when she had not. It had all happened too quickly to give her time to show any emotion. But it made no difference. He was convinced that inside she should be feeling revulsion.

Steeped in misery, she turned back to Delilah and began to remove the bridle. She had thought the major obstacle in her way was his father. But she had been wrong. His hand was a far bigger obstacle. Unfortunately, unlike George Bunting, it was not one she could spit back at when it challenged her. It needed to be handled with a delicacy she was not sure she possessed. She was more accustomed to charging at things like a bull at a gate. She gave a sigh. Maybe George Bunting was right when he said they had a lot in common. She *was* like him! It was not a very comforting thought.

* * *

The mood that greeted Hannah when she went into the kitchen was nothing compared to the fury of the following day. Jed had still not returned. It was not the first time he had spent the night away from home. But it was the first time George Bunting's precious car had been out of his sight for more than a few hours and he was like a raging bull, his language turning from crimson to blue. At which point Hannah raged back at him for his obscenity and Sam ushered her quickly out of the house and into the peacefulness of the yard.

'He's best left alone,' he told her. 'Going back at him is only giving fuel to his fire.'

'He knows I won't put up with that sort of language,' she protested. But seeing the wisdom of Sam's words agreed to leave the breakfast pots to be washed later and went to hose the milking parlour down.

It was a suitable job for working out her anger. The hose swished around furiously, the force of the water pelting the stone slabs of the floor until they were so clean they almost sparkled. As she rinsed out the pipes and tanks of the milking machine, she reflected on the unfairness of life. George Bunting with his grand parlour, while her father had still been struggling along in the old cowshed, milking by hand. The moment they had been installed with electricity, George Bunting had gone out and bought himself this fancy machine . . . and doubled his herd. He had not been forced to sit back and wait until he could afford it.

To add insult to injury, the cause of her bitterness chose that moment to walk through the door. 'Where's Sam?'

She glanced at him blandly. His voice had returned to normal and the tightness that had vibrated his jaw and turned his cheeks pink had gone. But she was not fooled into believing he had let the matter pass. It was only a brief respite and if Jed failed to turn up again tonight they would go through the same performance later. 'He's mending the gate in the top west.' She continued to busy herself with cleaning the pipes and did not look at him.

It was a moment before he said, 'What are you doing after this? I'm going into Derby to look for Jed – do you want to come with me?'

Her face was to the wall and her grimace went undetected. 'I'm taking Delilah for a ride. Then when Sam's finished he needs me to help round the sheep up.' When the gate was mended they were bringing the ewes down into the top west ready for the tupping, so they could keep an eye on them. It was necessary, to make sure which ewes were serviced by which ram, and if they became pregnant. Sam had not asked for her assistance but two would get the job done a lot quicker than one. Besides, she had no intention of going anywhere with George Bunting. 'If Jed is anywhere to be found you'll find him by yourself.'

He hesitated, seemed about to speak, changed his mind and walked out.

After finishing cleaning the parlour, Hannah went straight to the stables, saddled and bridled Delilah and set off up the Tor. As she rode across the yard and went through the gate, she did not notice that the Land Rover was still in the barn, where it had been the previous day.

Delilah cantered along the path, her hooves kicking up the dust of the dry soil. It was another beautiful warm day and the sheep nibbled lazily at the coarse grass or dozed in the sunshine. When they reached a point level with Sam down below, Hannah reined in and called and waved to him. He waved back, shouted something she could not make out, laughed, then flapped his hand to tell her to go on her way and let him get on.

Urging the mare to a gallop, she covered the rest of the Tor in minutes, spent a few more enjoying the view, then turned back. Swallows swooped in the cloudless sky and a couple of skylarks hovered, thrusting out songs that seemed much too loud for their tiny bodies. It was a perfect day and she soon forgot George Bunting and his bad temper.

Sam had finished the gate and was walking back to the house, when she stopped to look. She waved to him again, then turned Delilah away from the steep edge and returned to the footpath running down the centre of the plateau. She had not gone far when she sensed a movement out of the corner of her eye.

'Finished already?' George Bunting called, as he came riding over the brow of the hill on the eastern side.

Hannah pulled Delilah up and stared at him woodenly. He never came riding up the Tor. He liked to parade himself on Samson only where people were going to see him and think how wonderful he was, dressed in all his finery. It was knowing she was not likely to meet him that made her always choose that path.

'You're not going back already?' He pulled Samson up alongside Delilah.

'I thought you were going to find Jed?' Or rather your car. She was in no doubt which one was most important to him.

'I'll do that later. It might take me some time and Samson needed a run. So I thought I'd join you.'

She did not ask why, if he had been coming to join her, he had not come straight along the path, instead of creeping up on her over the brow.

'Let's give them a race. Pitting them against each

other is good for them. They run faster with a bit of competition.'

'Delilah has already had a gallop.' It was a lame excuse. The mare was capable of far more than she had been put through. But Hannah was nervous. She could not understand why he had suddenly chosen to come that way. And the unexpected softening of his manner, after the blood and thunder of earlier, was doing nothing to ease her mind. It was so unlike him. Even at his best he was never so calm, and his worst rages usually took days to simmer down.

He eyed the chestnut thoughtfully. 'She looks all right,' he pronounced. 'She can manage a chase to the end.' He jerked his head in the direction Hannah had just come from. Then his eyes narrowed. 'Or are you frightened of me beating you?'

She hesitated only for a moment. What harm could he do while sitting on Samson's back? she asked herself. All she had to do was make sure she remained firm in Delilah's saddle. If he made any move to dismount she only had to bolt out of his way. She was over-reacting because of his earlier mood, she told herself, and tossed her head in a manner that closely resembled the mare's own action. 'Think you can, do you?' Taking up the imaginary gauntlet she tossed it back in his face. Before he had time to reply, she had spun Delilah round and was leaning over the mare's outstretched neck as she raced back across the Tor.

Within seconds the sound of Samson's thundering hooves were close by her ear. She glanced round. His head was by her leg. In the next moment his head was level with Delilah's. She spurred the mare on. 'Come on! Come on!' She would not let him win. The chestnut inched ahead, only to be caught by Samson again. Her knees pressed tighter to the mare's flanks, willing her own need to win into the horse's flesh. 'We can do it!' she shouted. George Bunting's throaty laughter mocked her desperation, fuelled her determination. She forced the mare on. Samson might have the longer stride, but he was carrying the heavier load. George Bunting must be twice her own weight and Delilah, herself, was much leaner and more nimble than the heavy, muscular stallion.

Again Delilah inched ahead, again Samson caught up. It happened several times before Hannah had the feeling he was playing with her. He never went ahead, just allowed her to, then he caught up.

He was toying with her, she realized, but still could not listen to the voice of common sense that told her she should stop this right now, turn round and go home and leave him to his silly games. They were almost there and she would not give him the satisfaction of seeing her chicken out.

In the next moment it was all over. Samson suddenly shot ahead as if he had been fired from a cannon. Hannah's vision was filled with the sight of his great silver backside moving further away, along with George Bunting's; the flap of the navy blue jacket bouncing madly on the grey breeches. He waited until he was right at the end, reining Samson round into a skidding turn at the very edge of the steep incline.

She followed, determined to show she matched him for skill, if not speed. Reining the mare at the last minute, she performed a perfect duplication of his own masterful turn, only in the opposite direction. It was not until Delilah came to a standstill that Hannah realized she had her eyes shut, and her teeth were sunk almost right through her bottom lip.

'Very impressive.' As he came up to her side, he inclined his head in a manner of recognition of her capability. 'If I had known I had some real competition I would have done this before.'

She only just stopped herself from giving a derisory snort. Who did he think he was fooling?

'You go well together,' he said.

'I've always had an affinity with animals,' she said, thinking he was still referring to her riding ability.

He laughed. 'I mean the colour. You almost match.'

'Not quite.' She dropped her gaze and stared at the back of Delilah's neck. The chestnut of the mare's coat did closely resemble her own colouring, but the sprinkling of white that made her a roan lightened the colour, making it less intense. 'I'll have to start going grey first,' she replied, using flippancy to cover her embarrassment at the personal direction the conversation was taking.

'That's a long way off.'

She did not have to look at his face to know there was a smile on it. It was in his voice. It was an odd, uncommon sound that increased her unease and tightened her fingers round the reins. 'Sam's wrist seems to be back to normal now.' She said the first thing she could think of to change the subject.

'It's been right for weeks!' His tone conveyed that he thought it had been a stupid statement to make.

She stared at him coolly. 'No it hasn't,' she pointed out. 'You've only had to watch him using it to know it was still causing him pain.'

For a long moment he returned her stare. 'Meaning that *I* have been neglectful in not running round after him like a wet nurse!' he finally stated, angrily.

Normal service resumed, Hannah thought, and smiled grimly. But at least she understood this George Bunting better than the deceptively considerate man who, for a few minutes, he had pretended to be. Unwisely, she felt she could handle this man, and when she spoke, her voice was sharp and provoking. 'You could show him a bit more consideration. You'd be lost without him. You couldn't run the farm on your own.'

He gave a bark of sarcastic laughter. Frightened by the sudden noise, the horses skitted and tossed their heads. 'Where do you think he's going?' he enquired scornfully, pulling Samson easily under control while Hannah still struggled to calm Delilah. 'Who would have him? He wouldn't last five minutes out there.' He cocked his thumb in the direction of the village. 'Not unless a circus was passing. He'd make a good sideshow.'

'You bastard!' She was too incensed to be concerned that she was sinking to his level of vocabulary. 'How can you say that about your own son?'

'*My son!*' he bellowed, his cheeks turning a violent crimson. 'He's *her* son. He's not a Bunting!'

'Oh no! And I suppose Jed is? For all your cursing and yelling at him, you secretly admire Jed. He's what you think a *real* man should be. You're blind . . . and stupid! Too stupid to see further than the end of your arrogant nose. Sam is worth twenty of Jed and you put together.' She reined Delilah round, preparing to move away from him. But she could not prevent herself pausing to have a final stab. 'I feel sorry for you,' she snarled, icy cold eyes pivoting viciously to his face. 'What are you? A tin-god in his make-believe palace. Counting the money that you think can buy everything.' She gave a snort of derision. 'You have nothing worth giving to anyone and because of that you have nothing yourself . . . nothing in here!' She slapped her hand over her heart.

The blood drained from his face, his cheeks turning to the grey of the sheeps' fleeces spread around the Tor. His mouth stretched into a tight, bitter line. 'Why, you little bitch!' he growled, just as she urged Delilah to move, too late. In an instant he lunged forward and had hold of the mare's rein, jerking her head violently round. Delilah gave a startled whinny and tried to rear up on her back legs. He held her down. She skitted one way, then the other. Samson joined in and it appeared as if they were performing a dance in time to some unheard music.

'Let her go!' Hannah swiped at his arm. But he held fast.

'I'll show you what I've got!' He tugged hard on the

mare's rein, drawing her closer to him. When she was in reach he dropped the rein and lunged for Hannah's arm. Fortunately Delilah was so frightened by the raised voices that she slewed away and he was almost unseated as he hung on to Hannah's arm.

'Get off me!' she screamed, jerking her arm fiercely in an attempt at getting it free.

'Not until I've finished with you.' He tugged at her arm. She felt herself slipping from the saddle. Tightening her legs round the horse's body, her free hand grabbed frantically for a hold on the bridle round Delilah's head. She found it, and when he tugged again thankfully she remained firm. 'I've waited too bloody long and I'll wait no more. I'll make you have to marry me.'

'Never! I'll not marry you. I'd throw myself off the Tor first.'

'Not before I've had what's due to me!' he blazed, giving an almighty tug on Hannah's arm and closing the gap between the two horses.

Samson's body crashed sidelong into Delilah. The terrified mare reared. Hannah lost her hold on the bridle. She grabbed for it again, missed, her fingers fastening round an ear. Delilah let out a panic-stricken cry and performed several erratic sideways prances. George Bunting held fast to Hannah's arm and Samson was dragged along with them. The stallion took exception to this. He bucked, throwing himself away from his excited mate. The action left George Bunting suspended precariously between both horses.

It was a split second decision for Hannah. Taking her foot from the stirrup could have been a foolish move, bringing her crashing to the ground. Fortunately it did not and once again her feet provided her ultimate weapon against him. As her toe crunched into his cheek she wished she had been wearing hard riding boots like himself, instead of rubber wellingtons. But it did not matter. The knock was sufficient to make him lose his grip and land on the ground in an ungainly heap, emitting a string of expressive oaths.

She did not wait to see if he was hurt. Reining Delilah hard round, she thrust her heels into the horse's flanks and sent the mare flying across the Tor in the direction of the house, fighting to get her foot back in the stirrup as they went.

Once her foot was safely secure again, Hannah glanced round, making sure he was not close behind. He was not. But he was standing up, about to thrust his own foot into Samson's stirrup. Her fear increased. She urged Delilah to greater speed, knowing that once George Bunting was seated it would not be long before he was by her side.

'Keep it up,' she begged, as the house and farmyard came into view and she heard the ominous thunder of hooves closing in behind. As if sensing her rider's need, Delilah thrust herself forward. The sound of Samson's hooves came nearer and nearer, filling Hannah's ears. 'No!' she screamed, digging her heels harder and harder into the mare's sides. 'I'm sorry. I'm sorry,' she apologized to the horse, hating herself for having to be brutal. But she knew Delilah must be getting tired and she was terrified she would slacken off before they had reached safety. Neither dare she glance round to see how close her pursuers were, for fear the slightest movement might slow the mare down.

When Delilah skidded through the gates and into the yard, Hannah had the feeling her lungs were going to burst, so great was her relief. 'Thank you!' she said with extreme feeling, knowing the mare's lungs must really be about to explode. But there was no time to stop and pet the horse and show her true gratitude.

'Sam!' she screamed, leaping to the ground. 'Sam! Sam!' She raced for the back door, praying he was somewhere around. If he was not, her only refuge was the bathroom, the only door with a bolt on it.

She was still screaming his name as she threw herself

at the door, just as it opened and she careered right into his arms.

'What is it?' he demanded, gripping tight to her arms and peering anxiously into her eyes: wide and putting him in mind of a frightened calf.

'He . . .' she gasped, then had to draw deeply on her spent breath and was unable to continue.

'What . . . ! What is it?' Her appearance made the blood drain from his face. He had to shake her before she could find her voice.

'He . . . he tried to . . . to . . . attack me.' She could not say rape, even though she knew that would have been her fate.

'He what?' Sam paused, his gaze freezing on her own. 'Who?' he questioned, though he knew the answer.

'Your . . .' she began.

He did not give her time to finish. 'Where is he?' Pushing her roughly aside he took two purposeful steps into the yard. Then came up short.

Anxiety and fear trembled through Hannah's limbs. She wanted no repeat of their previous fight, nothing that would get Sam injured all over again. 'No!' she insisted, grabbing his arm to hold him back. That he put up no resistance confused her. She looked round. Her mouth dropped open and her hand fell slowly from his arm. In the yard Samson and Delilah stood side by side. Their heads hung low and steaming breath clouds snorted from their exhausted lungs. George Bunting was nowhere to be seen.

Chapter Nine

'Where is he?' Hannah's eyes rapidly scanned from one side to the other. She stood on the back of the tractor, clinging on to Sam's shoulders as it bumped and juddered over the uneven terrain. 'He should be here!' When the tractor reached the flat plateau she had expected to see an irate George Bunting marching back over the Tor. But the only signs of life were the sheep and birds.

'Did you come straight across?'

'Yes.' She gave a sigh. 'I saw him get back on Samson.' She paused. She had seen him about to get back on Samson. 'Perhaps Samson ran off without him,' she added hopefully.

Sam shook his head. 'If he had he would be walking towards us, wouldn't he?' He glanced round at her, the bleakness in his eyes sending a chill through her.

She gave a nod, then began to scan the countryside once more. He had to be here, she told herself. He could not have just vanished.

'There!' she suddenly cried, jabbing her finger frantically towards a dark patch in the grass. She could not see clearly what it was. But it was dark enough to be a navy blue jacket. Her heart stilled in her chest and, although she did not realize it, she stopped breathing.

It was George Bunting. Hannah had not thought her heart could sink any lower, but it did. He was lying flat on the grass. He was fully conscious. His eyes watched her as she leapt from the tractor and sank to her knees by his side. But he did not speak. The anger and rebuke she had been expecting did not come flooding from his lips in a stream of vitriol, and something deep inside her went very cold.

'Dad?' Sam sank to his knees on the opposite side of his father and took hold of his hand. He glanced worriedly at Hannah. But she could only bite her lip and stare at his father's ashen face. 'What hurts?' He bit his own lip as he turned back to the figure on the ground.

It was a moment before he said, 'It's my back.'

There was a distant quality about his voice. A shudder rippled over Hannah's flesh. She tried to deny what her mind was trying to tell her. 'If we hold you up can you walk?' she asked. It was all she could think to say.

His only response was to stare into her eyes with an emptiness that increased the numbness in her flesh.

'What is it?' she begged, looking anxiously to Sam as if he could give her the answer, before turning back to the bleak face on the ground. His expression was so strange: resigned, blank. She did not know what to call it. But she knew it frightened her. He was so quiet. Too quiet. That he had uttered not one swear word or angry accusation, increased her fear. It was so unnatural, so unlike him.

'What is it, Dad?' Sam repeated the question, the gentleness of his voice conveying all his anxiety.

When finally George Bunting replied, 'I can't feel my legs,' Hannah had the feeling all the blood in her body trickled slowly out through her feet . . . to be replaced by icy water.

*   *   *

The waiting was interminable. The ambulance could not get on the Tor, so Sam took the Land Rover with the two ambulance men and a stretcher. His father then had to be transferred to the ambulance waiting in the yard. Sam went to the hospital with him. Hannah stayed behind to look after the farm.

It seemed to be becoming a habit – waiting for news from the hospital. Twice for Sam, now his father. She wondered just where Jed had got to. Lightning could not strike twice in the same day . . . could it? She hoped not, as she unbridled Samson and Delilah, fed and watered them and let them loose to run in the top field. But as she walked back up the yard, she could not rid her mind of the picture of a dark green Jaguar smashed into a wall, and Sam bumping into his bloodied and battered brother somewhere at the hospital. It was not a pleasant thought, but at least it kept her mind from dwelling solely on George Bunting.

Fortunately her worries for Jed proved unfounded. At ten-minutes-past-twelve the Jaguar rolled into the yard.

'Where's dinner?' He looked around the neat and tidy kitchen, the empty gas stove.

Wanting feeding as if he had just walked in from a morning's work, Hannah thought bitterly. 'There's bread and cheese in the pantry,' she snapped. 'You'll have to get your own.' Food was the last thing she could think about.

'What's biting you?' He looked her up and down, his nose curling as if he was looking on a dirty rag.

She sat woodenly, elbows resting on the table, her eyes, which seemed the only part of her that was alive, fixing him coldly. His dark-blue blazer with shiny brass buttons and the pale-grey, perfectly creased trousers, made him look totally alien to the farm. Looking like a tailor's shop-window dummy was how he always looked when he went out. But under the present circumstances his smartness appeared obscene to her. It enraged her and she found her voice stuck in her throat and she could not speak.

'What are the others having? Why can't I have the same?' His voice and expression took on the tone of a spoilt child, acting as a goad to her anger.

'*Because there is no-one else here!*' The chair scraped noisily across the floor as she pushed it back and leapt to her feet. She was choked by guilt, overwhelmed by the feeling that whatever had happened to his father, she was to blame. She needed an outlet, something to hit, thump, scream at and tear into. Jed was that outlet. 'And if you'd been here, where you should have been, you would know that!' she blazed.

'Who the hell do *you* think you're speaking to?' he demanded, his chin lifting, his eyes narrowing to peer down his arrogant nose.

'You!' she returned confidently. Her own chin rose in challenge. Then her anger wilted into despair. Her chin dropped again and her voice softened, as she said, 'Your father has been taken to hospital. He's fallen off Samson. I think he's broken his back.'

'The silly bugger.'

A gasp flew from Hannah's lips, her eyes pivoted to his face. 'Is that all you can say?' She knew him too well to have expected any outright compassion, but she had thought even he could find it in his heart to rise above contempt. 'Don't you understand what it could mean? He couldn't feel his legs. He might be paralysed. Unable to walk!' She clutched her arms as a shiver ran up them.

Jed pulled a packet of *Senior Service* from his pocket, took one out and lit it with a fancy tortoiseshell lighter. As he took a long, thoughtful draw, his eyes seemed to light up, his lips curling in a smile.

She shook her head, unable to comprehend how he could be so calm, so unfeeling. 'Your father might be crippled,' she pointed out stiffly.

He gave a nod.

'Which means I shall have to take control of the reins far earlier than expected.'

She wanted to laugh as she watched him saunter confidently to the table, pull out a chair and sit down. But suddenly her body was filled with the same numbing coldness she had experienced on finding his father lying on the Tor. She shook her head as if the action would dismiss what he had just said. He could not really be serious. Thinking he was going to take over the farm! He couldn't run it, the animals would all be dead within a month. 'Your father is not dead!' she pointed out stiffly. 'And you do have a brother!' One that is as good a farmer as his father, she thought, hoping that his ability would, for once, outweigh his hand.

'A brother! He's a cripple. You don't think the old man will leave it to him.'

'He's not leaving it to anyone!' Hannah screeched, her fury increased because the sentiment of the words very closely emulated those his father had spoken on the Tor: the very ones that had provoked the argument which had caused the accident. 'Even if he can't walk he'll still be here. We don't know for certain what he has done! I only said I *thought* he had broken his back.' In her own mind she was more than certain, and she knew the ambulance men had been of the same opinion. The way they had moved and carried him with extreme gentleness had spoken volumes.

Jed did not reply. He remained quietly puffing on the cigarette, a thoughtful expression in his eyes. When finally he spoke it was to instruct her to get his dinner . . . as if he had already jumped into the boots of the lord of the manor!

She wished she had previously found the strength to obey the small voice telling her she should be preparing a meal for when Sam got home, instead of sitting idly at the table. If she had there would have been saucepans on the stove, the milk jug on the table: something to tip over him; something to spoil his debonair clothes; something to wipe the smug smile from his lips. But there was nothing to hand that she could toss or throw to show her true feelings. So she wheeled away, grabbed her wellingtons and rushed out of the door, not stopping to put them on until she was in the yard. If he wanted to eat he had to find it for himself. Despite having a great need to hear something of George Bunting's condition, in that moment, she hoped

Sam would not return for ages: so that she would not have to go back into the kitchen and, in preparing something for Sam, have to feed his brother, as well.

She got her wish. It was late evening before Sam returned.

She was just closing up the milking parlour after doing the milking single-handed, when she heard the sound of an engine coming up the lane. As the Land Rover swung into the yard, she was waiting. 'What . . . ?' she began, as she pulled the door open for Sam to get out, but the bleakness of his face stilled her voice.

Shaking his head he climbed out of the cab.

He looked so tired and drawn, the unnatural pallor of his face blended into the greyness of the dusk light and she wanted to throw her arms around him and comfort him. But she only said, 'Jed's back.' An unnecessary statement: Sam had parked the Land Rover next to the missing Jaguar and he could see it with his own eyes.

He looked straight into her eyes for a long moment, knowing she was waiting for him to speak, to tell her. 'He'll never walk again,' he finally said. It sounded blunt, but he did not know a better way to put it. However he began, whatever words he chose, they only put off the moment of grim truth.

She had known, deep down inside she had known what she had done to his father. But hearing the words struck the horror deep, wiped away the slender thread of hope that she might be wrong. 'Oh, Sam!' She drew a great noisy gasp and clapped her hand over her mouth. Her head fell forward and she closed her eyes tight, but tears still managed to squeeze through. 'I'm sorry!' It was her fault. George Bunting was an invalid and she was to blame. He would never work the farm again; never walk the hills; never ride Samson. 'I'll look after him. You won't have to worry. I'll do everything for him.'

'It isn't your fault!' Sam grasped her by the arms, shaking her gently until she lifted her head and he could see her face. 'You are not to blame and I'll not hear you say so. He only has himself to blame!' It was not the first time he had had this conversation. After the doctor had explained plainly what had happened to his father and told him he had no chance of walking again, George Bunting had returned to fighting form. He had immediately laid all the blame at Hannah's feet.

Sam had soon put him straight on where the real blame lay, but he knew his father would not let the matter rest. He would make sure Hannah knew he held her responsible. And if he realized she also held herself responsible, he would make her life hell. 'He'll have to use a wheelchair, but he'll be fine otherwise. It's only his legs. Nothing else has been affected.'

'Only his legs!' Her face crumpled in renewed despair. 'It couldn't be worse – not for someone like your father. How will he manage? What will happen to the farm?'

'The farm will continue in the way it has always done,' Sam assured.

'How . . . ?' She shook her head and gazed at him bleakly. 'How will *you* manage on your own?' It was impossible. He'd never do it. She knew he was only trying to put on his best face for her, and that made her feel even more responsible.

He sighed and gave a shrug. 'I don't know,' he replied, suddenly realizing she deserved honesty. He broke into a thin smile. 'It isn't so bad. I've got you to help me. And Jed will have to pull his weight.'

She gave a grim smile. But thought better than to make any mention of Jed considering himself the new owner. Sam had enough to concern him without having to contemplate taking orders from his brother. Besides, she knew Jed would make his assumed status known quickly enough.

'I'll do all I can. But . . . ' She gave a shrug. 'Your father will need someone with him.' The prospect of spending her days with George Bunting was not very pleasing, but she knew she had to do it.

He shook his head very determinedly. 'No!' he insisted. 'I've had a long chat with the doctor and we haven't got to mollycoddle him. He must be made to do things for himself. They were quite sure it's only his legs that have been affected, the rest of his body still works as it did before and he must be made to use it.' The last bit was true, the doctor he had spoken to had said his father must be made to do things for himself. But no-one had mentioned the word mollycoddle; he had added that for her benefit. He was not prepared to sit back and watch her turn herself into a martyr.

She gave a twisted grimace. She could not imagine George Bunting being made to do anything . . . if he chose not to. 'Oh, Sam, he'll be awkward. And it is my fault, no matter what you say.' Her face crumpled again.

'No, it isn't!' His voice rose in anger and he shook her forcefully. He had been burning with impotent rage for what his father had tried to do. She had not said the word rape, but he knew that that was what his father had been up to. Just thinking about it made him want to kill and as far as he was concerned his father deserved to suffer.

'It is,' she insisted. 'If I hadn't raced away. If I hadn't gone back across the Tor with him in the first place.' If I had not stayed here because I wanted to be with you. She looked sadly into his face, unable to speak the last thought. She gave a sigh of regret. 'If I had never come to live here,' she finished bleakly, and wondered what she was trying to do: push the blame all the way back to the oak tree that had fallen on her old home.

'Hannah!' he said firmly, giving her another shake. 'My father deserves no compassion. If you had not run away he would have raped you!'

For a long moment she could only stare into his eyes, the dullness of resignation, deep in her own, slowly giving way to understanding. The horror of George Bunting's injuries had masked the real cause of them. Hearing Sam speak the word she had been unable to utter, put everything in a better perspective. 'Yes,' she finally agreed, and her relief was so great she threw herself against him, wrapping her arms tightly around him. 'Thank you,' she whispered, and pressed her face close to his chest.

She could hear his heart beating beneath her ear. It was a warm, comforting sound and she pressed herself closer to it. For the first time in months she felt safe, as if she really belonged. Her arms tightened around him and, not really knowing what she was doing, she lifted her face, offering her lips to him.

In an instant his eyes were suddenly hostile, as if filled with pain. 'Don't, Hannah!' His voice was rough and he pushed her away. 'Don't do something you will regret.' He held his right arm straight, his hand pressed to her shoulder, holding her back.

She shook her head, unable to understand. 'I won't regret it, Sam.' Her voice held the plea that filled her eyes and, like a child needing the comfort of a cuddle, her arms went out to him.

'No!' The hand on her shoulder tightened, his fingers biting painfully into her flesh. 'You don't know what you're doing. You're upset.'

She shook her head. She did know what she was doing. She knew what she was doing more than anything she had done over the last months. But she could see he was determined and was not going to be moved. Her arms dropped defeatedly to her sides. 'I'm sorry.' She looked away, unable to bear the stark refusal of his gaze. Seth, the oldest collie, was sitting by her feet. She had not noticed him before, did not know how long he had been there. His soft, dark eyes looked up at her, as if he understood her despair and was offering comfort. She smiled tightly, gave his ear a scratch. 'They need feeding,' she said, happy to have found something to take her away from Sam, from the memory she wanted to forget, yet feared she never would.

'I'll do that,' he said, gently, his voice returned to normal.

She walked away as if he had not spoken. All she could think was that he did not want her. His brotherly affection was just that. For six months she had endured George Bunting and Jed, because she wanted to be with Sam. And now he had made it plain she had wasted her time. That she had made a fool of herself, as well, made the pain worse. Before going through the door, she paused and looked up at the dark grey, stone walls. Bunting's Claw! The derogatory name was not aimed at Sam, but at the house. Suddenly it felt like a prison: a claw holding her, keeping her there. All she wanted was to turn and run away and never set eyes on the place again. But she could not. George Bunting might be master of his own fate but she could not walk away and leave him, or Sam, in the mess that she had caused just by being there. She had to stay and nurse George Bunting, look after the house and help on the farm. And, with the knowledge that he did not reciprocate the love she felt for him, see Sam every day.

Chapter Ten

Sam never spoke of the time when Hannah had thrown herself into his arms. Neither did Hannah, she felt too ashamed. At first there was a certain reticence about him whenever she was around, which only strengthened her theory that his rejection was because he did not feel the same. It made her uncertain and uneasy in his company. Strangely, it was George Bunting's return that eased the situation.

Once he was home, Hannah was so busy that she never had time to bother whether Sam was around or not and the tension that had filled the house for the long weeks of his father's hospitalization was forgotten. Sam returned to his usual self: treating her like his little sister. She returned to being grateful that he considered she was, at least, worth that, while she struggled through the days that seemed to have no beginning and no end. George Bunting proved to be as awkward as she had expected, demanding her attention at all times of the day and night, and giving her very little time to help Sam in the yard.

'Help yourself!' Hannah demanded, going red in the face as she struggled to lift George Bunting's heavy weight from the bed. She dropped him into the wheelchair with a thud that gained her a scowl. 'Your arms aren't useless!' The struggle had caused some of her hair to come free of the rubber band it was stuffed in and she shoved it back from her sweating face, giving a weary, phew! 'You could do more for yourself . . . if you tried!' He did it on purpose. When she was not available he was well able to get himself in and out of the wheelchair.

'Sometimes I can, sometimes I can't,' he replied without concern.

Aye, she thought drily, and turned to straighten the bed. And sometimes I'm here and sometimes I'm not. He gained great satisfaction from making her pay for the error of her ways. It never occurred to him that his accident was his own fault. She was always to blame for running away from him – as he often reminded her. He had even had the gall to tell everyone she had been doing it because he had asked her to marry him. Which he said he only suggested to give her respectability: to save her becoming the topic of wagging tongues in the village who thought it wrong that a young girl should live in a house with three men. It was a story he had told so many times he seemed to have come to believe it himself.

The bed-making finished, she turned to him. 'What are you going to do today?' she asked.

'I thought I might indulge in a game of football,' he replied sarcastically.

Settling her hands on her hips, she glared at him. The doctor had told them it would take some time for him to come to terms with his new situation. But it was eighteen months since the fall, and she was getting increasingly fed up with his continual displays of childish petulance. 'There's a mountain of bills want sorting out. I haven't got time . . . what with all the Christmas preparations and everything.' Since the accident she had taken over the farm's finances and kept the account book in order. But he was capable of sitting behind a desk and she had purposely left this month's bills unattended, with the intention of getting him to do them. Not that he had shown willing. She had told him twice before – without any success.

'What Christmas preparations? What is there to celebrate? We don't go in for all that hogwash here!' His mouth set in a mutinous line and he flung his arm wide, as if throwing something repugnant away.

Her gaze hardened on his obstinate features. 'Well, I'm here now!' The past two Christmases had gone by with little acknowledgement: the first, when she lost her old home, she had not been aware of herself; then last year his accident had still been too fresh in everyone's minds to allow much festivity. But Christmas was Christmas and she did not care how little they had celebrated before, this one was not going by unnoticed. She had already replaced the box of tatty decorations that looked as if they had not been used since the turn of the century. And Jed was picking a tree up when he went to market. 'It will be celebrated in true style.' She tossed her head in a way that meant business. 'If you don't want to join in you can stay in bed!' With another toss of the head she turned away and hurried from the room, a flow of obscenities following her.

The accident had not affected his vocabulary, she thought drily, and closed the door noisily against the tirade. To save having to get him up and down the stairs, the small sitting-room had been changed into his bed-room and, as she turned into the hall with a weary sigh, she heard a chuckle coming from the kitchen. With another sigh, she went in.

'Dear Papa at his most beguiling,' Jed said, smirking at her with the arrogance that made her feel she would gain much pleasure from hitting him. He was sitting rocking back on a chair, his long legs, wearing the shiny black riding boots that had belonged to his father, resting on the table. He was dressed in black trousers and black sweater and his hair was standing up at the front in the silly quiff he had taken to wearing recently . . . which she hated.

'Get those boots off my clean table.' She stormed forward, aiming a hefty thwack at his legs. 'You've walked through the farmyard muck in those!' She glared at the boots which had been his father's trademark. 'And if *he* catches you in them he'll throttle you, wheelchair or not!'

It irritated her to see Jed in the boots; not because they had belonged to his father, but if he was wearing them it meant he was parading around like cock of the walk, and not doing any work. Which meant Sam was doing it all . . . as usual! At least his father had been able to wear the fancy boots and get on with something. But boots or not, Jed had never had the same ability. The fact that his father had soon put a stop to his visions of grandeur, making it very clear that despite the wheelchair he was still in charge, had not helped Jed to pull his weight. And now his father was never in the yard to see what he was or was not doing, he exerted himself even less.

Laughing, he stood up and rounded the table. 'Why did you refuse to become the lady of this house?' he questioned, stopping right in front of her and looking down into her eyes with the mocking gleam she had come to know so well. 'You do so enjoy playing the part.'

His gaze washed intimately over her face and her green eyes flashed with warning. She knew he was only taunting her. There was no real intent in him. He only did it to embarrass her, or irritate Sam if he was around. But it aggravated her all the same. 'I'm playing no part!' she snapped. '*I* work for my living. It's a pity everybody in this house doesn't do the same!' Spinning away from him she picked up the basket to go and collect the eggs. She had long before come to realize there was no insulting him, but it never stopped her trying.

'Why keep a dog and bark yourself?' he said, stopping her in her tracks.

The basket shook in her hands and she clasped it tighter, fighting the desire to throw it at his smug face. That it was Sam he was deriding, increased her anger. Sam kept the place going, doing the work of four men, while his lordship Jed spent his time drinking, womanizing, and, of late, gambling heavily.

'Be careful!' she warned, glaring at him with the same

ice that was in her voice. 'Even a dog can bite the hand that feeds it!'

Throwing his head back he gave a roar of laughter. The black quiff came loose, bouncing against his forehead and falling down to touch the top of his nose. He swept it back with a cocky toss of his head and her lips tightened, so did her hands on the basket. She hated that tuft of hair; the way he greased it and fixed it; the way his hands were continually smoothing over it to make sure it was still in perfect shape. She did not like it one bit, but she thought it suited his vanity and what he was: a waster; a nothing.

'But some masters like to be bitten.' He moved forward, ran his finger down her cheek.

'And some bitches are not particular who they sink their teeth into!' Recoiling from his touch, she brought the basket up in front of her, ready to strike if he touched her again.

He gave another bark of laughter. 'Oh, Hannah!' he dragged her name out suggestively. 'If only you put your fiery spirit into other things *you would be wonderful*!' The last was also dragged out lewdly and his eyes narrowed on the fullness of her breasts.

'Not for you I wouldn't!' she spat back. Even for Jed this was going too far. Knowing that to stay was only providing him with sport, she turned to hurry away and leave him standing there. But his next comment was below the belt and not only stopped her feet, but also the breath in her lungs.

'No,' he snarled mockingly. 'You'd never have a real man. You prefer to hang around for *him*!' He gave a bark of nasty laughter. 'He'll never have you. You'll never get him!'

That he knew of her feelings for Sam confused and angered her. But nothing was revealed in her expression as she turned to him, her gaze cold and blank. 'And how would you know what a real man looks like? You don't think there is one looking back when you look in the mirror, do you?'

'More so than that cripple out there,' he sneered, waving his hand dismissively towards the door.

'Sam is no cripple!' she hissed through her teeth, fury vibrating through her cheeks and turning them to a colour that closely resembled her hair. Then she wheeled away from him, throwing herself at the door and yanking it open, before a sudden thought made her stop.

'Oh, by the way, I saw Bill Riley up here earlier,' she said, realizing she had a means to fight fire with fire. 'I thought I should mention it.'

'Old man Riley!' he gasped, and she almost laughed. 'What was he doing?'

She gave a shrug. 'I don't know. He had his dogs and gun with him . . . so I imagine he was rabbiting.' Not giving him time to reply, she walked out of the door, closing it behind her with a feeling of victory. It was all a pack of lies. She had not seen anyone round the farm, there rarely was at that time of year. But on her last visit to the village she had learned that Bill Riley's unmarried daughter, Glenda, was pregnant. And everyone was of the opinion Jed was the culprit. It did not surprise her that he was getting the blame, ninety per cent of all the illegitimate babies for miles around were laid at his feet. If supposition was to be believed he was the father of the county – a theory that boosted his over-inflated ego no end.

Clutching the basket tightly to her in protection against the biting air, she gave a grunt of disgust and hurried across the snow-covered yard. The other babies might be pure fable, but this one definitely belonged to him, she told herself. The look of horror at the mention of Bill Riley's gun had given him away. She shook her head. Glenda had never been very bright but she had thought her to have more sense than be sucked in by Jed's smooth tongue.

'What's wrong?'

She stopped short. Until he spoke she had not been aware of Sam standing by the stables. She gave a shrug, embarrassed that he had caught her out. 'Just your brother making me as childish as he is.' She felt suddenly ashamed of the lie and bent down to stroke Peg, as the puppy ran to her feet. 'Hello, girl,' she said, ruffling her ears and rubbing her nose against the soft fur. Peg was one of the last litter of puppies. Her black and white coat closely resembled her father's lost Sal and Hannah had immediately asked if she could have her for her own. She had not been sure George Bunting would agree to her having a dog in the house, but he had put up no objections and Peg now had a bed in the kitchen. But Hannah's idea of having a constant companion had been short-lived. Peg was from good working stock and the confines of the house were not to her liking. She had soon taken to following Sam whenever he went out. Had it been one of the others Peg had attached herself to, Hannah would have been annoyed. But she quite liked the idea of Peg belonging to both of them and that Sam had someone to look after him when he was out on the hills. It wasn't much, but it made her feel they shared something in common.

'What's he been doing?' Sam came up to her. 'Has he been bothering you?'

'It doesn't bother me.' She stood up, shaking her head in denial and sending the long red pony-tail shimmering down her back.

Sam turned away; stared blankly across the snow-covered hills.

She gave a grimace. It was always the same. He could not bear to look at her. She studied the tiredness on his averted face, the skin drawn tightly over cheek bones that seemed to have lost all their natural colour. The high spots of red at the corners of his mouth and the tip of his nose, caused by the coldly biting air, only accentuated his paleness. She looked at the huge chunky sweater:

where it had once fitted snuggly to his broad shoulders, it now hung loosely. She gave an inward sigh. He was doing too much and it was beginning to wear him down.

'What's Jed doing?' he suddenly asked. Then, taking the thought right out of her head, added, 'I don't suppose there is much danger of him coming out here to get stuck in!'

She dropped her head and watched Peg snuffling in the snow. There had not been much danger of Jed coming into the yard before, but now she had told the silly lie about Bill Riley there would be even less chance. Jed would make himself scarce by either vanishing altogether, or hiding himself away in the house until he felt the coast was clear.

'Oh, Sam!' She gave a regretful sigh, then told him what she had done to Jed.

She had been expecting retribution. But he threw his head back and laughed in a way she had not heard in a long time. It lightened the strain in his eyes and brought a bit of colour back to his cheeks.

'I shouldn't have done it.' She dropped her head but there was a smile on her face. She could not feel guilty about anything she did to Jed.

'Rubbish. It's what he deserves. I only wish it would serve to make him run for his life, but I doubt we could get rid of him that easily.'

'But you wouldn't want him to leave?' She frowned uncertainly. 'He does help a bit. It would mean more work for you.'

'Helps a bit!' he spat drily, the strained weariness returning to replace the brief amusement. 'He goes to market and does the shopping. And that only because it gives him a chance to get near a pub, or the greyhound stadium. We'd be better off without him.'

She gave a nod then, unable to dispute what he was saying. When Jed went out he always came back reeking of beer and, from doing the books, she knew the amount of money he took out of the farm was ten times what Sam took. Financially they would be better off without him. But she could not believe Sam would be better off if he had to do all the running about for supplies, as well as everything else.

He had turned back to gaze over the hills once more and again she stared at his face, tauter now with the addition of anger. His black hair, usually slicked back and bearing no resemblance to Jed's silly quiff, had lost all its softness and shine. It looked dull and flat, as if all the life had been squeezed out of it. Something had to be done, she told herself. If he continued working this way he would crack up. Then where would they be?

'Is there really no chance of finding a farm-hand?' she asked. A few weeks back he had accompanied Jed to market in an attempt to take someone on.

He shook his head bleakly. 'The name Bunting is too well-known in the farming community. As soon as you say it they start walking backwards.' He gave a grunt of self-derision. 'Even before they've seen this.' He swept his deformed hand in front of her nose.

'Well, if it was before they'd seen it, it was nothing to do with it,' she replied pointedly. 'So stop selling yourself short. It's your father they won't work for . . . not you!'

He gave a shrug, looking unconvinced.

'We'll have to find a housekeeper,' she suddenly said. 'Then I'll be able to work out here.' She paused, tossing over the previously unconsidered idea. She was a fully experienced farm-hand. It seemed perfect. She could not understand why she had not thought of it before. 'We should be able to find someone who's never heard of the name Bunting,' she continued, when Sam just looked at her in disbelief. 'Your father might be famous in farming circles, but I doubt the entire population of Derby has heard of him.'

'No,' he agreed carefully. 'But they would not be here long before they had. Do you really think you'll find someone who would put up with him?' His expression was full of doubt. 'Whoever is in there . . .' he jerked his head towards the house, '. . . has to be nursemaid, as well. Nobody would put up with him the way you do.' His eyes fixed her pointedly. It never failed to amaze him how patiently she jumped to his father's commands, using only her tongue to administer a few sharp words when anyone else would have thrown something at him.

'I'm going to have a try.' She tossed her head determinedly. Then, her feet slipping and sliding on the frozen snow, she hurried to the chicken coop before he had time to change her mind.

He still had a go. 'You'll be wasting your time,' he called after her. But she did not reply and he went into the stable with Peg running at his heels, wondering why he was wasting his breath. There was no stopping her when she was determined, and she was determined about this. But her determination was not enough. His father would be just as determined it was not going to work.

Peg sat watching him, as shaking his head in despair he began to rake the soiled straw from the stalls. He knew, even if Hannah could find someone willing to take on the job, it would mean more trouble than it was worth. His father would play-up, making the woman's life unbearable, until she walked out in disgust. He wanted Hannah looking after him. Sam had seen it often enough: the victorious look in his father's eyes because he had got her. Maybe not in the way he would have wanted, but he had succeeded in getting her with him for the most part of every day. And night, as well . . . when he chose to be particularly awkward. Playing on her sympathy, trying to make her feel responsible for his condition.

Putting the rake away, Sam took the fork and began to lay fresh straw on the clean floors. He paused, leaned on the fork and shook his head once more. There were times when his father's treatment of Hannah made him feel physically sick, when he would have liked to take him and his wheelchair to the edge of the Tor and drop him off.

Heaving a great sigh he began to fork the straw once more, lifting it and tossing it across the floor with heavy movements that matched the feeling in his heart. If only he himself did not need her help so much, he would have insisted she go and find herself somewhere better to live. But he could not do everything himself. The farm alone was proving more than he could handle. It would have been impossible for him to manage the house, and his father, as well. But it was no life for a young girl, stuck up there with the three of them. She was at the age where she should be having fun, enjoying herself. It wasn't natural, forcing her to live like a nun. And he knew enough about that subject to know how painful it was. But his position was different.

Suddenly letting out a loud groan, as if of pain, he flung the fork through the air, spearing it forcefully into the pile of new hay at the far end of the stable. Peg gave a frightened yelp and cowered in the corner, but he neither saw nor heard her distress. The prongs went deep, the handle shivering from the impact, just as something deep and intense shivered inside his own body. The turmoil he had been fighting since the day Hannah threw herself into his arms, reared up, pressing at his chest like a great weight that threatened to choke him. Until that day he had felt safe with his feelings, thinking she would never have looked at him in that way, never have considered him as a man. But she had and he would never know how he had found the strength to push her away.

He was as bad as his father, he realized sadly, his head falling forward and his arms hanging impotently by his sides. He should have made her go then, straight away. Letting her stay was being unfair to her, and was putting himself through agony. But despite telling himself each morning that today he would tell her she must go, he had never found the strength to do so. He wanted her there for himself: wanted to see her; wanted to be near her.

And that wanting was just as evil as his father's because he could never have her as he truly wanted. He would not let himself.

Lifting his left hand, he stared at the two thickened digits: the curse of his life. He turned the hand, this way, that way. No matter how he held it, it was still obscene, did not look human. It was not human, and neither was he as long as it was attached to him.

His head lifted slowly and he turned to the axe hanging among the array of tools on the wall. It would be better if he cut it off, had no hand at all. The axe was in his right hand, his perfect fingers closed tightly round the wooden handle, when Peg whimpered. As if knowing what was in his mind, she ran to his side. Standing on her back legs she rested her front paws against his thigh, and whimpered again. He looked down into her large, dark, troubled eyes and, as if she had actually spoken, knew what she was trying to say. It was no good. It would make no difference. Severing the hand would not take the curse away: it would still be there inside him, in the blood that ran through his veins. Lying in wait until the day it could rear its ugly head once more.

He suddenly sent the axe flying through the air, pinning it to the hay close by the fork. Then he wheeled away. 'Come on, Peg,' he ordered, and hurried from the stable. He did not stop in the yard but marched straight across and out of the gate, taking the path on to the Tor. It was not like him to turn his back on duty, but work would have to wait. He had to get away and find peace and quiet, before he exploded.

Chapter Eleven

The following day Hannah set her plan in motion. The Christmas cake was in the oven and the pudding was boiling in the steamer on top of the stove. George Bunting had made himself scarce, grumbling about the kitchen being filled with steam.

She had to smile, as she listened to the wheelchair going down the hall and into the office. Not that she expected him to do the accounts, which yesterday he had once again stubbornly ignored, but having him out of the way gave her the chance to make a telephone call without him listening in. She did not want him to know she was looking for a housekeeper until it was all settled and past his interfering.

Listening for any noise to indicate the wheelchair was returning, she approached the telephone. She had looked up the number of the Labour Exchange earlier and, taking the scrap of paper with the number written on it from her pocket, she dialled quickly, wanting to get the call over and done with before she was found out.

When a female voice answered, Hannah explained what she needed, keeping her own voice low. She hoped they were going to be able to help, saving her the job of having to put an advertisement in the evening newspaper, where George Bunting might see it.

There followed a long probing questionnaire: was the position living in; how big was the house; how many occupants?

With one ear still listening out for any tell-tale signs of the wheelchair's return, she quickly answered. Then she explained the position would include a certain amount of nursing, not telling them exactly how much, made it very clear that she was the only person to be spoken to concerning this matter, left the telephone number and ended the call. Thoughts of getting a return call sent her heart fluttering. She hoped it would happen when she was alone.

Face that when the time comes, she told herself, got the mixer out and began making the mincemeat for the mince pies. By eleven o'clock two large jars of mincemeat stood on the table and the mixer was clean and packed away. She topped up the water in the steamer beneath the pudding, then went to the office to find George Bunting.

He had the wheelchair positioned by the window and was staring at the dogs in the yard. His look of dejection brought her up short. His predicament was his own fault. She had got over her feelings of responsibility and now never allowed him to convince her she was in any way to blame. But all the same she hated seeing him stuck in the wheelchair. He had been so strong and fit and it was painful to see him reduced to this.

He turned to look at her and the bleakness in his gaze instantly changed to the gleam of accusation she was more accustomed to.

'Are you all right?' she asked. She wanted to go out in the yard and help Sam, and she wanted him to keep an eye on the steaming pudding for her. But she did not say so straight away – it was best to find out what mood he was in before making any requests. She glanced at the desk, at the pile of untouched bills. 'Are you going to get these done?' It was worth a try, she thought, and swept her hand casually over the desk.

He gave a grunt and turned back to the window.

She gave an inward sigh of despair. But refusing to be beaten, turned to her initial reason for seeking him out. 'I want you to watch the pudding,' she said, keeping her voice casual and relaxed. 'The water will need topping up. There's plenty in the kettle, you only have to pour it in. I'm going to give Sam a hand in the yard and it will boil dry before I come back.'

'What if I scald myself?' He took on the petulant look of a child. 'I can't go throwing boiling water about in my condition!'

'Nobody is asking you to throw it about,' she pointed out, biting her lip against giving a sharp retort and a provoking suggestion that he stop being pathetic. 'You are quite capable of pouring a drop of water into a saucepan.' Then, seeing a chance to pave the way for the new addition to the household, she said, 'Sam needs the help.' She doubted he would allow himself to see with his own eyes the strain Sam was under.

'Why? What's he doing?' he demanded, proving her last thought to be correct.

She gave a sigh. 'He's running a farm,' she replied drily. 'Single-handed! For that other lazy lump does nothing.'

He gave a shrug that, had she not known him so well, she would have taken for nervousness. 'Jed will help if you tell him what to do. You're needed in here.' His voice was strangely docile, but it strengthened, as he added, 'You're supposed to be in here!'

'I'm needed out there!' She could keep hold of her temper no longer and jabbed her finger angrily towards the window and yard. 'Jed might have jumped to it when *you* told him, but he's never here for us to tell him anything.' She gave a groan of frustration and lifted her hands in despair. Did he really not see what went on? Or did he not want to see? It was the latter, she told herself, and stared unrepentantly at his tight-lipped mutiny. She gave another sigh. 'The lambing is only a couple of months away. How do you think Sam will cope with that? Even if Jed is around you know how useless he is at that sort of thing!' she finished pointedly, reminding him of how Jed would have let his cow die if she had not been there to take over the calving. 'Sam can't manage the entire lambing on his own . . . no-one could!'

'You can help him,' he replied, making her eyes open wider. 'Your father taught you well enough.'

For a moment she was lost for words. 'I can only help him if I'm out there,' she finally pointed out. 'But I'm supposed to be in here!' She tossed her head in disbelief.

He looked cornered, realizing he had dropped himself in it. Then the petulance returned. 'Sam can manage. He knows what's what.' He thrust his arm out angrily, as if sweeping the subject away and dismissing her with it, and knocked a vase of chrysanthemums from the windowsill. 'Damnation!' He swiped furiously at his trousers as water ran down his leg. 'Why the hell do we have to have blessed flowers around the place? They must cost a fortune at this time of year.'

'They make the place look like a real home,' she threw over her shoulder, as she hurried to the kitchen to get a cloth and wondered how she could ever think that sombre house could be a 'real home' to anyone . . . except to him. It was, after all, his pride and joy. The thought, along with his last comment about the price of the flowers, put an idea in her head.

She stopped just inside the door to the office and fixed him meaningfully. He would not listen to reason so he had to be made to see everything in black and white. 'Whether you can see it or not, I am needed out in the yard. If you don't believe me, take a look at those books and see what is happening to your precious farm. The way number one son is spending it at the moment it won't only be the stock you lose, you'll lose the whole damned lot, house and all!' She sank to his level of language, hoping he might understand it more clearly. The threat of losing his palace would, before the accident, have been enough to have him raging like a bull. He could still rage, but the bull was no longer there and his commotions now were more like those of a demented donkey, kicking out at anything just because it happened to be there.

It worked. His back visibly straightened and more real

determination flashed in his eyes than she had seen since he had come out of hospital. 'What do you mean?' he demanded. 'There should not be any problems with money!'

'Take a look for yourself.' Finance was not a real problem, at the moment. But if Jed continued to take money out faster than they made it, it soon would be. She did not tell him so. She wanted to get him looking at the books for himself. 'And while you're at it you can do those bills. After you've cleared that mess up and put the flowers back in the vase.' She tossed the mopping up cloth across the room to land on his knee. 'And don't forget the water under the pudding,' she added, and turned and walked away.

'Where are you going?' he shouted angrily.

'In the yard,' she returned without stopping. 'If I want this place to survive, we've all got to do our bit . . . haven't we?'

There was no reply. The bubbling steamer on the stove was the only sound in the unusually quiet house. She hoped it indicated he was actually thinking about what she had said. Nevertheless, she topped up the water under the pudding. She had no hopes of coming back to find the pudding attended to, or the flowers cleared up. But she did feel a bit more confident that he would now look at the cash-book and see exactly what Jed was doing. Which might lead to Jed having a few of his pleasures curtailed and, if she was really lucky, might get the bills sorted out, as well.

It was not until she stepped out into the yard that she wondered if she had put her foot in it. She was not sure Sam would approve of what she had done. If Jed had his wings clipped it would mean he spent more time at home. And having Jed hanging round the place, like a bullock at milking, was not an appealing prospect.

* * *

It was mid-afternoon when the return call came from the Labour Exchange. Fortunately, Hannah was in the kitchen and answered the call herself. But Sam and his father were also there.

'Yes,' she said carefully, feeling the tell-tale colour creeping up her cheeks. She turned her face quickly to the wall and prayed George Bunting would not find anything odd in her manner.

It was a different female voice to the one previously, and it told her they had three possibilities. 'When would you like them sending to you?'

'Oh!' For a moment Hannah was too taken aback to speak. She had thought the Labour Exchange would ask her to go to them, meet the candidates there. 'No! No!' she suddenly rushed out. Feeling both sets of eyes in the room turning to her, did nothing to calm her down. 'I'll come . . .' she began. Where? she asked herself. It was not possible for them to come to the Tor, not without George Bunting seeing them. 'Let me think,' she said, playing for a few moments of time. It all had to be handled very carefully, on both sides. She gave a sigh, wondering how she had ever thought it could work. 'It's a long way up here and miles from the bus route. I'll come to Derby.'

'It's most unusual,' the voice said stiffly. 'I would have thought the ladies would want to take a look at the place and see what they might be taking on.'

No they wouldn't, Hannah thought. 'How about the first Friday of the new year?' she suggested, ignoring the woman's doubts. Friday was market day and she could get a lift with Jed. 'In the café on the bus station,' she added, the only place she could think of on the spur of the moment.

'Well . . .' the woman sounded more doubtful.

'At ten o'clock,' Hannah put in.

'You can't see them all together!'

No she couldn't. But she did not know how to get around that, with the listening audience. Fortunately the female clerk saved the day. Pushing her previous doubts aside, she said, 'I'll arrange them at half-hourly intervals.'

'Yes,' Hannah readily agreed, breathing a secret sigh of relief. 'And thank you,' she added, and quickly put the receiver down. Only then did she realize she had not taken any names and would not know who she was looking for.

'Who was that?' George Bunting fixed her with a questioning stare.

'Silvie,' she said, finding an excuse in Aunt Renee's daughter, and turning her attention quickly to the pile of ironing she had been in the middle of when the telephone rang. 'She's got me a Christmas present. She wanted to bring it up here.' The iron flew rapidly backwards and forwards and she kept her head down, fearing if he saw her face he would also see the lies for what they were. 'I thought if she came here Renee would come with her. I didn't think you would approve of that so I've arranged to meet her in Derby.' She hoped he would be too grateful at her consideration for him, to find it odd that Silvie should suddenly buy her a present. Her cousin had never contacted her once in the two years she had been there, so it was pretty obvious there was no great affection between them.

George Bunting made no further comment and she could only assume his silence indicated he had accepted her explanation. But Sam's silence, and the telling expression in his eyes, told her he knew exactly what the call had been about.

'Did you do those bills?' she asked, seeking a change of subject and not expecting a favourable reply.

'Yes,' George Bunting replied bluntly, taking her so much by surprise that she stopped ironing and looked up with her mouth open. Sam also turned to his father with a similar expression.

'You can both stop catching flies!' he insisted huffily. 'I did the blasted bills. And I want to see Jed the minute he gets in!'

As if part of the same clockwork machine, Hannah and Sam turned to each other in astonishment, then back to the stony face in the wheelchair.

'Stop looking at me as if I was some blasted freak!' he stormed, and spun the wheelchair violently around and headed for the door. 'I did the bills. And the flowers. And the damned pudding!' he stressed meaningfully, not looking back as he rolled through the door and down the hall.

'How did you manage that?' Sam shook his head in disbelief. He had long given up any hope of his father getting back to doing anything but taking his frustration out on the rest of the world.

'I don't know,' she replied honestly. It had not been the first time she had got at him to do something. It was a regular occurrence. In fact, there were times when she had the feeling she was playing right into his hands: their arguments seeming to be the high spot of his day. 'It must have been the house,' she said. 'I suggested he was in danger of losing the farm and the house, hoping it would make him pick the cash-book up. But I never thought it would actually get the accounts done. And the rest . . . well . . . !'

'Why?' Sam looked puzzled. 'Is something wrong?'

'Not really,' she was quick to reassure. She had never worried Sam with Jed's excessive spending, foolishly hoping Jed would see sense for himself and stop the gambling, which was where most of his money went. 'I just thought your father should see what Jed was doing before things got difficult.'

'The greyhounds!' he stated plainly, and rubbed the back of his neck.

His weariness seemed to increase right before Hannah's eyes and she wished she had used other tactics on his father. 'It's nothing!' She gave a careless shrug. It had not been her intention to add extra worry to his shoulders.

He gave a heart-rending sigh. 'Why didn't you tell me?'

'You've got enough on your plate.' She returned to the ironing, trying to make it appear the trivial household task was of more importance. 'Besides . . .' she finally added, when he remained unconvinced, '. . . he isn't incapable.' She cocked her finger at the door his father had gone through. 'He'd be surprised what he could do . . . if he only tried.'

Sam gave a nod. 'You seem to have pulled the right cord. Now he's started let's hope he keeps going.' He stuffed his hands into the pockets of his jeans and rocked back on his heels. 'But I wish you'd told me about the money. It isn't your place to go worrying about things like that. We should . . .' He had been about to say we should share the problems. But the comment was too personal, might give her the wrong impression. He measured his words carefully, then amended to, 'We should discuss the books. I suppose it's my fault for not taking an interest.'

She shook her head, seeing nothing odd in his manner. 'I'm quite capable of looking after the money. If there had been any real problem I *would* have told you. Besides, hopefully your father will be taking charge of it again from now on.'

'Aye, hopefully.' He pursed his lips and looked thoughtful. 'But it might not last when we get the new housekeeper!' he added meaningfully.

'Oh, stop trying to put me off!' She plonked the iron down and fixed him with an irritated glare. 'We don't know until we've tried. If it doesn't work then you can tell me you told me so!' She picked up the iron again, taking her frustration out on one of his shirts. Her own doubts were bad enough, without him adding his own to them. 'We need someone – anyone!'

'You're right, I suppose.' His agreement was far from convincing.

She gave a sigh and stared at him again. Then softening, said, 'There are three possibles. Do you want to come with me to see them?' Getting him involved might give him a bit more enthusiasm, she thought.

But he only shook his head. 'And frighten them off before they get here,' he said drily.

'Oh, Sam!' she snapped angrily. 'When will you learn?'

'Learn what? How to keep my hand in my pocket when anyone else is around? How to never offend anyone by taking something from them with it?' His face contorted with bitterness. 'I learned all that a long time ago. I know my limitations. What I can and can't do.' His eyes hardened on her face and the pain in them was like ice spiking her skin. 'Nobody knows better!' he ground, whirled away, grabbed his wellingtons and, not stopping to put them on, went out with them in his hands.

Oh Sam! she thought, staring down at his half-pressed shirt with despair sinking like a brick in her stomach. What was the matter with him? She could not understand him of late. He had not been himself for some time and she could not believe it was all due to the strain of overwork. Turning to the window she watched him cross the yard to the cowshed, head and shoulders bent against the onslaught of snow that clung wetly to his dark hair and thick, brown sweater. She wished he would talk to her more. But the longer she had been there the more distant he had become. He was still kind to her, but the closeness that had evolved in her first weeks at the Tor had diminished, rather than grown. There were times when he was distinctly cool. And times like yesterday: when he vanished for a good three hours, his only explanation that he had been checking the walls.

In the snow! She had not been able to keep suspicion from her voice, when she questioned him. A deep snow lying heavily against the dry-stone walls, was one of the greatest reasons for them collapsing. But she received no further explanation, so bit her tongue against pointing out it was useless doing any checking until the snow had gone.

Where he went, or what he did, was not her business, she reminded herself, turning back to the ironing board. But instead of picking the iron up she leaned heavily against it, her eyes clouding with tears. She tried to deny it, but deep down inside she knew the reason for his coolness. It was her own silly reaction when she learned of his father's injuries. If she had not thrown herself at him and made her feelings so obvious, he would still be the same. And she would still feel she had a chance, and had something worth living for.

* * *

Jed did not come home that night. He did not grace the farm with his presence until the early evening of the following day. Until he arrived, Hannah had been waiting for him, wanting to see him get his comeuppance. But when he staggered through the door she changed her mind, wished he would go away again: the state he was in was going to cause more trouble than her own few minutes of pleasure was worth.

Even from the distance to the door, she could smell the drink on him. He was in desperate need of a shave, and his silver-grey suit and black shirt were so creased up they could have spent the night squashed under someone's mattress.

She was alone in the kitchen, making pastry for the mince pies. Sam was washing the milking parlour down after milking and his father was in the office . . . still attending to the cash-book. She glared at Jed coolly. 'Where have you been?' she questioned, disapproval stiffening her voice.

'Have you missed me?' He gave a leer, staggered across the room and dropped the car keys on the table. Then he came up behind her and wrapped his arms around her waist, pulling her hard against him.

'Let me go!' She swiped her floury hands angrily at

him, leaving white dust all over his sleeve. 'Get off me this minute!' She kicked back with her foot, landing him a hefty one on his shin.

He jumped away, laughing, but at least letting her go.

She dived her hands back into the flour and kept her attention fixed on the contents of the mixing bowl. 'I suggest you get yourself cleaned up,' she said pointedly. 'Your father wants to see you!'

'What does he want?'

As he spoke his voice came closer once more. She quickly turned to face him, pressing her floured hands hard against his chest to ward him off before he was close enough to get his arms round her again. 'Get up stairs *now*!' she insisted, fury gleaming from her eyes as they fixed his face. 'And get yourself looking half-respectable before *he* sees you!' She gave him a shove, sending him reeling backwards against the sink. It was not difficult, the state he was in. It made her wonder how anyone could get themselves into such a sodden condition so early in the evening. 'Go on!' She flapped her hand at the door, sprinkling flour over the floor. But she had no concern for the mess; when his father saw him in this state there was going to be more to clean up than a bit of flour. Whatever condition he had arrived home in the fur would have flown, but if he did not get himself into some sort of shape his father was going to go berserk.

Laughing at her concern, he closed in on her again. Her hands went up automatically. But the sound of the back door opening, brought Jed up short.

'Brother dear!' he said mockingly, turning to see Sam standing in the doorway, Peg at his side.

Sam did not speak. His gaze went slowly from Hannah's shocked face to her hands, still held out in protection, then to the white marks on Jed's sleeve and the two perfect floury hand prints on his chest. 'What's going on?' he demanded, his expression turning to thunder.

'Nothing!' Hannah insisted anxiously, seeing the way

his mind was working. She was not lying. Jed irritated her but he never frightened her. She never had the feeling she could not handle him.

Sam was not convinced. 'Has he been touching you?' He stepped forward, balling his right hand into a fist and the left into as much of a fist as it would go.

Jed gave a bark of mocking laughter. 'What's the matter, little brother? You can't have her but that doesn't mean the whole world is banned.'

Realizing what was going to happen, Hannah gave a cry of protest. Sam did not reply. He took the last paces with lightning speed. Peg followed him, ears back and teeth bared, ready to sink them into the cause of her master's distress. Hannah made a grab for the collie, pulling her back just in time. She did not see Sam crack Jed a mighty thump under the chin, but she heard the crunch, then the thud, as Jed was laid out cold.

'Oh no!' She pushed Peg away and dropped to her knees by Jed's inert body. 'Can't you Buntings have an argument without resorting to fists?' she enquired angrily, staring anxiously at Jed's face. His mouth was stuck in a silly smile and he still seemed to be more drunk than unconscious. She gave a sigh and looked up into Sam's unconcerned face. 'What did he mean?' she asked. 'You can't have her!' she added pointedly, when he remained dumb.

'Nothing.' He gave a dismissive shrug. 'He's drunk. Doesn't know which way up he is.'

She was not sure Jed had been drunk enough not to know what he was saying, his other speech had been coherent enough. But she could see she was not going to get any more from Sam without a struggle, and no matter what he was to her, his brother was more important at the moment. She looked back to the silly expression on Jed's face, at the thin trickle of blood coming from the corner of his mouth. 'Get some water,' she ordered.

'Leave him! He'll be round in a minute.'

Sam's lack of concern incensed Hannah. 'Get some water!' she snapped, fixing him coldly. He was acting more like Jed than himself. For several seconds he stubbornly returned her glare. Her mouth had to tighten into a mutinous line before he finally moved, took a cup from the cupboard and filled it with water.

She held her hand out to take the cup. But he passed her by, slinging the full contents hard into his brother's face. Splashing the floor, and Hannah.

She had no time to complain. The shock of the cold water did the trick and Jed began to rouse. 'What the . . . ?' He rubbed his chin and focused unsteadily on Sam.

In the next moment George Bunting's voice bellowed from the door. 'What's going off?' he demanded, as all three heads turned to see the wheelchair rolling into the room. As he waited for a reply his stormy glare ricocheted between Sam's and Hannah's faces, making it obvious he considered the third member of the party to be beyond explanation.

'Nothing that isn't taken care of,' Sam replied.

His father gave a grunt, dropped his gaze to Jed. 'I want you!' His voice was filled with all the command of the old George Bunting.

What a time to return, Hannah thought, staring into his face, which was once more full of the arrogance of the George Bunting she had first known. 'Let him get cleaned up first,' she said, trying to gain Jed a bit of time to sober up.

'Now!' George Bunting slapped his hands against the wheelchair's arms, making his impatience clear. 'I want him now!' he repeated unnecessarily. 'In the office.' He directed the order at Sam, waving his arm erratically in the air. 'Get him up. Get him in there. I won't wait another minute.'

Hannah could only look anxiously on, as Sam bent forward, grabbed the lapels of Jed's coat and hoisted him to his feet. There was something so cold and detached about him that she gave a shudder, seeing his manner to be that of his father. The Sam she knew and loved would never have struck first, she thought. She was too full of concern for what was to follow to remember it had been her he had been protecting, and could only look on in despair, as George Bunting spun the wheel-chair round and went out of the door, confident his orders were going to be obeyed.

Sam made to grab Jed's arm, but Jed pushed him away. He straightened his jacket and smoothed his hand over his ruffled hair, gave Sam a leer, and went after his father. He swayed slightly, but the staggering had decreased. He appeared to be considerably more sober than a few minutes ago. But Hannah was sure he was still in no fit state to face one of his father's full-frontal attacks.

His father had no such doubts. In the next moment his voice was bellowing through the walls, seeming to shake the rafters. 'What the hell have you been play-ing at?' he demanded. 'What gives you the right to go taking money the way you have?'

With a sigh, Hannah returned to the pastry. Well you wanted him back to normal, she told herself, wondering how she could have forgotten exactly what 'normal' was.

'I work for it!' Jed countered heatedly. He sounded stone cold sober now.

Work for it! Hannah could not believe her ears. She turned to Sam in open mouthed astonishment. 'Did you hear that?' It was an unnecessary question, she imagined anyone within a radius of five miles would be able to hear.

Sam gave a snort of disgust. 'He thinks he does work for it. It's hard graft lifting all those pint pots.'

'Where's it been going?' George Bunting continued. 'Don't tell me it's all gone on ale, or women . . . unless you've had to start paying for it!'

Hannah grimaced at the crudeness. Then wondered what she should expect. If George Bunting had not been the way he was, had bashed a few more morals into his eldest son, then Jed might be a bit more virtuous. She was so busy trying to imagine a virtuous Jed Bunting, that she missed his muffled reply.

But she did not have long to wonder what it might have been. 'Greyhounds!' his father bellowed. 'Bloody greyhounds! You've been gambling *my* money away!'

'*My money!*' Jed countered, his voice returning to full force.

'No it isn't. It's my farm! My money! And it will be until the day I'm dead and buried. No son of mine is going to gamble it all away. From now on you'll get your dues, the same as Sam. Not a penny more!'

Hannah kept her head down, her hands working the pastry as if it was dough. She would rather not have been hearing all this, and she wished Sam was not, either.

'Ah . . . Dad!' Jed began to whine pathetically. For several seconds all they heard was how he could not keep up appearances on such a small sum, and that it was not fair.

Hannah did not think it was fair, either, but not in the same way. She thought it was criminal that he should even get the same as Sam, when Sam did everything and Jed only a cat's whisker above nothing.

She was pleasantly surprised to find that George Bunting was of a similar opinion, when he went on, 'And if you don't start doing something to earn your keep, you'll get nothing. No money, no farm . . . nothing!'

'You can't do that!' Jed hissed. 'This will all be mine one day and you've got no right to keep it from me now.'

The breath caught in Hannah's throat. She turned sharply to Sam, seeing the tension entering his jaw and his lips tighten. He would not leave the farm to Jed! It was Sam who did all the work, Sam who deserved it.

She relaxed a little, when she heard George Bunting say, 'Who says it will be yours?'

Jed gave a coarse laugh. 'You'd never leave it to *him*!'

Angry spots of red leaped into Sam's cheeks. Hannah reached out, laying her hand on his arm, it was all she could do. It was impossible to think of words sufficient to comfort him in the deathly silence that followed, moments seeming to stretch into eternity.

When finally he spoke, George Bunting's voice was calmer, but still clearly heard. 'I'll not leave it to be washed down the drain,' he said.

Hannah bit her lip, praying that this was the moment when he was, at last, going to put Sam before Jed. But her hopes were short-lived.

'You'll get it,' he announced. 'But only in trust for your children. There'll be conditions. You'll never get your hands on all the money.'

Sam suddenly whirled away and hurried to the door, banging it noisily behind him. Peg almost got her nose chopped off as she raced after him, but was not fast enough.

The collie whined, unable to understand why she had been left behind.

'Come here, girl.' Hannah wiped her hands and went to Peg, stroking a consoling hand over the soft black and white fur of her neck. 'He'll be back,' she said, reassuring herself as much as the dog.

The next moment Jed came blazing into the kitchen, swept the car keys from the table and stabbed his finger at Hannah with such vehemence he could have been laying a curse on her. 'You can tell him, *I* take no conditions. He'll want me before I want him!' he spat forcefully.

Then he slammed out of the door before she could tell him he was wrong.

Chapter Twelve

On Christmas Day Hannah got up extra early. She had stuffed the turkey the evening before so it was all ready to put in the oven, leaving her free to help Sam with the milking and feeding. Holiday or not the animals still needed attending and she wanted Sam to have as easy a day as was possible.

There had been more snow during the night, several inches coated the yard and roof tops and icicles hung from the gutters. The dogs poked their noses round the stable door but not even they were willing to step outside, unless forced to. Everything was white for as far as the eye could see and the farm looked perfect for the festive season. It had the appearance of a scene from a greetings card. Even the usual dark severity of the house seemed to brighten, the warm glow of the lights from the windows turning it into a welcome haven of warmth in the sea of icy coldness.

When the milking was completed, Sam returned the cows to their shed and stocked them up with fresh water and feed. Hannah went to the large sheepshed to do the same there. All the sheep were brought down off the Tor for the harsh winter months. It meant they needed constant supervision, but it was necessary: many would have been lost in the deep snows if they had been left out.

'Phew! It's a cold one!' Hannah announced, rushing into the kitchen and straight across to the fire to warm her numb fingers.

'Boots!' George Bunting delighted in pointing out her error.

'I can't do anything until my hands have thawed out.'

She glanced at her snow covered wellingtons dripping all over the clean tiles. It was only water, not mud. It would soon mop up. Then she looked at him, sitting at the table. It was a pleasant surprise to see he had got himself up, she had not expected it. She made no comment, fearing it would earn his displeasure and a return to his awkward refusal to do anything. 'Have you had any breakfast?' Her hands finally warm enough to unfasten her coat, she took it off, followed by her wellingtons.

'No,' he replied bluntly, as she carried the boots to their rightful place by the door.

She gave an inward grimace. It had been a silly question. Expecting him to get himself up *and* feed himself was too much in one day. 'I'll have it ready in a few minutes.' She mopped the wet footprints from the floor, then dropped some bacon into a pan and cracked two eggs.

By the time Sam came in his father's plate was half empty and a large bacon sandwich was keeping warm under the grill for him.

'Is it getting bad out there?' his father asked, as Peg undid Hannah's good work by shaking her coat all over the floor, before paddling a fresh trail of footprints across to the warmth of the fire.

'The lane still looks passable. But if we have much more like last night it won't be for long.'

'Have we got plenty of feed in?'

Sam gave a nod and pulled a chair from under the table and sat down. 'I've made sure Jed got double the usual quota for several weeks before it all started.'

Hannah placed the bacon butty and a large mug of tea in front of Sam and he began to eat. His father returned to his breakfast and for a time the only sound in the kitchen was the crackling fire and the crunching of Peg's teeth on dog biscuits.

Hannah began to wash the dirty frying-pan and gazed out of the window at the water butt standing by the stables, its frozen contents expanded to stick up over the top by several inches. Sam's mention of Jed had brought him to her mind and she wondered where he was. It was not usual for her to be concerned for him, but the sparkling hills and sharply dangling icicles, although pretty enough when warm and safe, were hostile and treacherous for anyone caught out in them. And the sky hung low and was filled with thick, grey clouds that promised more snow to come.

'Where will Jed be?' she finally asked, unable to keep the thought to herself any longer, as she put the clean frying-pan away in the cupboard. They had seen neither hide nor hair of him since the argument with his father. He had taken nothing with him, except the car. But he could not live in the car, not in this weather. It was cold enough to freeze the breath as it left your lungs.

'I don't know and I don't want to know,' Sam snapped.

'But . . .' she hesitated, feeling unchivalrous for needing to pursue a subject that he plainly did not. 'It's cold out there. Do you think he'll be all right?'

George Bunting almost choked as he took a swallow of tea and began to laugh. 'Don't worry about Jed,' he said, after finally managing to control his coughing enough to speak. 'Wherever he is I can assure you of one thing – he'll be warm!'

Yes, she thought, watching the hardness entering Sam's eyes and wishing she had never opened her mouth. He put the half-eaten sandwich down and pushed the plate away. She began to think the cold air of the yard had affected her reason . . . showing concern for Jed!

'Is the pantry well stocked up?' George Bunting turned her attention back to him. 'It's no good having plenty of food for the stock, if we've got nothing for ourselves.'

'We could survive till August.' She had spent all summer bottling, pickling and preserving. The top pantry shelves were crammed with jars and bottles. The bottom ones were laden with tins and packets and bags of flour and sugar and dried yeast. She knew well enough what winter could be like on the hills and this one was showing every sign of being a special. They did not need much more snow to fall before the Land Rover would not be able to get down the lane and they were cut off until the thaw came. It could only get down now with the help of the snow-plough fitted on the front. She only hoped the weather would hold off long enough to get the intended housekeeper up there.

'Have you got much more to do?' She turned to Sam, turning her mind to a subject she could do something about. Today was supposed to be a rest day for him. After milking and feeding he had agreed to leave everything else and put his feet up, until the process needed repeating later in the day.

'A bit.' He pushed himself up from the chair.

'Well, don't be long!' she warned. 'And don't get frozen.'

He walked out without speaking and she had the awful feeling she had been the one to spoil the day she had been working so hard to make perfect.

*   *   *

'Merry Christmas, Hannah. Maybe this was not such a bad idea, after all.' George Bunting lifted his glass to her and smiled in the way that reminded her why he had always had the women running after him.

'I really can't believe you never celebrated Christmas before.' She spoke quickly, covering the embarrassment she was experiencing from thinking of George Bunting in that way. She lifted her own glass but only took a sip, fearing too large a taste would show her dislike. It had been his decision to have the wine. Judging from the fancy label she guessed it was an expensive bottle, but that did not make the taste any more palatable to her. It was too strong and left a strange after-taste on her tongue.

But he seemed to be enjoying it and it had put a bit of colour back into Sam's cheeks.

'We did when Mum was alive,' Sam said, bringing a smile to her face. Usually he did not speak of his mother, none of them did. The only time she had heard the woman mentioned was when George Bunting had been handing over her old clothes, or talking about Sam being 'her son'. It was nice to hear him calling her 'Mum'. 'But . . .' he gave a shrug, '. . . it didn't seem worth it just for us. Not with the farm to see to.'

Her smile tightened. She could not imagine Jed missing out on the festive spirit, and she was sure his father would have known where to find some. So it had only been Sam who missed out. 'Well, that has all changed now I'm here!' she said, very determinedly. Then forgot herself and allowed her smile to warm on his face.

His eyes immediately darkened. He dropped his head and stared at the table top, his right hand toying nervously with the knife and fork lying on his empty plate.

Hannah quickly got up and cleared the plates away and began to dish out the plum pudding and rum butter. She had only smiled at him, for heaven's sakes. Was it a crime? Should she go around with a mask over her face? She gave an inward sigh of despair, once again kicking herself for bringing Jed into the conversation earlier. He had not forgotten it. He had been strangely silent and withdrawn since coming back into the house, and she could not think of any other reason for it.

'I was thinking after lambing maybe we'll cut the flock down,' George Bunting suddenly announced. Sam and Hannah both looked round sharply. But he did not see either of the astonished gazes, he was staring down into his dish of pudding with his spoon poised ready for the attack, as if it had taken him some time to summon up courage to speak.

'What?' It was all Sam could say.

Hannah was taken by equal surprise and sat there with

her mouth open. But, cutting down on the sheep! On his precious stock!

'Why?' Sam asked, still as stunned as she was.

His father lifted his gaze to him. 'Something has to go. You can't keep on doing it all single-handed.'

Hannah bit her lip to stop herself explaining that Sam would not be doing it single-handed for much longer. The housekeeper would get there before the sheep were depleted. But it was a good sign. If he was seeing reason enough to realize things could not go on the way they were, he might be only too happy to accept someone else looking after him – if it meant he could keep all his sheep. She picked up her wine glass, holding it to her lips to conceal her smile of pleasure. She had heard of the season of goodwill, but finding George Bunting turning human and showing he did have a heart beating inside that great chest, was something she had not bargained for.

It was Sam who spoilt the magic. 'You don't think Jed will be back then?' he asked, the cautious note of his voice making her frown.

His father shook his head. 'He'll be back.' It was said with the confidence of certainty.

Sam gave a grunt of disgust. 'Oh aye! I forgot. He's got to come back and collect his inheritance!'

It was spoken with such venom. Hannah's astonished gaze flew to his angry face. His father was making a gesture towards him and he was throwing it back in his face. And he should have been able to see the way her own mind was working; should have known his father's new attitude would help initiate her plans to get a housekeeper. His plans should be cultivated, not stamped on.

The glass in her hand was plonked noisily on the table. She glared at Sam. 'Stop it!' she demanded, matching fire with fire, too angry to remember this was the day she had been determined to nip any arguments in the bud – stop them before they started.

He glared back at her, an iciness in his eyes that touched

her skin with the same strength of the biting air outside.

'Stop it!' she repeated. Her voice was still firm but no longer so hostile. 'Your father has just offered to cut the flock so you have less to do. That is what you should be talking about . . . not Jed!'

'You're telling me I should be grateful,' he said, his voice as cold as his expression. 'Why? So I don't make a complete cock-up and there's nothing left for him to pass on to my *dear brother*!' He jumped up from the table so quickly his chair toppled backwards. He did not stop to pick it up. He was at the door, thrusting his feet into his wellingtons, before she turned round.

'Where are you going?' she asked, despair and defeat dulling her voice.

'For a walk,' he announced grimly, and was out of the door with Peg only just making it in time before it slammed on her tail.

For several moments Hannah could only stare at the debris of the dinner table. At least he had eaten his first course, she thought, looking on his untouched plum pudding. The dinner was supposed to have been perfect, a time to bring them back together as a family. Only they had never been a family so did not know how a family should act. It had all been a waste of time.

Looking up, she found George Bunting's face holding a slightly ironic smile. It was the last straw. In frustration she slapped her open palms down on the table. 'It's all *your* fault!' she blazed, venting her rage on him. 'If you'd learn some sense this continual bickering could end.' She paused, fixing him knowingly. His smile did not vanish, it actually increased. 'That's it, isn't it? You enjoy the arguments, the constant tension. It's how you get your kicks.'

He threw his head back and gave a roar of laughter. 'I can't deny it adds spice to my life.' He fell suddenly serious. 'After all, there's sweet little else that gives me any excitement.' His eyes glittered at her in the way she had not seen since before his accident. 'It's only my legs that are useless. Everything else still works.'

Had he not been confined to a wheelchair, she would have been up and out and away from him. But she was confident she could move faster than he could manoeuvre the chair and so she remained seated, and hardened her gaze on his. 'And why should I be interested in that bit of knowledge?' she enquired stiffly.

'Damn it, Hannah!' He lifted his hands, bringing them crashing down against the wheelchair's arms. 'I could still father more sons. I need another son. One to take over. Jed's no bloody good and . . .'

'Sam!' she inserted hotly, jumping up and pressing her hands into the table top, as her angry eyes flashed fire into his. 'Go on, say it!' she demanded. 'Say Sam is no good, either. And I'll tip the whole damned table up on top of you!'

His cheeks turned the colour of the berries on the holly decorating the door. 'Sam's no good to inherit. He'll never marry. He'll not have anyone to pass it on to. This house has always been owned by Buntings, generation after generation. I'll not see it stop now!'

'How do you know Sam will never marry?' Her voice scoffed at the thought, but there was a coldness creeping into her flesh, where previously there had been heat. 'He's only twenty. Give him time.'

'He'll never marry.' He spoke with a confidence that sent a sickness to her stomach. 'And I'll have no-one to hand over to, only Jed. Is that what you want?'

She gave a snort of disbelief. He was trying to play on her own dislike for Jed, trying to make her believe no-one would ever consider having Sam for a husband. Well he was wrong. She would have Sam . . . if he would have her! Pushing the unpleasant thought aside, she said, 'Is it anything to do with me? If you're daft enough to leave all this to Jed . . .' her arms swept through the air then returned to the table, '. . . then its destruction rests on your own shoulders. It has nothing to do with me!'

'Of course it is!' he stormed. 'It's your fault I'm in this mess.' He pushed himself hard away from the table, sending the wheelchair careering backwards so it was in full view. 'It was *you* who put me in this thing!' His hands slapped against the arms once more.

She gave a dry laugh. She had heard it so many times yet it never failed to amaze her that he could be so blind to his own faults.

'It was you!' he repeated fiercely.

'*No, it was not!*' She thumped her fists on the table to emphasize her point.

'If I wasn't sitting here I could be out looking for another wife and not having to bother with someone who's of the opinion her virginity is something special. I want another son. You owe me that!'

She gave a gasp. 'I owe you nothing. *Nothing!*' she repeated, tossing her head in offence. Rounding the table she closed in on him, stopping so close to the wheelchair that he had to bend his neck back to look up at her. 'You are the most stupid man I have ever known. You think you can make me feel so guilty that I'll agree to bear you more children. Oh, sorry!' She tossed her head with such contempt that the long red pony-tail flicked over the front of her shoulder. 'I forgot,' she added sarcastically, tossing the hair back to its rightful place. 'It was *sons* you ordered. What would you do if they happened to be daughters? Put them in a sack and drown them in the river?'

'Hannah . . .' he began, making to grab her wrist. She shook him off. 'You could be the mistress here instead of the hired-hand.'

'I'll be no mistress to anything,' she spat. 'Least of all to a man who can't see any further than the end of his nose.' She gave a dry laugh. 'More sons! Do you want to produce a string of perfect little Buntings to show the whole world it really was not you that was affected.'

'It wasn't me!' His denial was so vehement that she knew she had hit the nail right on the head. 'There's been Buntings round here for years and not one of them less than perfect.'

'That is a matter of opinion,' she replied drily. 'The most perfect Bunting I have seen has just walked out through that door.' She stabbed her finger towards the back door, not thinking that her words were giving too much away.

He fell silent and she was scraping the uneaten pudding and rum butter into an old newspaper, before he spoke again. 'Would you marry Jed, if he asked you?' he enquired, watching her carefully.

She was brought up short by the unexpected question. Her mouth dropped open, then she gave a very definite, 'No I would not!'

'But you'd marry Sam?' It was spoken with such quiet confidence that a shiver ran over her flesh.

She tried to backtrack over what she had previously said, but was too confused to think straight and remember she had called Sam 'the most perfect Bunting she had seen'.

'Wouldn't you?' he prompted, at her lack of response.

'That's a rather stupid question.' Her voice was sharp, as she decided attack was the best form of defence. 'You can't just order marriages to suit your convenience. Just because I won't agree to have your children, don't think you can get me to agree to being a brood mare for your grandchildren!' She tipped the empty dishes into the washing-up bowl, turned on the tap and busied herself with the washing-up. She was not sure where his line of questioning was leading: whether he really thought he had found a way to continue the generations of Buntings; or if he was just angry that she would have his son and not him. Whichever it was she was not prepared to continue the conversation and wanted it brought to an end.

'You haven't said no . . . not like you did for Jed.'

She gave an inward sigh, realizing she had fallen into his well-laid trap. The second reply should have matched the first. But how could she have denied convincingly what her heart wanted so much? Anger increased by the addition of embarrassment, she spun round on him. 'And I'm not going to say it! Neither am I going to say "yes". It's too ridiculous to waste breath on. You think you can manipulate people, twist their words to mean what you want them to mean. Oh . . . !' she gasped in frustration, and spun back to the sink, diving her hands into the water and clattering the pots about with unnecessary zeal. 'Isn't there anything you want to watch on the television?' she asked, needing him to go, wanting to be alone with the misery his prying had invoked.

He did not reply, but he took the hint. His hands slowly turned the wheelchair and he rolled out of the door.

Christmas Day! she thought sadly. Her mind filled with memories of cosy Christmases past and tears prickled her eyes. 'Oh Dad!' she whispered, taking a pause from the washing-up to gaze out over the hills.

Why did she stay there? she suddenly asked herself. Then she caught sight of a hunched figure trundling through the snow on the Tor, a black and white dog running excitedly backwards and forwards in front of him.

A tight smile pulled at her lips, and she knew exactly why she chose to stay at the splendid, yet coldly unloving house on the Tor.

Chapter Thirteen

The big freeze continued and so did the snow. The Land Rover only just made it down the narrow lane into the village, the snow-plough blades seeming far too small to attack the bank of snow that lay before them. On several occasions it came to a juddering halt and Hannah's heart leapt into her mouth. But Sam would reverse, make a fresh run forward and the frozen snow would crunch and yield, and Hannah would breathe again. Even so, had it not been that the prospective housekeepers were due to be interviewed, she would have insisted they turn around and go back home.

'Are you sure you're doing the right thing?' Sam asked.

'Yes.' She replied without hesitation, although she was not sure if the question had been directed at the reason for her journey, or at the conditions and he was showing his own doubt that they were going to get back up the lane again. Since Christmas Day speech had been very limited between them. She did not know if it was because he was uncertain about her plans to bring the housekeeper in, or if his father had told him of their conversation regarding who she would and who she would not consider marrying.

George Bunting had not revived the subject of her willingness to marry his younger son, but she could feel him watching her very carefully every time Sam was around and she had grown ever more nervous and apprehensive that he was about to open his mouth. Neither had it done anything to convince her that this morning's journey was going to be worthwhile. Having a score to settle with her would only make him more obstinate and determined to get his own way. And having him thinking she would prefer his deformed son, over himself, was one very big score.

Despite her doubts, and the little voice that had risen at some point every day telling her to telephone the Labour Exchange and cancel the appointments, she had stood firm. She had gone too far to back down, she told herself. Or to let George Bunting win before he even knew there was a fight on.

She did make one call to the Labour Exchange, when she was certain George Bunting was busily employed in the office, to find out the names of the women she was to interview. There was a Mrs Ada Lancaster, aged fifty-nine; Miss Clara Jowitt, fifty; Mrs Rhoda Spencer, the youngest, at thirty-seven.

When the Land Rover stopped outside the bus station, the sight of the bleak, grey platforms covered in dirty ice and slush, only increased her doubts. Several red, double-decker buses stood waiting, seemingly without cause. Their seats were mostly empty and there was only a handful of people about. Only the brave – or the idiotic – had ventured out in the awful weather.

'I'll pick you up here at half-past-eleven,' Sam said. 'Don't be late!' he added, his eyes fixing her pointedly to emphasize the warning.

She promised she would not and pulled up the hood of her warm, woollen coat, fastened it close round her ears and got out. Then she ran as fast as the slippery platform would allow, to the café halfway down the right-hand side. She was already ten minutes late for the first woman. It was not until she reached the café door that she heard the Land Rover rev up and move away. She wondered if he had been waiting for her to change her mind and run back.

The café was as deserted as the bus station's platforms. There were three workmen in overalls at a table by the door, a woman with a young boy and a battered old suitcase sitting in the middle and, right at the back, a woman who looked to be the right age for the one Hannah was looking for. Her eyes rested on the woman and her heart sank. She was wearing a scruffy, brown coat with a moth-eaten fur collar, her frizzy, grey hair was half stuffed inside a thick brown hairnet, the rest stuck out in all directions, and a cigarette dangled unsteadily from her bottom lip.

No! she thought despondently. There was no way she could present George Bunting with such a person. For a moment she hovered uncertainly, considering turning round and walking out again. But the woman looked up and caught her eye and she knew she had to go through the motions, at least.

'Mrs Lancaster?' she questioned, even though she already knew the answer, as she forced herself to move forward. 'I'm Hannah Critchlow.'

'Hello, ducks. I was just beginnin' to think you weren't botherin'.' She pulled the cigarette from her mouth, gave a deep rattling cough, stuck it back again and sucked at it noisily.

Hannah cringed. 'It was the snow,' she said, pulling a chair out and sitting opposite the woman. 'We live a long way out. It's rather bleak. Cold and damp.' She tried to make the prospects look very unappealing.

It did not work. Fifteen minutes later, after she had emphasized George Bunting's faults and added a few extra for good measure, Mrs Lancaster was still of the opinion she was just what Hannah was looking for.

Hannah knew she was most definitely not. 'I'll write to you,' she insisted, almost having to physically push the woman away. 'I have several other people to see before I make a decision.' She gave a hefty sigh of relief when the woman finally took the hint and left, a fresh cigarette dangling from her lip, as if stuck there by glue.

It was cold in the café and Hannah fetched a cup of coffee, needing it for a bit of warmth and also thinking it necessary to buy something before they threw her out for being there under false pretences. When she sat down again the woman with the boy caught her eye. The woman smiled nervously. She returned the smile. She had the feeling the woman wanted to speak to her, but the boy began to complain about the cold and the woman's attention immediately turned to him.

Sipping at her coffee, Hannah watched, as the woman took out her purse and deliberated over the contents for several seconds. Finally she took out a few pennies and dropped them into the boy's hand, telling him to go and ask for half a mug of hot chocolate.

Half a mug! Hannah could not believe her ears. But the boy did not seem to find anything odd and went eagerly to the counter, coming back clutching the mug as if it was gold.

An icy blast of air turned Hannah's attention to the person coming through the door. Her heart immediately sank again. Even before she came striding purposefully towards the table, Hannah had the awful feeling that the amazon of a woman who stood giving each of the café's occupants an intense scrutinizing look down her long nose, was her second candidate: Miss Jowitt, aged fifty!

She glanced at her watch: exactly ten-thirty. Punctuality to perfection? She looked up at the woman again. She must have been every inch of six feet tall, with a great bosom encased in a navy blue fitted coat that gave the impression of a uniform. Her hair was cut so short if she had not been wearing a skirt she would have been taken for a man. And her hands and feet were large and masculine enough for any navvy.

She bit her lip, having the feeling Sam had been right. It had been a stupid idea. The entire morning was going to be wasted.

Fortunately the isolated position of Bunting's Tor put Miss Jowitt off. Heaving her body out of the chair and her great bosom into the air, she apologized very politely for wasting Hannah's time. Then she marched out of the café with her arms swinging in a manner that would have looked perfect on any military parade ground.

Again Hannah gave a sigh, but this time it was accompanied by a smile. It would have served George Bunting right, she thought, and almost burst out laughing as she contemplated his expression if she had presented him with Miss Jowitt for his new nurse.

Pushing her amusement aside she glanced at her watch again. The super-efficient Miss Jowitt had only taken up ten minutes of her time and the last woman would not arrive for another twenty minutes. She was considering whether it was worth hanging around for another disappointment, or if she would be better employed going round to Sam at the market and admitting she had been wrong, when the woman with the young boy came across to her.

'Are you Miss Critchlow?' the woman asked nervously.

Hannah was taken aback. 'Yes,' she replied cautiously, looking the woman up and down. She seemed to be painfully thin beneath the camel coat she was wearing, which had obviously seen better days. The edges of both pockets had been ripped, but they had been neatly mended and it was spotlessly clean. The toes of her brown leather shoes had been scuffed clean of any colour and her thick, lisle stockings were covered in darns which, like the repairs to the coat, had been performed very neatly. She had the air of someone who had fallen on very bad times and remembering the boy's half mug of chocolate, Hannah's heart pulled for the woman.

'I'm Rhoda Spencer. I have an appointment with you.'

Hannah looked puzzled. It took several seconds for the penny to drop and the name to mean anything to her. 'Oh . . . yes . . .' she stammered, pulling herself together. 'I'm sorry. It was seeing you with the boy.'

The woman's pale cheeks coloured and she looked uneasy. 'I . . .' she began uncertainly, then hesitated.

'Sit down,' Hannah instructed, thinking if she did not do so very rapidly her thin frame might collapse.

Rhoda pulled the chair out and sat down. She did not speak right away, but seemed to be weighing her words.

Hannah watched her. 'What is it?' she finally asked.

'I didn't mention David.' Rhoda looked up, fixing Hannah with uncertain eyes. 'I thought it might put you off.'

Hannah looked puzzled all over again. 'You don't mean you would bring the boy with you?' Her voice displayed the incredulity of the suggestion and her confusion increased. 'I'm sorry, it isn't . . .'

'Please!' Rhoda cut in.

Hannah did not miss the note of desperation in her voice, and she fell silent, staring at her in disbelief.

'Listen to me first,' Rhoda begged. 'Before you say no.'

It was a fair enough request and Hannah gave a nod, feeling she had to agree . . . but only to listen, not to anything else.

'He's a good boy. He wouldn't get in the way. He could do little jobs to help . . . he's always helped me out. Where I've been before,' she added, a little too quickly.

Hannah continued to look uncertain. There was something about the woman she found odd and unexplainable, yet there was also something about her that she took to. She looked across at the boy sitting by the side of the battered old suitcase. Like his mother, he was thin and his cheeks were terribly pale. He looked as if a good meal would not do him any harm. 'How old is he?' she asked, trying to push the memory of the half mug of chocolate away. She was in no position to allow compassion to rule her judgement. George Bunting would go berserk if she brought a child to the Tor.

'Eight. He would be at school during the day. He

wouldn't get in the way!' The desperation was back on the last.

'The school is a long walk from the farm.' Hannah looked from the boy to the mother and wondered why she was even bothering to continue the conversation.

'He isn't frightened of walking.'

Hannah stared at the table, where the woman's hands were clenched into tight fists, as if clinging on to the grim hope that *she* was not going to let them down. A great weight of responsibility suddenly pressed down on her. She gave a sigh. But even the thought that the decision was ultimately George Bunting's and, if she took them on, it would only be to have them thrown out again, could not stop her asking, 'Where are you working at present?' The moment she spoke she asked herself why – the only answer was the haunted look in the woman's eyes.

'I'm not. I worked for an old gentleman who died four weeks ago. I haven't been able to find anything since then . . . not with David.' Her eyes filled with tears and she quickly dropped her gaze to the floor. 'I really need a job . . . and somewhere to live.'

'You don't have anywhere to live?' Hannah gasped, her disbelief evident. She stared at the top of Rhoda's bent head. Her dark brown hair had the same curl as the boy's. It was clean and freshly washed, but it had a dull, lifeless quality about it. It reminded her of the way Sam's had begun to look.

Rhoda looked up then, shaking her head. 'We've been in lodgings. But with no work I can't afford to stay there any longer.' She snuffled back her tears and wiped her eyes. 'I'm sorry,' she said embarrassedly.

Hannah fell silent, not knowing what to say. She looked at the boy once more, at his thin little legs, at his clothes. Like his mother he was clean and tidy, but his grey coat was not thick enough for the present icy spell. He was wearing short trousers and no hat or gloves. His knees, hands and ears had all turned pink from the cold.

Feeling her heart turning inside her chest, she called him over. He came timidly, clutching his mother's hand the moment it was in reach.

'It's all right,' Rhoda reassured, wrapping her arm protectively around him.

They made such a pathetic picture, clinging to each other so tightly. Hannah gave him a smile of reassurance. 'I just want to know how you would feel if your mum came to work for us?' She kept her voice soft and gentle, somehow sensing it was necessary, as she gazed into his big, brown eyes which had the startled, apprehensive appearance of a frightened calf. 'I'm not saying she is,' she added carefully, more for his mother's benefit than his. She was still not sure she knew what she was doing and she did not want the woman's hopes raised, only to squash them again. 'But if she did it would mean you had to live on a big farm miles from anywhere. There wouldn't be any friends for you to play with. Would you mind that?'

He shook his head slowly from side to side, his wide eyes never leaving her face.

'Wouldn't you miss the friends you have now?'

Once more his head moved from side to side.

'You'd have a long walk to school . . . would you mind that?'

Again his head moved and she realized, if she expected to find a reason for a refusal from him, she was going to be waiting a long time. She bit her lip and toyed with her fingers on the table. The woman needed the job and she and the boy needed somewhere to live. But . . . she looked up into Rhoda's pleading gaze . . . was she strong enough to tackle George Bunting? She was as sad and pathetic as her son, and Hannah had the awful feeling George Bunting would make her life hell. But how could she turn them away?

'You'd have to be strong,' she suddenly said, realizing the time for turning the pair away had long passed and that she, herself, was no longer strong enough to do it:

not now she knew they were homeless. 'The owner of the house is a cussed man. He needs a firm hand.' Once more she explained George Bunting's bad points, this time adding no embellishments.

'I can do it!' Rhoda stated, a confidence entering her voice and manner that surprised Hannah.

She pondered for a long moment. 'I really don't know how he'll take to the boy,' she said, then quickly turned to him, concerned her unthinking comment might have alarmed him. 'Mr Bunting can't walk,' she explained gently. 'He has to stay in a wheelchair and it makes him irritable. He shouts a lot. He does it to everybody, so he might shout at you. But his bark is worse than his bite.'

The boy's eyes widened with the addition of fear and he turned anxiously to his mother. 'Will he smack me?'

They were the first words he had spoken and Hannah was so taken aback by the question that it was several seconds before she could speak. 'Gracious no!' she gasped, confident that not even George Bunting would resort to using fists on one so young. 'He might shout and bellow but he wouldn't smack you.' She looked at Rhoda in confusion.

'He's a bit timid,' she explained.

Hannah gave a nod, then checked on the time. It was quarter-past-eleven. Sam would be back soon and she recalled his warning not to be late. 'When can you start?' she asked, throwing caution to the wind. If she did not take the woman on she would always have on her mind what might have happened to them. She just hoped they were such a pathetic sight that even George Bunting's hard heart would be touched.

'Straight away,' Rhoda replied, nodding to the battered suitcase.

'You mean now?' Hannah could not conceal her shock. 'You've got everything in there!' She stared in disbelief at the old case. It wasn't even a large one.

Rhoda gave a nod. 'The sooner the better.'

'Well . . . !' Hannah scratched her head, yet again lost for words. She had expected to have time to put the idea to George Bunting before actually presenting them to him. But . . . ! She gave a shrug. Presenting him with a *fait accompli* might work in her favour . . . and theirs! 'You'd better come with me then,' she said, and stood up. Relief swept over Rhoda's face and Hannah imagined a hint of a smile even found its way to the boy's young mouth.

But as she picked up her bag, she wondered what it would take to make a smile reach those big, soulful eyes. Her confidence slipped. Whatever it was, she doubted he would find it at Bunting's Tor.

'Have you had any breakfast?' she suddenly asked, turning her mind to less stressful matters.

'Yes,' Rhoda replied.

The reply had been too quick for Hannah to believe. 'Well, it's almost dinner-time and the journey back might take a long time. So . . .' she reached into her purse, pulled out a ten shilling note, and handed it to the boy, '. . . go and get some sandwiches and biscuits to eat on the way.'

He gazed at the note as if he had never seen one before. 'Go on,' she had to urge, before he finally took it from her and hurried across to the counter.

'Thank you,' Rhoda said meaningfully.

Hannah smiled, but inside she was asking herself what she had done.

Sam's expression repeated the same question, when he pulled the Land Rover up in front of Hannah and realized she was not alone.

'All our problems answered in one.' Her voice sounded far too cheerful, as she pulled the passenger door open. 'One housekeeper,' she announced, pushing Rhoda into the cab. 'And one farm-hand.' She lifted David up, passing him on to his mother's knee and being shocked by the lightness of him. He looked thin, but he felt no heavier than a handful of feathers. She did not wait for

Sam to reply but picked up the one suitcase, threw it into the back, then squeezed herself into the cab with them all. 'What was market like?' she asked, changing the subject.

'Cold,' he replied drily.

'So was the café.' She fixed him with a pointed glare. 'This is Rhoda and David. Rhoda knows what to expect. She's done something similar before.' She was speaking too fast, attempting to explain away her rash behaviour. 'And it won't be long before David is a fully trained chicken and duck keeper. So stop looking so disapproving. You'll frighten them off!'

Sam opened his mouth to speak, then changed his mind. He turned to the two uncertain faces pinned to his own, and smiled embarrassedly. 'Sorry,' he apologized. 'It's just that I didn't expect to find you waiting today.' His gaze settled on David, his eyes narrowing with uncertainty.

'There was no point in delaying when they were free,' Hannah put in, wanting to get her own explanation in before Rhoda started telling him they had had nowhere else to go. She would tell him all that, in her own good time. For the present she wanted him to think she had grabbed them because they were too good to miss, not because she had given way to a moment's softness. 'Shouldn't we be going!' she pointed out, fixing Sam with a look of annoyance. His frowning gaze seemed to have got stuck on the boy and she was concerned that it might be upsetting him. She had prepared them for George Bunting, but she had not felt it necessary to add that his son might be equally unwelcoming.

'All right!' Sam flashed her a knowing glance. 'Point taken.' He engaged the gear and moved away. They were on the outskirts of the town, before he spoke again. 'No offence intended, Rhoda.' He glanced a friendly smile at her. 'It was such a shock to find she'd got it all signed, sealed and delivered.' He flashed Hannah another telling

204

glance. 'Then I should have known she wouldn't mess about.'

'There wasn't any need,' Hannah countered, but felt her tension decreasing greatly. She needed him on her side for the fight she knew was to come from his father.

'Sorry if I upset you, David.' Sam gave the boy a conspiratorial wink. 'It's these women, you know. They have you so you don't know which way up you are at times.' He broke into a smile that put the smile back on Hannah's lips and, to her surprise, also brought one to the boy's. It was thin and weak but it was a smile, and it even put the hint of a sparkle in the big sad eyes.

Perhaps it wasn't going to turn out so bad, after all, she thought, and settled back in the seat, happier. But only for a moment.

In the next, David asked, 'What did you do to your hand?'

Hannah's tension leaped back and her spine stiffened. Her gaze spun anxiously to Sam, seeing the tightening of his lips and the pain filling his eyes. His hand did not matter to her and she had forgotten it was there and had not thought to make any reference to it.

'Hush!' Rhoda demanded. 'That was rude.' She smiled apologetically at Sam. 'I'm sorry. He's too young to understand.'

The reprimand caused David's eyes to fill with tears and he buried his head in his mother's shoulder.

Hannah stared at Sam and shook her head. 'I never thought . . .' she began.

'It doesn't matter,' he quickly cut her off. 'Come on, David,' he urged, turning his attention back to the boy, as silent sobs began to lift his thin little shoulders. 'I didn't do anything to it. It was how I was born.' He gave the boy a gentle nudge on the arm, with the deformed hand. 'It's nothing to be frightened of,' he assured. 'Look at it.'

Was she really hearing this? Hannah could only look on with her mouth open, as David slowly lifted his head.

Sam had returned the hand to the steering wheel to get round a tight corner. When the road straightened out again, he glanced the boy a warm smile and held his hand out for him to see clearly. 'It doesn't hurt me and it won't hurt you. It's just how it was made, not like the other.'

David stared at the hand for several moments, then he turned to his mother. 'Sorry,' he whispered, his eyes filled with remorse.

'It isn't me you should be apologizing to,' she pointed out gently, brushing a consoling hand across his brown curls.

He turned back to Sam. It was several more moments before a second, quietly whispered apology left his lips.

Sam shook his head. 'It doesn't matter. But I don't want you to be frightened of it. You've got to get used to it if you're going to live with us.' He glanced the boy another smile as they stopped at a junction. 'I have to run the farm and you'd be no good as a farm-hand if you daren't come near it.'

A smile flooded David's face. It was so unexpected that Hannah actually gave a little gasp and Sam flashed her a reproachful glance.

'Have you got cows?' the boy asked, seeming not to notice Hannah's reaction.

Sam gave a nod. 'And sheep and horses. Along with chickens and ducks and dogs.'

'Can I see them all?'

Sam gave a laugh. 'You'll not be able to miss the dogs. The minute they hear the engine there'll be a reception committee waiting to give you a good sniff.'

'Will they bite me?'

Sam looked round, his eyes filling with compassion. 'No, they won't bite you. You'll be quite safe. There's nothing at the farm that will harm you.'

A lump came to Hannah's throat. Sam had not been at the café to learn of the pair's dire straits, yet he seemed to understand the boy far better than she did. She did not know how, but she was grateful he did, as the smile she conveyed across the cab told him.

Except for having to cling on tightly as the Land Rover skidded and slewed up the steep, final incline of the lane, the journey back to the Tor proved less hazardous than the journey down. Hannah's prayers had been answered and the snow had held off. Although the sky had increasingly darkened the closer they got to home, the first flakes did not fall until they were passing through the large, stone gateposts and entering the yard.

If it was possible, Hannah imagined David's big brown eyes grew even larger and wider, as he got his first sight of the house. Fortunately, his moment's apparent fear disappeared as, true to form, dogs came hurtling from all directions, yapping out an excited greeting.

'Can I feed them?' he asked, just as excitedly.

'Of course you can,' Hannah readily replied. She smiled, wondering how eager he would be after experiencing it once and having all the bowls knocked out of his small hands; which she knew was bound to happen. But her smile vanished as she got out of the Land Rover and turned to the dark, grey walls of the house. It suddenly looked very sombre and even the silver icicles hanging from the roof lost their glitter, as she contemplated the occupant waiting inside.

She turned to Sam. 'Hang on out here for a minute. Let me go first and make sure he's not in the kitchen.' She wanted to let him know about Rhoda and David, before they walked in on him. She turned suddenly to Rhoda and placed a hand on her arm. 'Don't worry,' she forced a smile to her anxious lips. 'He'll be all right . . . eventually. It just might take a bit of time before he accepts you totally. He likes to make a fuss about everything.' She glanced at Sam and knew, from his tight-lipped grimace, that he was hoping she was right as much as she was hoping she was right.

There was only one way to find out, she told herself and closed the door on them, took a deep, steadying breath and walked quickly to the house.

The warmth of the kitchen wrapped around her, as she stepped inside and slipped her boots off. George Bunting was nowhere to be seen, but the pan of broth she had left on the stove ready to be warmed up the moment she got back, was already bubbling away. She gave a grimace of approval. It was a good sign. If he had thought to light the gas ring he must be in a fairly amiable mood. She listened for the sound of the wheelchair moving down the hall, coming to meet them after hearing the Land Rover's engine. There was no sound of the gently rolling wheels. She quickly returned to the door and gave Sam a sign that it was safe to bring the others in. Then she went in search of George Bunting, hoping all the cloak and dagger stuff was not scaring the wits out of Rhoda and David . . . especially David. The boy was so insecure and clung so desperately to his mother. She hated to think what could have happened to him to make him so timid. Or what would happen to them both, if George Bunting played true to form and she had to take them back.

She found him in the office, sitting by the window . . . with a full view of the yard!

The best laid plans, she thought despairingly. He did not turn and acknowledge her arrival and she stood silently and watched his gaze move very deliberately across the yard to the back door. Her heart sank. She knew his eyes were following their new residents as they crossed the yard on their way from the Land Rover to the house.

When his gaze had reached the back door, then fallen to the floor, she spoke. 'Here you are!' she said, her voice excessively cheerful.

He turned the chair round to face her, slowly bringing his eyes up to hers. 'Who are they?' he demanded bluntly.

She stared mutely at the tightening line of his mouth and the glitter of defiance suddenly sparkling from his eyes. Her heart took another dive, but she knew there was no time left to pussyfoot around. 'It is Rhoda Spencer and her son David. Rhoda is our new housekeeper . . .'

'Like hell she is!' The words were spat like shot from a gun.

'Keep your voice down!' she demanded, placing her hands on her hips and tossing her chestnut mane in a manner that echoed more of the arrogant Samson, than the gentle Delilah whose colouring it emulated. She had had the entire length of the journey back to consider her speech and work out how best to tackle him. Her thoughts had not been very productive but she had at least made up her mind not to be messed with. And the sooner he came to realize she was not going to back down, the better it would be for him, as well as her. It was going to work. She was determined it was going to work. And she was not going to let him spoil things before they had even begun. 'I've gone to great trouble to find someone suitable. Someone I thought you would approve of,' she added, to stress her point and make it clear she had not only been thinking of herself. Rhoda needed the job and they needed a housekeeper. If only she could make him see half the sense of her actions, she was sure it would work out. She was hoping that Rhoda would be determined to put up with anything so long as David had a decent home to live in.

'We don't need anybody . . . suitable or not!'

'*Oh yes we do!*' she stressed, keeping her voice low in the hope that he would take her lead and keep his own voice down, and Rhoda and David would not have to hear. 'We need someone out in the yard to help Sam.'

'Yes!' he countered hotly, not sharing her qualms about being overheard. 'In the yard, not in the house with you!'

'*I* shall not be in the house.' She spoke slowly, as if speaking to a halfwit. 'I shall be out in the yard. *Rhoda* will be in here with you! That way the farm will keep going and you can keep all your sheep!'

She had hit the right spot. He looked piqued, but fell silent. She held her breath. Bringing up the subject of his suggested cutting of the flock had been a good move. She knew he had not really wanted to do it. Cutting down would have shown the rest of the world he was struggling, might even have made them think he was short of money: which would have shamed his arrogance.

He gave a grunt and screwed his mouth into a belligerent line, giving himself the appearance of a spiteful child. It was an expression she knew well but one she had not expected to see so soon. It meant he felt cornered, that he was aware her opinion was the one with the most strength. He didn't like it, but for the moment at least, he would concede, albeit ungratefully, and only until he had had the time to conceive some just retribution.

'And what's the kid doing?' he suddenly asked. 'Are we giving him free board and lodging? Am I expected to pay for his keep?'

That he could be so petty, incensed Hannah. But she did not allow it to show. Keeping her voice steady, she said, 'David's keep will be taken into account with Rhoda's wages.' It was only then that she realized Rhoda had been so eager to take the job they had never got around to talking terms. 'He's a bright lad. He'll do little jobs around the place,' she added, trying to persuade him the boy was not totally useless.

He gave another grunt.

'So you had better come and meet them properly, hadn't you?' She favoured him with an expression befitting a strict school teacher, and held the door open for him to pass through.

He did not reply and his features remained obstinate, telling her all was not well. But he did move the wheelchair slowly across the room and she sent up a grateful thank you. It was only the first step, she reminded herself, as he passed her by and gave her a glare that would have cracked glass. Then he rolled himself down the hall and she followed behind, praying he would not frighten them away in the first sixty-seconds.

David crept closer to his mother, when the wheelchair and its occupant glided through the door. Sam was standing by the sink and Hannah's gaze went anxiously to him, a question in her eyes.

He gave an almost imperceptible nod, just enough to tell her what she did not want to know: they had heard every word.

Hannah turned to Rhoda, seeing the taut lines of anxiety drawn across her brow. She opened her mouth to speak, but Rhoda beat her to it. 'Hello, Mr Bunting,' she said, standing up and offering her hand to him.

Hannah could see Rhoda was nervous and found it amazing that her hand was actually steady. 'This is Rhoda,' she hurriedly said, when he hesitated to take the offered hand. She gave his wheelchair a little shove forward. Then, realizing it was what she would have done to a reticent child, wished she had never moved. He lifted his eyes, casting her a warning glare. She edged back, giving the wheelchair space. 'From now on Rhoda will be in charge of the house and assisting you.' She forced herself to sound confident.

He gave a grunt and Rhoda finally decided he was not going to take her hand and pulled it back.

Hannah ignored him. She went to David, pulling him away from his mother's skirt. 'And this is David.' She rested her hands on his shoulders and held him in front of her. 'He is very keen to learn all about farming. As soon as he knows what to do he will be taking over the chickens and ducks.' She did not mention the dogs, knowing how fiercely possessive George Bunting had been of his collies – before the accident. 'Aren't you, David?' she added, trying to persuade at least one word from his lips.

George Bunting stared silently at the boy, with an intensity that would have made a grown man cringe. But finally David managed to reply, 'Yes . . . Mr Bunting,' very timidly.

George Bunting did not reply and Hannah had the feeling she was drowning and was watching the lifeboat vanishing over the horizon.

'He'll be a big help,' Sam insisted, leaping to her aid. 'I don't know why we never thought of it before – taking on a housekeeper with a built in farm-hand.' He gave David a reassuring wink and pulled a chair out and sat down at the table. 'Let's get that broth inside us before we start work,' he said.

Hannah quickly agreed, jumping to the instruction, grateful to move on and have the first introductions over with.

The meal was a quiet affair. George Bunting did not speak. Hannah tried to act naturally, as if nothing was out of the ordinary. And it was left to Sam to keep the sparse conversation going and make Rhoda and David feel they had not walked into a mausoleum.

'I'll take you up and show you your room and let you get settled in,' Hannah said, the meal over and wanting to give Rhoda a few minutes to herself – and give her the chance to back out – if she wanted to. She would understand if Rhoda had decided she could not take the position after all.

'Why don't you come with me, David?' Sam suggested. 'I'll show you the yard and the animals.'

His eagerness was immediate, then waned and he turned uncertainly to his mother.

'Go on,' she said, and he needed no more encouragement. He jumped up from the table and was at the door before Sam was on his feet.

'Have you got some wellies?' Hannah asked.

David nodded and Rhoda went to their suitcase standing by the wall and pulled out a pair of old black ones.

George Bunting watched her every move, taking in the battered exterior of the case, the meagre contents inside. Hannah wanted to scream at him to stop. His silent gaze was making her feel nervous, she dreaded to think what it was doing to Rhoda, at whom it was aimed. It did finally stop. Rhoda handed the boots to David and George Bunting's gaze left her, and settled on the boy as he sat on the floor to pull them on to his thin legs.

'Haven't you got any long trousers?'

It was George Bunting who had spoken and the room was suddenly silent. David's eyes pivoted fearfully to his mother and Hannah's astonished gaze went straight to Sam.

It was Rhoda who replied, 'No, he hasn't.'

'Get him some thick socks and let him borrow your wellingtons.' He directed the order at Hannah.

'We're only going across to the sheds,' Sam pointed out.

'It's no trouble.' Hannah hurried to the laundry basket, knowing she had several pairs of clean socks in it and wanting to shut Sam up before he upset his father. If this unexpected show of concern indicated he was having a change of heart, then she was willing to do anything, no matter how strange were his demands.

'Come on,' she said, dropping to her knees in front of David and ignoring his mother's protests that they did not want to be any trouble. She tugged one of his wellingtons off and pushed the long blue sock on to his thin leg, then followed it with one of her own wellington boots. 'Let's get you all nice and snug,' she said. It was not until she pulled his second boot off, that she noticed it had a large hole worn right through the sole. She glanced up at George Bunting. There was nothing in his bland expression to tell her he had seen the hole, but she had the feeling it was the cause of all his fuss. She gave a secret smile, wondering if she had found a spark of softness in his hard heart, after all. Maybe there was hope for him yet. And if there was hope for him, there was hope for the rest of them.

'There you are.' She helped David to his feet. 'We'll have to find you something warmer to wear than this.' She looked at the thin fabric of his coat. 'But it will do for now. You're not going far and if you start to feel cold, tell Sam to bring you back.'

'He'll be all right,' Rhoda insisted.

Hannah could see the woman was concerned that they were causing too much trouble and she gave her a smile of reassurance. Then she turned to watch as David ran to Sam, and without concern grabbed his nearest hand to hold on to as they went out. It was his left hand and Sam's momentary surprise soon turned to a smile of affection. A lump came to Hannah's throat and, as the door closed behind them, she turned quickly to the table and began to clear the dirty dishes away, needing something physical to take her mind away from the emotion that was prickling her eyes and threatened to choke her.

'Is it all right?' Rhoda looked anxiously to George Bunting.

'Of course it is. He'll be fine with Sam.' Hannah got her reply in before him. She was anxious that Rhoda might make too much of a fuss, and put his back up.

Rhoda smiled tightly. 'I know he'll be safe with Sam,' she said. Then to Hannah's alarm, insisted on pursuing the matter. 'But I don't want him to get in the way of your work.' Her face crumpled and she dropped into a chair and began to sob.

Hannah went straight to her side. 'What is it?' she asked, glancing anxiously at George Bunting to see how he was taking the display of emotion. His face remained bland and unreadable and offered her no hope.

'It's . . . just . . .' Rhoda looked up with tears streaming down her cheeks. 'This morning I didn't know where we would be or . . . or what . . .' Her voice failed and she collapsed in sobs once more.

'Hush,' Hannah said, a note of panic in her voice. 'Don't upset yourself. Everything will be all right.' She glanced at George Bunting once more, again receiving no indication of what his reaction was going to be.

Fortunately, it was only moments before Rhoda pulled herself together. She wiped her eyes and turned to George Bunting. 'Please don't send us away, Mr Bunting,' she said calmly. 'David won't get in the way. I promise you he won't. Just give us a chance and I'll do anything you want.'

Hannah bit her lip, as she stared at him, waiting for his response, fearing the emotional outburst would be Rhoda's downfall. She was certain he would hate it and use it as a weapon against her.

For several heart-stopping moments he remained silent.

'Anything!' Rhoda repeated.

It was seeing the flicker of interest enter his eyes that made Hannah wake up to what Rhoda was saying. She bit her lip again. The woman did not know what suggestions her words would put in his head. But if she intervened it would get Rhoda thrown out. She bit her lip harder and kept her thoughts to herself, telling herself she would have to make sure Rhoda understood exactly what he was like, at a later date.

Finally he said, 'So long as you get the work done you and the boy have a home here.'

'Thank you, Mr Bunting. Thank you. You're a gentleman,' Rhoda said with feeling.

Hannah wondered how long it would be before he changed her mind on the last. But for now it did no harm for Rhoda to think of him as a gentleman. It certainly did not displease him, as the upward tilt at the corners of his mouth only went to prove.

He lifted his gaze to Hannah's face. 'Show Rhoda where everything is,' he said, and turned bleakly to the single case. 'Is that everything you own?'

Rhoda gave a nod. 'Yes,' she said. 'Not much for thirty-odd years.' She attempted to joke, but there was real pain in her eyes.

He turned to Hannah again. 'Get those old clothes out.' He did not say his wife's old clothes, but she knew those were the ones he meant. 'There should be something suitable for Rhoda. And something that can be fixed up for the boy.' He turned and wheeled himself out, leaving Hannah to stare after him with an open mouth. Then she sent up a prayer of thanks to some unseen guardian angel who she knew must have been by her side that day.

Chapter Fourteen

The journey from Derby with Rhoda and David turned out to be the last for some time. The snow came thicker and faster and the following day Sam announced, for the benefit of anyone who had not noticed the great banks of white stuff for themselves, that they were now snowed-in.

To Hannah's surprise, Rhoda was not upset by the isolation. In fact, it appeared to please her. She began to relax in her new home, and so did David. He adored all the animals and was only too eager to get out in the yard and help Sam. His pale cheeks turned to a healthy pink and he began to look more like an eight-year-old should look.

George Bunting continued to be a real surprise. He still did plenty of arguing with Sam and Hannah, but he never raised his voice to either Rhoda or David. He didn't do much speaking to them, either. But Hannah was quite overwhelmed that he had managed to find a little compassion in his heart for the desperately needy pair.

Sam also began to look better. The healthy glow of outside work returned to his face and the dark circles left his eyes. The lightening of his workload was doing him good; but Hannah was of the opinion Jed's absence was helping him more. There had been no word from Jed in the four weeks since the day he rushed out of the house after the argument with his father. If George Bunting missed him, he never spoke of it. And she knew no-one else missed him. Secretly she wished he would never come back . . . for Sam's sake. Now they had Rhoda's assistance there really was no need for him.

Unfortunately, Hannah did not think there was much chance of getting her wish, and Jed vanishing off the face of the earth. Like the proverbial bad penny, he would turn up again . . . when he ran out of money. In fact, she imagined it was only the inability to get up there in the snow that had kept him away so long.

'Don't fall!' Hannah smiled, as she watched David run through the snow with not a care for the slippery ground, the egg basket swinging in his hand. A sharp wind was whistling over the Tor, freezing the breath as it left your lips and lifting patches of dry snow to whirl like dust in the air. But David was no longer worried about the cold. He was wearing a navy blue coat of a thick woollen material, with green corduroy dungarees. Both had been cut down from garments belonging to the late Mrs Bunting. His head and ears were covered with a bright orange woolly hat, which matched his mittens and high necked jumper, also made from a sweater of Mrs Bunting's, which Rhoda had carefully unpicked and knitted up again.

Rhoda had the ability to work marvels with a needle. Hannah shook her head in wonder, as she picked her way carefully across a particularly bad icy patch, worried that if she fell the bag of corn in her hands would go everywhere. Rhoda could do things that she would never have considered attempting. She could produce a garment from something that had looked like an old rag, and she did it with amazing speed. Hannah had sat on many evenings, unable to take her eyes away from the clicking knitting needles and an ever-growing part of a jumper, scarf or hat.

'Come on, slow coach,' David teased, grinning impishly at her awkwardness, and swinging the basket high in the air.

'It's a good job there aren't any eggs in that.' The scold was good-natured and accompanied with a laugh. It was good to see the difference in him. February began in a few days and he would have been at the Tor for one month.

But the change that had come over him in that short time was unbelievable. He seemed to grow with every passing day: in body; in confidence; in contentment.

Reaching the coops, he dropped the basket and bounded back to Hannah. 'Let me take the corn.' He leapt round her legs, reminding her of one of the dogs, and tried to get the bag out of her hands.

'Hang on!' She held on tightly, seeing his eagerness doing what she had feared her slipping would do: spilling the contents all over the snow. 'It's too heavy for you.'

'No it isn't.' He looked greatly offended and she had difficulty stopping herself laughing and insulting him all over again. 'But you said I could be the chicken and duck keeper,' he protested.

'And so you can.' She hitched the bag higher, taking it out of his reach. 'As soon as the snow has all gone you can take full responsibility for the birds. But until it has, I'm taking no chances of you falling and not being missed until you've frozen solid.'

He was only partly placated. 'But if I can't carry the bag . . . how can I feed them on my own?'

'You'll have to put some in a bucket.'

'I could put it in the basket,' he said eagerly.

Hannah laughed. 'Only if you want to get there and find it's all fallen through the bottom.'

The prospect of laying a trail for the birds to follow, put a smile on his face and a sparkle in his eyes. Hannah smiled with affection, recalling the sadness that had filled his eyes before. She hoped it would not return when the snows went and he had to begin leaving the Tor every day to go to school. Like his mother, the imprisonment seemed to suit him. It was as if he felt safe up there. Safe from what? she wondered, as he turned away and bounded back to the coops. Her smile vanished as she tried to think what could have happened to make an eight-year-old afraid of the outside world.

'Take those to your mum,' Hannah instructed, as they walked back round the stable to the yard. This time David was by her side, walking very carefully, the basket with its precious cargo of eggs clasped very tightly in his hands. 'I'm going to find Sam and bring him in for dinner.' Leaving him to go to the house alone, she turned down the yard.

'Don't forget Peg,' he called, never taking his eyes off the eggs.

'I won't,' she assured, and had to smile. He was always so careful and had never broken one. She shook her head. It was not as if they needed them. Being cut off from the rest of the world meant nothing was getting out, as well as in, and they had more eggs than they knew what to do with. It was the same with the milk. Until the lorry could resume the daily pick-up, they had enough to bath in.

'Sam,' she called, as she went into the milking parlour, but he was not there. She stopped and looked around at the gleaming metal and clean floor. He had obviously done the washing-down and she realized he would be out the back, pouring the unwanted milk down the drain. It was such a waste. But the cows still had to be milked and there was nothing else they could do with it.

When she stuck her head out of the back door, he was fixing the manhole cover back in position, the depressing deed completed. 'Are you going to be long?' she asked.

He never got time to reply. A loud wail suddenly filled the air, coming from the direction of the yard.

'David!' she gasped, as Sam's astonished gaze pivoted to her face. In the next instant she had let the door slam on him and was racing back to the yard.

She was halfway across the milking parlour when she heard the door behind her open again and knew Sam was following. The wailing increased and she quickened her steps. It was such a terrified sound and it filled her with trepidation. She could not think what could be causing the boy such grief. As she flung herself through the parlour's front door and across the yard, Sam was right there with her.

'What!' she gasped, coming up short and causing Sam to cannon right into her. In the middle of the yard was Jed, David slung over his shoulder like a sack of potatoes. At his feet lay the upturned egg basket, broken shells and bright orange yolks spattering the white snow. 'Leave him alone! What do you think you're doing to him?' she demanded angrily, fear for David, and frustration for Sam, shaking violently through her limbs. He was the last person she had expected to see. She could not begin to imagine how he had got up there. Flown up on one of his acquaintance's broomsticks, she thought, her bitterness curling into a tight ball inside her, as she rushed forward to David's aid.

Sam beat her to it. 'Put him down! He lives here,' he insisted, the quiet threat in his voice promising far more retribution than any loud shouting. He snatched David from his brother and held him tightly in his arms.

'I thought the little runt was stealing our eggs,' Jed announced proudly, dusting his shoulder down as if something distasteful had been there.

'I know exactly what you thought.' Sam settled a hostile glare on Jed. 'Well don't go judging everybody by your own standards. This is David, he is our new housekeeper's son and if you'd been around, like you should have been, you'd have known that!' He turned his attention to David then, making it obvious who he considered to be of most importance. 'It's all right, David.' His voice was gentle, soothing, and he fastened a reassuring gaze on the boy's distraught, tear-stained face. 'It's all over. There's nothing to be frightened of. This is my brother.' On the last his voice tightened, conveying the disgust he felt for his sibling. David's sobbing ended, but his body still trembled and he wrapped his arms tightly round Sam's neck and buried his face into his shoulder.

'You've frightened the life out of him,' Hannah hissed, feeling her hate for Jed double in that moment. Resting her hands on her hips, she moved forward, stood on tiptoe and thrust her angry face into his. 'You great bully! You knew he wasn't stealing anything.' She gave a groan of frustration and despair. 'Why did you come back?' Her voice tightened with bitterness on the last.

He tossed his head and gave a bark of laughter. That he showed no remorse, fuelled her anger and hardened her gaze on him. 'This is *my* home!' he ground. 'I have every right to be here. Or had you forgotten?'

'I hadn't forgotten!' She gave a sarcastic snort and let her disapproving gaze run slowly down to his feet. His trouser legs were wet well above the knees, the black leather of his shoes looked to be soaked to such an extent they were past redeeming. He had walked up. The thoughts of him trekking up the hills would have made her laugh, if she had not suddenly asked herself why. He never walked anywhere, considering himself too good to waste his energy on the practice of common men. To do so in the present circumstances must mean he had a real reason – and his reasons were always suspect. He could have run out of money, she thought, as she returned her gaze to his face, fastening her eyes coldly to his. But she did not think so. He was wearing a black leather overcoat and a pair of black leather gloves. They were new, she had never seen either before, and their quality emitted an aura of wealth that surpassed even his usual extravagant tastes.

Spending more of Sam's hard earned money, she thought bitterly. 'It would be impossible for the peasants to forget the lord and master,' she grated sarcastically, grabbing hold of his tie and bringing his face down closer to her own, so he could feel the full force of her hate at close quarters. That it was silk her fingers fastened on, spurred her anger, and she gave it a sharp tug, making him gasp in pain and grab her hand to stop her doing it again. 'And just so *you* don't forget! This is also David's home now. And he doesn't get bullied by anyone, least of all somebody who does less work than himself.'

Ripping her hand away, he jerked himself free. 'I see the icy weather has done nothing to chill your temper,' he growled, glaring at her as he straightened his tie.

The sound of the farmhouse door opening cut off her sarcastic reply. George Bunting and his wheelchair appeared in the doorway. A worried and anxious Rhoda stood behind, trapped by the chair that was blocking the way and stopping her getting to her son.

Hannah could only stare at him. It was the first time he had ventured to the door since coming out of hospital. For over a full year the nearest he had got to outside was sitting at a window. She did not know if it was the prodigal son's appearance, or David's predicament, that had brought him. But she hoped it was the latter.

'How the hell did you get up here?' He fastened his stony features to Jed's face.

Jed gave a sneer. 'Hello, father. It's nice to know you missed me!'

'How did you get here? Where's my car?' his father demanded, ignoring the sarcasm.

'I walked.' Jed strode arrogantly towards the door. 'And seeing how I could not get up here, I had to cover my expenses somehow.' He stopped right in front of the wheelchair and stared unrepentantly into the eyes that were a mirror-image of his own. 'So I had to sell the car,' he concluded, with a lack of concern that made Hannah gasp, as she contemplated the reaction that was to come.

She did not have long to wait. 'You what?' George Bunting's face turned crimson. For a moment she had the feeling his anger was so great it would give him the strength to actually stand up and grasp Jed by the throat.

'Did you expect me to live in the gutter?' Jed's haughty reply showed no remorse.

'I don't expect you to go off in *my* car and sell it without my knowledge.' George Bunting's fingers turned bloodless from the tightness of his grip on the wheelchair's arms. 'You had no right!'

David gave a whimper and Hannah turned, just as Sam said, 'Hush, it's all right.' He gave her a telling grimace over the boy's head. She returned the same, thinking how useless the words were. It was never all right at that house – not for long, anyway.

'You can't have sold it without my consent,' George Bunting stated baldly. 'You haven't got the papers. I've still got the log book. You can't sell it without that.' His eyes suddenly narrowed, his lips clamping so tightly that the corners of his mouth turned as white as his fingers. 'You haven't sold it,' he began, speaking with the certainty of sudden realization. 'You've lost it in a game.' His eyes opened wide, challenging his son to deny the fact.

Hannah held her breath, as she was sure everyone else did. For several seconds even the wind seemed to cease whining over the hill. The tense silence stretched, seeming to have no end, as they all froze, waiting the next move.

It came from Jed. He shuffled nervously and the soft crunching snow beneath his feet sounded loud enough for an avalanche. 'I had to sell it,' he began. 'I . . .'

'You've gambled my car away!' His father's voice slashed through the air like a knife, cutting off his worthless excuses. 'Well, you'll never get your hands on the log book.' His anger visibly trembled through him, the wheelchair rattling from the force. 'That's why you're here, isn't it?'

Jed's increased nervousness proved his father had hit the nail right on the head. His father gave a mirthless laugh. 'That car is mine. You either get it back or I report it stolen to the police.'

Hannah bit her lip – to stop herself laughing out loud. Jed had really done it this time. The last thing his associates would want was the police getting involved, as George Bunting well knew.

'There's no need for that,' Jed insisted. 'I told you I sold it, fair and square. Do you want to make me look a right idiot?'

Jed's squirming held no sway with his father. 'There's no need for me to make you look a right idiot, you manage it very well on your own.'

For a moment Jed's face hardened and it appeared he was going to square up to his father. Then he thought better of it. 'I had to do something.' His voice had taken on the whining quality of the wind. 'I had no money. But if you give me some we can buy it back.'

'We!' His father blazed. 'It is *we* who have to buy it back?'

'Do we have to discuss this standing here, with all the . . .' he hesitated, his gaze sweeping over Sam and Hannah.

'Peasants watching,' she inserted for him.

He sneered at her.

But his father was having no more. 'There is nothing more to discuss,' he pointed out firmly. '*You* lost the car *you* will get it back. And until you do you don't get another penny from me.' He craned his neck round to Rhoda. 'Get me back inside,' he ordered, and she pulled the wheelchair away from the door and into the kitchen.

Jed immediately followed. Hannah turned to Sam with a grimace of resignation. Their peace and tranquillity had been brought to an end sooner than she had expected, and in a far worse way than she had expected. Of all the things for Jed to go and lose at a card game, his father's treasured Jaguar had to be one of the worst. 'I wish there was a chip shop round here,' she said drily, the prospects of having to follow the others inside for dinner, holding no appeal. With Jed present she would rather have not set foot in the house at all.

Sam gave her a grim smile to show he shared the same feelings, and David lifted his head. It was the first sign of interest he had displayed since burying his head against Sam's shoulder. Hannah smiled and patted his shoulder. 'Come on, buster. It's time to get fed.'

But the distress on his young features did not lessen. 'I want fish and chips,' he said, and clung tighter to Sam. 'I don't want to go in there.' His watery eyes lifted to the back door and Hannah felt something tighten inside her.

'There's nothing to fret about,' Sam assured, giving the boy an affectionate squeeze. 'He won't hurt you. And we'll all be in there with you.'

'I don't like him,' David stated with feeling.

Join the club, Hannah thought, raising her eyebrows over the boy's shoulder at Sam. 'If we don't get any warm food inside us we won't be strong enough to look after the animals. Then what would they do?' she asked, playing on his love for the animals.

His face puckered in a deep frown and he toyed with his orange mittens. Then he looked into Sam's face. 'But we won't stay in there after?' he asked, with a note of anxiety that made Hannah's lips tighten into a grimace again.

Sam shook his head. 'We'll be out just as soon as you've cleaned your plate. Now, what do you think your mum will have made for us? Stew and dumplings? Shepherd's Pie? Or sausages?' He quickly began the daily game of seeing who could guess what was for dinner: the winner being allowed to take a caramel from a large tin Hannah had got in for Christmas, which had not been opened until David arrived.

'Sausages,' he said, his eyes brightening, his worries for the moment pushed aside, as Sam carried him across the yard. But they came back the moment they stepped into the kitchen, even though the cause of his distress was nowhere to be seen.

'Where's he gone?' Sam enquired stiffly, and his father jerked his head upwards to indicate the bedrooms.

Settling himself in, Hannah thought irritably, as she pulled her wellingtons off and went to the sink to wash her hands. But at least he had done them a favour by making himself scarce.

'Shall I set another place for dinner?' Rhoda looked uncertainly at George Bunting, a knife and fork poised in her hand, as she dithered about whether she should make a place for Jed or not.

Hannah was wiping her hands and, before George Bunting could reply, tossed the towel at Sam, and said, 'No. I'll take it up to him.' She was prepared to do anything to keep him out of the way.

'You'll do no such thing,' Sam put in angrily. 'If he can't come down to get it himself, then he can go without.'

Hannah glared at him. 'I think, under the circumstances . . .' her gaze flicked pointedly to the back of David's head as he washed his hands, '. . . that it would be better if Jed stayed where he was.'

Sam's gaze followed and he stared at the boy for several seconds. 'All right,' he finally agreed, with reservation. 'But don't make a habit of it. If he thinks he's got a wet nurse we'll never get rid of him.'

Hannah knocked on Jed's door and he immediately called her in. He was lying on the bed, one hand behind his head, the other holding a *Senior Service* thoughtfully to his lips. The fancy silk tie was hanging loose around his neck and the top two buttons of his black shirt were unfastened. His snow-dampened trousers had been slung over the back of a chair and his legs were bare. As she walked through the door, his lips pursed in a knowing smile and he exhaled a large cloud of smoke.

'Where do you want this?' she asked, showing no concern for his state of undress; she knew he was expecting her to cringe with embarrassment and she was damned if she would give him the satisfaction. Besides, she was too well acquainted with the man inside to be overtaken by lust at the sight of his hairy legs. Without waiting for his reply she made her way across the room to put the tray down on top of the drawers by the window. She could feel his eyes watching her every step of the way. He let her get to the drawers and lay the tray down, before he finally spoke.

'Here!' he said, patting the cabinet by the side of the bed. 'I'll have it here.'

With a grimace she picked the tray up again. 'Don't strain yourself,' she said drily, plonking the tray on the cabinet, with such force the cutlery rattled and the tea spilled over the cup and filled the saucer.

His reaction was so fast that she was taken completely by surprise. Before she could turn away, he had lunged across the bed and had hold of her wrists. 'I hope you'll be gentler with *me*,' he said, his eyes glittering with malicious intent as he twisted her flesh in a way that caused her so much pain she could do no other than gasp and follow his command as he pulled her down on to the bed.

When she was flat on the bed he pulled her arms up above her head and leaned over her, bringing his face down close to hers. 'Now let's see if the peasants really know how to treat their lord and master!' he ground, returning the insult she had thrown at him when finding him with David.

Each word blasted the stench of second-hand tobacco fumes into her face. Her nose curled with distaste and she turned her head to the side and tried to wriggle away from him. She managed to move the bottom half of her body a little, but her wrists were held tightly by his hands and she could not free them and get away completely.

Laughing at her ineffectual attempts he threw his leg across her chest, pressing it there to keep her still. But his leg was bent and his knee was very close to her throat.

In an instant her head reared up and her teeth plunged through the thin covering of skin and flesh, right down to the bone of his kneecap. For the second time in her life she was tasting Bunting blood, but she was too angry to notice.

He gave a yelp and let her go. She did not wait to give him a chance to grab her again, but was off the bed and grabbing for the tea cup. The next moment the hot liquid hit him hard in the face and he let out a string of curses eloquent enough to match his father.

'Don't you ever try that again!' She glared at him fiercely, but he did not see. He was too busy trying to rub his stinging eyes and clutch his painful, blood-smeared knee all at the same time. Her lips curling with contempt, she tossed the empty cup down on the bed by his side and hurried to the door, rushing out and closing it noisily behind her. As she turned away, she cannoned straight into Sam.

'What's wrong?' he demanded, grabbing her by the arms and giving her a shake. 'What is it? What's he done?'

'Nothing,' she assured. 'It was nothing. Leave it.' He did not look convinced and, putting her aside, he moved towards his brother's bedroom door. She grabbed his arm and pulled him back. She knew if he went into that room there would be a fight. Not that Jed was in any condition to put up much resistance, but resorting to fists was no way of going on, and she was not going to allow it to happen over her. 'Let it go, Sam.' She fixed him meaningfully. 'It's over and I don't think he'll try it again.'

He hesitated, his gaze swinging from Hannah to the closed door and back to Hannah.

'Why did you come up here?' she asked, tightening her hold on his arm, not sure she was winning this fight.

'I heard something. It sounded like a cry.'

'It was a yelp. But who did you hear give it?'

'It sounded like him.' He jerked his head at the door and his confusion increased. 'I think!'

'It was him,' she confirmed, and had to smile at his bemusement. 'So don't you think that tells you something?'

He gave a nod. 'It tells me he was up to something.'

'It also tells you he didn't win.' Her smile deepened and she shook her head at him. 'Oh, Sam, it wasn't anything, really.' She gazed into his troubled eyes, and she saw something there that made her forget herself so that, almost unconsciously, she moved to lift her hand to his cheek and would have touched him. But he moved faster. He turned his face away with a jerk, as if her hand had been fire, her fingers a flame about to burn him. His whole body followed, turning from her, not so violently, but enough to make her lose her grip on his arm, and the way her hands fell impotently to her sides echoed her loss better than any words.

It was several seconds before he looked at her again. 'If he ever did anything to you I would kill him!' Fierce intent vibrated from his voice but she could only nod her head. Her voice was lost in the emotion that clogged her throat. It was no idle threat. He meant every word. If he knew what Jed had tried to do he would have gone right in there, grabbed him by the throat and shaken him until his neck broke. He would not have been able to control his anger, not in the way he was able to control the emotion, the passion she had seen burning in his eyes just then. It had gone far deeper than his usual concern for her, so deep that she realized his feelings matched her own for him – feelings which, at times, she feared would take her sanity.

It was a shock to know he was not so immune to her as she had thought. It should have pleased her, but it did not. That he was willing to let his anger loose, yet able to hold back the feelings that could have changed both their lives, hurt her far more than the physical pain of Jed's assault. Turning quickly from him, she hurried to the stairs, stopping only when she reached the top. 'Dinner will be waiting,' she said, glancing back at him and waiting to make sure he came downstairs with her, and did not do as he had first intended and go in to Jed.

It took a moment, but then he moved from the spot to which he seemed to have become glued. When he reached the stairs he did not stop, but went straight past and hurried down before her.

Wasn't life ironic! she thought, as she followed slowly behind. She had, without any effort on her part, managed to find herself underneath two of the Buntings. Yet the only one she would willingly lie beneath, didn't want to know.

Chapter Fifteen

The snow continued to fall thick and fast and Jed settled himself down to a life of idleness. Hannah's feelings swung from irritation that he did not feel it necessary to lift a finger to help and that his father did not see fit to make him, to a certain relief that he did, at least, keep out of their way by staying in bed for most of the day. Surprisingly there were no more arguments. George Bunting appeared to have taken the attitude that he had said his piece, and was, like the rest of them, waiting for the snow to clear. But in his case it was so that his car could be returned, rather than an urgent need to be rid of his elder son. Rhoda seemed to have settled down again and had accepted Jed's presence far better than Hannah had first thought possible. But David was a worry. The boy had not ventured out of the house for the entire week. It had never happened before. His eagerness to get out in the yard usually had him standing at the door in coat and boots long before Sam was ready to go. And he was not eating as well as he had been doing: leaving half of the food on his plate, where before he would have gobbled it down with a speed that put a smile on everyone's faces.

'Do you think he will go when the snow does?' Hannah connected the last cow to the milking tubes and straightened up and rubbed wearily at her neck. Every morning she got up praying that this would be the day the thaw set in. But she wished she could believe that was all it would take to get rid of Jed. He was obviously in real trouble over the car and she had the awful feeling that he might choose to lie low until the dust settled – which could take weeks.

'I shouldn't hold your breath.' Sam was lining up the

empty churns, ready for filling, and the last one was slung up against the rest with frustrated force. It made a clatter that disturbed the cows, something he would not normally have done.

Hannah sucked on her lip, wondering how it was possible for one person to cause so many problems for so many people. Sam moved down the line of cows, pausing at each to study the milk slurping down the tubes. When he was content all were working well, he turned to her. 'The lad isn't very happy . . . that's what concerns me most of all.'

'I know.' She gave a grimace. 'What I can't make out is if he's staying inside with his mother for his own protection, or if he wants to be there in case she needs protection.' She felt it might be the latter. David had grown so attached to Sam that she was sure he would have felt himself to be safe, so long as Sam was there.

Sam shook his head bleakly.

'I wish I knew what had happened to them before they came here,' Hannah continued, on a sigh.

'It doesn't take much working out. David is terrified of men. Do you know what happened to his father?'

She shook her head. 'Only that he's dead. Rhoda told me she was a widow. But not how or when.' She hesitated. 'Do you think he has bad memories of his father's death?'

He gave a shrug and turned back to study the cows. 'I don't know about that. But I do know the man must have beaten the living daylights out of the both of them.'

'No!' Shock left her mouth open. She remembered the very first words David had spoken, 'Will he smack me?', when she had been explaining that George Bunting might get angry with him. 'He wanted to know if your dad would hit him.' She gave a little gasp of self-reproach, astounded at how dim she had been. Sam had seen it easily enough and yet she had not once considered that David and Rhoda could have been ill-treated in that way.

233

Her thoughts had been along the lines of poverty. She could well imagine any mother's nerves being at breaking point: if she had not known where they were going to sleep at night, or where their next meal was coming from. She had assumed David had been astute enough to also be aware of the problem. 'But he's never been afraid of you,' she pointed out. 'Even at the beginning . . .' She had been about to add when he first saw your hand, but thought better of it. It had never failed to amaze her how David had disregarded Sam's deformity and she knew it surprised him, too, but he never spoke of it himself.

'Takes one to know one,' he replied stiffly, and hurried down the line to the first cow and began removing the milking tubes.

'Oh Sam!' Again she was guilty of lack of thought. His own mistreatment had made it easy for him to see the same in others, while her own happy childhood had blinded her to the more unpleasant side of life. She began moving the freed cows towards the door, ushering them outside so the next batch could come in and be milked.

Sam was fixing the tubes to the second lot of udders, before she decided it was time to speak out. 'David doesn't find your hand repulsive, so can't you now believe there are other people out there who don't give a damn?' she asked.

Straightening up to his full height, he fixed her with a gaze that matched the coldness of the snow outside. 'Do you expect me to take the opinion of *one* very frightened, very insecure little boy. You can't judge anything that David does as being natural. I don't know why he clings to me, but I can only assume it's because he doesn't see me as a real man!' He spun away, returning to the cows and turning his back on her.

'You don't really believe that!' Her voice lifted in anger. 'He's taken to you because he can see the real you, inside, beyond the hand that you seem to feel is all people see of you!' Frustration at his own refusal to see the facts trembled through her and increased her anger. 'I'm not a man! But David hasn't taken to me in the same way.' Clenching her fists she looked heavenward and gave a loud groan of despair. 'I don't believe you at times. The lad likes you, I'd even go so far as to say he loves you. Yet all you can do is be suspicious of that affection. No-one will ever believe you're worth anything . . . until you start believing it yourself!'

He stood up then, rounding on her with blazing eyes. 'I know what I'm worth!'

'Oh yes! And it amounts to nothing.' She tossed her head, her pony-tail flicking like the tail of an angry cat.

He brought his left hand up, pushing the pincer-like claws up to her nose. 'You think because one person can turn a blind eye to this, I should presume that everybody else is going to. One person in the whole world! That only leaves a few million left to convince.'

For several moments they glared at each other in tight-lipped fury. Then Hannah said, 'Two,' very quietly, but with great meaning.

He wheeled away. 'Forget it!' he grated.

'No, I won't forget it!' Grabbing his arm, she forced him to look at her. 'You can push your hand into my face a thousand times, it won't make any difference. Like David, I can see beyond it to the real you.' Her anger suddenly ebbed, leaving her weak with defeat. 'Oh Sam, why can't you see it for yourself?' she said, the slow shake of her head displaying her sadness.

The hardness of his gaze softened. He lifted her hand gently away from his arm and held it while he spoke. 'It's no good, Hannah,' he said. 'I don't want to hear you speak this way.'

The hurt of the words was lessened slightly by the regret that clouded his eyes. 'Why?' she asked simply.

He shook his head. 'I've never given you any reason to believe I thought the same . . . and I don't!' The last was emphasized, but gently.

She stared at her hand, lying in his, and wondered why, if he spoke the truth, he did not let her go. 'Why?' Although the word was repeated, her mind had turned in another direction. She lifted her eyes to stare at him steadily. 'There's a reason. Jed said you couldn't have me. What did that mean?' She had often pondered over the comment: you can't have her. Which, at the time, he had dismissed as his brother's drunkenness.

'It meant nothing. He was just trying to cause trouble. You know what he's like for opening his mouth and trying to get you going.'

She had the feeling he was lying. The reply had been too fast, the words too sure, as if he was reciting a well-rehearsed speech.

But he let her hand go then and returned to the cows with indecent speed. And she took herself off to attend the sheep in the crowded sheepshed, knowing, no matter what she tried to say, the conversation was at an end and she was not going to get any better explanation from him.

*   *   *

The meal that evening was no less strained than all the others throughout the week. Jed had not got out of bed until the middle of the afternoon, but since then had made his presence felt in the house. The tension filling the kitchen had touched Hannah the moment she stepped through the door. Rhoda was a bag of nerves and David sat at the table, staring at the tablecloth, seeming to be too terrified to move. Even George Bunting had a strained look about him.

It was obvious something had happened. Having no intention of asking what, with Jed present, Hannah could only assume he and his father had been at it again. She exchanged a knowing glance with Sam, then sat down, hoping the meal would be over quickly.

Sam was the only one who spoke throughout the meal.

Forcing himself to be cheerful, he tried to draw David out of his protective shell. But the boy was too far inside and the door firmly closed. He managed to shake his head twice, and nod once, to Sam's questions, but his voice had left him completely and his lips remained clenched tightly together, not even opening to allow food to pass.

Hannah looked questioningly at Rhoda. But her only response was a frightened, barely perceivable shake of the head. It was enough to tell Hannah it was not a subject to pursue at that moment and she returned to her meal, once more praying that the snow would soon go, and Jed with it.

The first course was almost at an end when the telephone began to ring. Hannah immediately leapt up to answer the call, grateful for the brief respite from the sombre table.

'Hi sweetheart! Is Jed there?' A male voice enquired.

She stiffened, taking instant offence at the over-familiarity. She did not bother to reply to the voice but held the receiver in Jed's direction. 'It's for you!' she said, her voice lifting to make her disgust loud enough for both him and the caller to hear.

'Female, I presume.' His eyebrows made a suggestive twitch and, as he took the receiver from her, he let his fingers brush her hand.

Her lips tightened and her gaze hardened on him. Let him find out the hard way, she thought, as she turned and walked away. He did, and as she sat down again at the table she found it difficult to keep a smile from her lips.

'How the devil did you find out where I was?' he demanded, but with more dread in his voice than anger.

Hannah glanced at Sam, but the ironic tilt of her own eyebrows was not reciprocated, and from the angry glitter of his eyes she knew Jed's over-familiarity had not gone unnoticed, and that it was giving him more concern than his brother's own welfare. Why? she asked silently, looking him straight in the eye. He had told her only that morning he had not given her any reason to believe he harboured any special feelings for her. Well, he should be sitting right where she was sitting and seeing what she was seeing, then he would know why she found it difficult to believe him.

'Like hell you will!' Jed blazed into the receiver, turning Hannah away from her morose thoughts and making her look round at him. 'I told you I'd get it, and I will!'

George Bunting's attention was also diverted, although his was from the food on his plate. Placing his knife and fork down very deliberately, he turned to the telephone with sudden interest.

'I don't know when. It's the snow. We're up to our armpits in the blessed stuff. There's no way I can get back to you tomorrow.'

It was the car! Hannah dropped her elbow on to the table and rubbed at her temple. This was going to resurrect the argument and spoil the rest of the evening. It was movement at the end of the table that brought her head up again, sharply. George Bunting was gliding the wheelchair quietly across the floor. She glanced anxiously at Sam, but his attention was fixed on his father and he did not notice her. Rhoda's gaze was also fixed on George Bunting, and even David had managed to lift his downcast eyes to watch.

Jed had his back to the room and did not see what was happening. His father stopped the wheelchair right next to him and stared at the side of his face, his silence aimed at drawing Jed's attention down to his level.

It was not many seconds before Jed felt the presence. 'You'll have it as soon as the weather picks . . .' His voice trailed away as he turned to see his father there. In an instant the receiver was snatched from his hand.

'What the devil . . . ?' Jed tried to grab it back. But his father proved that, despite the wheelchair, his arms had the greater strength and easily held him off with one hand, while the other lifted the receiver to his ear.

'I don't know who you are but I'll tell you this. That is my car and I'll have it back!' He gave a snort of laughter, mocking the reply he received. 'He hasn't got it and he isn't getting his hands on it. What you have is stolen property and, unless my son wants every bone in his body breaking, he will be telling the police exactly who you are within the next ten minutes.' He slammed the receiver back in its cradle and glared at Jed.

'You can't!' he gasped, the colour draining from his face. It made him look like the weasel he really was, Hannah thought, as he continued to cringe and plead with his father. 'You wouldn't,' he begged. 'They'll . . . they'll . . .'

George Bunting's lip curled in distaste at the pathetic sight of his son. 'If they don't *I* will!' he declared meaningfully. Then wheeled himself back to the table and returned to his meal as if nothing had happened.

Everyone round the table followed his example, not daring to do anything else. But Jed's appetite was lost and he hurriedly left the kitchen, preferring the seclusion of his own bedroom – which Hannah could readily understand. She had never seen him that way before. He was frightened for his life. Not of his father. For all his threats and promises, she knew George Bunting would go no further than a good hiding. But the fear on Jed's face had shown that he knew his other associates would have no such scruples. She put her knife and fork down and pushed her plate away, the remainder of Rhoda's home-made steak and kidney pie unpalatable. She looked at David, his head was down again, eyes glued to his knees. He had not eaten a thing.

He was going to waste away, she thought, pushing herself up from the table and beginning to clear the dirty plates away. She was at the sink when she saw the bowl of chocolate blancmange standing by the side of a lemon meringue pie. The pie was George Bunting's favourite: Rhoda had soon learned to pander to his tastes. But the blancmange was for David. 'Why don't you take your pudding into the sitting-room and watch television?' she suddenly suggested to him. He loved watching the television and would sit with eyes glued to the screen and not hearing a word that was said to him. She hoped if he sat in front of it with a dish of blancmange on his knee, he might forget himself and begin eating.

'Don't want to,' he said, shaking his head, but not looking up.

He never refused a chance to get the television on. She turned to Rhoda, hoping she might come up with some solution to the problem. But Rhoda was busy with the teapot, filling George Bunting's cup, and had her back to Hannah. Making her pander to him again, Hannah thought, irritated that he put his own needs before the boy's. She glanced at Sam in exasperation, then had a sudden thought. 'Why don't you go and watch television, as well?' She stared at him in a manner that dared him to refuse. Sam's mouth opened, then closed again. David looked up. She was not sure if he was happy with the suggestion, or about to refuse again. Not giving him a chance, she dished out two bowls of blancmange and pushed them across the table. Then she looked pointedly at Sam and jerked her head at the door, telling him, in no uncertain terms, to go. It worked. As soon as Sam got up, David did. She watched them go through the door, Peg diving after them, and felt a little happier in the knowledge that she had been right: David had not wanted to go alone, fearing Jed would catch him that way.

Rhoda was busily fussing round getting George Bunting's lemon meringue pie and so Hannah began on washing-up the pile of plates and dishes from the first course. Rhoda had soon learned how to keep him sweet she thought, and found the thought surprising. Although she had grown in strength since coming to the Tor, Rhoda still dithered a lot. She did not give the impression she would be able to control anything, yet she could manage George Bunting extremely well. The woman must have hidden depths, she thought, and smiled to herself as she scrubbed the burnt crust off the edge of the steak and kidney pie dish.

Hannah had finished washing and was drying the dishes when the door opened and Jed walked back in. His cockiness had returned and he swaggered across to the table and poured himself a cup of tea.

He did not sit down, but stood with his back to the fire to drink it. No-one spoke and the only sound was the crackling flames and the clattering of crockery as Rhoda got up and began clearing the remaining dishes from the table.

Jed drained the tea cup before he finally spoke. 'As soon as the snow has gone I'll go down and get the car back,' he said, returning the empty cup to the saucer which was still on the table.

His father looked up at him. 'You will go tomorrow morning – snow or no snow!'

Jed gave a dismissive laugh. 'Don't be ridiculous. I can't go in this. Do you think I'm stupid?'

'I know you're stupid.' George Bunting never raised his voice, but his quiet certainty was far more powerful than his usual yelling. He fixed his son with a gaze of steel. 'You proved that this afternoon. And I am not having you in this house a moment longer than is necessary.'

Hannah's eyes widened. It had been obvious something had happened, but she had not expected to hear George Bunting say it was just cause for sending Jed away. She turned questioningly to Rhoda, but Rhoda kept her head down and did not look at her.

'You got up here in the snow, you can get down again in the snow,' George Bunting continued. Jed only stared at him, seeming to be lost for words. 'You will leave first thing. And you won't take anything away that you didn't bring with you!' With that he rolled the wheelchair away from the table, picked up the evening newspaper from the dresser, positioned himself on the opposite side of the fireplace to Jed, and began to read.

Jed hovered for a few minutes and on several occasions looked about to speak. But he finally thought better of it and walked out and returned to the seclusion of his bedroom; obviously deciding to give his father time to change his mind, before he brought the subject up again.

It was much later before Hannah found out that George Bunting had banished his son because he had tried it on with Rhoda. David had gone to bed and she was alone in the sitting-room with Sam, watching the late evening news.

'What do you mean *tried it on*?' she questioned uncertainly. 'Do you mean he was arguing with her?' She could not really believe that even Jed would sink so low as to make a play for the insecure Rhoda.

Sam slanted a glance at her. 'He tried it on!' he repeated plainly. 'As in he had her over the table and her blouse got ripped.'

'No! Where was your father?' She hesitated, as she was struck by a sudden thought. 'Where was David?'

'Oh, David was the audience. It was his screams that got Dad there.'

'Oh no!' It was no wonder David had looked scared to death all through dinner. She had long wanted Jed to vanish off the face of the earth, but at that moment she wanted to kill him herself, rid the world of his loathsome person once and for all.

'Oh yes!' He fixed her meaningfully. 'And if somebody hadn't tried to cover up for him when he tried it before, it might not have happened.' His voice was sharp with anger directed at her and she knew exactly what he was talking about: when he had met her coming out of Jed's room, on Jed's first day back at the Tor.

'That isn't fair! You can't blame me for what happened.' She sat back in her chair, shocked by the charge.

He gave a shrug and a resigned sigh. 'I don't know,

Hannah. He's got away with murder all his life, because people let him.'

She knew what he meant, but she had no answer. Jed was Jed and would always be so. She looked at him bleakly. 'But it isn't my fault and I won't have you saying it is.'

He got up then, went to the television and turned it off. Then he stood with his hands stuffed into his trouser pockets, rocking back on his heels and looking down on her. 'I know. I'm sorry. I'm just so damned angry that it happened. The lad will never get right if he has to go through that sort of thing at regular intervals.'

'He won't.' She smiled at his concern for the boy. 'I think you're exaggerating a bit. It is only the once! And from what I've heard your dad saying I don't think Jed will get another chance. He told him he has to leave tomorrow.'

He gave a grunt. 'I'll believe that when I see it.'

Yes, and she would too. Although she had to admit there had been something very final in George Bunting's attitude earlier. 'Was David all right when you were watching television?'

He gave a nod. 'Yes, he seemed to have pushed it away.' He hesitated and shook his head. 'If you'd only let me go into Jed's room that day.' Her sharp retort was cut off, as he added, 'I should have gone in. I should have settled him once and for all. I don't know why I let you stop me.'

That he was taking some of the blame himself, soothed her anger and there was no harshness in her voice, only a quiet resignation, when she said, 'It would have changed nothing, except that you would have had an almighty ruck – and probably got hurt.'

'I can handle him,' he put in, taking offence at her suggestion of inferiority.

'I was meaning both of you!' She glared up at him as he hovered by her chair, but there was a hardness in his eyes that she did not like to see and she dropped her gaze and stared into the dying flames of the fire, before she said, 'You would both have got hurt: been cut, bruised, battered. But inside you would still have been the same people. It wouldn't have made any difference to either of you.'

He gave a weary sigh and sank down into the chair again. 'Yes, I suppose you're right.' He fell silent then and for a time Hannah matched him. For all her objections to his charges of blame she did feel guilty. But she had been doing it for him; trying to save him getting into a fight; trying to stop him getting hurt. Her thoughts had all been for Sam and not once had she considered that her actions were designed to let Jed get away with his misdemeanours. That had been her last intention.

'Do you think your dad will get his car back?' she finally said, steering the subject, not away from Jed, but at least away from her feelings of responsibility.

He shook his head. 'I don't know.' His voice was flat. 'They are obviously amateurs. Real crooks wouldn't waste time wanting the log book. They'd already have had it sprayed a different colour and have produced their own paperwork.'

Hannah smiled. She was too innocent; or too trusting. It had never occurred to her to wonder why they were getting so het up about the log book. Trust Jed! He thought he was so brilliant. But even as a villain he was second rate. 'Is there anything he's good at?'

'Aye, making trouble. I just wish I knew of a way to wipe him out of our lives.' Resting his elbows on his knees he leant forward, clasped his hands before him and seemed suddenly to have the weight of the world pressing down on his shoulders. Every inch of him echoed with despair and something tightened in Hannah's chest.

'Don't take on so.' She fell to her knees in front of him and placed her hands over his. 'You aren't responsible for what he does. Besides, he won't be here much longer.' Even if Jed did not do as he was told and go tomorrow, he would not hang around for longer than was necessary: farm life was far too quiet and unexciting for his tastes.

He looked up into her face with a bleakness in his eyes that increased the tightness in her chest. 'I only want to keep you safe.' The words slipped out before thought, and he hesitated uncertainly. Then, realizing what he had said and, at the same time, realizing he was allowing her to touch him, to hold his hands, he suddenly pulled back. 'I feel responsible for you all; David, Rhoda, and yourself.' He put her at the end, because he knew that was where he had to put her.

She smiled tightly and sat back on her heels and dropped her offending hands into her lap. 'Your dad stood up for Rhoda perfectly well,' she said, turning her gaze to the fire so as not to have to look at the rejection clouding his eyes. He had reacted as if her fingers had suddenly turned to flame. 'So I don't think you need to worry too much about us.' Her voice had tightened with her hurt and she wanted to grab his hands and thrust them before his eyes and say: Look, they are not burnt! My touch has not branded your flesh and neither has your touch poisoned mine.

But he stood up then and was across the room, before he said, 'I'll go and see everything's all right.'

She watched him go and she did not, as on other nights, jump up and follow, but remained where she was. Having all the sheep down off the Tor and filling the enormous wooden sheepshed made the final nightly check up of the animals and the yard take twice as much time as usual, but tonight he would have to do it all himself. Only that morning she had, once more, tried to persuade him of his worth, but he would never listen. She was no closer to proving he was just as much a man as the next one, than she had been on the day she first arrived there.

With a sigh that echoed her dejection and movements heavy with her weariness of it all, she pushed herself upright.

Yet again Jed had managed to cause disturbance, even though he was not aware of it. If he had not tried to molest Rhoda, Sam would not have felt responsible and she would not have felt the need to comfort him; and Sam would not now be outside on his own and she would not be feeling as if her world was caving-in.

She was at the door before her thoughts turned back to Rhoda and the event that had started it all, and she was saying a silent thank you to George Bunting for leaping to Rhoda's aid, when she suddenly came up short. Would he, she wondered, have acted so promptly, or even at all, if it had been herself Jed was trying to molest, instead of Rhoda? She could only think the answer was no, and her eyes widened and she saw the other woman in a very different light: one she had never considered before. And she could not stop herself wondering if Rhoda's tender loving care went a lot further than lemon meringue pie.

Chapter Sixteen

Despite his father's insistent order, Jed did not leave the following day. During the night a blizzard took up, lasting into the morning. The drifts in front of the house came halfway up the windows and the yard was so full of snow it came over the tops of your wellington boots.

George Bunting softened enough to tell Jed he could stay until the snow had gone, but only on the condition he got the shovel out and cleared the yard. He had to work for his keep and he was not having him hanging round like a leech. So Jed got the shovel out and, for two weeks, did nothing but shovel snow. As fast as he cleared it away, more fell. But he did appear to have learned a lesson. He kept himself to himself, they only had to suffer him at meal times, and there were no further arguments or incidents.

But even his quiet presence filled the house with tension and, on the first day that passed without any fresh snowfall, Hannah breathed a sigh of relief.

Sam stood just outside the farmyard gates, at the point where the hill dipped suddenly downwards. He rested his hands on his hips and studied the snow-covered countryside. Everything was white, with dips and hollows like sand dunes in a desert. The snow had banked up on both sides of the walls and there was not even a tell-tale sign of grey stone to help him pinpoint the hidden lane's position. But he knew it well enough and his eyes travelled down the line, not missing one unseen bend or buried slope. 'I'm going to have a try,' he finally said.

Hannah bit her lip. 'It looks a bit deep to me.' Her own

gaze followed his, cutting an imaginary line beneath all the whiteness.

'If I get a bit done it will help.' He glanced round, as if seeking her approval, and she gave a nod. 'It might take all week to get to the village, but we'll do it in the end.'

She gave another nod. It would be a start, and clearing a stretch every day would take them closer to Jed's departure. She was sure Jed himself was so fed up with having to shovel snow that he would be away the first chance he got, whether his father still insisted or not. George Bunting had not continued to remind Jed of his leaving date, but she doubted he would soften and go back on the order again. She had the impression that he was as sick of Jed's presence as they all were. She also had the feeling he had only softened in the first place, because he considered he had a better chance of getting his car back if he did something to keep Jed sweet.

'I'll get the shovels.' Spurred by her need to see the elder son depart, she hurried to the stables and took two shovels down from the wall. She had no intention of letting Sam go alone. If the snow proved too much and the Land Rover got stuck he would need her to help dig him out.

'Is this sensible?' she asked, as Sam drove slowly out of the yard and brought them to a halt in front of the wall of snow. In reality it was between two and three feet high, but suddenly it took on the proportions of a dam wall.

'Probably not,' he replied, but engaged the gear and moved slowly forward. The top snow was quite soft and moved without much trouble, but the bottom was frozen solid and the snow plough blades crunched and screeched alarmingly as they made contact. The Land Rover juddered unsteadily against the force, the skidding tyres squealed and spun, and Hannah clung tightly to her seat.

It was a slow job. Forward a few inches, then back again

to take a fresh run at it, until they came to a grinding halt and had to reverse once more. But, little by little, a narrow track was beginning to form.

'At this rate we won't make the village until July,' Hannah said, judging his earlier reckoning of a week to be grossly understated.

'We will!' Determination puckered Sam's face, as he took another run forward. 'If we don't get back to normal soon David is going to be ill.'

She gave a nod, knowing that 'normal' meant losing Jed, rather than the snow. 'But he will have to go to school then,' she pointed out. 'He might not like that, either. He's so happy on the farm, with the animals. I'm not sure he'll settle to anything else.'

Sam glanced her a frown. 'Maybe not.'

'Have you ever spoken to David about their life before?' she asked. If the boy would open up to anyone it would be him, and they had had plenty of chance when they were alone together in the yard.

He shook his head. 'If he wants to talk about it he'll do it himself.'

She knew he was right and fell silent for a time. But her thoughts remained on David and Rhoda, then moved to Rhoda and George Bunting. She had not been able to forget his reaction when Jed had tried it on with Rhoda. She was now convinced he would not have reacted the same had it been herself Jed was molesting. After all, she knew as well as anybody that he had not been beyond a spot of rape and pillage himself in the past. She found it odd. Rhoda's pampering of him in the kitchen was obvious to everyone, but she was beginning to think it definitely went further. What she didn't know was why. If Rhoda really felt she liked the man and was happy to show him affection, then it was nothing to do with her. But if Rhoda was only doing it because she felt she had to, to keep a home for David, that was another matter. She wished she had the courage to try and broach the subject, but she wasn't even sure there was anything going off, and she didn't want to put her foot in it.

'Your dad seems to have taken to Rhoda far better than I had expected,' she said, fishing to see if Sam might have come to any of the same conclusions.

'It would be difficult for anyone not to take to her . . .' he tugged at the gear stick and sent the vehicle rocketing forwards, '. . . the way she looks after him.'

'She looks after all of us.'

He gave an amused laugh. 'Yes, but if I have to eat another slice of lemon meringue pie I think it will choke me.'

She laughed then. 'I know what you mean.'

'He's never been so well looked after in all his life. She treats him the way she treats David. Even *he* is not daft enough to pass up a chance like that.'

No, she thought. He was not daft enough to pass *any* chance up. If he thought he was in with one he'd soon latch on. The conversation increased her concern, but she did not get a chance to continue the subject. They had reached the ruins of her old home and, as her gaze fell on what was left, her mind was suddenly tugged in another direction.

There was nothing to show the cottage had ever stood there, except a mound of virgin white snow. The one corner that had been left precariously standing had given way beneath the weight and no longer stood like a beacon to mark the spot. The cowshed was the only evidence that at one time something had been there. But even that had collapsed, the roof had all but vanished and the two main walls had fallen in, supporting each other like a pair of playing cards.

A lump came to her throat. There was nothing to show that once the cottage had stood there, happy, full of life and love. The sight was too depressing to even allow her mind to conjure up the picture of the little building standing in sunshine, as she usually remembered it. She turned away, wishing they had not come that far. Tears pressed at her eyes and she gave a snort of derision. 'If the gale had not got us this lot would have,' she said, her voice taut and bitter.

'Hush, Hannah. Don't go upsetting yourself.' Sam frowned at her deeply, feeling to blame for bringing her this far. But she never spoke of her father, or the cottage, and he had not thought.

The gentleness of his voice was her undoing. She dropped her face into her hands. 'I'm glad dad died and didn't have to see this,' she sobbed.

In an instant Sam switched the ignition off. Before the engine had completely died away, he pulled her across the seat and into his arms.

'Oh Sam!' she sobbed, tears flooding from her eyes and on to his coat, as she buried her face against him. 'We'd have been homeless. We'd have had nowhere to go.'

'Hush.' He stroked his hand down her hair. He did not point out that she had been homeless with nowhere to go. He knew it was her father she was thinking of more than herself and so he held her tight, continued to stroke her hair, and spoke gentle reassurances to her.

When finally she looked up her eyes were pink and swollen and his coat had a large wet patch on it. 'Sorry,' she whispered, the bleakness in her eyes softening as it fastened to the compassion in his own. For several moments they only looked at each other. She could feel the warmth of him, even beneath the barrier of the two thick coats. She felt safe, like before, when she threw her arms around him and clung to him. It was such a good feeling and it forced all her sadness and bad memories away. She lifted her hand and traced a finger beneath the line of his bottom lip. 'Sam . . . ?' she began, but never got time to finish the question.

His right hand grasped her chin, lifting her mouth to receive his kiss. His left hand pressed into her back, forcing her to him as if he would never let her go again.

It began gently, his mouth moving softly against her own, as if he was as surprised by himself as she was. The tip of his tongue traced along the inside of her lips and she shivered and a little laugh of pleasure rose in her throat. She lifted her arms and wrapped them tightly round his neck, pulling him closer, greedy to get more of him now he had finally yielded and torched the spark that had been waiting so long for him.

His kiss deepened, becoming more urgent and demanding. She responded in kind, pressing herself as close to him as the bulky coats would allow. But it wasn't enough. She quickly slipped the zip of her own windcheater, then reached for his: an action she was soon to regret. His coat was only half-open, when his hand closed on hers and stopped her going any further.

'What . . . what's wrong?' she asked, bewildered and confused. He looked suddenly so grim. His mouth was a tightly compressed line and his eyes were filled with something she did not understand.

'Fasten your coat. You'll freeze.' His voice had an emptiness to it that chilled her far more than the frozen snow on the ground outside. He pushed her back into her own seat, turned round and thrust the engine back into life.

'Sam?' She reached over and placed her hand on his arm.

'Don't!' He growled painfully. He clung tightly to the steering wheel and his head dropped forwards, his forehead resting hopelessly between his hands.

'I don't understand.' She shook her head, her confusion growing. 'Why?'

He turned on her angrily, eyes blazing, and knocked her hand away. 'Is that how you want it? In the back of a filthy Land Rover?'

She shook her head. Put like that, no it was not. A thin smile came to her lips. It was just the situation, she told herself, and her hand went back to his arm. 'We can find somewhere. We can . . .'

Before she could finish her hand was grasped and thrown so viciously away that she flinched. 'When it happens make sure it happens with someone who loves you!' There was bitterness in his voice of an extent she had never heard before. It cut her to the core, reaching even to her vocal chords and making speech impossible. She could only watch in numb silence, as he thrust the gear into reverse with such force she feared the stick might break off in his hand. The Land Rover skidded and slewed, as he made a space in her old farmyard big enough to turn round in. Then it careered forwards, along the narrow track they had cut between the high bank of snow on either side.

Hannah clung to the seat, too wounded by the brutality of his angry rejection to open her mouth and tell him to slow down, before he killed them both.

*　　*　　*

'Is something wrong?' Rhoda looked up from the pastry she was making for a meat and potato pie for dinner. She looked both worried and concerned.

Hannah gave a grim smile. 'Whatever gave you that impression?' she asked drily, knowing exactly what. It would have been difficult for anyone living there not to have realized something was amiss. For the last two days Sam had been like a bear with a sore head to everyone, including David, and especially to Hannah. 'Nothing of any importance. He'll get over it.' But she wasn't sure she would get over it. She was still smarting from his cruel rejection. 'What do you want getting?' Changing the subject she went to the cupboard and checked the supply of dog food. Yesterday Sam had completed clearing the lane, they now had a track cut through all the way to the village. Jed could now leave and he was doing so that morning. Sam was taking him and was going to replenish their dwindling stocks at the same time; he had told her to get a shopping list written out. Or rather he had ordered her to do it, which seemed to be the only way he could speak to her at the moment.

'Flour and sugar are the main things.' Rhoda hesitated and thought for a moment. 'Some fresh lemons, if he can get any. And another of these.' She held up a plastic lemon filled with juice. 'So I don't run out.'

Hannah smiled to herself as she added the items to the list. Can't have the master going without his lemon meringue pie, she thought.

'Can I collect the eggs?' David looked up from the slice of toast he was devouring, jam all round his mouth. With Jed present he only picked at his meals so Rhoda had taken to filling him up in between.

Hannah turned to the boy in amazement. Then she broke into a smile, but it was more from pleasure than amusement at his appearance. He had not gone out into the yard while Jed had been there and the question had been a sign of his return to normal – even before Jed had actually gone. 'Of course you can,' she said, putting a smile on his jammy face.

David fell serious. 'I'll do it later,' he said.

Hannah gave a nod, understanding that 'later' meant after Jed's departure. She turned to Rhoda. 'Is that all you need in the kitchen?' she asked, changing the subject before her obvious pleasure embarrassed the boy and made him change his mind.

'I can't think of anything else.'

As Rhoda spoke, Sam appeared at the door, but did not come inside. 'Haven't you got that list done yet?' he demanded impatiently. 'And where is he? I want to be off!'

'It's here.' Hannah flapped the sheet of paper at him and gave him a scowl. 'I think he's saying his goodbyes,' she added. She did not know where Jed was, but she had the feeling if he did not get an answer from her he would insist she go and find his brother. And she had no desire to see Jed before he left, whatever the reasons. 'Do you want anything putting down?' she asked, knowing if he had a lot to remember he liked the farm stock writing down along with the household. He shook his head and she noticed the dark rings had returned to his eyes. She turned quickly away. She was still too angry with him to want to feel any concern for him.

'Aren't you eating that?' she asked, turning her attention to David and the slice of toast now lying half-eaten on his plate. 'You'll not grow any muscles,' she teased, and tried to pretend the dark presence hovering at the door was not really there.

'I will,' he protested, and pushed his sleeve up and bent his arm.' 'Look! There's one!'

She gave the soft mound a gentle prod. 'So there is,' she said, affecting a very serious expression. 'We'll have you cattle-rustling yet.'

'Can I?' he asked, his excited gaze swinging to Sam. 'Will you take me?'

Sam was still stuck in the doorway, hands stuffed in his pockets, head bent, seeming to be giving deep contemplation to the toe of his wellington boot.

'Will you, Sam?' David repeated urgently.

Sam's head slowly lifted. 'What . . . oh . . . yes . . . sometime,' he replied, far too distractedly to know what he was talking about.

David's face fell and Hannah flashed a scowl at Sam. Just the thought of Jed's departure had made the boy a different person. But if Sam carried on this way he would take over where Jed had left off, and David would be back in his shell. To make things worse, she felt responsible. She was the one he had kissed. She was the one he was angry with. That was where it should have stopped. He had no reason to take it out on the others.

'Tell him I'm waiting outside,' Sam suddenly said. Then he wheeled round and banged the door noisily behind him, leaving Hannah to look bleakly at the shopping list still in her hand.

'Oh . . .' Rhoda turned to the closed door. 'I was just going to tell him we needed washing-powder.'

'It doesn't matter.' Hannah waggled the list in the air. 'I imagine I am supposed to run after him with it.' Picking up the pen she quickly scribbled washing-powder on the bottom, then went after him.

The Land Rover was in the middle of the yard, but Sam was nowhere in sight. She called his name. There was no reply. She went across to the stables, the barn, the milking parlour. She finally found him in the sheepshed. His hands were stuffed in his pockets in the same way as when he had hovered at the door, but now his brooding contemplation was directed at the sheep in the wooden pens.

'Won't be long,' she said, walking to his side and mimicking his stance. Come the end of the month the lambs would start arriving and they would be in one of the busiest periods of the year.

He did not reply.

'You forgot this.' She held the shopping list out to him. He stared at it as if she was offering him poison. When he finally reached out to take it, she held on and refused to let go. His expression took on a great weariness. It made her feel like a playful puppy he had had enough of, but at least he was looking at her, instead of past her as if she did not exist. It was small comfort. 'We can't go on like this,' she said flatly.

'Like what?' His voice conveyed lack of understanding but no questioning frown came to his eyes.

With a sigh she let the shopping list go. Keeping him looking at her was getting her nowhere, and was very painful. She had the feeling she was defeated before she had begun.

'I'm ready! Sam! Where are you?'

She gave a grim smile. Jed, as usual, getting in the way, she thought bitterly.

Without speaking he turned to walk away.

'No!' She grabbed his sleeve, holding him back. 'He can wait for a few minutes. We need to talk.' He looked at her coldly. It was as if he had switched himself off to all emotion and a shiver ran over her flesh. 'This is unbearable, Sam.'

For a long moment his empty gaze stared into her pleading eyes. 'Yes,' he finally agreed. 'So maybe it would be for the best if you were the next to leave.'

If he had slapped her across the face she could not have been more stunned. Her mouth dropped open, her hand leaving his arm as if burnt. 'You can't . . .' she gasped, then words failed her and her head shook in disbelief. 'You can't mean that.'

But he meant every word and his next words proved it. 'We have Rhoda now,' he said. 'We could get by without you.'

'But . . . but the farm?'

'David is useful. He will get more so as he gets older. I don't think you have any need to worry yourself about the farm.' With that he turned and walked out, leaving her to stare stupidly after him.

Hoist by your own petard, she told herself, when she finally pulled herself together enough to move. Rhoda and David, brought there by her own scheming, were to be her usurpers. It was ironic. She wanted to laugh and cry at the same time. She heard the Land Rover going out of the yard. Jed was leaving. The moment she had been waiting for had come. But she felt no joy, no pleasure. She felt oddly devoid of any emotion, as if Sam's coldness had rubbed off on her, drawing all the feeling from her. She began to replenish the feed troughs and raked out the soiled bedding and put down new, but she was only half aware of what she was doing.

When all the animals had been attended to she did not go into the house, but out of the yard and down the hill. She could not face the others, could not speak to them and pretend everything was all right. She needed to be alone and she could think of only one place to go.

The lane was icy and her feet slipped and slid, but she carried on. She stopped once, when she came to a holly bush, and broke off a sprig and took it with her. The bright red berries had all been stripped by hungry birds and she grimaced at the dull green leaves. But it was better than nothing.

She did not stop again until she reached the mound of snow that marked the position of her old home. Leaving the lane she walked up the yard, in the tracks where the Land Rover had turned round. She did not want to think of Sam. But she could not stop herself recalling the occasion the tracks had been made. Suddenly it was as if he was there with her. She could feel the touch of his lips on hers. She gave a startled little cry and her hand flew to her mouth, wiping away the unwanted feeling.

Seeking something to turn her mind in another direction, she hurried forward and clambered up on top of the wall of snow where the track came to an end. If she had stood up she would have sunk right up to her thighs and not been able to walk. So she crawled on all fours to where she guessed the remains of her father's bedroom lay buried beneath. There she stuck the holly sprig upright, to stand proud like a little tree.

For several minutes she stayed there, sitting back on her heels, thinking of her father, her mother, her life before. The wind was icy, turning her nose the colour of the berries stolen from the holly and clouding her vision. But she shed no tears. The passing of time, although not healing the wound, had given it a hard scab, and she now knew the futility of tears. They would not change anything; would not bring anything back. She was still sitting there when Sam and the Land Rover came up the lane, and went flying straight past.

'Thanks for the lift,' she muttered, her gaze sadly following the vehicle as it quickly climbed the slippery hill;

which she knew would be hell for her feet. It wasn't until it vanished through the large impressive gateposts of Bunting's Tor, that she turned back and took one last look around. There was nothing to see, she thought, wondering just why she had come. No animals filled the snow-covered fields. No birds flew in the icy air, even though the sky, for once, was blue. Whichever way she looked there was snow and more snow. But at least it had given her a few minutes of freedom, she told herself, and began to crawl back across the snow to the track, so she could stand up again before her knees froze solid.

The slippery hill proved to be as bad as she had expected. For every three steps forward, she slipped two back, and getting up was taking her twice as long as getting down had done. Her progress was not helped by the legs of her corduroy trousers, which were saturated from kneeling in the snow. They clung icily to her legs and her knees began to ache and stiffen, and the going became even slower.

She asked herself why she was going back. It would have been much easier to sit on her bottom and slide all the way down the valley to the village. It would have pleased Sam, he wanted her to leave. But she would not have known what to do when she got there, she told herself, just as she saw the Land Rover pulling out of the yard and coming towards her.

Stopping where she was, she pressed herself into the snowy bank, giving it room to pass by. She could only think Sam had forgotten something and expected him to go straight past, as he had done before. She was very surprised when he stopped.

He pushed the window down and stuck his head through. 'Where have you been?' he demanded.

'For a walk.' Her voice was stiff. She could not believe he had been concerned for her. He was only angry because she was putting him out. Well she had not asked him to come and fetch her. 'You can carry on to wherever you're going. I'll take myself back.'

'I've come to find you!' he pointed out, speaking as if she was a wayward child. 'Where did you walk to?'

'The cottage,' she replied, biting her lip against asking him why he had bothered, if she was such a nuisance to him.

'You weren't there when I came past.'

'Yes I was.'

'I didn't see you.'

'I was on my knees.'

'On your knees!' His astonishment brought the snapped retorts to an end. 'Whatever for?'

She gave a dismissive shrug and remained silent. It didn't matter any more, and it did not concern him.

He gave a sigh. It sounded like despair, but she thought it was more likely to be irritation. Then he jumped out of the cab. 'Get in!' he ordered. 'You must be frozen.' She did not have time to protest. The next moment she was shoved through the door, across the driver's seat to the other side of the cab. 'Why didn't you tell someone where you were going?' His voice was stiff with annoyance, as he followed her into the cab, started the engine and drove off.

'I didn't think anyone would miss me.' Least of all you, she thought bitterly.

He gave her a sidelong glance and for a moment she had the uncomfortable feeling she had spoken the last aloud. 'I thought you'd gone,' he finally said. 'I thought . . .' He fell silent.

She wondered what his second thought would have been. But she would not ask. 'Where else would you have expected me to go?' she asked drily. She was hardly overrun by friends and relatives to visit.

He shook his head and they drove on in silence. When they reached her old home, he turned into the yard to turn round. She held her breath, hoping he would not stop like the time before. He immediately reversed and set off up the lane again, and she experienced a sinking disappointment.

He did not speak until they had almost reached the Tor. 'We didn't know where you were,' he said, without looking at her.

She smiled grimly. So it was *we* who had been worried. He had not come of his own accord. The others had sent him. 'Did Jed go quietly?' She changed the subject.

He gave a nod. 'But he'll be back just as quickly . . . when he's in trouble again.'

'Isn't he still in trouble?' His father had made sure he never got anywhere near the car's log book.

'I think he might have found a way to pay off his debts.'

'How?' she asked, glancing at him questioningly.

'I caught him in dad's old bedroom. He had mum's jewellery box out. I think he was emptying the contents into his pockets.'

'You think! You didn't stop him? Was there much of value? Would it cover the car?' She was appalled that he could let Jed get away with it.

'Yes. No. Yes. I don't know, it depends how much he took.'

Her head shook in disbelief. He might think Jed would use the jewellery to pay off his debts, but all she could think was that Jed was now let loose with a fresh supply of money to fritter away. He would probably give it away for a quarter of its true value, just to give himself an evening's entertainment. 'I can't believe you did that,' she said, and turned away from him in disgust, as they went through the gates and into the yard.

He stopped the Land Rover, reached for her with his left hand and pulled her round to face him. 'I wanted him gone!' he stressed, the claw-like fingers biting into her flesh. 'What are a few baubles worth, measured against a peaceful life . . . especially a lad like David's!'

She was not sure if she wanted to laugh or cry. If she had thought he was so relaxed with her to forget his hand, she would have been laughing. But she was not so foolish. His lack of self-consciousness was not due to familiarity. It was due to anxiety and not for her, but for David. 'Yes,' she suddenly said, giving her agreement because she wanted to end the conversation. Her thoughts were suddenly so depressing that she had to get away from him. 'I wasn't thinking.' Pulling away from his grasp, she jumped out of the cab and hurried across the yard.

Seeking seclusion she went into the sheepshed and sank down on a bail of hay. There she recalled all the kindness Sam had bestowed on her. The little things he had done when she first came there. When she was homeless . . . penniless . . . broken! Only half a person . . . just like he thought he himself was!

Her head dropped on to her chest but she felt too numbed by her newly realized understanding to cry. Now she had grown strong again she did not need a crutch to lean on any more. So Sam had turned his attention to David, whom he felt needed him more than she did. And he would keep his attention on the boy until he had grown strong enough not to need him any more. Then Sam would back away, stopping all the little kindnesses that she had misread for affection, because he did not feel he was worthy enough to love a whole person.

She looked up bleakly, meeting a row of puzzled sheep stares as they poked their heads over and through the slats of the pens. 'What do I have to do to prove his hand is of no consequence?' she asked. All she received for reply were more puzzled stares and a couple of bleats.

Chapter Seventeen

For the next few days George Bunting and Rhoda both treated Hannah with the care of a delicate china doll: as if they were of the opinion that one false move and she would crack – or at least pack her bags and walk out. It would have amused her, had she not realized it was because Sam had let it be known he had told her to go. She felt humiliated and angry that he could talk freely to the others when he was ignoring her and speaking only when forced to because they were the only two people out in the yard.

They did not hear from Jed and the car did not suddenly appear in the yard, which George Bunting had thought would happen after his threat of going to the police. He was not aware of the missing jewellery and Hannah had no intention of telling him. He became increasingly more irritated by the lack of his car but, strangely, he never got into a blind rage about it. He convinced himself that Jed had got it back and was riding round in it again, and no-one was stupid enough to squash that theory.

'Another couple of weeks and it should all begin,' Hannah said, not for the first time, as she came up by Sam standing in the sheepshed, silently contemplating the pregnant ewes. She did not know if he would answer or in any way acknowledge her presence. There were times when she had the feeling she must have turned invisible, or he had gone deaf. But she still spoke whenever she came upon him, in the hope that it might urge him to resume normal friendly relations.

He gave a nod. 'Yes.'

It wasn't much. She bit her lip, pondering the reasons for his coolness. She could not believe he really wanted her to leave . . . or perhaps she did not want to believe. She turned away with a sigh. 'We're getting low on cattle cake.'

'I'll get some from market.' His voice was flat and the sheep remained of more interest to him, for he did not once turn to look at her.

Suddenly it all became too much. 'Is this to be it?' she demanded, exploding with frustration.

He turned to her then, his face blank, uncomprehending.

'A couple of weeks to lambing! The cattle cake is low! The stables need more hay! The parlour floor needs scrubbing!' She wheeled away from him, her fists, balled in impotent rage, hammering the air. 'Damn it, Sam! I'm worth more than that!'

He dropped his head, stared at the hay strewn across the stone slabs of the floor, then he closed his eyes tightly, as if that would make her disappear.

'No!' She grabbed his arm and spun him round to face her. 'I'm here! You can't shut me out. I won't let you. I love you, Sam.' She did not expect the truth to make any difference to his coolness and she was not sure why she was speaking this way. It was as if her voice had suddenly taken on a will of its own and her tongue was working by some other means than her own brain. 'There are times when I ask myself why, and there are times when I can't find any answer. But I love you and there's nothing you can do to stop me feeling that way. And it isn't fair of you to even try.'

His head shook with a determination that hardened his gaze and drew his lips into a tight, angry line. 'That's where you're wrong!' he blazed, and threw her hand from his arm with a ferocity that sent her reeling backwards into the bales of hay piled by the wall.

'Why?' she cried in frustration, wishing he would give

her a reason, other than his own bloody-mindedness, for the futility of her desires. But she was speaking to the sheep; he had gone, leaving the shed door swinging open behind him and the icy air blasting in.

By the time she had gathered herself enough to run after him, it was too late. He was through the gates and out of the yard, heading purposefully up the path on to the Tor, the black and white figure of Peg streaking after him, frantic at having been left behind.

Well, two could play at that game, she thought, knowing that his jaunts over the Tor in search of peace and solitude were never short. He would be away for at least two hours, possibly more. He need not think she was going to be doing the work and waiting patiently for his return.

Marching over to the house she stuck her head round the door. 'I'm off into the village,' she announced to Rhoda, who was the kitchen's only occupant, and closed the door before Rhoda had time to reply. Then she hurried out of the yard and down the lane in the opposite direction to Sam.

It was dry now, though it had rained all night and the snow was going fast. Dirty grey remnants clung beneath the walls, where the snow plough blades had pushed it in great mounds. But the lane was clear and it did not take her long to reach the bottom of the hill.

The lane flattened out as it curved into the tight bend around the duck pond before going into the village square and she saw the first signs of life since leaving the farm. People milled about like gnats after a downpour: not having anywhere particular to go, but happy to be free after being confined to their own hearths, by the snow.

Her first call was at the grocery shop that stood in the corner of the old market square.

'Hello, Hannah.' Mrs Fletcher's thin face crinkled into a smile that made her pale complexion appear warm and welcoming. She was a skinny little woman whose meagre flesh seemed to lack the addition of blood. Her appearance was not helped by the large white apron she always wore wrapped tightly round herself, which gave the impression of a shroud and accentuated her paleness. But somehow when she smiled, her face lit up and the lack of colour in her cheeks was suddenly unnoticeable.

It never failed to amaze Hannah how much the woman's appearance could change in a moment, and there was a twinkle of amusement in her eyes as she returned the smile.

'Not seen you for a while. Then I imagine the Claw's had its fair share of snow – we've had enough down here.'

'The Tor! Mrs Fletcher,' Hannah corrected, bridling at the slur against Sam, even though she knew it was not aimed directly at him.

Mrs Fletcher gave a chuckle that folded her old face like a concertina. 'Aye, if you say so.' She inclined her head meaningfully, as if about to impart a confidence. 'But it'll take more than you to change its name in people's minds.'

Hannah gave a grimace. She held no illusions that she had the power to change the local way of thinking, but she would not let the derogatory name go by without making her feelings felt.

'Anyway, what can I do for you?' Mrs Fletcher rested her bony old hands on the dark oak counter and fixed Hannah pointedly.

'A quarter of liquorice allsorts, please.'

Mrs Fletcher took a large glass jar from the row filling the shelf behind her, unscrewed the lid and poured the sweets into the silver pan on the scales. 'Glenda Riley's not got long to go now,' she said, screwing her tiny eyes up to peer at the needle as it wobbled to stillness on the scale.

'No, she won't have.' Hannah kept her voice casual. She had the feeling the woman was trying to lead her and she was not getting involved in this one. Whether Jed was the father of Glenda's baby or not was no concern of hers.

Mrs Fletcher obviously did not agree. 'What's that Jed think of it all?' she asked bluntly.

'Jed?' Hannah shook her head as if she did not understand. 'Why should Jed have anything to think of it?' She felt more than a bit of a sham, but the store was the heart of all the local gossip and she knew that if she so much as uttered one word on the subject, it would be all round the village before she had got back to the farm.

Mrs Fletcher gave a sideways glance of disbelief and tipped the sweets from the pan into a paper bag. Twisting the top closed, she pushed it across the counter. 'He who plants the lettuce doesn't always eat the salad,' she quoted, nodding her head knowledgeably.

Hannah did not reply. She dropped a shilling into the scrawny hand that was held out before her and shoved the bag of liquorice allsorts into her pocket. 'Is Glenda keeping well?' she asked, steering the conversation without totally changing it, as Mrs Fletcher counted the change into her hand.

'Oh aye. Glenda's blossoming.' The thin shoulders shivered with indignation. 'Quite proud of herself . . . the silly madam! It's her dad that's taking it bad. I wouldn't like to be in that Jed's shoes if Bill ever gets his hands on him.'

Hannah was reminded of the time she had told Jed that Bill Riley was up the Tor with his gun, and she found it difficult to keep her smile to herself. 'When is the baby due?' she asked, still refusing to make any comment on Jed's part in the matter. If Glenda was daft enough to get sucked in by him that was her problem.

'Two weeks time, or should be. Myself, I think it could be any day now.'

Two weeks! Not long. Hannah wondered if George Bunting was aware he was about to become a grandfather.

It could be fun to tell him, she thought. It might please him . . . if it was a boy! She stopped her thoughts right there. A grandson appearing on the scene would not be good for Sam, she realized, and decided to keep George Bunting in the dark about the next generation Bunting – if that was what the baby really was. They only had Glenda's word for it because she couldn't see Jed ever admitting anything that might incriminate him and spoil his fun.

The shop door opened and Timmy Waldren and three of his friends tumbled through, each with a threepenny bit clutched in his hand to buy sweets to eat on the way home from school. Mrs Fletcher was immediately bombarded with requests for the prices of humbugs, gobstoppers and cherry lips. Hannah took the chance to escape.

She was halfway across the square when she met old Madge Cresswell coming in the opposite direction. 'Hello, me ducks.'

Madge was not wearing her hearing aid, so Hannah shouted her response loudly. 'How have you been getting on with all the snow? Has someone been doing your shopping for you?' Madge was not very good on her legs at the best of times, but when it was snowy or icy she became an immediate recluse. A few years back she had slipped on the ice and broken her hip and she was determined it was never going to happen again.

'Mopping? What mopping?' Madge put her shopping basket on the floor, rested her hands on her hips and frowned into Hannah's face.

Hannah smiled. 'Shopping!' she stressed. 'In the snow! You haven't been coming out – have you?'

'Oh no!' Madge flapped her hand in the air, then picked up her basket once more. 'Me gentleman – he's been doing it for me.'

'He's still with you?' Hannah looked surprised. It was a couple of years since the artist gentleman had just pipped her to Madge's spare room, and supposedly he had only been staying for a few months.

'What's to do?' Madge leaned her ear closer to Hannah's mouth.

'He's . . . still . . . with . . . you!' she mouthed, loudly and clearly.

Madge caught it that time. 'Oh yes!' she replied very definitely. 'He's a perm'nent fixture now. Likes it here, he does. Why . . . you weren't looking for a room again?'

'Not at present,' she replied drily, her voice dropping away as she began to wonder if that was what she should be doing. Hanging around waiting for Sam to wake up was proving to be a fool's errand. She glanced bleakly round the cottages surrounding the square. Except for the odd lick of paint every now and again it was all just the same as it had been for years. Progress had not touched the grey stone walls. Just like herself, she thought. For all the progress she was making with Sam, she could still be in the same position in ten years' time.

'No, I shouldn't think it is very pleasant.'

Hannah turned back to Madge with a frown. It took her several seconds to realize the old lady had misheard her again, but the penny finally dropped. Shaking her head, she broke into a smile. Madge without her hearing aid was like trying to communicate with someone from another planet. Lifting her hand she waved goodbye, considering that would be quicker than speaking the word and then having to hang around repeating it. Still smiling, she turned and walked across the square, leaving Madge to continue to the shop.

She had nothing particular to do and could have turned up the lane that led directly back to the Tor. But she had a perverse need for Sam to be the first to arrive home, so that he would miss her. Or if not exactly miss her, at least know she had been out.

So she took the lane which travelled close to the river and led out of the village in the same direction as the Tor, but keeping to the valley basin. After about one mile she would take to the fields and walk up the hills. Knowing she was going in the right direction, even though it would take her half as long again as going by the direct route, made her feel less guilty for her childishness. It did not wipe it completely away, though, and she found her feet beginning to hurry of their own accord.

It began to rain as she reached the long row of dark stone cottages at the village limits. Beyond were only fields and hills, and Bunting's Tor looking down from high above. The rain quickened as she passed the end terraced cottage, where Patty Swain conducted her questionable business. She smiled to herself, recalling the time she had told George Bunting that Patty was more particular than to have him. Pulling the neck of her coat more tightly to her throat, she bent her head and hurried on, wishing she had, after all, taken the more direct route.

She did not hear the car, or see it until it skimmed past so close it almost knocked her over. The lane was verged by grassy slopes too steep to walk on. But they were her only defence and, when she realized the car had stopped and was about to reverse back up the lane towards her, she leaped frantically on to the steep bank. She gave a gasp of fright as her rubber boots skidded down the wet grass and almost had her laid out full length on the lane. But as she picked herself up and saw it was George Bunting's dark green Jaguar, her shock turned to surprise . . . and then to anger.

Damn Jed! she thought furiously, as the car pulled up by her side. But it was not Jed who got out of the driver's door and came towards her.

He was of average height but had a stockiness about him that told her he had a powerful body and was not a man to be tangled with. His hair was a shiny brown cap, slicked back with so much grease that the rain drops falling on it rolled off with the efficiency of water off a duck's back. His dark grey suit looked expensive and of the type Jed would flaunt himself in.

A tiny shiver of fear ran down her spine. But it was soon wiped away, replaced by a burning anger, as he strolled confidently up to her, a leering smirk plastered on his lips, and said, 'Hello sweetheart.'

She knew immediately that it was the same man who had spoken to her on the telephone: the same words; the same voice. Offence at the over-familiarity bristled through her, just as it had done the day he called Jed and she had been unfortunate enough to answer the phone. 'I'm surprised to see *that* car around here – where everybody knows who the true owner is!' Her eyes hardened and fixed pointedly on his smugly satisfied face.

He gave a laugh, but his pale eyes remained emotionless as they washed over her. 'Hannah Critchlow I presume! Jed said I would not be able to miss that hair. He also said I should find you easy enough – if I came up to the farm. But I never imagined it would be this easy.'

Her body stiffened, ice running down her spine. For the first time in her life she hated her hair, wishing she had plain, ordinary, mousy locks. But her annoyance with her crowning glory was nothing compared to her uneasiness at the realization that he knew her name. He knew who she was and he was actually looking for her. That Jed was a part of it increased her alarm.

'And why would you be wanting me?' she enquired, tilting her chin in a manner that belied the uncertainty rippling through her limbs.

He pulled no punches. Looking her straight in the eye, he said, 'We don't take threats from anyone . . . least of all cripples. Jed's father needs teaching a lesson. Seeing that he seems to be a bit short on fatherly love where Jed is concerned, we'll see what he thinks of you.'

She almost laughed. Perhaps at one time she might have held a bit of sway with George Bunting, but Jed was badly out of date if he had reported she still had the same

271

power. His father would more than likely laugh in their faces – and thank them for ridding him of a nuisance.

He had got the wrong one. It was Rhoda he should have been looking for, she thought. But she did not tell him that. Realizing that, once again, Jed's associates were showing themselves up as less than competent, she set her gaze squarely at him. 'So, if you were looking for the farm, why were you travelling down this lane?' She took pleasure in pointing out his error; even though she found it ironic that he should take the wrong lane at the very time she was walking down it.

'That's the Buntings' place.' He glanced over his shoulder, up the hill towards the Tor. When he looked back to her his beady eyes had narrowed into dark little slits, telling her he thought she was lying.

The rain came heavier and, as she gave a nod, sprayed off her hair and dripped from the end of her nose. 'Yes. That is the Buntings' place.' She saw no point in lying. If he got it wrong this time he would only go back to Jed and get it right the next time. Besides, she wanted the conversation brought to an end so she could get back to the farm and get dry. 'So . . . what is it that I have to tell George Bunting?' Her voice and expression conveyed her weariness with it all.

He shook his head, his grin returning. 'Nothing,' he stated baldly. 'He doesn't listen to words. But he might start listening . . . might come round to our way of thinking . . . if we've got something to barter with.'

It took only a moment for Hannah to realize what he was intimating. She was supposed to be their 'something to barter with'. He intended to kidnap her, take her with him, hold her prisoner – until George Bunting had given in to their demands and handed over the car's log book. Without bothering to point out that he had got it wrong again, she spun on her heels and hurried back along the lane in the direction she had come from, wanting to get back to the safety of the cottages. If it came to a toss up between herself and his car, she was under no misapprehension that she would come out on top in George Bunting's eyes.

He did not let her get far. His hand closed around her arm and she was almost pulled off her feet as he spun her round to face him. 'Oh no you don't! You're coming with me.'

She had sensed his strength, but even so the power with which he threw her back against the car surprised her, as well as winded her. Fighting to regain her breath, she lifted her hands and lashed out at him. But her defence was feeble and made no impression on him. 'You'll never get the log book. George Bunting won't let you have it. His car is more precious to him than I am.'

He gave a harsh laugh, easily captured her flailing hands and pinned them to her sides. 'I hope for your sake that isn't true. George Bunting needs teaching a lesson. We don't like people who threaten us. We take revenge, one way or another. Now get in!' Swinging the car door open, he grabbed her by the back of the neck and bent her double, forcing her down and into the car.

This was Jed's way of getting back at her, she thought anxiously. He knew, as well as she did, that she no longer held any sway over his father. But he had seen a way of putting her in her place once and for all. The alarming thought made her fight harder. She struggled and kicked with all her might, but the man was far stronger and she was halfway on to the car's back seat before she knew what was happening. In the next moment a voice rang out. The man froze and the forceful pressure on her neck ended.

'I said, if I was you I'd back off!'

Feeling her opponent do just that, Hannah straightened up. At first she was confused, then she wanted to laugh. Patty Swain stood in the centre of the lane, the rain battering down on a black and white polka dot umbrella held over her blond head. Her heavily made-up eyes, filled with an insistence that she would be obeyed, never left the man's face. Her blood-red mouth was puckered in a determination that could not be ignored. Her white dress looked out of place in the pouring rain. So did the white high-heeled shoes that increased her height, which in bare feet must already have been close to six feet. She looked like an Amazon and Hannah wanted to rush forward and hug her, so great was her relief.

But the man gave a snarl, and when he spoke Hannah's relief began to diminish. 'Patty Swain!' He tossed his head on contempt. 'Just who do *you* think you're talking to?'

'Small fry, lad.' Patty's tone made it obvious she held him in no awe. 'Now I don't know what you're playing at, and I don't want to know. But I do know you're letting her go.' Her head jerked towards Hannah, sending her white blond curls bouncing round her face.

'And just who is going to make me?' His hand fastened tightly to Hannah's arm again, biting through the wetness of her soaked coat sleeve and into her flesh so that she had to grit her teeth to keep her pain hidden.

'I am!' Patty insisted. 'Because if you don't listen to me you'll find yourself listening to Jerry Stone.'

Hannah had never heard of Jerry Stone. But the name meant something to the man. His grasp on her arm immediately loosened and uncertainty claimed his smile. But only for a moment. His hand soon tightened again and his sneer returned. 'You don't frighten me,' he said, but Hannah noticed the confidence was no longer so strong in his voice. 'I'm taking her with me.' He shoved Hannah back inside the car. She kicked out again with both feet, making contact with one heel and causing him to swear colourfully.

'Let her go!' Patty's voice slashed through the air as violently as the rain that bounced noisily off the car's metal body. 'Let her go now! I don't give out idle threats. If you don't get your hands off her right now Jerry Stone will know about it before you've got yourself back to Derby.'

He hesitated, glaring mutinously into the heated threat of Patty's gaze. She did not speak again, but just stood there, the rain billowing off her umbrella and splashing up her legs and over the white shoes, as it bounced up from the ground almost as fiercely as it fell from the sky. It was several long seconds before he finally let Hannah go and dropped his hands to his sides, his lips working but unable to find any sound.

Rubbing at her sore arm, Hannah stared at the rain running in rivulets over his greasy hair, down his neck and inside the collar of his shirt, the pale blue cotton darkening as it soaked up the liquid. It pleased her to think it must be feeling very uncomfortable and it never occurred to her that she should be taking the chance to get away from him.

Patty had to say, 'Come here, luv. Get yourself under this brolly with me – you're getting soaked,' before Hannah realized she was free to move and hurried to Patty's side, just as she was adding, 'And if anything happens to this girl – if anybody touches her – Jerry Stone will be the first to hear about it. Do you understand me?'

He gave a belligerent nod and Hannah shivered and hoped Patty was not going to live to regret sticking her neck out to help her.

'Good,' Patty stated meaningfully. Then she took Hannah's arm and turned her away and led her back to the first cottage, which was her own. As they were going through the gate, Hannah could see Madge Cresswell had finished her shopping. She was standing outside the front door of her cottage on the other side of the river. She seemed to be watching them, but Hannah knew it was no good calling to her: she would never have heard at that distance, even without the addition of the thumping rain and the roaring river. The next moment the Jaguar's engine leapt to life and she turned to see the car speed off down the lane, and she forgot Madge Cresswell.

'Thank you,' she said, feeling relief sweeping through

her and only then realizing how tense with fear she had been. 'Who is Jerry Stone?' she asked, hesitating on the doorstep, her father's words of warning about never associating with Patty ringing in her ears.

'Let's just say he's the king rat in these parts – that's all you need to know.' Patty gave her a gentle shove. 'Are you going in? Or have we got to stand here till we shrink?'

Realizing that her doubts were out of order and, under the circumstances, her father would be the first to understand, she pulled her wellingtons off and parked them by the door. Then she walked into a neat little sitting-room filled with furniture of a quality that quite took her breath away. Immoral or not, Patty's trade was obviously very profitable.

Patty took Hannah's wet coat and draped it over the ornate brass fireguard enclosing the very welcome fire that roared up the chimney. 'Sit yourself down. I'll make us a cuppa. I think you could do with one after that.' Pressing her into one of the two red moquette fireside chairs, she went through to the back kitchen of the two up, two down cottage, deposited the wet brolly in the sink and took a clean towel from a cupboard. 'Get your hair dried off with that.' She dropped the towel on to Hannah's lap and returned to the kitchen to put the kettle on. After a few minutes she came back with a silver teapot on a silver tray and Crown Derby china cups and saucers.

Hannah was busy towelling her hair, but she paused to look up when Patty walked in. 'I hope I'm safe to hold that!' she said, nervously eyeing the delicate Derby Posy pattern flowers, knowing her limbs still felt shaky and having visions of the delicate china chattering in her hands like teeth in several degrees of frost. Then feeling gauche and awkward she quickly returned to rubbing her hair and changed the subject.

'Does Jerry Stone live in Derby?'

'I told you to forget Jerry Stone. Him and his kind aren't for the likes of you – and neither was he.' Patty's head jerked towards the window. 'Whatever was he doing in George's car?' Picking up the teapot she began to pour.

Finally putting the towel down, Hannah gave a sigh. 'It's a long story.' She suddenly had the feeling she had better keep her mouth shut. George Bunting would not appreciate her telling the whole village his business.

'Oh aye!' Patty put in knowledgeably. 'And I'll bet my last tanner that Jed is at the heart of it.'

Hannah grimaced and took a sip of tea, and felt very guilty for not telling Patty the truth, after all the woman had done for her. If it were not for Patty she would not be sitting there now and it seemed very ungrateful to be unforthcoming. But George Bunting's fury weighed heavier than any offence Patty might take. In search of something to say, she looked around the cosy little room that had come as a shock to her. 'You've got it nice here,' she said, hoping her change of subject did not sound so false it appeared insincere, for the words were spoken honestly. She did not know what she had expected Patty's home to be like. But she certainly had not imagined the neat and tidy furnishings, or the delicate china they were drinking from. Somehow she had come to think the inside of Patty's home would be grubby and not very nice. She didn't know why. Patty herself always looked very presentable as she tripped around the village in her high-heeled shoes and glamorous clothes – totally out of place – but no-one could ever have said she looked dirty or shoddy.

But Hannah had no need to worry. Patty was a master at knowing when to pursue a matter and when to drop it – in her line of business she had to be. 'How's George getting on?' she asked, sensing her visitor's discomfort and providing the remedy herself. 'Driving everybody mad, as usual? Or is he mellowing with age?'

Hannah smiled, Patty's lack of concern returning her confidence. 'I think he is mellowing with age. Although

I'm not stuck in the house with him all the time now. So perhaps it's just that I miss most of it and Rhoda gets it all.'

'Who's Rhoda?' Patty picked up a packet of cigarettes and offered one across the small, walnut table that stood between the two chairs. Hannah shook her head and Patty took one herself, stuck it into a black and gold holder and lit it with a dainty mother of pearl lighter. 'Is she a friend of yours?' she prompted, after taking a long draw and blowing the smoke up in the air above her head.

Hannah gave a nod, seeing no reason to lie. 'Rhoda is the new housekeeper. You'll be seeing her soon. She's got a young son. He comes down to school.'

'A lad!' The perfectly pencilled eyebrows arched in surprise. 'I'm surprised George took a kid on.'

'He didn't.' Hannah grinned sheepishly. 'We needed help and I did it before he knew what was happening.'

Patty gave a screech of laughter and clapped her hand on the chair arm. 'If he let you get away with that, he is definitely mellowing!'

Hannah gave a smiling nod. On second thoughts she was not quite sure mellowing was the correct word, but she knew what Patty meant.

'I always had a soft spot for the old devil.'

It was the last thing Hannah had expected to hear and she could not conceal her surprise.

Patty laughed. 'Don't look so shocked. I'm still capable of having feelings – just like anyone else.'

'Oh . . . I didn't . . .' Embarrassment coloured Hannah's cheeks.

Patty shook her head. 'It doesn't matter. It's the natural mistake to make,' she said, shaking the matter off and immediately returning to the previous subject. 'If truth be known, most women round these parts would have had him – of my generation, that is. He could have had his pick if he hadn't been so toffee-nosed.' Her smile was touched with a fondness that made Hannah suddenly wonder just how well she knew him. 'I've told him that many a time,' she concluded, picking up her cup and taking a drink, the sentiment lingering gently on her face.

'He'd appreciate that.' There was a touch of dryness in Hannah's voice, as she recalled the occasions she had tried to point out some error of his ways – and the response it had received.

Patty's head shook in fond remembrance, sending her blond curls bouncing round her face. 'But of course by the time I was telling him, he already knew it for himself.'

Meaning it was after Sam had been born – the son he considered imperfect. Bitterness tightened Hannah's mouth. She withheld the sharp retort that sprang to her mind. It was not for Patty and snapping at her would prove nothing. But, despite taking a moment to calm herself down, when she spoke her voice was still harsh. 'If he could stop being ashamed of Sam for long enough to see what he really is, he'd realize which of his sons was more of a man.'

'Here, luv!' The hand holding the cigarette dropped into her lap and Patty leaned forwards and rested her free hand on Hannah's arm. 'I wasn't saying nothing against Sam. Don't tar me with the same brush as the rest of this lot.' The holder, plus cigarette, was jabbed towards the window in the direction of the village, indicating she was referring to the residents of Aldale. 'I was talking about things . . . well . . . personal. Perhaps I should keep my tongue still. Here, have another cuppa.' Without waiting for Hannah's reply, she refilled her cup.

Hannah wondered if she was being entertained in the manner Patty's usual 'guests' were entertained. The thought put a smile on her face.

'That's better.' Patty lifted the black and gold holder to her lips and took a long draw, blowing the smoke out again, as she said, 'I thought for a moment there I was going to get a black eye.'

Hannah gave an embarrassed laugh. 'I'm sorry. It wasn't you I was getting at. It's just . . .' Her voice trailed away and she returned to toying with her damp hair.

'It's just that you have a soft spot for Sam,' Patty put in knowledgeably.

Hannah blushed furiously and her finger curled more rapidly in her hair.

'Nay, luv, don't take on. There's nothing wrong in fancying a fella.'

'But there's not much point in it if they don't like you.'

'Has he told you that?' Patty stubbed the cigarette out very deliberately, then laid the holder down by the side of the brass ashtray.

'As good as.' Hannah looked bleak.

'Why . . . what did he say?'

Hannah bit her lip, wishing she had never begun the conversation. Sam's constant rejections were not something she wished to discuss. 'He told me to leave,' she said bluntly.

A smile tugged at Patty's crimson mouth. 'Is that all?'

She was being laughed at and Hannah tried to appear affronted, but only succeeded in looking more embarrassed and ill at ease.

Inside, Patty's smile broadened, but she kept it hidden, sensing her guest's discomfort with the personal subject. 'How many times has he told you to go – once, or does he make a habit of it?'

'Once.' The word was little more than a whisper and she could not lift her gaze from the blue socks on her feet, as they poked from beneath her damp, brown corduroy trousers.

'Ignore him!' Patty's voice rang with the confidence of someone who knows exactly what they are talking about. 'It was probably only his anger speaking for him. And even if it wasn't, it's up to you to change his mind for him.' She clapped her hands together as if in prayer. It made Hannah smile, considering the woman of ill-repute in a religious devotion.

'Men are strange creatures,' Patty continued.

Hannah's eyebrows rose in expectation. She wondered if she was about to be taught a few tricks of the trade.

'You have to ignore half what they say, and take the other half with a pinch of salt. Unless you think there is a real reason why you should do as he says, you stay put. Dig your heels in and make him see you mean business.'

Hannah shook her head. Patty made it sound so easy. 'I've been doing that almost since the day I moved in up there.' Resignation dulled her voice, but then she suddenly looked up with a smile. 'You never mentioned his hand!' She could not believe that anyone, except herself, could be discussing Sam so intimately, without bringing his hand into the conversation.

'Now why should I?' Patty asked, sitting back in the chair once more. 'I dare say that is the biggest part of the problem. But if you're patient and show him it doesn't make any difference to how you feel, you'll overcome it.'

'Do you really think so?' Hannah wished she could believe. But in her own mind she felt she *had* shown Sam his hand was of no consequence – yet it did not seem to have made any difference to him. Turning to the brass carriage-clock on the mantel, she saw it was getting late. 'I'd better be getting back,' she said, and pushed herself out of the chair with regret. At the Tor there was never much chance for her to be alone with Rhoda for any length of time without someone joining them, and she had quite enjoyed being in female company for a change. She only wished she could have come there under more pleasant circumstances.

She was just about to pick her damp coat up, when a mighty thudding at the door caused them both to look round in surprise.

'Dear God, they get earlier!' Patty grumbled, glancing at the clock and getting up to answer the persistent knocking. 'Don't they expect you to have any time off!'

Hannah hurriedly thrust her arms into her coat. She was horrified that she was about to come face to face with one of Patty's customers. But Patty seemed to have no qualms about her meeting them and did not hesitate in hurrying to the door. Hannah shrank up against the wall, pushing herself into the corner of a large walnut bureau, hoping Patty would keep the gentleman talking while she crept out behind his back.

She was too busy praying it was a stranger and not someone she knew from the village, to instantly comprehend Patty's startled gasp. It took several moments before it sank in that what Patty had said was: 'Sam!'

Hannah pinned herself tighter to the wall. The blood rushed to her head, then just as quickly drained away again. She felt sick. She felt faint. The red and cream roses on the carpet performed pirouettes before her eyes. But no! Not Sam! Not Sam! She could stand anything, anything – except finding out that Sam was one of Patty's *clients*.

'Where is she?' he demanded, pushing Patty roughly aside and charging into the room.

'She's in the parlour, luv. But what's the hurry?'

He did not reply. His strides were so long and purposeful that it only took him two to get across the room and come face to face with Hannah, huddled in the corner, clinging to the ridiculous hope that he might not see her.

'What the hell are you doing here?' The words were spat through tight, fury-trembling lips. His right hand, balled into a fist, thumped continuously at his thigh. The claw flapped agitatedly in the air only inches from her nose. But it was the anger and accusation that darkened his eyes, which made her flinch and press her body harder against the wall, needing the closeness to keep her upright.

'I . . .' Patty began, but never got the chance to continue.

'Shut up!' he blazed. 'I don't want to hear anything *you've* got to say.'

'Sam!' His insulting manner instantly brought Hannah back to normal. 'Don't be so rude!' she hissed, her mouth stiff with offence. That it was Patty, who had been her saviour, whom he was aiming insults at, only increased her anger. Straightening herself up and leaving the support of the wall, she glared mutinously at him. 'I could ask the same thing?' she pointed out meaningfully.

'Children! Children!' Patty positioned herself between them, one hand raised in each direction. 'Now why don't you both calm down and talk things through sensible. I'm sure you'll find it much more fruitful.'

Sam's stony gaze pivoted warningly to Patty's face, instantly dismissed her, and turned back to Hannah. 'What the hell are you doing here?' he repeated, just as heatedly as before.

Patty gave a sigh. 'Suit yourselves,' she said, and moved out of the way. 'Have a scrap if you like. But don't break anything!' she warned, before vanishing into the little back kitchen and leaving them to it.

Hannah settled her hands on her hips, lifted her chin in defiance and thrust her face into his. '*I* was having a cup of tea with Patty! What's your excuse for hammering on the door as if your breeches were on fire?'

All the colour drained from his face and it was several moments before he could control the quivering in his cheeks enough to speak. 'I was looking for you!' he finally hissed through his teeth, as if to open his mouth further would have broken his jaw.

She jerked her head in disbelief. 'So you just happened to choose Patty's door.' Her voice dripped with sarcasm.

'I was told you were here!' he retaliated, taking the wind from her sails.

'How?' She was bewildered and appeared to visibly

shrink several inches, as she took her hands from her hips and ran them over her hair in confusion.

'Madge Cresswell phoned the farm. At least her lodger did it for her.'

'What?' Hannah was totally bemused now.

'Madge was concerned because you'd told her you were looking to find a place to live and she'd seen you come in here.'

Hannah gave her head a shake, trying to find some sense in all this. 'I didn't tell Madge I was looking for a place.' She recalled seeing Madge standing over the river watching them as they came inside, but she had not bothered trying to shout to her because she would never have heard. She couldn't hear you when you were standing right in front of her. 'Oh yes!' She suddenly remembered the conversation in the market square. 'I didn't say anything of the sort to her. She can't hear what you're really saying, so she makes it up herself.'

'I thought she was talking out of the top of her head when she said you'd come here. But she was right, and I was wrong. What I want to know is why? Whatever possessed you to come into a place like this?'

'Saints preserve us!' came from the kitchen, a moment before Patty's blond head appeared round the door. 'Don't sweat lad. I wasn't thinking of taking on an apprentice.'

He spun round furiously. 'Then I'd thank you not to invite her in here again,' he blazed.

'Sam!' Hannah rushed at him, pulling at his arm. 'Stop it!' she insisted. 'Patty has been nothing but kind to me and you have no right to speak to her that way. If it wasn't . . .'

'Oh aye!' he spat drily, shaking his arm free of her grasp and cutting her off before she could explain all that had happened. 'I wonder why?' His disbelieving gaze washed slowly over her face, taking in the green eyes, still wide with the memory of the fear that had filled her earlier.

For several moments he lingered on the softly dishevelled hair that hung freely round her shoulders. It was very rare that she let it free of the rubber band that usually held it tethered behind her back. That she had done so here, for this woman, added fuel to his anger, and his bitterness was so great he could not believe that Patty did not have ulterior motives for bringing Hannah into her home. 'Are you getting too old for it?' he demanded nastily. 'Need a bit of new blood to bring in the money?'

'Sam!' This time Hannah screamed out his name, appalled by his attitude. It was so unlike him. She could not understand it.

But Patty shook her head and there was a smile on her face as she came into the room. 'I've had far worse said to me and I can still laugh.' She was speaking to Hannah, but when she reached Sam she stopped right in front of him and stared him straight in the eyes. 'It's a pity you can't still laugh, lad. Or at least give a smile to accept your good fortune.'

He stared at her blankly.

'As I see it . . .' Patty continued, '. . . if I hadn't been around to see what I saw, then Hannah would not be here now. She could have been anywhere . . . *with anybody*!' she added significantly. 'So, instead of chewing her ears off, you should be counting your blessings and taking her home – where she really belongs!'

The colour returned to his face in a hot flush. His gaze swung from Patty to Hannah, then back to Patty. 'Why, what has happened?' he asked carefully.

Patty's smile was victorious. 'At last!' she breathed with feeling, and turned to Hannah. 'Are you going to tell him, or shall I?'

Despite Hannah's account being very brief and sketchy, Sam listened intently, never speaking a word until she had finished. Even then he did not get the chance to say much, for Patty pushed him into a chair and gave him her own account. It was far more graphic than Hannah's and even included the man's name, as well as the name of the man he worked for, and where they could be found.

It was a very different Sam who walked out of Patty's cottage. 'Thank you,' he said, feeling both duly humbled for jumping to the wrong conclusions, and embarrassed that he did not know how to express his true feelings in words.

'Think nothing of it.' Patty shoved him out of the door after Hannah. 'Just make sure it never happens again. Don't let her go roaming off on her own until you've got things sorted out. Or the new housekeeper or her kid,' she added warningly.

Sam nodded. Jed had always been trouble but he had excelled himself this time. He would never forgive him for this. For putting Hannah in danger. And Rhoda and David. Patty was right there, until it was sorted out they were all in need of protection.

'Give my love to George,' Patty called, as they climbed into the Land Rover.

'I will,' Hannah assured, and had to smile as she closed the door and contemplated his reaction. But they had not gone far before her amusement turned to dread. Thoughts of what could have happened suddenly hit her and she began to tremble all over again.

'It's all right,' Sam assured. His voice was gentle, but he did not take his hand from the steering wheel to offer the physical comfort she craved.

She attempted to smile, but it was rather thin and weak. What was it Patty had said: dig your heels in and make him see you mean business. Well she could dig her heels in, but she could only make him see what he wanted to see. And if he had not seen her as a desirable woman by now, she doubted he ever would.

Chapter Eighteen

As it turned out, there was no reaction to the relayed greeting of affection from Patty. After learning what had almost happened to Hannah, George Bunting was too angry to take much notice of anything else. The first thing he did was to give her, along with Rhoda and David, very firm instructions that they were not to leave the house without an escort. The second thing he did was telephone the police and report his Jaguar as stolen. He did not give them the names that Patty had imparted to Sam. He did not want Patty getting into any bother. Besides, he did not think there was any real need. The men were obviously riding round freely in the car, assuming that no-one would involve the police, so he was confident they would pick up the green Jaguar without much trouble. There were not that many of them on the road round those parts and he was certain that it would be very easy to spot.

Unfortunately his confidence was unfounded. The car returned to the Tor that same night – but not in the way George Bunting would have chosen.

'You look tired. Do you think you'll sleep?'

Hannah gave a nod and smiled across the table at Sam. Rhoda had just taken his father off to help him into bed, David had been in bed for a couple of hours, and they were alone for the first time since coming back from Patty's. 'I feel all right now,' she assured. After getting back to the Tor and having to go through everything all over again, as she related the story to George Bunting, she had had yet another attack of delayed reaction. Her arms and legs had turned to jelly and she had felt quite giddy. But it had not lasted long and she was fine now, and her main concern was that his father should get his car back quickly and put an end to it all.

'Do you think Jed will be all right?' she asked. She got up and went to the sink, where the pile of dirty dog bowls was waiting to be washed. If the police recovered the car Jed would have to find some other way to cover his debts, she thought, as she turned on the tap.

'I don't give a damn if he is or not.' There was no anger in his voice, as she would have expected with such a statement, just a cold, calm certainty that made her shudder far more than if he had thumped the table and shouted loud enough to scare the sheep in the shed right at the far end of the yard.

'He is your brother!' She paused and glanced round at him. She did not like Jed and would be perfectly content never to have to see him again, but she did not like to hear Sam speak in such a coldly unfeeling way. It was so unlike him.

He gave a disgusted snort. 'Tell him that! He has never been happy to accept that *I* am *his* brother. I don't see why I should feel sorry for him now. Not after causing all this trouble. David has just got settled in at school. He's liking it. And now I don't know if we should send him or not!'

'They couldn't get at him when he's inside school!' It was a statement not a question, an alarmed statement. 'They couldn't,' she repeated, trying to convince herself as much as Sam. 'And you or I always take him and fetch him back.'

'It'll be only me from now on.' The sombre tone of his voice sent a shiver through her.

'Oh Sam!' Her mind filled with the awful imaginations of David meeting up with the man who had accosted her, and of what would have happened to him. 'We mustn't let David out of our sight.' Folding her arms around herself in protection, she turned to the comforting warmth of the blazing fire. 'We can't let it happen to him.'

Sam was up from the table in a moment and by her side. 'We won't,' he assured. 'But it's you that concerns me more at the moment. To think what might have happened to you if Patty hadn't . . .' His voice trailed away and his chest heaved on a sigh filled with the dread of his imagination. 'Oh Hannah!' He pulled her into his arms and held her tight, as if to let her go would be releasing her back to danger.

At first she was too surprised to react. Then when she finally looked up into his face it was too late. There was no reciprocating smile to the one his unexpected reaction had put on her lips. Something had made him realize what he was doing and he was quick to amend his error. His arms released her so suddenly that she stumbled backwards and physically shivered from the loss of the heat of his body, which, though only brief, had seemed very warm, and extremely welcoming.

'I'm sorry. I didn't mean to do that.' He moved away, putting the length of the kitchen between them, making her feel she had some nasty, contaminating disease.

She shook her head. 'It doesn't matter,' she was quick to assure. He looked so bleak. She did not want to believe he was ashamed of holding her in his arms, but that was the only description she could put to his expression: shame; guilt; inexcusability. And all she wanted to do was take it away before he was telling her to leave again, trying to rid himself of his own problems by getting rid of her. Turning back to the sink she completed washing all the bowls, dried them and put them in the cupboard. She wished she could understand just a little of what went on inside his head. For a moment he had shown real care – but only for a moment. It was better than nothing and at least it showed there was something there for her to work on, she told herself. But as she turned to him and found his bleakness had increased, rather than diminished, she changed her mind, knowing the last thing she wanted was to be privy to the thoughts which at that moment clouded his head and appeared so depressing.

'I'm off to bed,' she announced bluntly, leaving him in the kitchen before he had time to object, or tell her something she did not want to know.

She had been lying in bed listening to the darkness for some time, before he came upstairs. She did not feel sleepy, but the rhythm of a gently hooting owl on a nearby branch, was lulling her fractious senses into an opiate state of only half-awareness. Suddenly the bark of a hunting fox shattered the calm, making her jump and startling her back to reality. The owl fell silent and, as she listened intently for the return of its call, the soft footsteps began to climb the stairs, followed by the light running steps of Peg. She had the feeling he stopped outside her door and hovered uncertainly. She held her breath. But then she heard the click of his own door closing and she thought she must have imagined it. Wishful thinking, she told herself, and turned over in the hope that she might find some rest. She also hoped the strange yearning that seemed to be affecting her more and more of late and which could become so intense it caused a physical pain in her stomach, would not bother her tonight.

But, as on other nights, when she heard the click of the light switch turning off in the room across the corridor, she began to think of him lying there – within calling distance, yet miles apart. At first it was only a tightness, as if her muscles were about to revolt over something she had eaten. Then the ache began, and grew until she had the feeling some little creature was gnawing at her innards. Pressing her hands to her stomach she bit her lip and groaned under her breath – just as the silence shattered and a lightening flash sliced the darkness, and a mighty explosion ripped through the night.

She sat bolt upright in bed. The walls trembled and the sound of shattering glass seemed to be all round her. And there was a strange roaring and a flickering light dancing on the bedroom walls. In an instant she was out of bed. Grabbing the curtains she tore them aside. From the sound of the breaking glass she had expected the window to be broken, but it was intact. Down in the yard a car burned furiously. Long fingers of flame licked up into the darkness, reaching way up past the guttering of the roof. As if hypnotized her shocked gaze moved up to the top of the vivid orange tongues, then back down to the car at the bottom.

Was it the Jaguar, she asked herself? The flames and smoke were so intense that she could not see properly. But she had the feeling it was George Bunting's car. Just then a gust of wind fanned the flames dangerously close to the stables.

The horses! The dogs! They were all shut in for the night and could not escape. 'Sam!' she screamed, whirling away from the window and flying across the room, shocked that she could have wasted even one second just standing and staring.

They barrelled into each other as they both came racing out of their bedroom doors at the same time.

'What's happened? Do you know?' Sam's bedroom window was on the wrong side to see the yard and his face was pale with the additional uncertainty.

'There's a fire! A car. I think it's the Jaguar. It's close to the stables.'

'Christ!' He was only wearing pyjama bottoms but there was no time to consider propriety. Pushing Hannah out of the way, he hurtled down the stairs four at a time, Peg close at his heels. 'Call the fire brigade,' he threw over his shoulder.

Hitching her nightdress above her knees, Hannah chased after him. At the bottom of the stairs she met Rhoda coming out of George Bunting's room. 'There's a fire,' she gasped, in too much of a hurry to stop and wonder why Rhoda was coming out of his room dressed only in her nightdress.

'I know. I'm going to get David then I'll come and help.'

'Call the fire brigade,' Hannah shouted, passing the order on to Rhoda, considering she, herself, would be better employed assisting Sam out in the yard.

When she reached the kitchen Sam had gone ahead and was already outside. The back door was open and Peg sat peering out, having obviously been ordered to stay that way. Not stopping to assess the damage Hannah stepped out, then took a step backwards as the intense heat met her. It was George Bunting's Jaguar, at least what was left of it. But she had no time to consider what his reaction would be to seeing his prize possession going up in flames. 'Sam!' she called, lifting her hand to shield her face. She could not see him, yet the orange glow lit up the entire yard. 'Sam! Sam!' she repeated anxiously, just as he rushed round the side of the stable with the large-bore hosepipe in his hand, water already gushing from the end.

'Get the dogs and horses out,' he shouted, having to lift his voice above the roar of the flames. 'And don't get too close. I think what we heard was the petrol tank going up. But I don't know if anything else will explode.' He gave the hose a mighty tug to get the length he needed. Then he tossed it to the back in a wide arc, sending the pipe waving like a wriggling snake before straightening out. In the next moment the water was hissing and spitting as it bombarded the flames.

Hannah would have preferred to let him get the horses. They were both going to be terrified and need a great deal of strength to get past the flames. But the hose pipe was a large one, kept specifically for the danger of hay fires and it took Sam all his strength to control it when the water was blasting through. She doubted she would have been able to hold it, and keep the water gushing on to the right spot. So she did not have much choice.

With the spray hitting her she raced barefoot through the mud to the stable door. The heat was even more intense on that side of the car and the acrid smoke filled her nose and throat and stung her eyes. Samson and Delilah were going to be beside themselves with fear and she prayed she was going to be able to get them out safely.

The dogs were not such a problem. Their frantic barking indicated they were already clustered round the door waiting to get out. As she pulled the door open, the first sight of the flames made them fall silent and back off. But she only had to shout, 'Away!' and Seth, the oldest and wisest, cut a quick path along the front of the stables and round the back of Sam. Once he had moved the rest quickly followed and Hannah hurried inside to the horses.

Delilah's fear was of the frozen type. She huddled trembling in the corner of her stall, her terrified eyes staring at the door, where all the noise and light and stench were coming from. Samson was another matter. His eyes rolled large and white in his grey head, panic-filled breaths came in fast panting snorts from his flared nostrils. His hind hooves kicked so violently at the wall between the stalls that Hannah feared it would soon collapse.

'Like it or not you've got to move,' Hannah said, speaking more to herself than to the horses. She grabbed a bridle from its hook on the wall and quickly threw it over Delilah's head. Fortunately the mare was too terrified to make any protest and be awkward and the straps were soon secured. Hannah then grabbed a blanket from the shelf and tossed that also over the horse's head. There was a little, frightened whinny, but nothing else. Holding the blanket secure, Hannah gave a gentle pull on the rein. Delilah took one step, then dug her heels in and refused to budge.

'No! Please! Come on. Move!' Hannah begged. Using force would only add to the mare's fear and she had hoped to avoid it. But Delilah would not be cajoled into movement and force was necessary. Needing both hands free, Hannah quickly tucked the blanket into the straps of the bridle and hoped it would stay put and prevent the timid mare from seeing the flames at close quarters. Taking the rein in both hands, she curled the leather several times around her palms so that it would not slip. Summoning all her strength, she gave one long pull. Then another, and another.

It took several attempts before Delilah finally moved forward. But once she had got her moving, Hannah kept her moving. When they reached the door and the roaring became louder, Delilah pulled back and became skittish. Hannah held on, forcing the mare out into the yellow floodlit yard. The flames did not seem to have diminished at all and still reached high into the sky, although Sam's hosepipe was keeping them well away from the stable wall and clearing a safe path for them to walk.

'Are they all right?' he called, his anxiety roughened by the effects of smoke and his voice having a dry, rasping quality.

'Yes,' she returned on a gasp, as she fought against exhaustion to regain her breath. There wasn't much point in saying no, she told herself. He was in no position to come and help. Then, as if in answer to her prayers, Rhoda was by her side and adding her strength to the reins. Hannah never knew if the addition of another body made Delilah give up, or if she suddenly realized she was going in the right direction to get away from it all, but she suddenly stopped resisting and moved forwards at an eager trot.

'Thank heavens!' Hannah laughed with relief, and quickly handed Delilah over to Rhoda. 'Shove her in the top field and come back and help me with Samson,' she said, hurrying back to the stables and hoping Samson might have calmed down a bit.

He had not. His eyes were rolling faster, his kicking was more vicious and three of the planks of the dividing wall of the stall had been smashed through by his frantically thrashing hooves. She had the bridle in her hand and was gritting her teeth ready for battle, when Sam suddenly came to the rescue. 'Rhoda has taken the hose. Go and help her.'

Hannah hesitated uncertainly. Rhoda would be struggling to hold the hose. But Samson looked as if he was a ten-man job. 'You can't . . .' she began.

'*Go on!* Rhoda needs you.' He jerked his head towards the door and took the bridle from her hand. 'I'll manage this one.'

She doubted the last. But the hose and keeping the flames away from the stable wall was more important. So she left Sam there and hurried to Rhoda's aid. Rhoda was fighting just to keep herself upright and the water spout directed where she wanted it to be. Even with Hannah's help the hose proved difficult to hold and seemed to have a will of its own which constantly fought against their grasp, and she knew Rhoda shared her relief when the first clanging ring of the fire-engine was heard coming up the lane.

Unfortunately, it coincided with the moment Sam got a bucking Samson to the stable door. There was no blanket over his head, Sam had given up after the third time it had been shaken off, and the fast approaching noise, coupled with the sight and sound of the flames was too much for the frightened stallion. He reared on his hind legs, threw his great head back with a startled whinny and pawed madly at the air. His silver coat, along with his frightened eyes, appeared to have turned pink in the glow of the flames and made him look even more wild and uncontrollable.

Sam was almost dragged off his feet as he clung on to the reins, fearing what the horse might do to himself if he got free and ran wild. His eloquent curses rose above the roar of the flames and Hannah thought his father would have been proud of him.

'Can you manage this on your own?' Hannah turned hopefully to Rhoda. Now the fire brigade were almost there their hose was not so important, and Sam definitely needed help. Rhoda gave a nod and Hannah did not waste a moment. She raced to Sam's aid. He was going in all directions, as Samson bucked and pranced and got far too close to the burning car for comfort.

'Keep back!' Sam warned, as one of Samson's front hooves almost caught him on the side of the head.

'No,' she insisted, more concerned for Sam's safety than for her own. 'It will take two, or you're both going to end up on the bonfire.' Grabbing hold of the bridle she clung on to Samson's head.

At that moment the fire-engine shot through the gates, bells clanging and lights flashing, then came screeching to a halt, its wheels sending a spray of mud and muck in all directions. Samson let out an ear-shattering squeal and once more stood back on his hind legs and reached up into the sky – and lifted Hannah right up off the ground.

'Don't let go!' Sam called frantically, fearing she would drop and fall beneath the flailing hooves. He dug his heels into the ground and used all his might to drag the stallion down again. But his bare feet found no grip in the mud. When Samson brought his front hooves crashing back to earth and skittered suddenly backwards, Sam went face forward into the mud. He was dragged along the hard mucky ground for several feet, until Hannah's frantic cries to let go sank into his unsteady brain and he found the sense to open his hands and let the rein go.

Sensing freedom, Samson immediately bolted off, Hannah still clinging to his head. She was tossed around like a rag doll, but Sam's warning not to let go rang in her ears as she shared his anxiety that she might end up beneath the hard, trampling hooves.

She tried to talk to Samson, calm him down. But her voice came in ragged gasps as her breath was knocked from her by the constant pounding against the great, solid bulk of the stallion's ribs. She fell silent, praying her fingers were strong enough and her hands would not lose their tenuous grip.

The horse was heading down the yard and, at first, Hannah was thankful for that. If he had gone the other way and through the gate and down the lane, there was no telling where they might have ended up. But, when she saw the wall at the bottom of the yard getting closer yet his speed not hesitating, she had a change of heart. Having an open gate to run through would have been greatly preferable to being dragged over a stone wall. But fate had taken things out of her hands and all she could do was squeeze her eyes tight shut and bite down hard on her lip, and wait for the moment of impact.

When she felt Samson's body reach and stretch up into the air, she bit even harder on her lip. The toes of her left foot scraped against stone. Then she was flying through the air – alone. She had lost her grasp on the bridle, but the jolt of the lift had thrown her upwards and outwards, away from Samson. On a scream of panic she barrelled through the air as if shot from a cannon, coming to earth with a breathtaking thud that crunched her bones and rattled the teeth in her head.

At first she could only sit there, gathering her wits and trying to work out which way up she was. Then she began to feel her arms, legs, ribs. Her hands went everywhere, prodding and patting. She was bruised and sore, but nothing was excruciatingly painful. She could not believe she had got away without any major injuries and was giving herself another all-over prod, when she heard Sam calling her name. Her nightdress was up round her thighs, but it was not until she heard his voice that she thought to pull it down and cover her modesty.

'Are you all right?' His voice was anxious as he leapt over the five-bar gate and hurtled across the grass, skidding to his knees by her side. 'Christ! Are you hurt?' He put his hands on her shoulders, as if he would shake a reply from her if she did not give one quick enough. He peered into the shadows of her face and repeated the question. The fire was lighting up every part of the farmyard on the other side of the wall, but where she sat was sheltered by the wall's own dark shadow and he could not see her clearly.

But he was facing the fire and she could see every part of him. A mucky stripe ran up the entire length of him, where Samson had dragged him along the ground. It covered the front of his pyjama trousers, smeared his naked chest and caked his hair. And his eyes appeared like two large, very white, hard-boiled eggs in the sea of mud that was his face. He looked so sad and funny at the same time and all she wanted was to throw her arms around him and hold him, taking comfort for herself, as well as giving it to him. But she held back, recalling how she had felt earlier when he had taken her in his arms for a few precious moments, then backed away as if she was infected. No affection at all, was better than having it thrown back in your face, she told herself.

'Yes . . . yes, I'm fine,' she suddenly said, and turned her head away from him, unable to bear the concern that seemed to be multiplied tenfold in the staring white eyes. It seemed so genuine. It was genuine, she told herself. He did care. But what she wanted from him was much, much more than mere care. And much, much more than he was prepared to give. 'Where's Samson?' she asked, changing the subject of her thoughts. She peered all around. But the night was too dark and the hillside dipped away into a consuming blackness that the eye could not invade. The errant stallion was nowhere in sight, neither was Delilah, who was also somewhere in that same field.

'He'll be in the bottom meadow by now. Don't worry about him. When he calms down he'll come home.' He stood up, for a moment gazed down at her as if about to speak the deepest secrets of his mind, then thrust out his right hand and helped her roughly to her feet.

Her legs were shaky and the suddenness of his action made her stumble and falter.

'Careful!' Catching her in his arms, he pulled her up against the support of his own body and for a long moment looked down into her eyes with an anxiety that was bordering on fear. 'All right now?' he finally asked.

She gave a nod. He would never know how all right she felt at that moment, with his arms wrapped tightly around her and his naked, if somewhat muddy chest pressed against her. She gave a thin smile and lifted her hand, resting it against his arm. A shiver ran through his flesh. 'You're cold,' she said, suddenly becoming aware of the coolness of the night.

He shook his head. 'No,' he said, and a great sadness hung in his voice and put a frown on Hannah's face. But before she could question him he put her away, holding her at arms' length. 'We'd better get back,' he said. 'They might be needing our help. Can you walk now?'

She gave a nod of agreement, even though it was the last thing she wanted to do, and he turned her round and guided her to the gate without speaking again.

The firemen had soon got the blaze under control and the car was nothing more than a smouldering hulk when they got back to it. It looked a sorry sight.

'Oh dear!' Hannah glanced at the open back door of the house. George Bunting was sitting there in his wheelchair. Even at that distance his face appeared grey and unmoving – so lacking in emotion that he could have been etched out of stone. 'What is going to happen now?' She turned back to Sam with a resigned grimace.

'I don't think much more can happen,' he replied drily, staring at the smoky remains and watching the firemen rushing here and there. He suddenly turned to her, looked the soiled, damp, cotton nightdress up and down. 'I think you had better go and get something else put on.' He cast a pointed glance around the yard and at the firemen.

Suddenly reminded of how little she was wearing, she blushed to the roots of her hair. That she was wearing nothing but a nightdress had not concerned her before – when Sam was the only man around. Now the firemen were there to see her – and also George Bunting – though from the absence of expression on his face she did not think the latter was taking much notice of her. 'I think you're right,' she agreed, quickly turning away.

As she hurried across the darkened yard, she was pleased to see the damage to the house was not so bad. The twin lights outside the back door had been smashed by the blast, so had the ones by the stable, milking-parlour and sheepshed. The two that stood guarding the large stone gate posts at the entrance to the farm were still intact and so were the two further down the yard. The downstairs lights in the house had been switched on to help illuminate the yard and she could see that all the windows on that side had been blown in. It looked a mess. But all the walls were still standing and there was no major structural damage.

Thank heavens, she thought, as she reached the door and the statuesque figure sitting there. 'Can I come in?' She had to ask the question, after hovering there for several seconds and seeing no signs of him moving to let her get past the wheelchair.

For several more seconds there was nothing. Then his eyes suddenly pivoted to her face. 'You're not hurt?' His voice was gruff, empty.

She shook her head, realizing he must have witnessed it all. She knew how impotent he would have felt, how frustrated at not being able to do anything, and she wished he would rage and bellow and get rid of his anger. But there was nothing. 'I hope Samson is OK,' she said, having a final attempt at poking some response from him.

'He'll be all right. He'll come home when he calms down.' His flat voice echoed Sam's earlier reassurance. His chest rose on a silent sigh and he turned his gaze back to the remains of his treasured car.

She gave a sigh, wondering why people like Jed ever got the chance to live in the first place. He was neither use nor ornament to man or beast. 'Can I come in!' she repeated wearily, and held the filthy skirt of her nightdress out for him to see. 'I need to change,' she pointed out slowly and precisely, as if he could not see it for himself. The white cotton background now looked grey and it was difficult to separate which marks were the yellow daisies of the pattern, and which were splashes of mud.

But he seemed to be hypnotized by the smouldering wreck and the acrid stench of burning leather and scorched metal, and it seemed like an eternity before he looked sharply round at her for the second time. 'Yes,' he said bluntly, and gave a mighty shove to send the wheelchair careering backwards until she could step past him. Then he immediately rolled the chair forwards again, taking up his silent position in the doorway.

Hannah turned into the kitchen. Then groaned when she saw Rhoda sweeping up the broken glass and crockery. 'And I thought we'd got away without much damage!'

Rhoda gave a grimace. 'It could have been worse.'

Hannah gave a nod and turned to David. He was sitting on the table with his arms wrapped tightly round Peg's neck, who was sitting on the table with him. She had to smile. 'What are you doing up there? You look like the monkey on the table.'

He grinned impishly. 'Keeping out of the way,' he said. 'Has the fire-engine gone? Can I come out and see it?'

Before Hannah could reply, Peg gave a little whine and rested her front paw on his leg. 'There's your answer. Peg knows you shouldn't go out there. Don't you, girl.' She ruffled the collie's black and white neck. 'You keep him here, Peg. Don't let him move.'

Peg answered with another whine and David moaned. 'I want to see the fire-engine.'

'Well you can't. So just be told.' Rhoda straightened up with a dustpan full of broken glass in her hand, her out-of-character sharpness making Hannah turn in surprise.

'Are all the downstairs rooms in this mess?' she suddenly had the feeling she should be helping.

But Rhoda shook her head. 'It isn't as bad as I first thought. This is the worst – with all the broken pots.' Her gaze travelled bleakly round the ravaged kitchen. The shelves were still securely on the walls, but their contents of crockery and cooking pots were all spilled over the floor. 'Look at that.' She lifted her favourite copper saucepan and stared at the large dent in the bottom. 'Ruined!'

Hannah went to her and placed a hand on her arm. 'It could have been worse,' she repeated, and looked into Rhoda's disturbed eyes, then glanced pointedly at David. 'No-one has been hurt.' They would soon put everything back together again – things could have turned out very differently.

Rhoda gave an understanding nod. 'Yes, I know that. It's just . . . just . . .'

It was Hannah's turn to nod then. She understood that Rhoda had not needed her to point out what could have happened. She turned to David and bit her lip. Wrapped up snug and warm in his bright blue dressing-gown and bright red felt, zip up, bootee slippers, he was quite unconcerned. In fact he thought it was all a bit of an adventure. But . . .

Shaking her head she turned away, grabbed a brush and began sweeping furiously, working her anger and fear away in activity. If David had been injured! If it had been David the man had pounced on that afternoon instead of herself! The consequences were too horrible to consider. And they had done nothing to deserve any of it. It was Jed the men should have been getting at. Not his father. Not Sam. Not Rhoda or David. Or herself. Jed! Who had the uncanny knack of beginning all the trouble yet leaving others to reap the rewards. It did not seem fair or just. But at least the car was well and truly gone. No-one in their right mind would want to argue over the discoloured heap of metal that now sat outside. She just hoped that meant an end to it all.

Chapter Nineteen

The last remnants of the deep snow vanished in the increasing heat of the spring sun. The hedgerows sprang into blossom and the hills became verdant once more. In every direction there was green as far as the eye could see and life, as the sheep and cows returned to the fields and birds filled the air.

The lambing began and the days at the Tor sped by in a hectic whirl. Each night Hannah fell into bed tired, but with a certain contentment, as she contemplated the new little lives which had come into the world that day and marked another day gone by without any word from either Jed, or his villainous associates.

Fortunately the need for sleep stopped her dwelling too long on the less satisfactory side of her life. Since the night of the fire and meeting Rhoda coming out of George Bunting's room, Hannah knew that Rhoda regularly spent her nights in the downstairs bedroom. On several occasions she had got up at dawn to relieve Sam of a long night's vigil with one of the ewes, and she had always heard Rhoda creeping up the stairs and returning to the room next to her own. Strangely it no longer concerned her in the same way. Rhoda was an adult and old enough to make her own decisions, she told herself. And Rhoda seemed more than content with her life at the Tor. There was nothing in their day-to-day lives that suggested she was living under any threat or pressure. But knowing of their night-time trysts did not help Hannah's own frustration.

Realizing Rhoda and George Bunting were sharing the closeness and intimacy she craved from Sam, only made her own unfulfilled yearning more difficult to bear. She tried to forget the night of the explosion. It should have been easy, the mangled, metal wreck had been carted away and no-one ever mentioned that night. It was a taboo subject for George Bunting and he had soon made it known to everyone else that he did not want to hear one word spoken on it. But the silence could not wipe the memory from her mind. Not of the explosion, the fire, or the fear and panic. But of the feel of Sam's arms holding her tightly to his half-naked body, the warmth of his flesh despite the coldness of night and a liberal coating of mud. She could remember it so clearly, as if the mud had pressed an imprint of him on to her own body, which could not be washed away. Every time she thought of it she could feel him as if he was really there. It strengthened the physical pain that now prodded at her stomach every night. So each day she worked herself like a donkey, in the hope that exhaustion would cut the time between falling into bed and sleep to the absolute minimum.

'That's it!' Gratitude rushed from Sam's voice and a smile of victory spread over his face. He looked tired but happy, as he tugged off his wellingtons before dragging a chair from beneath the table and sinking gratefully on to it. He had been supervising the final delivery. The last six ewes had all given birth that day, the first at ten o'clock that morning and at regular intervals until the last at ten o'clock that night.

Hannah immediately leapt up and dished out two bowls of broth from the bright, shiny saucepan simmering on the gas ring – one of the new set bought to replace the ones damaged in the explosion. One bowl she placed in front of Sam, the other she put down by the hearth for Peg. The collie gave a whine of gratitude and dived her nose in; loud slurping sounds followed.

'What did you get?' Rhoda looked up from the navy blue school jumper she was knitting for David.

'Twins. Two ewes.' Sam brushed his hands over his hair,

bringing them to rest behind his neck as he gave a great yawn.

'We've done well.' George Bunting put the *Derby Evening Telegraph* down and turned to his son. For a moment there was a look of pride on his face that was so unexpected it brought Hannah up short, as she came back to the table with a mug of steaming tea. Could it be the loss of his car had made him see Jed in his true light – and with it Sam? Had he finally seen which son was worth the most? But then he said, 'Not one lamb lost. Are they all strong stock?' and she realized it was thoughts of his expanding wallet that had put the smile on his face.

'Why don't you come out tomorrow and see for yourself,' she suggested, speaking to George Bunting but not looking at him, as she placed the mug down by the side of Sam's bowl of broth. He still did not venture out of the house. She did not know why, no-one did. He never offered any explanation, other than a blunt refusal to go any further than the back door.

He gave a grunt. Agreement or objection? Hannah was not sure, but guessed it was the latter.

'David will be up at the crack of dawn.' Rhoda said.

Hannah smiled, knowing Rhoda had been tactfully changing the subject. Jumping to his aid, she thought, and found it rather amusing that George Bunting would allow anyone to leap to his defence. He was definitely mellowing, she told herself. 'Are you sure he's in bed now?' she asked, and glanced questioningly at the other woman. David had been very unhappy at being sent to bed before the last lambs were born. But, with school in the morning, his mother had insisted. Although Hannah would not have taken any bets that his head was on the pillow and his eyes closed.

'I don't care what time he gets up,' Sam put in meaningfully. 'So long as he doesn't expect me to get up with him.'

Hannah grimaced. Two nights ago Sam had not got

to bed until four o'clock, only to be woken at six by an excited David, who wanted to see the triplets that had been born the previous day, before he went to school.

'He won't wake you up again,' Rhoda promised confidently.

Hannah hoped Rhoda knew what she was talking about. Sam looked on the brink of exhaustion. It was always the same at lambing time, when births insisted on happening in the dark hours. It would only take a couple of nights' uninterrupted sleep to get him back to normal, she told herself, and studied his face with the concern that was a natural part of her emotions, where he was concerned. 'Have you got to go out again?' Even though today's lambs had been co-operative, and not put off their arrival until the small hours, she expected he would want to make a last check on them before going to bed.

Confirming her theory, he said, 'I'll have a final look,' and pushed the empty bowl across the table, stretched his arms above his head and gave another yawn. 'Then it's a hot bath and bed!' he declared with feeling, and pushed his chair back and stood up.

'I'll come with you.' Hannah was by his side as he thrust his feet back into his wellingtons. She did not expect he would find anything to do which would keep him outside for very long. But, if he did, it would be done twice as quickly by two.

As Sam went out of the door, Hannah glanced at Peg. She was curled up in front of the fire. The sound of the door caused her eyes to open and peer blearily at Hannah. Then they closed again and she made no move to follow. Too warm and full of food, Hannah thought with a smile, and hurried after Sam, leaving the collie to the comfort of the hearth.

The sheepshed was bathed in the soft yellow glow of the four hurricane lamps hanging one in each corner. Most of the ewes were settled down for the night with their babies. Hannah breathed in, drawing the warm sheepy aroma deep into her lungs. It was the smell of contentment, she had always thought, and it always put a smile on her face.

The smile was still there as she went around extinguishing the lamps, while Sam checked on the latest arrivals.

'Everything all right?' she asked. He was crouched down in the pen with the mother and the twins of the last delivery. Leaning over the fence, she peered at him in the dim light of the one remaining lamp.

He gave a nod. 'We can shut up shop.' He stood up, stretching the kinks out of his curved spine. Then he came out of the pen and was fastening the gate, when he suddenly stopped and turned to the door. His face crinkled in a frown that darkened his eyes and increased his tiredness.

'What's wrong?' Hannah followed his gaze, but they had closed the door behind them to protect the newborn lambs from the cool night air, and all they were looking at was the wood. 'What is it?' she insisted, uncertainty lifting her voice.

He turned troubled eyes to her. 'Did you hear anything?'

She shook her head.

'Nothing?'

She shook her head again. 'The dogs aren't barking.' Nothing could get into the yard without the dogs noticing, she told herself.

'I heard something. I definitely heard something.' Sam spoke as if trying to convince himself. But Hannah could hear nothing, only the snufflings and shufflings of the sheep, and she shook her head. Or perhaps she did not want to believe there was something, or somebody out there. She did not want to think they could be about to have a similar experience to the night the car had exploded in the yard.

Sam was at the door before she could stop him.

'No,' she begged, reaching his side and laying a

restraining hand on his arm. She did not want him to go out until they knew for sure what he was going out to – and perhaps not even then.

Sam did not share her concern. Pressing his ear to the wooden door, he listened for several moments. Then he pushed the door open just wide enough to squeeze through. 'Wait here,' he ordered, in a hoarse whisper.

'Not on your life!' she returned, intending to whisper but anxiety putting a squeak in her voice. She had no intention of letting him go alone, he might need her help. Besides, if there really was trouble out there, she was going to meet it head on, not wait around to let it creep up on her unawares.

'Wait here!' he insisted, favouring her with a hard chastizing glare.

'No!' Her voice held equal insistence, her gaze the same determination. She gave his arm a nudge. 'Get on with it,' she urged.

He gave a sigh and stuck his head round the door and looked over the yard. When he had gone into the house before supper, he had switched all the lights off, except the one by the back door, which stayed on all night. The single lamp cast a gentle glow over the centre of the yard, but it was not bright enough to reach the dark corners. All the outbuildings were cloaked in shadows and strange angular shapes stretched across the yard. Nevertheless Sam had the feeling the yard was empty.

'What is it?' Hannah felt her tension increasing and could stand his silence no longer. She shivered, though not from the cold.

Sam gave a shrug. 'I don't know. There's nothing noticeable. But I'm sure I heard something.'

'The wind. An animal,' she offered, trying to convince herself, as much as him. 'Perhaps it was a fox. I had better go and check the coops.' She wished Peg was out there with them, instead of curled up in front of the fire, all warm and safe.

'*You* are checking nothing! Stay there.' His eyes fixed her warningly, then his left hand shoved her back inside the shed and he closed the door on her.

It had been the claw that had pushed her back. Once again he had forgotten himself enough to touch her with it. For that moment his anxiety had overcome his revulsion of his deformity. Just as it had done on the night the car had burned.

If only he could forget himself all the time, she thought, and tugged the door open and chased after him.

'What are you doing!' He glanced round with annoyance when she came up to his side. He was standing in the middle of the yard, looking all around.

'I couldn't stay there . . . doing nothing!' she whispered. 'Besides, there isn't anything.' She looked around, letting her gaze linger on the dark shadows and hidden corners. There was nothing out of the ordinary. 'You must have imagined it. The dogs would have barked.'

'I di . . .' He did not get time to voice his disagreement. A car engine suddenly sprang to life and he flew to the gate, where the sound was coming from.

Hannah chased after him. But before they could get through the gates the car was away, the only evidence the diminishing sound of the engine and the glowing beam of the headlights moving through the night.

'What is it? Can you make it out?' Hannah gasped, clinging to Sam's arm and catching her breath after the mad dash across the yard.

He shook his head. It was just a dark shape behind the wedge of yellow light that sliced through the darkness. 'It's a car,' he stated. 'So that narrows the field down considerably,' he added drily.

'What were they doing?' Whatever it was, she hoped she and Sam had caught them before they did it. She glanced nervously back into the yard. There was nothing there, she reassured herself. Nothing was going to go bang in the night.

Again Sam shook his head. 'We'd better check everything,' he said. But neither of them made any attempt to move until the car's lights had gone unsteadily round the bend that took them past Tom Rowbottom's duck pond and into the village, and suddenly vanished from sight. It was as if they feared taking their eyes off it would make the car turn and come back again, Hannah thought, as she kept her gaze fixed on the darkness for several more seconds.

It was Sam who moved first. 'They could have been after the birds.' He hurried back to the sheepshed to get a lamp, so they could see the coops in the darkness behind the stables.

'You don't think it was Jed's friends . . . do you?' Hannah asked, as he came hurrying out of the shed, the lighted hurricane lamp swinging in his hand.

He gave a not very reassuring shrug.

'Let's go look for the worst then,' she said, leading the way to the chicken coops and hoping to find just that. If someone had been poaching the birds then it meant they were unlikely to be Jed's associates.

But the coops were intact. The birds were all safely locked inside. Nothing had been touched. The cows were the same and none of the equipment in the various sheds had been moved or noticeably tampered with. The stable was the last building to be checked and that proved equally pointless. Samson gave a snort of disgust at having his rest disturbed and the dogs began to yap as if it was breakfast time.

'It's too late now!' Hannah scolded. 'You should still bark even when you're locked in!'

Sam laughed, the tension leaving him as he realized they must have disturbed the prowlers before they'd had time to cause trouble. Holding the lamp up high he gave the dogs a contemptuous snort. 'They were so full of food they couldn't rouse themselves. Somebody must be feeding them too much!' He slanted an admonishing glare at Hannah, but he could not hold it for long. And his relief soon became apparent in the smile that tugged at his mouth and softened his eyes.

The fact that whoever had been in the car had gone without leaving a trail of disaster behind, made Hannah's relief equally potent. Spurred by Sam's lightheartedness, she flicked her gaze over his own expanding frame. Having her sharing the workload had certainly been good for him. Despite his present tiredness, his face had lost the strained pallor and returned to the old Sam. His body had regained the lost weight, plus some. There was no fat on him, just muscle. He was more well-built now than she had ever known him to be. Contemplating the body beneath the brown jumper took her back to the night of the explosion. She was in his arms, could feel the strength of him pressed to her.

'And I think somebody must be feeding *you* too much, Sam Bunting,' she declared, quickly turning her mind to less intimate thoughts and taking a mischievous pinch at his midriff. She moved to dodge away then, but Sam was quicker. His hand caught hers, imprisoning it against him.

'Oh, you do, do you?' His eyebrows lifted expressively and his dark eyes narrowed, returning her teasing in feigned retribution. Without taking his gaze away from her, he reached across and hooked the lantern on to one of the many nails protruding from the wall.

'Yes,' she countered, thrusting out her chin and laughing into his eyes. 'If they're not, what is all this?' She rested her free hand on his arm, ran it up and over his shoulder and down his chest. She paused there, feeling the muscles tensing beneath her fingers. Only then did she realize what she was doing.

In an instant her laughter died. Her gaze, suddenly serious, locked with another of equal intent. 'Sam,' she whispered, her lips parting invitingly on his name. He did not move. His expression was frozen, as if carved in stone. She did not know what he was thinking. But she did know she had touched him and he had not backed away. Gaining strength from that knowledge, she let her hand move again. Gently it brushed across his chest and she felt the same tautening response. The fingers clasped around her other hand also tightened. With increasing bravado her fingers traced the solid curves of each individual muscle. She smiled, thankful he had not put his coat on and she only had his woollen jumper as a barrier.

'Oh Sam!' she mouthed wonderously, her need for him swelling inside her and banishing all her uncertainties to the darkest corner of her mind. In the next moment she lifted her arm, curled her hand around his neck and pulled his head down. She met no resistance. His lips came down on hers with a hunger that matched her own. His arms went around her, crushing her to the length of him. Her hands cupped his head, her fingers sliding into the softness of his hair and pulling him closer. Now she had got him she was greedy for all he had to give, and she was not going to allow a sudden retreat – like the day in the Land Rover outside her old home.

She had no need to worry. Sam's passion was equal to her own and withdrawal was the last thing on his mind. The years of frustration, of seeing her and wanting her, yet telling himself no, suddenly exploded within him. She was no longer the frightened young girl who had been forced by circumstance to move in with them. She was twenty now, a young woman who knew her own mind, who knew all about his hand – and she was not pushing him away. She wanted him as much as he wanted her. A moan rumbled up from his chest, one of self-derision. She had never hidden the fact that she wanted him and he wondered how he could have been so stupid for so long.

Hannah gave a responding moan and pressed herself more closely to him, and he knew that his stupidity was well and truly over. Cupping her buttocks, he lifted her so that her feet left the ground, grinding her pelvis against his hardness. The hardness that before had always been relieved by self-gratification, but was now going to find its true home.

Throwing her head back, Hannah gave another moan. She had longed for this, but her imagination had fallen far short of the intensity of feelings his touch would release. She felt she was flying and drowning all at the same time. His mouth searched her exposed throat, lips nibbling, teeth grazing skin whose every nerve-ending seemed suddenly to have leapt to tingling life.

'Sam! Oh Sam!' she murmured, her head falling drunkenly on to his shoulder, as his hands went beneath her sweater and tugged her tee shirt free of her trousers. For the briefest moment she was sending up thanks that she had long ago stopped wearing his mother's old vests. Then his hands were travelling over bare flesh, cupping her waist and searching beneath her bra for the fullness of her breasts, and the only awareness left to her was of Sam and what he was doing to her.

Suddenly she was hoisted up in the air, high in his arms, as he carried her to an empty stall and placed her gently on the bed of straw. He was with her all the way, his body covering hers. She could feel every inch of him and his weight crushed her breasts with a pain that was so exquisite she cried out against his mouth, as it came down on hers.

In the next moment they were covered by leaping, bouncing, yapping dogs.

Hannah squealed: first in fright, then in frustration, while Sam swore with the vivacity of a true Bunting, as he threw himself off her and rolled on to his back to get the excited collies away.

'Damn dogs!' he blazed, sweeping them angrily away. 'When you're needed you're nowhere to be seen. And when you're not needed you're all over the place.'

For a moment Hannah could only stare at his furious face. Then she looked at the dogs, forming a semi-circle round their feet, tongues hanging out and all ready to pounce the moment the fun started again. Biting her lip she turned back to Sam. His lips were clamped so tightly together that his cheeks vibrated, and the rage in his eyes should have turned each one of their uninvited guests to stone.

She felt it too: the anger directed at the dogs; the sinking disappointment that the moment she had been waiting for had not, after all, arrived. But suddenly she saw the funny side. She did not want to show her amusement and she bit down harder on her lip, but she was powerless to stop the smile breaking out on her lips, or the bubble of laughter that rose in her throat.

Sam glanced at her. For a moment all the animosity that had been directed at the dogs, was aimed at her. Her smile vanished and her teeth pressed so hard into her bottom lip she could not understand why she was not tasting blood. She dropped her gaze and stared at her feet, and waited for the recriminations to begin – not at the dogs, at herself. Now they had stopped she was sure he would regret what he had done, blame himself, turn that blame on her – just as he had done on that snowy day outside her old cottage.

It was several breath-stopping moments before he moved, then it was only the slightest twitch at the corner of his mouth. But it was enough to show her he was also seeing the funny side, and trying to stop himself. Only when she released her breath on a grateful sigh, did she realize she had been holding it all in. Her smile returned, grew and blossomed. She threw her arm across his chest, buried her head against his shoulder and began to laugh. He was not angry. He was not going to reject her all over again.

When he lifted her chin with his finger and looked deep into her eyes with an emotion she had feared never to see, he thought the tears rolling down her cheeks were of mirth. Only she knew they were of joy. A joy that

315

expanded, as he bent his head and kissed away each tear and, with the tip of his tongue, licked the damp streaks from her cheeks.

Unfortunately, it was not long before Derwent joined in again, attempting to push his nose between their faces. With a sigh of frustration, Sam dropped his forehead against Hannah's and stared into her eyes with resignation. 'If we don't surrender gracefully, we're in danger of getting licked to death.'

She nodded in agreement and lifted her hand and traced a finger down his cheek. 'You . . . er . . . could . . . come to my . . . room.' Her voice was small and uncertain. She was not sure he would welcome her being so forward. 'Later. When . . .' She hesitated. It was only what Rhoda and his father were doing, she told herself. But she wanted to see some sign that he was not disgusted with her suggestion, before she went any further.

As if he could see all the uncertainties inside her head, he smiled fondly. Then, squashing all her worries with one little word, said a very simple, 'Yes.'

Holding the persistent Derwent aside, he planted a brief kiss on her lips. Then he helped her to her feet and brushed the straw from her clothes and pulled it from her hair.

The love she felt for him glowed softly from her smile, as she stood and allowed him to attend to her clothing for her, enjoying the intimacy that, once again, was performed with both hands. It had now become quite natural for him to touch her with his left hand: the part of him that he detested. The loathing might not have gone completely, but it had gone in her presence, washed away by the need for her. The thought warmed her inside. She was pleased his need had been just as great as her own and that it had overcome his own revulsion of the deformity. She did not point that out to him. It was best if the realization came to him of its own accord, along with the acceptance that he was no less a man for the slight error in his physical make-up.

After pronouncing her respectable once more, he urged her to the door, letting her reach the lighted yard before dousing the hurricane lamp and plunging the stable into darkness. Leaving him to secure the stable door, she went slowly across the yard, savouring her new-found happiness, thinking nothing could ever go wrong in her life again. Then she saw it . . .

In her euphoria she had forgotten the reason why they had been checking on all the buildings; had forgotten Sam hearing intruders; had forgotten the car. Now she was remembering. Standing on the back doorstep, illuminated so clearly by the yellow light from the single bulb above the door that she could not understand how they had missed it, was a large cardboard box.

Her hand flew to her throat. 'Sam!' she called, her voice little more than an urgent, dread-filled whisper.

His steps quickened behind her. 'What?' he asked, coming up by her side.

She stood very still, holding back in a strange limbo of fear of the unknown. She could not drag her eyes away from the box. She wanted to know what was inside, yet at the same time feared the answer.

'What is it?' Sam moved forward to peer down at the carton. The lid was closed and there was no indication of what might be inside.

She pulled him back. 'Come away. It might explode.' All she could think was that it was another present from Jed's so-called friends.

Sam looked at her bewilderedly. 'It's all right. It's only a box.' He took her hand and held it tightly in his.

'But you don't know what is inside!' It *was* a bomb, she was telling herself, just as a strange whimper came from beneath the lid. She almost jumped out of her skin.

Sam's head spun round in open-mouthed shock. 'There's something inside,' he said, unnecessarily. Then, before she could stop him, he crouched down and lifted the lid.

'Bloody hell!' He froze, mouth once more hanging open, as he stared at the contents.

'What . . . what is it?' Hannah did not want to look, but she found herself moving forward and sinking to her knees by his side, as if her body was suddenly being controlled by some outside force. She looked at Sam, he looked at her. Then he pulled the lid further aside. She also froze.

Suddenly it was all clear. They had not disturbed the car before it had accomplished its mission, as they had thought. Sam *had* heard noises, *had* heard someone creeping about. But nothing had been stolen or tampered with because their unknown visitor had not been there to take anything. Their purpose had been in the opposite direction – to bring; to leave something there they obviously did not want.

'But why here?' she found her voice to ask stupidly, unable to lift her stunned gaze from the carton's contents. 'Who . . .' she began, before words failed her.

'In their right mind would leave a baby on the Buntings' doorstep!' Sam completed for her.

'It . . . it must be a mistake.' She stared at him woodenly. 'It doesn't belong here.'

He shook his head. 'There's no mistake. See . . . it's a Bunting all right!' he said, as he pulled the white shawl aside to reveal a pink and white baby with a mop of dark hair – and a left hand which bore the unmistakable shape of Bunting's Claw.

Chapter Twenty

'*It isn't mine!*' Sam blazed.

How many times had he denied the child was his? How many times had his father called him a liar? He looked to Hannah, seeking support. She shook her head, unable to respond. She wanted to help him, wanted to hold her hand out to him and deny the accusations his father was flinging with liberal persistence. But how could she when she did not know?

She looked across the table at Rhoda, sitting with the baby cradled in her arms. The perfect mother, she thought bitterly. Why? she asked herself. Why had it to come now, when everything was going right? She did not want to believe it was Sam's child. It was too painful to think he had been with someone else while he had been pushing her away. But the evidence was right there before her eyes.

It was Rhoda who attempted to intervene; just as it had been Rhoda who had picked the baby up, held it and cuddled it as if it was her own – while the other three had hung around doing nothing. As if they were of the opinion it would go away if they ignored it, Hannah thought, as she watched Rhoda stand up and walk across the kitchen, bouncing the baby in her arms.

She stopped right in front of George Bunting. 'It does not have to be Sam's,' she said gently.

'Of course it's his!' He swiped his hand through the air, aiming an invisible object at his son. 'You only have to look at it to know that!' His ironic glare accused Rhoda of stupidity.

Sam gave the groan of a wounded animal. He scraped

his hands over his head and brought them to rest behind his neck, the way he did when he was exhausted. 'I don't care what you can damn well see! That baby is none of my doing.' He brought his fists down on the table with a thump, making Hannah's eyes leap to him. For a long moment his injured gaze bore into hers. 'Don't tell me *you* don't believe me, either!' The bitterness of his voice made her flinch. He did not wait for her reply, but whirled away and turned his back on her, obviously sure he knew the answer for himself.

'Sam . . .' she began, but she did not know what to say and her voice trailed away in the misery that was engulfing her. The minutes before finding the box had been some of the happiest of her life. Now it had all gone, wiped away by a tiny black-haired baby with facial features that could have made it belong to any one of the Buntings – but with a left hand that made it belong to Sam.

The baby began to grizzle. Without giving her a chance to object, Rhoda pushed the tightly wrapped bundle at Hannah. 'It's probably hungry. I'll make up a bottle.' Fortunately, whoever had left the child had had the sense to leave the equipment needed for it. At its feet in the carton had been three tiny white nightdresses, four woolly cardigans, a pile of nappies, two feeding bottles and a tin of milk powder.

Hannah looked down at the little face, cocooned in the softest white blanket, now going all pink and wrinkled with dismay and making a lot of noise.

'Christ Almighty!' George Bunting oathed. 'Can't you shut it up?'

'Perhaps it's ill,' Hannah suggested, unable to conceal the note of hope that they might have a valid reason for taking it to a hospital – and leaving it there.

'It sounds healthy enough to me.' Rhoda sprinkled the prepared milk on to the back of her hand, to test the temperature. 'And babies do cry, George. When they

want something. So it's better to find out what they want –
instead of ranting and raving at them.' She favoured him
with a cool stare and received a thunderous glare in return.
Taking no notice of him, she took the wailing baby from
Hannah's knee, sat down with it and stuck the bottle in its
mouth.

The wailing was instantly overtaken by a noisy sucking
on the bottle's teat. Rhoda smiled down at the child, then
at George Bunting. 'What did I tell you?' she said.

He gave a grunt. Hannah gave a sigh. Sam gave a
groan. Then they all fell quiet.

It was Rhoda who broke the silence. 'You're all so fired
up about its hand you've forgotten the most important
thing.'

Hannah frowned.

'What's more important than *him* . . .' George Bunting cocked his thumb at Sam, '. . . passing that on!'
His hand clipped the air as if flicking something distasteful from out of his sight. 'I've heard enough jokes
about Bunting's Claw to last me several lifetimes. Now the
stupid bugger has given us another generation of it.'

'It is not mine!' Sam blazed afresh, rounding on his
father.

Hannah had the feeling he was going to grab his father
round the throat and drag him out of the wheelchair.
But then he wheeled away, arms, stiff and trembling with
impotent rage, dropping to his sides. He looked in so
much despair that she wanted to go to him, put her
arms around him and tell him everything was all right.
But everything was not all right. She felt cheated and, at
that moment, she did not know if she would ever forgive
him that.

Rhoda gave a heavy sigh and looked George Bunting
straight in the eyes. 'What is more important is whether
we are going to call it Jack or Jill,' she said meaningfully.
'We don't know what sex it is,' she added, as if speaking

to idiots, when the three other occupants of the room looked on in dumb stupor. 'And, as I said before, it does not have to be Sam's baby.'

'Whose else could it be?' he questioned sceptically, taking the words right out of Hannah's mind. She did not think there was another person in the whole of the county who was afflicted with Sam's hand.

'Jed,' Rhoda stated bluntly.

Hannah's gaze pivoted to the other woman. She shook her head, unable to take it in. It couldn't be. She could not believe Rhoda knew what she was talking about.

George Bunting was of the same opinion. 'Jed!' he scoffed. 'Jed hasn't got the disease. Jed's a Bunting through and through.'

Oh aye, he was that all right, Hannah thought bitterly, her head spinning round to see Sam's reaction to his father's thoughtless comment. As she expected, the blood drained from his face and angry tension vibrated his cheeks. He looked as if he had plenty to say, but only of words that would choke him.

'*Jed!*' Rhoda repeated plainly, making it clear she was on Sam's side. 'Jed has the same mother as Sam. Just because it doesn't show on the outside doesn't mean he hasn't got it inside. He could pass it on.' She spoke with a confidence that lifted Hannah's spirits.

George Bunting's face turned livid. 'Since when have you been a bloody doctor?' he demanded spitefully.

'I'm not,' Rhoda returned sharply.

Hannah's eyebrows lifted in amazement. She had never heard Rhoda be so masterful before, and to George Bunting, of all people. 'I might be wrong. But I don't think I am. What Sam has is not a disease. You can't catch it. It's there or it isn't. Sam has it, we all know that, passed on by his mother. And it's my guess Jed has it, as well, even though you can't see it. Just the same as his mother!' she laid particular emphasis on the last.

Hannah's gaze pivoted to Sam's. It was true. Their

mother had not had the deformed hand – George Bunting would never have married her if she had! It had never occurred to her before that Jed could be a carrier – just like his mother!

'So . . .' Rhoda persisted, '. . . if Sam says the baby is not his, I think it's time you started believing him.'

Hannah had never seen George Bunting speechless before and she felt she might have laughed out loud, if her mind had not suddenly presented her with an answer to all this. 'You think the baby is Jed's?' she asked. She wanted to believe. But that wanting was so great she feared she might be leaping to judgements that suited herself. Just because Jed could father a child with the deformed hand did not mean to say this child was definitely his.

'Yes.' Rhoda took the empty bottle from the child's mouth and gave a nod. 'It would make more sense.'

Hannah bit her lip, wondering if she should speak out. She was not sure George Bunting was in any mood to have Rhoda's theory proved to him. Jed was only the way he was because he had been the apple of his father's eye and allowed to get away with anything. Now, if what she was thinking was true, she was about to prove Rhoda's theory and taint Jed with Sam's deformity – which their father found so disgusting. But when she looked at Sam and saw the gratitude flowing from his eyes, directed at Rhoda, she knew she had to speak and show him he had more than one friend. She turned urgently to Rhoda. 'How old is it?'

Rhoda gave a shrug. 'I'm not sure. But it's very young. I wouldn't put it more than two weeks . . . perhaps three.' Laying the child across her knee she began to attend to its damp nappy.

Just right! Hannah felt relief sweep through her. With all the extra work of lambing she had not had time to visit the village, so did not know when Glenda Riley had finally given birth. But it was four weeks since she had been in the shop and Mrs Fletcher had said Glenda was due in two weeks' time, but could be anytime now. It fitted perfectly. 'It's Glenda's!' she suddenly announced, turning to Sam with a triumphant smile. But he looked sceptical and her smile instantly vanished.

'What are you talking about?' George Bunting demanded.

'Glenda Riley . . .' Sam put in drily, before Hannah had the chance, '. . . she was expecting and everybody was saying it was our Jed's.'

'*Saying!*' his father blazed. 'What does that prove?'

Refusing to believe any ill of the *perfect* son, Hannah thought bitterly. 'It *proves* that it could be Jed's,' she snapped, flapping an agitated hand at the child.

'And if we listened to everybody who *said* Jed was responsible for some little brat, we'd be taking on every kid in the neighbourhood.'

Hannah grimaced, knowing at least half of what he was saying was true. 'But on this occasion things are slightly different,' she said carefully. She did not want to go into details. Pointing out that the baby's hand made it an undisputable Bunting, which he could see for himself, would not help anybody.

'What the hell do you mean by that?' he demanded.

Fortunately Rhoda saved her having to reply. 'What Hannah means . . .' she inserted, looking him square in the eye with a certain gleam in her own, '. . . is that whichever one of your sons is the father, there's one thing for certain. This, George Bunting, is *your* granddaughter!'

'A girl!' His nose curled as if a nasty smell had passed beneath it.

Hannah bit her lip to stop herself laughing.

Having no such qualms, Rhoda did laugh. 'Aye, George,' she said, shaking her head in amusement. 'The Buntings have started producing females. Now that really is something to be ashamed of.'

With a snort he spun the wheelchair round, his arms

working furiously to get it rapidly out of the room, emitting a string of very expressive oaths as he went.

Hannah was too amazed to speak. She looked at Sam and shook her head, in confusion, and wonder. Then she turned to Rhoda: the quiet, timid little woman she had brought to the farm because she felt sorry for her. In that moment she realized there was no trace left of the Rhoda she had first met on the snowy bus station. She was not sure when, or how, the transformation had taken place, but it most definitely had. The woman who sat confidently nursing the baby and shaking her head at the door George Bunting had gone through had, in the same way as her son, blossomed since arriving at the Tor, both mentally and physically. She was not only more confident but had filled out bodily. The colour had come back to her cheeks and the bones did not appear to be stretching through her skin. Her brown hair shone and there was a glow about her. Put there by George Bunting, Hannah thought, finding the realization incredible.

'Thanks Rhoda,' Sam said, scraping a chair from beneath the table and dropping on to it with a weary sigh. 'But you're going to regret saying all that in the morning.'

She smiled at him warmly. 'He'll get over it. He's got to. The baby's here and, the way she was left, I don't see anybody coming back to claim her.' Standing up she passed the baby over to Hannah. 'Look after her while I go and settle him down,' she said, and went after the wheelchair.

'She's got it bad,' Sam said, on hearing his father's bedroom door close behind Rhoda. 'She must have to go after him when he's in that mood.'

Hannah gave a nod. They had never spoken of Rhoda's nightly excursions, but she had assumed he must have also heard the oddly timed comings and goings. 'Perhaps she knows she can calm him down.' She looked up, meeting his gaze. 'If one of us had spoken to him in that way he would not have made a muttering retreat. He would have raised the roof.'

'Yes,' he replied thoughtfully.

The baby stirred in her arms and Hannah's gaze dropped uncertainly to its face. She was not used to babies and she wished Rhoda would come back and take charge. But then its lashes flickered and closed on the deep, midnight-blue eyes and she relaxed. It was going to sleep and she could cope with a sleeping baby, she told herself, and studied the long dark lashes lying against the pink cheeks. With its cap of silky black hair the face was so like Sam's. Her doubts began to return. But it also looks like Jed, or even their father, she quickly reassured herself. Even without the deformed hand there was no denying it belonged to the Buntings. She gave a sigh. It had to be Glenda's. It just had to be.

'It isn't mine!' Sam stressed pointedly, as if reading her mind.

It was a moment before she responded with a nod, her gaze remaining fixed on the face peeping out of the soft white shawl. 'I believe you,' she said, but her voice, little more than a whisper, conveyed her doubt.

He gave a snort. 'But what if it doesn't belong to Glenda . . . will you still believe me then?' His tone was harsh and condemning on the last.

She looked up then, meeting the anger darkening his eyes and she knew how much she was hurting him. 'I do believe you, Sam. It was just the shock. I . . . I thought . . .'

'Because it had this . . .' he inserted angrily, thrusting his clawed hand in front of her nose, '. . . that it had to belong to me.'

She turned her head away, but not in disgust. 'Stop it!' she ordered angrily. 'I believe the baby is not yours. So there is no need to stoop to bullying tactics.' It was several moments before he finally removed his hand and the air between them crackled with electric tension. Not until it fell to the table with a resigned thump, did she turn to him and meet his eyes. 'I believe you, Sam,' she said with gentle sincerity. 'I'm sorry for doubting you.'

He gave a snort. The chair scraped noisily across the floor, and he leapt to his feet and wheeled away from her. 'But who else will believe me?' Clenching his right hand into a tight fist, he looked up at the ceiling in despair. 'Nobody!' he growled. 'They'll all look at it and see me!'

'Well let them,' she returned irritably. 'What does it matter what other people think?'

'What does it matter?' He turned on her so savagely that, had she not had the baby in her arms, she would have stood up, feeling the need to do so to protect herself. 'You haven't got a clue what you're talking about.' He thrust his face into hers, his dark eyes blazing with more anger than she had ever seen in him before. 'But she will have!' He swept his arm across the sleeping child. 'Wait till she goes down to the village and they all start whispering and giving each other sideways glances; when she goes to school and they treat her like a leper. Tell *her* it doesn't matter when she asks you why no-one likes her. Or why she is different. Or what she did wrong to be born that way.' By the end his voice had risen to such a height it seemed to be rattling the window panes.

Hannah did stand up then. She could not stop herself. She wanted to scream at him to stop his self-pity. But she knew, in a way, he was right. She did not know what she was talking about. How could she? It was something that had to be experienced to be understood fully. But that did not mean she had no perception of what the deformity had meant to him. The baby began to cry at being disturbed and she placed it on her shoulder and rocked gently – as she had seen Rhoda do earlier. Placated, it fell silent. 'You're not different.' She spoke with a gentle firmness that matched the determination in the gaze she fastened on his. 'Neither is this baby. It was not your hand that was your biggest drawback . . . it was your father. And this child won't know any of that.'

'Oh no!' He gave a snort of derision. 'What are you going to do . . . shoot him?'

'There won't be any need for that,' she replied confidently. 'Rhoda and I will be here to stop him. And I should have thought you would have come down heavy on him, as well,' she added pointedly.

He turned away again, but not before she had seen the humbling effect of her words. He shook his head. 'It won't work.' Stuffing his hands deep into his pockets, he stared at the floor. 'We can't always be there to protect her. We'd be doing her a favour if we dropped her in the water butt and put an end to it right now.'

'I'll pretend you never said that.' She glared stonily at the back of his bent head, appalled he was capable of such callous thoughts.

He gave a harsh bark of laughter. 'You needn't do any pretending on my part.' He turned his head, glancing cold eyes at her. 'It's what I believe in my heart,' he said, the equally cold certainty of his voice sending a shudder down her spine. She held the baby closer, as if fearing he might suddenly snatch her away and rush her across to the water butt.

'It comes from here,' he continued, and clapped his hand over his heart. 'One day she will feel it too and she will wonder why she was ever put on this earth at all.'

'Don't, Sam.' It was all she could utter. So intense had been the bitterness in his voice, the pain in his eyes too palpable to be hidden by his hate.

Despair slowly claimed him. His shoulders drooped and his gaze sank to the floor. 'Don't you see, Hannah? There's nothing for her to live for. There's no future for her. Just a day-to-day existence . . . locked away up here.'

Hannah could feel his pain reaching out to her. She shook her head. 'There is always a future, so long as there is life.'

'For you – maybe.' He looked up then and she could see the glisten of tears in his eyes.

'Sam?' she said uncertainly, her heart turning for him. She quickly placed the sleeping baby in the cardboard box of its arrival, and hurried to his side, placing her hand on his arm. 'If there is no future for you, there is no future for me.' She spoke gently, re-living the wonderful moments in the stable – before making the discovery that was to turn the evening upside down.

'*Don't!*' he ground, viciously flinging her hand away.

She looked at him bewilderedly. 'I don't understand. Sam! I love you, Sam. Does that mean nothing to you? Have you forgotten so quickly?'

His chest lifted on a mighty sigh and he closed his eyes, as if unable to bear the sight of her. But when he opened them again and looked right into her own, she knew he had not forgotten one moment of their inconveniently interrupted passion. But there was something else, something cold and dispassionate, something she did not like. Damn the dogs, she thought on a shiver, and had the awful feeling that what had almost happened out there in the stables was all part of the problem. 'Tell me, Sam,' she said, her voice weary with defeat. 'If nothing else, you owe me that.'

It was only a moment before he began to explain. Proving her feelings to be correct, he said, 'A long time ago I made a promise to myself that I would never have a child and be responsible for passing this on.' He lifted the claw-like hand, stared at it, then let it drop defeatedly to his side.

Hannah shook her head, wondering how she could have been so blind. 'He'll never marry,' his father had told her. 'You can't have her,' Jed had said. Why hadn't she realized the true reason for herself?

'I wouldn't wish what I've been through on my worst enemy,' Sam continued, tugging her mind away from herself and back to him. She looked up, meeting a gaze that bore right into her and reached some deep secret part of her that suddenly had the feeling of being torn in two. 'Because of that promise, I can never fall in love, never marry.'

'But it's too late,' she said, forcing herself to sound confident, though it was a million miles from her true feelings. 'You have fallen in love. Or was I wrong to think I meant something to you.' Her voice died away as she realized she had been speaking in the past tense.

'Oh Hannah!' He swept the fingers of his right hand through his hair, ruffling it and making it stand on end. 'You do mean something to me. But can't you see how impossible it is?'

'No!' Gaining strength from his words, she grabbed his hands, pulling them close and clutching them to her waist. 'It isn't impossible. Nothing is impossible. Not if you want it bad enough.'

The panic in her voice put a thin smile on his face, but the glisten of tears was still in his eyes. 'I couldn't live with myself if I passed it on. And I couldn't do that to you, Hannah. I couldn't give you a baby that wasn't right.'

'Oh Sam!' She lifted his hands and pressed them to her face. 'There's nothing about you that isn't right. Why won't you believe me? It's one hand. That's all! It doesn't stop you doing anything. It doesn't stop . . .'

'It does,' he put in fiercely, not giving her time to finish speaking. 'It stops me fathering a child.'

'But it doesn't stop you . . .' She brought herself up short, blushing as she tried to think of the right words. 'I mean . . . we almost . . . in the stable. There are ways to make sure you don't get pregnant.'

'And there are more mistakes running about than those that were intended.' His voice was harsh and a bleakness entered his eyes that caused her own to fill with tears. 'I was afraid it would happen. That's why I wanted you to leave.' His head dropped forward and he could not look at her. 'But I was too selfish to make you go.'

'Oh Sam!' She bit her lip, recalling his anger when he had kissed her, how he had told her to leave. She had been too hurt, too intent on licking her own wounds, to stop and wonder why.

'I'm frightened, Hannah.'

'Don't be. There's no need.'

'There is! There is!' He pulled away from her and turned his back on her. 'I don't want you to leave me. But I don't want to hurt you.'

Coming up behind him, she placed her hands on his shoulders and rested her cheek against the back of his shirt. 'Only if you hurt yourself, will you hurt me.'

He shook his head. 'No,' he said. He did not turn to her, but she could hear that the tears were running freely down his cheeks.

She tightened her hands on his shoulders. 'I love you, Sam. I only stayed here because of you. Don't turn me away now.'

'I know. I know.' He turned to her, falling into her arms and wrapping his own so tightly around her it could have been him who was begging not to be turned away. He buried his face against her neck and she felt the wetness of his tears running down her skin. Her own tears began to fall and they clung to each other, their shared love turning to desperation.

It was Sam who finally pulled away. 'It's no good,' he said, looking into her eyes with a bleakness that crushed her heart. 'We're playing with fire and we'll get burnt . . . sooner or later. It mustn't happen.' Putting her arms away from him, he turned for the door, shoulders bent from the great weight that was pressing down on him. 'It mustn't happen,' he repeated, as he went out of the room, then twice more as he went down the hall and up the stairs.

Hannah could only stand and stare at the empty doorway he had gone through. A noise turned her attention to George Bunting's room. A muffled laugh, a moan. She did not know. But she did know it meant Rhoda was still with him. And she also knew, despite what had happened in the stable, Sam would not be coming to her room tonight – or any other night.

Chapter Twenty-One

'I'll take David down to school.' Hannah pushed away from the table, stood up, and looked steadily at Sam. He had not spoken much to anyone throughout breakfast and, from the shadows under his eyes, she imagined he had found sleep as difficult as she had. Even David's lively chatter had been greeted by short, inattentive responses. Fortunately David was too interested in the Tor's new inhabitant, and did not seem to notice anything amiss.

Sam looked up at her over the rim of his teacup. 'And . . . ?' he questioned pointedly.

'Yes,' she said simply. He did not have to explain. Over breakfast his father had made it quite clear she should go and find out if her theory that the baby was Glenda Riley's held any strength. She was now more than certain the baby belonged to Glenda: the timing fitted perfectly. But she was going to find out for sure – even if she had to go up to Glenda and ask outright. 'You'll manage without me if I don't come straight back. I don't know how long it will take.'

He gave a nod and she went to the bottom of the stairs and called David to hurry up. When Sam took him down the lane to the village school, it was in the Land Rover, but when she took him it was hoisted up in front of her on Delilah's back. Going on horseback pleased the boy greatly, but it made the journey more time consuming and necessitated an earlier start. 'We're on the old mare,' she shouted jokingly, when he acknowledged her call, and broke into a smile when whoops of joy came flying down the staircase. At least someone is happy, she thought, turning back to the kitchen. Only to have her brief smile wiped away by the sombre face still sitting at the table. His brooding worried her. It made her wonder what he was about to say. And, if he did say it, would she like it?

Having the awful feeling she would not, she turned her mind back to David. She was amazed how he had accepted waking up to find their little stranger sharing his room. Instead of the childish jealousy she would have expected, David had fussed round the little girl and helped feed her the bottle his mother had prepared. He had objected strongly when he was forced to eat his own breakfast and then sent to get ready for school. He wanted to stay at home and help look after her, he protested. Just as if she was another newborn lamb out in the shed.

'We'll have to get around to giving you driving lessons,' Sam suddenly said, taking Hannah by surprise.

'It would help,' she agreed. Neither she nor Rhoda could drive and he was always saying they needed another driver. But there always seemed too much to do and he never got around to actually showing them how to do it. A smile grew slowly on her face. The first half of the night she had lain in bed wanting him to come to her, yet knowing he would not. The second half she had convinced herself the first thing he would do that morning would be to tell her she had to go again. But he was offering her driving lessons, just the way he had done before. And he was only doing that because he expected her to stay. 'Thank you,' she said, her smile lingering fondly on his face – even though it remained unmoving.

'Find out where that whelp has come from,' George Bunting demanded, coming through the door so quickly the wheelchair scraped the paint off the jamb. 'Damnation!' he cursed, glancing at the mark, then at Rhoda, who was following behind.

She shook her head at him, as if he was an errant child, and Hannah had to turn away to conceal the smile tugging at her lips. It was strange, she thought. Never in a million years would she have put George Bunting and Rhoda together, yet they paired up with the ease of rhubarb and custard, both bringing out the best in the other. It made her wonder if there would be a marriage announced soon and, if so, what that would mean to Sam. Rhoda was a natural mother. She would happily bear him a football team of little Buntings.

'I'll try and find out.' Forcing herself away from the depressing turn of her thoughts, she concentrated on the task before her. If the baby was not Glenda's she did not know where she would turn.

'Offer them money,' George Bunting tossed with a flippancy that made Hannah grimace. It was his answer to everything, she thought. 'We'll pay for its support,' he continued, rolling himself over to the table and taking up position opposite Sam. Not once did he look towards the cardboard carton, which Rhoda had now made up with sheets to look like a proper cot. 'But we won't have it here,' he concluded, with the air of someone whose word was law.

Hannah glanced at the box and was grateful the baby was sleeping peacefully, and not creating a noise that would have made him more determined it had to go. 'I'll see what I can do. But don't expect miracles. I can't go knocking on people's doors and asking, excuse me, did you happen to forget a baby on George Bunting's doorstep last night?' She turned to Rhoda, seeking assistance. If he thought he was going to get rid of the child so easily, he was in for a big disappointment. As Rhoda had said last night, the way she had been left made it very clear the baby was not wanted, wherever it was she had come from. If it was Glenda's she was only hoping to get the confirmation out of her. But she held no hopes of getting Glenda to take it back – not with that hand. Whether he liked it or not it belonged here. It was a Bunting and no-one else was going to take if off his hands.

Rhoda got the message. 'Now, George!' She took

on the not-to-be-messed-with stance that always made Hannah smile. 'Stop getting yourself all worked up. It's no good for your blood pressure. There's really no need. One more mouth to feed isn't going to make a great deal of difference to you.'

'One more mouth!' he blustered. 'This place gets more like the bloody workhouse every day – taking in waifs and strays off the street.'

Hannah gasped. Rhoda's lips tightened and she moved towards him, but Sam got there first.

'Take that back!' His clawed hand came down on the table with a mighty crash, sending the cups jumping noisily in their saucers. 'Do you hear me!' He threw himself over the table, grabbed the front of his father's sweater and almost dragged him out of the wheelchair. 'Take that back! Now! Or you'll find yourself a very lonely old man.'

His father's lips tightened mulishly. 'I wasn't meaning them.' He waved his hand airily at both Rhoda and Hannah. 'I was meaning that!' His hand swept round to encompass the cardboard box.

'*Her!*' Sam blazed, throwing his father back into his wheelchair and slamming his hands down on the table with such force his fingers turned white and bloodless. '*That* is a her! And, despite what *you* might think, she is a human being and will be treated like one.' His voice quietened, but was no less determined, as he added, 'And everybody else in this house will be given the same respect. So I think you'd better begin doing some apologizing.'

For several long moments George Bunting glared obstinately at his son, receiving equal animosity in return. No-one spoke. No-one moved. They were all waiting for him to make the first gesture. When finally it came, he turned to Rhoda. 'Sorry,' he said. 'I was speaking out of turn – to the both of you,' he added, but did not look at Hannah.

Sam's body visibly relaxed and he pushed himself off the table. The apology had been brief and curt, but it was more than he had expected to hear. He looked up at Hannah. Her own inclusion had been very cursory and he was looking for her reaction. It would be in her eyes and he knew he would see it; the way he could always tell what she was thinking by looking in her eyes.

Reading his action, she gave a little shake of the head. The apology was sufficient, trying to drag more out of his father would only prolong the tension. She had David to take to school and the other mission to perform. And she wanted to get on with it.

Sam smiled thinly. She was protecting his father, but that did not bother him as much as the great sadness shadowing her eyes – put there by himself. Not for the first time his guilt rose and swelled inside him. He should have made her leave right at the beginning, when he felt the first stirrings deep in his loins. Now those stirrings were a great fire that threatened to burn him up, and her as well. If he really loved her he should send her away now, protecting her from hurt, he told himself. And he did love her. Oh how he loved her. With her mass of bright-red hair and large green eyes that could look as bewildered as a kitten or as fierce as a tiger, she was the most beautiful creature he had ever set eyes on. But how could he send her away when she looked at him the way she did, in a way he had never expected to see anyone look at him? Not him, with the obscene hand that looked more animal than human.

'I'll be in the sheepshed if anyone wants me.' He spoke suddenly, wheeling away and hurrying to the door. He needed to get away from all human contact and be with the animals, where he could talk to his heart's content, revealing the deepest secrets of his soul. They were good listeners, the sheep and cows. Even Samson, at times, had become his father confessor. They never scorned or ridiculed him, which was good: he had enough scorn and ridicule for himself – especially after last night. Letting himself weaken to the point where it was only the dogs that had saved her!

It was only when Sam slammed out of the back door that Hannah noticed David peering nervously round the doorway from the hall. She hurried across to him. 'Come on. It's all right to come in.' She held her hand out but it was a moment before he put his own into it.

'What's the matter with Sam?' he asked.

Hannah smiled fondly and ruffled his mop of brown curls. He was not very keen on George Bunting, but he had got used to him. Jed he hated, and would always do so. But the gentle Sam he adored and he could never understand when his hero began to shout and bluster in the way more associated with the other two. 'Nothing is the matter,' she assured. 'Sam was a bit angry. But he's over it now. And it wasn't you he was angry with.' The uncertainty in the large brown eyes did not diminish and Hannah knew she had to think of something else. 'When you're ready you can run down to the shed and say goodbye . . . if you want to?' She had found the answer. His face visibly brightened and he rushed to the coat pegs by the door and, jumping up to reach, got his coat down.

Pulling a green felt deerstalker hat from the pocket, he stuck it on his head, leaving the ear-flaps hanging loose while he stuck his arms into the coat sleeves.

Rhoda was busy making sure her son was all fastened up, when George Bunting turned to Hannah. 'Offer them money,' he said.

It took her a moment to understand he was back on the subject of the baby. She gave a shrug. She did not think money, his cure for all, was going to have any effect, this time.

'I'll give them a lump sum. As well as the child's keep.'

It was ironic, she thought, going to fetch her own coat. He would pay a fortune not to have the baby where he could see it. All he could see was its hand. He was too blind to realize he would be giving away more than money could buy. Didn't he know what he would be missing? Of course he didn't, she told herself sadly. He had done it once before. Sam had not been banished from the house, but he had been banished from his father's care and affection. Yet the man was too stupid to see that he had missed out, as well as his son. She turned away from him, for the moment too angry to form words. Her coat was on and all fastened up and she was ready to go, before she said, 'What if I'm wrong and the baby does not belong to Glenda, after all?'

'It will,' he insisted, with a confidence that drew a gasp of astonishment from her.

'So now you accept the baby is Jed's?'

He looked cornered, then broke into a bitter smile. 'Not necessarily,' he stated baldly. 'Maybe the girl didn't want to admit she'd been near that.' He jerked his head in the direction of the yard, and Sam.

She glared into his hated face with open hostility, her hands clenching into fists of their own accord. 'You are the most despicable . . .' she began, then brought herself up short, remembering David was in the room. 'Come on, David,' she said, as she thrust her feet angrily into her wellington boots.

Having tacked up Delilah before breakfast, she had to hang around while David ran down to the sheepshed to see Sam before they left. She hoisted herself into the saddle and sat fuming. Even now, after all Jed had done, George Bunting could still look on Sam as the poor relation, the one only fit for scraps. Losing his precious car had done nothing to alter his feelings. The man was an idiot, she thought, just as raised voices came from inside the kitchen. She had to smile. Rhoda was giving him an earful about waifs and strays.

'I really wasn't meaning you. I didn't think what I was saying. It's that blasted kid. Aw . . . Rhoda! You know I wouldn't have said that about you.'

Hannah bit her lip. His whining reminded her of when he first came out of hospital; when he had tried to make her feel responsible; when he was of the opinion she owed him a debt. She gave a sigh. She really did hope Rhoda knew what she was doing.

Delilah began to stamp her feet, unable to understand why they were standing around waiting. Fortunately David came racing back up the yard then. Hannah hoisted him up in front of her and off they went.

As Delilah trotted down the lane with her chestnut head held high and proud, Hannah began to wonder just how she was going to approach Glenda Riley. She decided it would be best to make a visit to the shop first. Mrs Fletcher was bound to know when the baby had been born, and if it was a boy or a girl. She wondered if she would also know if it had two perfect hands, and if Glenda still had it. No, she thought, it was too soon for anyone to know if Glenda's baby had vanished. But Mrs Fletcher would hopefully give her a start, something to work on – before she went to face Glenda. She gave a sigh. She hoped Glenda was going to be in. And she hoped her father was going to be out.

They had reached the sharp bend that led directly into the village market-place, before she was to realize her worrying and planning had been for nothing.

There was never much traffic on the lane, but all the same she slowed Delilah to a walk to take the blind corner. They were halfway round when they saw the police car. Benny Broadhead, the village bobby, immediately held his hand up for her to stop and she reined Delilah up, pulling the mare into the grassy bank.

A rusty green crane and Derek Entwistle's blue builder's lorry were blocking the lane. At first Hannah was not sure why. It took several moments for the full horror of what she was seeing to become clear.

The crane's motor leaped to clanking life. The heavy chain dangling from the jib suddenly tightened. There was a lot more clanking and grinding, then a battered black car began to rise above the stone wall.

'What is it?' David's voice was filled with childish excitement at being able to witness the scene. Bracing his legs against Delilah's flanks he reached himself up to see better. He did not want to miss anything.

'Sit down,' Hannah insisted. 'A car has crashed.' David was too young to be seeing this, she told herself, and, fearing what they were going to see next, turned quickly to Benny Broadhead. 'Is there anyone in it?' she called, her voice filling with panic.

But Benny shook his head. 'We got them out first.' He came over to her, pushing his helmet back so he could look up at her without the brim getting in the way of his eyes.

'Who is it?' She glanced at the car, now swinging unsteadily over the back of Derek Entwistle's lorry. The front was all stoved in and unrecognizable. The back was dripping with water and duck-weed concealed the registration plate.

'It *was* Fred Riley and his daughter,' Benny replied, laying particular emphasis on the past tense.

'Oh . . . !' Hannah's hand flew to her mouth. She went cold all over. No, it couldn't be, she begged. 'They're . . .' She could not bring herself to speak the last. It was too awful.

Benny nodded sombrely.

'When . . .' Her voice left her and she gave a whimper. 'When did it happen?'

'Sometime last night – we think. Nobody is really sure.'

Somebody was, she thought, her fingers gripping tighter to the leather rein. But she could not tell Benny that she had seen it happen. She and Sam had stood and watched the car racing down the hill. They had seen its lights vanish. She had thought it happened suddenly. But the bend was so sharp and she had never thought that . . . that . . . they had gone through the wall and landed in the duck pond. 'How . . . how . . .' Her voice faltered. She did not want to ask, but she had to know. 'Did they drown?' she finally managed to get out.

Benny shook his head. 'Glory no. There isn't enough water to cover a car. They'd both got head injuries. And Fred's chest had been crushed by the steering wheel. It was bad. But I reckon it would have been quick. Doubt they would have known much about it.'

'Are you sure?'

'Sure as I can be. But one thing I do know: they must have been coming hell for leather down here. It's a puzzle. Fred was usually such a careful driver.' He turned to study the progress of the crumpled car. It was now on the back of the lorry and they were freeing it from the crane's rusty old hook. 'You'll be able to get through in a few minutes,' Benny assured, and tipped his helmet back into its proper position and walked away.

Lifting her face to the cloudy spring day, Hannah closed her eyes tightly, trying to cut out the awful pictures in her mind. They had stood and watched! Looked on while Fred and Glenda were dying. If only they had known. If only . . .

She gave a sigh. At least it put her in no doubt as to where the baby had come from. But why? Why couldn't Fred have just knocked on the door and said: 'Here, this is yours'? No-one could have disputed the claim.

'Are you all right?' David craned his neck round to look at her.

'Yes . . . yes, I'm all right. It's just . . .' She glanced at the battered car as the lorry finally began to move away. 'It isn't a very pleasant start to the day. Do you want to go back home?' She thought it might be best to give school a miss after the shock of it all.

But his response told her the shock was all one-sided.

'No!' he insisted excitedly. 'I want to tell them I saw it.'

She had to smile, even though she felt more like crying.

342

But she was grateful the childish lack of concern for the circumstances was sparing him from the real horror. 'All right,' she agreed, geed Delilah back into action and followed the lorry into the village square – but not too closely.

After leaving David at school, Hannah followed her plan to go to the village shop. She no longer needed Mrs Fletcher's assistance in proving the baby belonged to Glenda, but she was hoping the shopkeeper might be able to give the child's birth date, and also her name.

With all the excitement of the accident, Mrs Fletcher was in her element. 'What a morning!' she exclaimed, lifting her hands in the air the moment Hannah stepped through the door. 'You can't lie safely in your bed now without wondering what's going on outside.'

'Didn't you hear anything?'

'Not a thing!' The older woman dropped her hands on to her hips with a loud slap. 'Not a thing! Would you credit it?'

Hannah shook her head. No, she would not credit it. It seemed incredible that no-one had heard the crash, which must have made a considerable noise. She wondered if she and Sam should have heard it from the Tor. It was too far, she tried to reason. But she could not rid herself of the guilt that they should have guessed what had happened, and done something.

'Was someone looking after the baby for her?' She hoped her voice sounded natural and untouched by the jittering the question caused in her limbs.

'Oh glory be!' Mrs Fletcher's scrawny hands went up in the air again. 'Didn't you know? It was stillborn.'

'Stillborn!' Hannah could not conceal her surprise. Fortunately, Mrs Fletcher took it for distress and, nodding her head, looked duly sympathetic. 'When?' It was all Hannah could ask, as defeat swept through her like a tidal wave. She could not believe, after all that had happened, that the baby could not be Glenda's.

Mrs Fletcher screwed her tiny eyes up to peer at the calendar on the door. 'Three weeks tomorrow. Or so they say. Fred or Glenda didn't tell anyone at first. It was a bad business. Sort of turned Fred's head, so to say.'

Hannah's interest suddenly picked up. 'What do you mean?'

'Fred kept Glenda locked in the house to begin with.' Mrs Fletcher folded her arms over her flat chest and shook her head in utter disgust. 'He wouldn't let her show her nose outside the door. Poor girl. As if she had something to be ashamed of.' She gave a grunt. 'And at the start he'd tried to get her to get rid of it.' She gave another grunt. 'There's nowt so funny as folk. You can't imagine what could make a father treat his own daughter so.'

Hannah could. She could see it all clearly. At least, she hoped she could. Fred Riley had not only locked his daughter away, he had also locked his granddaughter away. He had made up the story of a stillbirth because he was too ashamed to let people see the baby – which had the Bunting's Claw! She gave a sigh. For all his offers, George Bunting's money was not going to get him out of this one: there was no-one left to take it.

It was not until Mrs Fletcher said, 'Well, what was you wanting?' that Hannah remembered she should be buying something. She quickly pointed to a bar of chocolate, the first thing her eyes rested on, handed over the money and left the shop. Mrs Fletcher had told her all she wanted to know, so now she had to go back to the Tor and tell the others. George Bunting was going to be over the moon at finding there was absolutely nothing he could do about it.

Sticking her foot in the stirrup, she threw her leg over Delilah's back and settled in the saddle. But as she turned the mare round and pointed her at the lane leading back to the Tor, a sudden, awful thought occurred to her: if everyone was of the opinion Glenda's baby had been stillborn, the baby at the Tor did not exist!

She pulled Delilah up and just sat there in the middle of the market-place. There were not many people around but she was totally oblivious to the few that were. Her insides were churning with fear. If George Bunting thought the baby had, supposedly, never been born, he would feel he was free to do anything with it. She gave a shudder, recalling Sam's instructions to put her in the water butt. It was only a threat spoken in the heat of the moment. She knew Sam could never have done it. But his father was a different matter.

The baby had to be brought into the open, she told herself, and considered going back into the shop and telling Mrs Fletcher. That would ensure that by the end of the afternoon the whole village was aware of it. But what if she was wrong? What if the baby was not Glenda's?

'Oh . . . !' In frustration she brushed her hand across her head, just as Dr Hallam's car went by. The doctor! she thought, wondering why she had not thought of him before. Surely he would know about the birth, know if there should be a living baby around somewhere. His car had been going in the direction of his surgery so she reined Delilah round again and set off after him.

* * *

'What?' George Bunting's face drained of all colour, then slowly turned to a dull puce. 'Fred Riley is dead?'

Hannah nodded. She had just relayed the whole sorry story to him and Rhoda.

'And Glenda?'

She gave another nod.

'Christ Almighty!' He stared woodenly at Rhoda, as she sat at the table, bouncing the wide-awake baby on her knee. 'Well, it can't stay here,' he declared.

'She has to. There's nowhere else for her to go.' Hannah crossed the kitchen, folded her arms and stared out at the yard. The flags need a good scrub down, she thought, looking at the mucky stones. She had better get this one over with and get out there, she told herself. She took a deep breath. In the village her plan had seemed like a good idea. Now, with George Bunting glaring at the back of her neck, she did not feel so self-assured. 'The doctor is coming up later on to take a look at her.'

'What! You told the doctor it was here?' he blazed.

'Yes.' Forcing herself to face his anger square on, she turned around. Getting the doctor to come up had been a deliberate ploy. Fortunately, she had been proved right: the doctor did know of the birth. Not that he had initially been very forthcoming.

'You can't expect me to tell you other people's business, Hannah,' he had asserted, very firmly.

But when she told him about the baby left on the doorstep, he no longer had to speak the words. The uncomfortable expression suddenly filling his eyes and the way his old hand clutched at his wrinkled chin, as if in a torment of indecision, confirmed what she wanted to know. And now George Bunting was aware the doctor knew of her presence, the baby was safe, at least from any physical harm.

'It's a good idea,' Rhoda said. 'Not knowing anything about her, it's best to have her checked over and make sure she's all right.'

George Bunting gave a snort. 'I don't care whether it is all right or not. It isn't staying here!' He balled his fists and bounced them against the wheelchair's arms. 'Why won't you listen to me? I don't want that blasted kid here and I'll not have it here.'

'Then where do you expect it to go?' Hannah demanded hotly.

'You can't throw her out, George,' Rhoda put in, firmly, but using the patience that always seemed to get her what she wanted. She stood up and put herself between the two heated opponents. 'The child is a Bunting,' she stated meaningfully. 'She is *your* granddaughter. And even at your most cussed, not even *you* would see your own flesh and blood out on the streets. So stop all your bluster and get used to the idea.'

His lips tightened mutinously. 'I don't want to get used to the idea,' he said, childish petulance filling his voice. 'We can't manage a child. You haven't got time to be doing with it . . . you've got me to see to.'

Hannah smiled grimly, she couldn't help herself. It was himself he was concerned for. Hadn't he said very much the same thing to her when she told him she was going to find a housekeeper. 'You thought you couldn't live without me waiting on you hand and foot,' she said pointedly. 'But now you've got Rhoda well-trained I'm sure you wouldn't swap back.' She cocked her eyebrows at him.

He gave a grunt and slanted a telling glance at her. 'Perhaps not!' he agreed carefully. But the victorious glint suddenly lighting his eyes told her very plainly she did not have a chance of swapping back to her old job – not that she would have ever suggested it. 'But we can't afford to take on a bloody nursemaid,' he continued. 'And Rhoda hasn't got the time. She's got David, as well, remember.'

'I'll be able to look after you all,' Rhoda confidently reassured him, as the door opened and Sam came in.

'Can you go shopping?' Rhoda asked without hesitation.

'Yes, this afternoon.' He kicked his boots off and came into the room. 'I'll combine it with picking David up. What do you want?'

'Milk powder, first size baby clothes, and a cot – if we can run to it? If we can't I'll fix a drawer up until she's bigger.'

'What?' Open-mouthed, Sam looked from Rhoda to his father to Hannah, then back to his father.

'Baby clothes,' Rhoda stressed meaningfully, bringing his astonished gaze back to her. 'A baby needs plenty of things. Perhaps Hannah should go with you?'

He turned to Hannah, still speechless. She gave a nod, even though she was not sure she would know what they wanted any better than he would.

He turned to his father. 'Will she?' he questioned, with a frown. 'Is . . . have . . . ?' Words failed him. He could not believe his father had given in so easily. He did not know what the women had done to make him change his mind, and he did not dare to voice the question for fear of putting his foot in it and making him change his mind back again.

It was Hannah who put an end to his confusion. 'Glenda and her father are dead,' she explained. 'So . . .' She gave a shrug.

'It seems we have got your brother's bastard whelp foisted on us, whether we want it or not,' George Bunting put in, finishing the sentence for her in a far more brutal fashion than she would have chosen.

Hannah gave a sigh of despair and Sam's chest heaved on a great, noisy indrawn breath. His right hand balled into a fist and the clawed hand rested heavily on the table and he glared at his father. '*She is not an it!*' he ground through angrily clenched teeth, the same anger trembling through his colour-heightened cheeks. Lifting his left hand he prodded the pincer-like claw at his father. '*You* will start treating her like the little girl she is, or I'll know the reason why!'

The pincer jabbed dangerously closer to his father's nose, which had taken on the arrogant tilt Hannah had not seen in several years. She gave a gasp. It had been a long time since she had witnessed one of their fights. But the way his father was glaring at Sam, and the tight set of his lips, had all the hallmarks of a return to the old ways of sorting their problems out with their fists. Not sure if she was about to stand between them and stop them, or if she was putting herself in a position to rush in and help Sam, she took a step forwards. Then she came up short, reminding herself that George Bunting was no longer in a position of superiority, and Sam would not hit him, not in the wheelchair.

But it was only a moment before she was reconsidering her theory. George Bunting swiped at Sam's hand. 'Take that thing away from me,' he growled, his nose curling as if some repugnant substance had been thrust beneath it.

A loathing equal to his father's spread over Sam's face. Hannah rushed forwards, certain she had been wrong and he was about to hit out. She grabbed his arm. But he shook her off.

'There's no need to worry.' He glanced round at her, his mouth twisted in a bitter smile. 'I share his name but there any similarity ends. I won't hit him. At least, not with my fists.' He placed his hands on the wheelchair's arms and brought his face down close to his father's. 'But I will hit you with my tongue. That child needs a home and she'll have one here. And she won't be treated like something the dog dragged in.' He lifted the claw again, holding it right in front of his father's nose. 'It's a hand! One hand!' he grated. The very same words Hannah had used to him. She bit her lip, feeling emotion rising to her throat. 'The rest of me is the same as you . . . normal!' He gave a sarcastic bark. 'If anything is *normal* about this family. Well she is the same.' He jerked his head towards the baby in Rhoda's arms. 'And I won't let *you* or anybody else say different.' He pushed himself up to his full height and stood glaring down his nose at his father, who had gone unusually quiet. 'And from now on she'll be called Jenny,' he declared, in a manner that brooked no refusal.

'I'm her grandfather! I should choose a name!' George Bunting's spine stiffened and he looked greatly affronted.

Hannah gave a gasp of disbelief. But she thought better than to point out only moments before he had wanted nothing to do with the child.

'So think of one,' Sam insisted. 'But do it now. I'll not have her called *it* any more.'

There was silence while Sam waited. It seemed an eternity before his father's broad shoulders lifted in a shrug, and he said, 'Jenny sounds all right to me.' It had a certain reluctance, but it was an agreement.

Hannah breathed again.

'Good!' Sam stated with feeling. Then he wheeled away, grabbed his wellingtons, and slammed out of the door.

The baby began to wail and George Bunting cussed.

Hannah felt it was wise to follow Sam into the yard and leave Rhoda to deal with his father.

Chapter Twenty-Two

Jenny Bunting proved to be the perfect baby. She was soon sleeping through the night and when she was not doing the same during the day, would lie contentedly playing with the string of brightly coloured rabbits stretched across the hood of her pram.

Despite pouring maternal affection all over the child, Rhoda still had plenty left for David, and to cosset the delicate ego of George Bunting. He had not become any happier about the child being there, but he seemed to have resigned himself to the fact that there was nothing he could do about it, and whenever Rhoda said they needed something she got it. The kitchen became cluttered with baby clothes, bottles and toys, and the cardboard box was exchanged for a very large navy blue pram and a pretty white cot with puppies painted on both ends. She might have begun life as an abandoned waif, but she was going to be treated like a princess from now on, was Rhoda's decision.

At first Hannah was stunned by how easily George Bunting agreed to pay out for the baby. It was several weeks before she realized he was doing it for Rhoda.

Once again Rhoda was displaying her innate ability to control him without him knowing it. Whenever the baby was in need of anything, she always said 'we' need, not 'Jenny needs', not 'the baby needs'.

'It makes him think I'm getting the things for him,' Rhoda explained, when Hannah questioned her one day. 'And you know how he likes to think people are doing everything for him.'

Hannah had smiled and nodded. She agreed with the

last, but she wasn't so sure about the first. He was doing it for Rhoda. It might have been his way of making Rhoda's life easier, so she had more time for him. But Hannah did not think so. She felt he was doing it for the woman he loved. She had the feeling that if Rhoda had asked him to burn the farm down and move into a wooden hut, he might have agreed. But she kept those thoughts to herself. Rhoda's relationship with the master of the house had still not been brought out into the open – even though it was now obvious to everybody with two good eyes and a pair of well-tuned ears.

Hannah could not understand why they did not get married and have everything above-board. It was not a thought that did anything to help her with Sam. It was three months since the night Jenny had been left on the doorstep, yet his views were still the same. His fear of becoming a father made him shun sex, and her with it. That he had nearly succumbed to his natural instincts on that night had only made things worse. Now he made sure he was never alone with her for too long. And when, by necessity, they were forced together, he kept his distance as if she had the plague.

'It's a beautiful day, why don't you come out and try it?' Hannah suggested to George Bunting, as she pulled her boots off before crossing the kitchen. She had popped inside for a mid-morning cuppa. At one time Sam would have been with her, but she knew if she suggested it now he would make some excuse about being busy. So she saved her breath, knowing he would come as soon as she had gone back outside again.

'I'm all right where I am.' He did not lift his nose from the morning newspaper. But Rhoda, who was sitting opposite to him and feeding Jenny, glanced her a thin smile.

Hannah shook her head. In the two years since his accident he had never ventured out into the yard. He had let Sam take him into town for two hospital check-up appointments, after that he insisted there was nothing they could do for him and he was not going any more. He had poked his nose out of the door twice: the first when Jed arrived and frightened David; the second when the car was ablaze. He had tasted fresh air four times in two years, not even that, because when the car was burning, the air he breathed was hardly pure. It wasn't natural, especially for someone who had loved and worked the hills. 'It would do you good,' she said, as she went to the sink and washed her hands.

'Says who?' He lifted his eyes to peer over the top of the paper, but his nose stayed where it was.

'Says me.' Pouring herself a cup of tea she joined him at the table. 'This weather won't last for ever and it's too nice to miss.' She turned to Rhoda, seeking support. But Rhoda was busy giving Jenny a bottle and, although she looked up at Hannah, she did not speak.

'You could get the gun down and go shooting,' she suggested. His shotguns had not been taken out of their case since the accident, yet before he had often gone out with one. He was a good shot. 'You could do that sitting down.'

His hands and the newspaper dropped sharply to his knees and he turned on her with a snort of disbelief. 'And where do you suggest I go? Over the Tor? Down to the river? Are you going to lay a railway track all over the hills for me to run on?'

'I wasn't meaning hunting.' She gave a sigh. She had spoken without thought and not given the right impression. Now he had lost his temper she may as well save her breath. But foolishly she continued. 'We could fit up a shooting range in the top field. We only use it for Samson and Delilah and we could take them over to the top west without much trouble.'

'A range! What with? Or are you going to stick empty cans on top of the wall?' Flinging the newspaper on to the table in an untidy heap, he spun the wheelchair round and careered out of the kitchen. 'You'll be giving me a peashooter next and expecting me to play with it,' he shouted angrily, a moment before his bedroom door closed very noisily behind him.

Hannah gave a sigh and rubbed her hand over the sleek cap of hair on the top of her head. 'I was only trying to help.' She tugged on her ponytail to tighten the slipping rubber band, and gazed at Rhoda with resignation.

'It's only because he's frightened.' Rhoda took the empty bottle from Jenny's mouth and put it on the table. Then she lifted her over her shoulder and began to rub her back. 'He worries that he will get himself into a situation he can't get out of. Get stuck somewhere or fall out of the wheelchair and not be able to get himself back in.'

'But he's in no danger in the yard. There's always one of us around.'

Rhoda smiled tightly. 'But he would feel stupid if anything happened and he had to wait for someone turning up to help him out. He's a very proud man.' Jenny provided the awaited burp and Rhoda put her down in the pram. Turning to Hannah, she said, 'It makes him feel as if he's been pushed back into childhood, or rushed forward into old age before his time.'

Rhoda's eyes filled with the compassion that was in her voice. It tightened a chord in Hannah's chest. When she looked at George Bunting she only saw someone whose own stupidity had put him in the wheelchair, and she had never taken the time to consider how he must really feel. She shook her head. 'I thought it was a good idea,' she said, gathering up the sheets of paper and fixing them together again. When the newspaper was returned to its original state, she stuck her nose inside and began to read – in the same way George Bunting had been doing before she upset him. She did not want to see the look in Rhoda's eyes. It reminded her too much of the expression in her own when she was thinking of Sam. The only difference was Rhoda's feelings were reciprocated, hers were only thrown back in her face.

She turned one page, then another. She glanced at the headlines but not at the small print. George Bunting's demise had quickly flown her mind, now it was filled with Sam. Two of the dogs began a scrap, their angry yapping and snarling reminding her there was a world outside and she should be getting back to work. She put the paper down, was about to close it and stand up, when the headline right at the top of the page leaped out at her. CONTRACEPTIVE PILL NOW ON PRESCRIPTION.

There was a pill that could stop you having a baby! She had never heard of it: then her knowledge of the subject was very limited. It only amounted to Miss Beighton, the deputy headmistress at her school, taking all the girls into a separate classroom and giving them their one and only lesson on sex education. It had taken all of fifteen minutes. The first five consisted of a very pink-faced Miss Beighton giving a brief description of a condom and what you did with it. The other ten minutes had been taken up by her vehement insistence that the only safe and moral contraceptive was abstinence, and that boys were something 'nice' girls kept away from. A theory which, judging by Miss Beighton's single state, Hannah had felt the middle-aged woman had clung to rather too long.

Her dad would have told her, if she had asked him, she told herself, as her eyes ran eagerly over the report. But living on a farm the process of procreation had never been a mystery to her. A baby, calf, lamb or foal, all were made the same way. And it wasn't until she got to know Sam that she had needed to change her thinking to how to stop them being made. Rhoda! she thought, but immediately pushed the thought away. Living under the same roof made it seem too personal.

But by the time she had finished reading the article she did not need anyone else to put her straight. It told her everything. Excitement began to bubble inside. This was exactly what they were looking for: her and Sam. It was the answer to their prayers.

'I'll be down at the barn with Sam,' she said, and had her wellingtons on and was out of the kitchen before Rhoda had turned round. She wished she could have taken the newspaper with her. But that would have looked odd and led to questions she would not have wanted to answer. And Sam could read it for himself, later, after she had told him.

She walked until she had reached the corner of the stables and was out of sight of the house and George Bunting's bedroom window, where he was more than likely to be sitting looking out. But once she was round the corner and out of sight she began to run. She raced down the side of the old stone building, along the back and past the coops. Alarmed by her haste, squawking hens and ducks went in all directions. But she did not stop until she had reached the first dutch barn, where Sam was busy forking bales of hay on to the trailer to cart up to the stables. It was a burning hot day. His tee shirt was soaked in sweat and clung to his chest like a second skin and his suntanned arms glistened as he swung the forked bale high over his head and tossed it on to the trailer.

But she had no time to stop and admire his appearance. 'Sam!' she gasped, breathless more from excitement than from the run. She grabbed his arm and swung him round to face her, and made the fork fall from his hands. 'There's a contraceptive pill,' she blurted out, unable to keep the news to herself a moment longer.

'What!' His whole face puckered in disbelief.

'A contraceptive pill. It's safe. It's in your dad's paper. I just read it.'

'Hold on!' He pulled away from her and rested his hands on his hips. 'What are you talking about?' He looked very serious.

'Oh, Sam! It's what we've been looking for.' She carried on speaking as if he had not asked the question. 'All I have to do is take this pill and I won't have a baby. They've just invented it.'

He gave a deep, weary sigh. His gaze swept round the surrounding countryside as if seeking some answer from the grass, the trees. When he could not find it, his eyes pivoted back to her face. 'They haven't just invented it,' he said, the sombre tone of his voice instantly wiping away her exuberance and making her feel very naive and stupid.

'You knew . . . !' She could not believe he had known about it yet not told her, not seen it as the way forward for them. She stared at him bewilderedly, wondering if she really did know him at all. 'What . . . what do you mean? It's in the paper. I just read it.'

'Well you haven't read it properly.' The fingers of his right hand raked through his hair. 'It's just come out on prescription,' he explained, slowly, as if speaking to an idiot. She felt even more stupid and naive. 'It's been around for a couple of years.' He gave a shrug, scooped the fork up from the ground and spiked it into the next hay bale with more ferocity than was necessary.

But Hannah did not see the frustration of his actions. She only saw he was turning his back on her and she would not let him dismiss the matter so easily. 'You knew all about it!' It was not spoken as a question, but thrown as an icily condemning statement.

He nodded his head. 'It doesn't make any difference, Hannah.' Jabbing the fork into the hay and leaving it stuck there, he rested his hands against his hips and stepped towards her. She would never have thought it possible for anything to make her move away from him, but she did then. Feeling a terrible hurt of betrayal she backed away from him. All she could think was that if he had not seen this as the answer to their prayers, then he did not want to see it.

He stopped short. His right hand came out to her then went back to his hip. His chest lifted on a sigh. 'That isn't the whole problem. Don't you see?'

She shook her head stiffly. 'No I don't see, Sam. I thought the problem was your not wanting to father a child.'

'It is!' Both hands raked through his hair, then dropped to his sides defeatedly.

She did not know why he should feel defeated. She was the one who had been fooled, tricked, who had lost out.

'Oh, Hannah! Don't make this any more difficult than it is.'

'I'm not the one who is making things difficult,' she snapped angrily. 'I was under the impression I'd found the answer to the problem. I won't say *our* problem, because it seems it has only been mine! You're changing your mind and I'd like to know why?'

'I am not changing my mind!' His voice rose to a pitch that frightened the hens and ducks and had them flapping noisily around again.

'From where I'm standing you are,' she countered hotly. Then wheeled away, would have left him standing there if he had not been faster.

Grabbing her arm he dragged her back and had her round facing his angry glare before she had managed to take the second step. 'I'm not doing this for me! I'm doing it for you! So what if there is a pill you can take. You only have to forget to take it – and then what?'

'I wouldn't forget,' she snapped, incensed that he thought she was not capable of remembering something as simple as swallowing a pill.

He shook his head. 'You can't be sure. Besides . . . I have no right to ask you to give up the chance of having children. It's my problem, Hannah. I shouldn't thrust it on to you.' His voice faltered and he seemed to crumble before her eyes.

All her anger drained away, leaving behind a great,

bewildering sadness. 'Oh Sam!' She reached out, laying her hand on his shoulder. 'It's you I want.' A note of panic entered her voice. She felt like a drowning man clutching at a straw that was rapidly being swept away by a current that was far stronger than she was.

Sam shook his head, a bleakness in his eyes that made him look suddenly old and tired. 'You're only twenty-one. How do you know you'll feel the same in ten years' time? Or worse, in twenty when it's too late.'

'I know,' she said simply. But, even as her love for him expanded inside her chest, he turned away from her. She dropped her head, stared at a single patch of pink clover fighting for survival in a sea of white clover and had the feeling she was seeing herself. Straightening her shoulders she stared determinedly at the back of his head. If she did not fight his obstinance, like the pink clover, the white would close over her head and all would be lost, including life itself, because Sam was her life. She had discovered that long ago and she had not wasted the last years waiting for him, to give up on him now. He might not believe the new pill was a solution but she did, and come hell or high water she would make him believe it in the end.

'I understand why you feel the way you do. But can't you see it's time you began to see things differently? It's time to let go of your father's warped thinking. That's all it was, Sam. It was all inside his head and instead of throwing it away, as he should have done, he let it grow and fester.' Going to him she laid her hands on his drooping shoulders and pressed her cheek against the warmth of his back. 'I love you and I want to spend my life with you. I don't look at you and see someone with a deformed hand. I see you, Sam! The man I love. It's the same with Jenny. She's just a baby, a little girl. Not a hand that happens to have a person attached to it.' She lifted her head and peered round into his face. 'Or is that the way you see her?'

359

He stared at her blankly. Then he shook his head. 'You know it isn't. But it's the way other people will see her.'

'No,' she insisted, and only just stopped herself from trying to shake some sense into him. 'They'll see her for what she is. If we make her feel inferior then she'll project that and be treated as inferior. But we won't. We'll make her know she is loved and wanted. We'll make her feel so important that she will never have cause to hang her head in shame because of one slight mistake in her make-up.'

He cast his incredulous gaze across the hills, then up to the sky. A sky lark hovered overhead. 'A slight mistake,' he repeated, ignoring the little bird's persistent song. 'Is that how you see it?' He turned to her, shaking his head in disbelief.

'That is how I see it because that is how it is,' she replied confidently, refusing to be put off by his persistent doubt.

'Stop it!' He suddenly threw himself away from her.

She was about to step forward and lay her hand on his shoulders again, but he glanced round and the bitterness in his eyes stopped her in her tracks. 'I meant what I said the night we found Jenny. We would have been doing her a favour if we'd dropped her in the water butt.'

'No!' she returned angrily, hardening her gaze on his. 'Jenny will have a good life. Rhoda and I will make sure of that – if no-one else can be bothered!' she added pointedly. He turned away again and it was to his back, she said, '*I* won't give up on her. And I won't give up on you, either. You might think I don't have the age or experience to know my own mind, but you're wrong. Just remember you are only one year older yourself and you seem to think you have it all worked out. Well maybe you're the one who's got it wrong. Only time will answer that one. But no matter how long it takes I'll still be here waiting. You won't get rid of me. Whether I stay happily or unhappily is up to you. But stay I will – until you finally come to your senses.'

He did not reply and she turned and walked away, leaving him standing there. She could do no more. It was now up to him.

Chapter Twenty-Three

The nights began drawing in and the weather turned wet and miserable. The end of the year was only two months away and Hannah was still waiting. Sam had never brought the subject of 'them' up again, and she stubbornly refused. It had to be his doing. She had laid all her cards on the table and he had to pick them up.

She could wait, she told herself every morning when she woke up, at the same time praying that this would be the day her waiting ended. Then she would fall into bed each night knowing that another wasted day had gone by, and hate was the only word she could put to what she felt for Sam. It was not what she wanted to feel. But her emotions were so torn that, for the long minutes until exhaustion pushed her into sleep, she lay in the darkness hating him.

'I think it's time to get the sheep down.' Sam gazed thoughtfully out of the kitchen window, hands stuffed into the pockets of his jeans.

Hannah was eating her breakfast and she looked up and gave a nod, as she got her mouth round a large piece of bacon. There had been no frosts yet, but for several days the air had been damp and misty, and a real pea-souper had descended the previous evening. You could smell winter was on its way, as her father would have said, and the sheep needed to be got off the Tor and into the fields close to the farm before the first snows appeared. 'I'll stay at home and help you,' David offered, looking round hopefully. He was playing with Jenny, who sat in the highchair chewing on a rusk and getting most of it round her face and in her hair. 'I could say I'd been sick,' he added, just as hopefully.

Sam shook his head, immediately squashing the eagerness on the boy's face. 'It's school for you, lad,' he said firmly. He glanced at his watch. 'And you'd better hurry yourself up about it.'

David went grudgingly from the room and Sam turned to Hannah. 'I'll go to the corn merchant's after dropping him off. It won't hurt to get extra stock in at this time of the year. It shouldn't take long. We'll get the sheep down when I come back.'

She gave a nod and returned to her bacon and eggs. It would take both of them, as well as the dogs, to get the whole flock down in one go. 'Don't forget Rhoda's order.' She nodded to the notepad where Rhoda jotted down all the household requirements.

He went across, tore the sheet of paper off, and studied it. 'Mostly baby things,' he said, and smiled with amusement as he stuck the paper in his pocket.

'I'm ready,' David announced flatly, as he appeared in the doorway with his coat hanging off his shoulders and his satchel dragging on the floor. He was making it obvious he was only going under duress.

'Fasten your coat.' Hannah fixed him with the warning glare Rhoda would have given, had she been in the kitchen to see the state of her son.

He grumbled, but fastened the coat. Sam got the packed lunch Rhoda had prepared before going to get his father out of bed, and put it in David's bag for him. Then he ushered him, still grumbling, out of the door.

*   *   *

By late morning Hannah had begun to wonder what was keeping Sam. The visit to the corn store should not have added more than half an hour on to the journey and he should have been back long before now. She had just finished cleaning out Delilah's stall, when she heard the engine coming up the lane.

Hooking the pitchfork on to the wall, she went outside to meet him. They would be hard pressed to get the sheep down before the light began to fade, she thought irritably. She ignored the little voice that told her she had been more concerned for him, than for any sheep.

When the vehicle came through the gate, she was standing in the yard, waiting. But it was not the muddy old Land Rover. Her mouth dropped open. It was a green Jaguar. For a moment she thought it was George Bunting's. It was the same colour, the same design. Then she saw the driver – Jed!

She gave a gasp: disbelief, despair, and more than a touch of amazement. It was almost a year since Jed's last visit and she had foolishly allowed herself to believe he had found pastures greener and they were free from his interference. And to turn up in a replica of his father's car – the very one blown up by *his* stupidity! His father was going to go berserk.

He swept the car so closely past her that she had the feeling she was going to lose the ends of her toes. But she stood her ground, refusing to move and be intimidated by him. As he climbed out he gave a lopsided leer.

Hannah kept all her emotions safely hidden behind a bland mask. As usual, he looked impeccable in his suit – if you found a tailor's dummy attractive. It was charcoal grey and, for him, rather classy and a far cry from the silver-grey Italian jobs he usually went for. He had got rid of the silly quiff, as well. His hair was slicked back in a shiny cap that put her in mind of the man who had tried to kidnap her. And the car! He must be going up in the world, she thought sarcastically.

'Still in charge of the mucking out, I see,' he said, flicking a disdainful glance over her mucky jeans and dusty appearance. Then he flicked at an imaginary speck on his jacket sleeve, making it plain it was deserving of more attention than she was.

Ignoring the jibe, she jerked her head towards the car. 'Been on a winning streak?' She pinned him with a meaningful gaze, making it plain she did not think he was capable of earning such money by working for it.

The silly leer returned. 'There you are spiking at me. And I'm doing you a good turn.'

She did not ask what good turn he thought he was doing her. She knew him well enough to know that if he was doing anything, it was for himself . . . and only himself.

The leer increased. He made a sweeping gesture towards the car. 'I've brought your dear old aunt to see you,' he announced, in the infuriating manner of someone who knows he is having the final, and most powerful punch.

Hannah forgot all about not allowing her emotions to show. Her gaze pivoted to the car. She had been too bound up with Jed's unexpected appearance to look for passengers. But, sure enough, sitting in the back seat like lady bountiful, was Renee.

'Oh no!' It was out before she could stop herself. Jed's eyes lit up with malicious glee. She was reacting exactly how he expected her to, she realized, and gave herself a very sharp mental kick. Letting him see her squirm was only adding to his pleasure. 'He'll kill you,' she stated baldly, hiding her own displeasure in that of his father's. He was going to be furious. Not only bringing the car to rub his nose in, he had brought Renee with it. She was too sure that Jed had committed the two most deadly sins that she did not stop to wonder why Renee, whom she had not seen since the day of her father's funeral, should suddenly want to visit the Tor.

'Hello, luv!' Now that she had been seen, Renee got out of the car. Her insincere smile creased her eyes into tiny points surrounded by wrinkles that were greatly accentuated with smeared turquoise eye-shadow.

Her scarlet-painted lips made a garish slash across her heavily-powdered face, which was so pale it could have been dipped in the flour barrel. Gone were the vivid cheeks smeared with rouge. Hannah was not sure which she preferred: the Red Indian war paint of previous years; or the ghostly spectre now before her. Renee had turned into an old woman and Hannah was put in mind of a dried prune.

She took a deep breath. 'Hello,' she replied shortly. She glanced at Jed, at the smirk covering his face. He was up to something. She turned back to her aunt. 'I did not expect to see you again.' She had no wish to see her aunt and she found no reason to conceal her true feelings.

'Oh luvvy!' Renee rushed forward and wrapped her in a bear hug. Hannah was not sure if she was going to be suffocated by getting her lungs crushed, or gassed by the obnoxious cloud of cheap scent. 'You and your sharp tongue.' Renee stood back and waggled her finger in front of her nose. Hannah was too busy breathing fresh air again to knock the impertinent finger away. 'She always did have a bark worse than her bite.' Renee turned her gargoyle smile on Jed. 'She got it off her mother,' she added knowledgeably.

Hannah stared from one to the other of their unwanted guests. She could smell a rat and, the longer this went on, the stronger the smell became. 'Why are you here?' she demanded. Under normal circumstances Jed would not have gone out of his way to bring Renee. He could never stand having to chauffeur her about when his father had ordered him to in the past.

'Jed's been staying with me for a few weeks.' Renee flashed him another sickeningly benevolent smile.

'Staying with *you*!' Hannah could not conceal her astonishment. But Jed staying with Renee! He had to be broke. She could not think of any reason, other than seeking charity, for Jed to abide living in the same house as her aunt.

'He's courting our Silvie,' Renee put in, cocking her nose in the air and hardening her beady eyes on Hannah's disbelieving stare. In the next moment all censure had gone from her expression and she glanced yet another benevolent smile at Jed. 'I think an engagement could be in the offing.'

Hannah wanted to laugh. She did smile, could not help herself. The vibrations at the corners of Jed's mouth told her clearly that his teeth were tightly gritted beneath his responding smile. Whatever reasons he had for being at Renee's and making up to Silvie, they certainly were not with a lifelong commitment in mind. She glanced at the car and his expensive suit. He did not appear to be down to his last shilling. Perhaps he was in trouble again and lying low? The thought deepened her smile. If that was the case the last person he should have been with was someone with a mouth the size of Renee's.

'Oh yes,' Renee persisted, proving Hannah's last thought not unjust. 'Our Silvie thinks the world of him. Make a lovely couple they do. Don't you?' Jed was favoured with another sickeningly sweet smile and Hannah tried to imagine the arrogantly cocky Jed walking alongside her dull, miserable cousin. Silvie was everything her mother was not, which Hannah could well understand. Having to live with her loud, brash mother was enough to send anyone running for cover.

'You'd better come in then,' Hannah suddenly said. She had no desire to prolong the conversation and be given all the intimate details of Silvie's and Jed's relationship. And the sooner they were in, the sooner they would be gone – and the sooner she would know what the visit was all about.

The finding out came far quicker than expected.

'We've got guests,' she announced drily, as she entered the kitchen and began to kick off her wellington boots. George Bunting was sitting at the table going through a pile of bills. Rhoda was peeling potatoes at the sink. They both looked round.

'Bloody hell!' George Bunting said with feeling, as his eyes settled on the tall man following Hannah. 'Look what the dogs have dragged in!'

Hannah breathed a sigh of relief. He had not seen Jed's arrival – and the car he had come in. If he had he would have been waiting, grabbing him by the throat the moment he set foot through the door.

It was then that Renee, who had been lingering strangely behind Jed, pushed him aside and stepped forward, making a very grand entrance. Hannah gave an inward groan and watched for George Bunting's reaction. But he was not the one to receive Renee's attention.

Renee's vicious little eyes went straight to the woman at the sink. A mean smile spread slowly over her scarlet lips. 'Hello, Rhoda,' she said, as Rhoda's hand went to her throat and all the colour drained from her face.

Hannah rushed to Rhoda's side. She did not know what all this was about, but it was clear Rhoda needed some moral support. 'You know each other?' She directed the question at Rhoda, but it was Renee who replied.

'Oh yes, we know each other.' Her spiteful voice made Hannah want to go and slap her. It was only knowing that Rhoda was in need of close support that stopped her moving. 'Rhoda lived across the road from me.' Renee persisted. 'Gave us quite a scare, she did. We all thought he'd done you in.'

Rhoda began to tremble violently and Hannah pulled her into her arms.

'Who?' George Bunting suddenly demanded. He thrust the wheelchair forward, bringing it right up in front of Renee and glowered at her with a ferocity that would have melted ice – but had little effect on her thick skin.

Oh no! Hannah thought. Rhoda had lied. She was not a widow. She was married – and he did not know. She had not thought anything could be worse than Jed turning up in a Jaguar, with Renee. She had been wrong.

As if reading her mind, Renee looked him straight in the eyes, and said, 'Why . . . Rhoda's husband, of course.' Hannah never took her eyes off George Bunting's face. But there was nothing, not even the slightest twitch of an eyebrow that gave anything away.

'He was always belting her around. Wasn't he, Rhoda?' Renee glanced at Rhoda, but received no reply from the bloodless lips. 'And the lad.'

Hannah's heart turned inside her chest. Sam had been right. Rhoda and David had been the victims of some brute. And they thought they had escaped him. Now these two were bringing it all back. Today's little trip had been to check the facts – before Renee opened her big mouth to Rhoda's husband.

'He reckoned he'd been looking all over for you.' Renee gave a harsh laugh and shook her head. 'But we never believed him: me, Vera Bennett, Mavis Jackson. We all thought he'd done for you. They'll be pleased to know you're safe and well.' Her face brightened on the last, but there was no sincerity in her smile. 'I couldn't believe it when Jed told me George had got himself a new housekeeper *and told me your name*! I thought it couldn't be right. But I was wrong. Vera and Mavis will be really chuffed.'

Hannah could not control herself a moment longer. Her anger increased because the woman standing in the middle of the floor was her relation, her own flesh and blood. She pushed Rhoda up against the support of the sink, then rounded on her aunt. 'There's no need to tell anybody anything!' she blazed, her fists clenching, as she fought the desire to take hold of Renee and shake her till her teeth rattled. But George Bunting cut her short.

He lifted his hand, holding her back. 'It doesn't matter who she tells,' he said, his voice deceptively quiet. But his gaze was rock hard, as it swung from Renee to his son, and his voice hardened with it, as he added, 'You've had your fun. Now get out of here. And take her with you.' He flapped his hand at Renee as if he was swiping at a fly. He looked up into her suddenly unsmiling face, his lips curling with all the disgust he felt for her. 'You're a bitter, spiteful old woman. You can't bear to see anybody else happy. Well, you can go and tell Vera Bennett, Mavis Jackson, *or anybody else you choose*!' He laid emphasis on the last and they all knew he was meaning she could go and tell Rhoda's husband. '*Because, whatever happens, we shall be ready and waiting. And you can tell him that, as well!*'

For once in her life, Renee was struck dumb. Leaving her that way, he spun the wheelchair round and closed in on Jed, who was still managing to hold on to his cockily sneering smirk. 'And you have stepped into this house for the last time!' He lifted a warning finger at his son and the smile finally vanished. It was replaced by an arrogant sneer that reminded Hannah very much of the man in the wheelchair, a few years back. 'If I ever see you inside that yard again, I'll take the shotgun to you.'

Rhoda whimpered and Hannah's mouth dropped open. She could not believe she was actually hearing Jed get his final comeuppance.

Jed gave an arrogant toss of the head, accompanied by a sarcastic bark. 'You'd never do it. I'm the only Bunting left who has all his faculties.'

Hannah drew a noisy breath. He was referring to Sam, but the statement had also encompassed his father. But instead of the expected explosion, George Bunting gave a mightily amused laugh.

He looked Jed straight in the eyes, a sparkle of victory lighting his own. 'You might think you're the only Bunting that is perfect, but I know differently.' He turned to Rhoda, changed his mind and looked to Hannah. 'Get Jenny,' he said simply. Then he turned back to his son. 'I told you you would never get your hands on this place,' he continued, as Hannah went out into the hall and had to disturb the peacefully sleeping baby. Lifting her from the pram she wrapped her in the shawl and hoped she was not going to begin protesting loudly about being woken up.

'You said it would go to my children,' Jed reminded him insolently.

His father smiled. 'And so it shall,' he replied confidently. 'Let me introduce you.' He held his hand out towards the child in Hannah's arms. 'Jenny Bunting. My granddaughter. *Your* daughter!'

Jed laughed. Fell silent. Then laughed again.

'It's true.' His father beckoned Hannah. She hesitated, unsure if he had ever held Jenny before – or any other baby. But he beckoned her again and she finally handed the child over.

He held the baby up to Jed. 'Don't you recognize your own daughter? Yours and Glenda Riley's.'

'She was lying. I never touched her.'

'*Oh yes you did!*' George Bunting bellowed, startling Jenny who began to cry. Hannah rushed forward to take her back but he pushed her away. 'He hasn't seen everything yet,' he insisted, rested the wailing baby on his knee and began to unwrap the shawl. When her left hand was free, he held it out. 'See . . .' he said calmly, '. . . she has the Bunting hand.'

Jed backed away, horror and fear encompassing his face and draining all the blood from it. It could have been a vampire his father was presenting to him, Hannah thought. His lip curled with disgust and his head began to shake, slowly at first, then with increasing speed. 'That isn't mine! It's his! It's got to be!'

His father shook his head, enjoying his son's discomfort. 'Jenny is your daughter! You have provided me with a grandchild so I don't need you any more.' He waved a hand through the air. 'She will get her fair share of all this. If she remains the only grandchild she will get it all – after Sam. If Sam has any children

371

then they will share it between them. But this is the only child of yours that will get anything. I will not recognize any other children you are responsible for,' he added, the steely determination of his gaze settling meaningfully on his son's colourless face.

Sam being given the farm! Being looked on as worthy to take it over – and to have an heir of his own. Hannah wondered if she should pinch herself to make sure she was awake. But then the sight of Renee made her aware this was no dream. Beneath all the powder her aunt's face had gone as grey as Jed's and Hannah realized George Bunting had unknowingly put an end to Renee's dreams. It was all clear now, at least Renee's part. She had failed to become mistress of this house herself so was now trying to get her daughter into the position. If the situation had not been so serious for Rhoda, Hannah would have laughed out loud.

'Sam!' Jed gasped, the scorn he held for his brother for the moment overshadowing his repugnance for the child his father was foisting on him.

'Yes,' his father returned, with a confidence that stunned Hannah. 'I have no intention of leaving this place to someone who cares so little for it they almost get it burnt down. You might have thought getting my car blown up was hitting me where it hurt, but you were wrong, it was you who got hurt. Until then I had had the foolish notion that you would one day grow up.' He gave a mirthless laugh. 'How wrong could I be? But at least *I* finally grew up and began to see clearly what was right before my eyes. This place needs a farmer so I am leaving it to a farmer – the only farmer left in this family! The only son left in this family,' he added pointedly. 'I wash my hands of you and you would do me a very great favour if I never had to see you again. Sam will get all of this. And if you can produce children, why can't he?'

Oh why wasn't he here! He should have been hearing

all this. Hannah despaired at whatever fate had kept him away so long.

Jed did laugh then. 'And who would have him? Let alone have his children?'

'I would!' The words were out before she knew what she was doing. But even had she been aware of her actions, she would have done the same. 'I would have Sam and his children – and be *proud* to do so!' Thrusting her chin out she met his vicious glare.

For several moments they stood like opponents frozen in the moment before encounter. Then suddenly he thrust out his arm, jabbing his finger at the baby on his father's knee. 'That isn't mine. I couldn't produce anything like that. It's his – and hers!' The finger came round to point at Hannah's nose. 'You can't fool me. You'll not make me believe I've got that inside me. Look . . .' he held his hands out for all to see, '. . . they're perfect. There's nothing wrong with me.'

George Bunting laughed. 'Oh, Jenny is yours all right. You say what you like, but you can't hide from this, can't run away from it. Wherever you go you take it with you.'

'No!' The word tore from Jed like the wail of a demented animal.

Hannah's lip curled in disgust at the pathetic sight he made. The big man finally brought down to size.

'I haven't got it! I haven't got it.' He turned to his father, a pleading in his eyes that further sickened Hannah. 'I'm your son.' Taking no notice of the baby on his knee, he grabbed his father's arms and began to shake them. 'I'm your son!' he insisted. 'I'm like you! *Not her!*' Repugnance curled his lip as he referred to his mother and he began to shake his father harder. The constant battering made Jenny's wailing increase and, forgetting her own problems, Rhoda rushed forward and grabbed the baby to safety.

'So is Sam,' George Bunting said meaningfully, as, with a calmness that stunned Hannah, he took hold of Jed's arms and pushed him away.

There was silence. Jed and his father stared angrily at each other and no-one dared move. Even Jenny, content now she had found Rhoda, fell silent.

It was Renee who broke the spell. 'Well, George, you've got yourself quite a little family here,' she said nastily. 'You must think you're very clever.' Going to Jed she tapped him on the shoulder and nodded at the door, telling him it was time to go.

Hannah wasn't sure if she was trying to get him away for his own good, before he got thumped. Or if she was ashamed of associating with him now she had seen his true colours, and was trying to save her own face. Knowing Renee she guessed it was the latter.

George Bunting shook his head. 'Oh no, Renee, I'm not clever. In fact I've been a right idiot. But it's a wise man who can admit when he's been wrong, and put it right.' He looked up into Jed's bloodless face. 'So, as I said before, you can get out of here and don't bother coming back. And take her with you,' he repeated pointedly, jerking his head at Renee.

'Come on, Jed. I'll not stay where I'm not wanted.' Her mouth contracted into a red blob that was barely bigger than her vicious little eyes. Then she grabbed Jed's arm and dragged him out.

'Send us an invitation to the wedding,' Hannah called, as they reached the door.

Renee stopped short. She did not speak, but her expression should have been enough to turn her niece to stone. Jed's stormy gaze was equally withering, but he had not lost his voice. 'There won't be any wedding,' he spat through clenched lips. Then he turned to the wheelchair. 'Just because you fathered a monster you needn't think you're pinning one on me.'

His father was saved from having to reply. Renee gave

Jed's arm a sharp tug. 'What do you mean no wedding?' she hissed.

'There was never any chance of me marrying that stupid bitch,' he ground, and shook his arm free of Renee's grasp and hurried out of the door. Renee chased after him, hissing and spitting like an enraged viper.

Like father like son, Hannah thought, and hoped the father would not see the car going out of the yard; or a few choice names would be coming from his lips, as well. Then she wondered why she was worrying about something so unimportant and turned quickly to Rhoda, whose problems were far greater than any injured pride George Bunting might experience at seeing his son driving off in a car like the one he had himself once owned. 'Oh Rhoda!' she gasped, and rushed across the kitchen and placed an arm around her shoulders. 'Why didn't you tell us?' As she spoke she wished the question back. George Bunting was the reason, she told herself, glancing anxiously at him and waiting for some unfavourable reaction.

But she was in for a surprise. As if reading her mind, he said, 'I already knew.'

'Oh . . . I . . .' She did not know what to say, so fell silent. Then got another surprise.

'Why do you think we've never got married?' he asked.

She gave a shrug, again unable to find a reply.

'You know what's been going on, so don't look so shocked.'

'I'm . . . I'm not shocked.' She felt colour rushing to her cheeks. 'Oh,' she gave a gasp of frustration, mostly aimed at her own inability to conceal her embarrassment. 'You've never talked about it before. I thought I wasn't supposed to know.'

'Only because of David.' He reached up and took hold of Rhoda's free hand. 'If she had tried to get a divorce her husband would have learned where she was. And she doesn't want David to have to see him ever again.' His voice was so caring and he looked on Rhoda so fondly. Hannah had never seen him this way before and a lump came to her throat. It was like looking at a different person. He was human, after all, she thought, then had the sudden recollection of a man walking up a tree trunk propped unsteadily against a fallen cottage.

Fortunately Rhoda took Hannah's mind away from her unexpected thoughts. 'Oh George,' she suddenly gasped, and dropped to her knees and buried her face in his lap. 'Will he come here?' she asked, and her shoulders began to shake with sobs.

'If he does, he won't get near you,' he promised, and lifted his hand and began stroking her hair.

Suddenly feeling like an intruder, Hannah reached down and took Jenny from Rhoda's arm. Then she carried the baby outside, leaving them alone together.

The Land Rover was standing over by the stables, but Sam was nowhere in sight. She was surprised to find he had returned, yet not come into the house. She went across to the stables but he was not there. Neither was he in the parlour or any of the sheds.

She was beginning to get worried when she spotted Peg, sniffing round at the top of the Tor's rocky western face. She had to screw her eyes up before she found Sam. He was sitting looking out over the precipitous edge, his blue jeans and green jacket blending into the coarse grass and rocky outcrops that surrounded him.

What was he doing up there? she asked herself. She looked down at Jenny, almost asleep again, and wondered what she should do? She didn't really want to take the baby up to the top of the windy Tor in the damp air. But she wanted to know what Sam was doing. Besides, she didn't want to go back inside the house just yet: Rhoda needed a respite to get over the nasty shock of having Renee and her spitefulness foisted on her.

The last did it. Hurrying to the stables, she took one of the old Barbour jackets down from the wall. There was quite a selection. For some reason no-one had ever found out, George Bunting had had an aversion to throwing them away, and even though he never went outside now to see if they were still there or not, neither Sam nor Hannah seemed to want to make the decision to chuck them out. The jackets were all too large for her, but were just right for today's needs. Lying Jenny on a bed of straw, she pulled the coat on and fastened the bottom buttons. Then she fitted Jenny inside the coat with her, fastened all but the very top button, and set off up the Tor. She felt as if she was pregnant, her hands clasped together beneath this great bulge in front of her.

Sam was staring out into the void of space before him. His eyes glued to some unseen point that she could not define. He was not seeing the rolling hills, the grey clouds, or the sparrows and starlings that flitted through the air. His vision was lost to something far deeper than the mere eye could see.

'Sam!' She spoke suddenly, bringing his head snapping round to see her approaching. 'What are you doing? The grass is damp.' It was a stupid statement. He was sitting down and must be able to feel it soaking through his jeans.

He turned to look at her but did not speak.

'I didn't know where you'd gone.'

'I had a puncture,' he said simply, excusing his earlier absence rather than his present trip up the Tor.

The wind gusted and flicked her pony-tail over her shoulder. She tossed it back. 'We've had visitors,' she said, hoping the news might drag some words out of him.

'I know,' he replied flatly.

'You saw them?' Her surprise was obvious. If he had seen them, she could not understand why he had not come to find out what they wanted.

He gave a nod. 'And heard.' He turned back to stare over the hillside. 'I was listening outside the back door for most of it.'

377

She was still bewildered. 'Then you heard your father tell Jed not to come back.'

He gave another nod and her confusion increased.

'Sam, what's wrong? If you heard that, then you know the farm is yours. It's what you wanted.'

'It isn't the farm I'm interested in.' He looked up at her and the great weight of his sadness reached out to her and pressed down on her shoulders. He jerked his head back towards the farm. 'He isn't the only one who's been a right idiot.' He gave an ironic snort. 'Like father like son!' he said bitterly.

'Well, your father said he had learned from his mistakes.' She eyed him cautiously, not daring to raise her hopes too high. 'So – have you done the same?'

For a long moment he stared down at the patch of grass growing up between his feet. 'Maybe it's too late for me.' He looked round sharply. 'Is it too late, Hannah? I heard what you said, as well. But I wasn't sure if you were just saying that to put Jed's nose out of joint. Besides, I don't deserve it. I know what I've done. I know what I've put you through. But you're still here and that must mean something.' His sadness shadowed his eyes as he looked up into hers. 'I wouldn't ask you to have my children,' he added uncertainly. He held out his hand, then drew it back as if expecting it to be rejected.

She smiled and shook her head. Then she sat down in the damp grass by his side and took hold of his hand, cradling it in both of her own. It happened to be his left hand, that being the one closest to her, but she had not noticed: fingers or claw they were still Sam; warm and alive and what she wanted. Lifting it up she pressed her lips into the palm. 'I meant what I said. I would be proud to have you and your children.' Her eyes misted and she was sure she saw the same in his.

'I won't hold you to the last. I still don't want children – and I never will.' His mouth drooped and he gave a sigh. 'I'm asking a lot of you, Hannah.'

But she quickly shook her head. 'Just hold me to you.' She dropped her head on to his shoulder, emotion clogging her throat. His arm was around her shoulders and he was holding her, before she could say, 'And will you stop going on about children. I've never said I wanted any.' If she had been like Rhoda it might have been different. But she was not a natural earth-mother type. If Sam had never brought the subject of babies up, it would never have crossed her mind.

'I love you, Hannah Critchlow.' Cupping her head, he pushed her windblown hair away from her face and spoke the words she had longed to hear. Then he kissed her, meeting her lips with a need increased by their long separation.

Hannah placed an arm around his neck and she clung to him, as if the wind might lift him up and carry him away if she let him go.

He pulled her closer, twisting her body so that it was facing him squarely. But there was something in his way and, having her cosy cocoon disturbed, Jenny began to grizzle.

'What . . . ?' He pulled at the neck of the overlarge coat and peered inside. 'What's she doing there?' He looked amazed, but was laughing. 'I wondered why you'd got that old thing on.'

Hannah also laughed. 'It's a long story. When did you leave the back door?' She guessed he had gone before Jed and Renee so had missed the bit about his father and Rhoda.

He confirmed he had gone into the stables when he heard Jed about to leave. 'I knew if I stayed there I wouldn't be able to stop myself belting him.'

She grimaced. 'Like father, like son.' She mimicked his earlier words. 'And I thought you were the gentle one!'

'That's why I got out of Jed's way. I wasn't thinking of his welfare. I was thinking of my own – and your reaction.' He looked sheepish. 'I knew I had to bow down and admit my mistakes, but I didn't know if you'd accept it. I thought you might have lost all patience with me by now. So I thought it best not to upset you by getting into a fight before I told you.'

'Oh Sam!' She shook her head in despair, then peeped inside her coat at Jenny. 'I'm glad you're a girl,' she said with feeling, and looked up into Sam's puzzled gaze with a smile. 'Or is it likely that female Buntings will also inherit the liking for using their fists before their tongues?'

'I hope not. But it is only against each other,' he said, in uncertain defence of the family trait. 'At least with me it is. I'd never set about anybody else, unless it was self-defence. I imagine Jed is a different matter,' he added, his voice becoming grim.

She wasn't so sure she agreed with the last. Underneath all the bravado Jed was a coward. But she did not want to talk about Jed. 'Well, he's gone now, so we should see an end to all the arguing and fighting, shouldn't we? *You* wouldn't hit a man in a wheelchair. Besides, I think you'll find your father is a reformed character now.'

He lifted his eyebrows questioningly.

'Your eavesdropping ended too soon. You missed the bit about your father and Rhoda.'

'Have they finally come clean?' It was said with an air of amusement mixed with a certain amount of relief.

It was a relief Hannah shared and it came out in a heartfelt sigh. 'Rhoda is frightened her husband is going to turn up now – thanks to Renee,' she emphasized pointedly. 'Anyway, it all came out.'

'I'm glad,' he confirmed, and glanced at his watch. 'We'd better be getting back before they send a search party out.' He helped her to her feet.

'What about the sheep?' she asked, hitching Jenny higher inside the coat and supporting her on one arm.

'We'll leave it until tomorrow.' He took hold of her hand and they began to walk back along the windy Tor. They had not gone far when he began to laugh. 'You know . . .' he said, smiling down into her eyes with a possessiveness she had longed to see, yet feared she never would, '. . . I'll bet it's the first time our Jed's ever done anything useful in his life.' They fell against each other and laughed as they walked along. Even Jenny joined in, with a series of coos and sighs and chortles coming from beneath Hannah's massive coat.

Chapter Twenty-Four

With a pale sun trying desperately to break through the November morning mist, Hannah and Sam were married. It was to have been a simple affair, but Rhoda had insisted on making Hannah a proper wedding dress. So the simple white shift Hannah had bought herself was discarded and she walked down the aisle looking like a fairy princess in lace and satin. She had drawn the line at a full, flowing veil. So Rhoda made strings of satin daisies and twined them down the length of her hair, which hung over her shoulders and down her back like a rich, red cloak.

The little church was packed to overflowing. Although Hannah was not sure if all the congregation had come to bless her union with Sam, or if they had turned out to get their first glimpse of George Bunting in his wheelchair. Rhoda was also causing some interest. They knew her only as the new woman who was living up there, and that only because she had a son who came down to the school. Not being able to drive she always left the shopping to Sam or Hannah and, apart from two visits to the school, had always been happy to stay at the Tor. Most of the inhabitants of Aldale had never set eyes on her before today and they did not know the cream and brown check-suit, worn with slim-heeled shoes and brown hair pulled back into a very elegant French pleat, were only for the occasion. She did not look like anyone's housekeeper and there was much eyebrow lifting and pursing of lips – especially as she had Jenny in her arms.

George Bunting gave Hannah away. At first she had not been sure about agreeing to that. She had thought to walk down the aisle alone, leaving her father's space empty.

But after all the months of self-inflicted imprisonment, he had surprised everybody by insisting he was going to be there at the church. Then, yesterday, he had surprised them even more by getting Sam to take him to his solicitors in Derby: so he could change his will.

After that Hannah had not had the heart to refuse. So, telling herself her father would have understood her reasons, she laid her hand in George Bunting's and listened to the gentle glide of the wheelchair as he escorted her down the aisle of the little village church.

Sam was waiting for her with a look in his eyes that told her everything she wanted to know, and made everything else of very little importance. He looked so smart and handsome in his dark grey suit, with a burgundy red silk tie borrowed from his father. He was so used to wearing tee shirts and sweaters all the time that, although he remembered to get a new shirt along with the suit, he had forgotten he also needed a tie.

When she reached his side he held out his left hand to her, without hesitation or concern. She took it willingly, folding her fingers possessively around the two thickened digits, her love smiling right out of her eyes and into his. He shook his head. 'I don't deserve you,' he whispered.

'Oh yes you do!' she returned emphatically, and turned to the front to allow the rosy-faced vicar to get on with the job of making them husband and wife.

No reception had been planned. Hannah had said there was no-one to invite. But she was proved wrong. When George Bunting began inviting everyone to The Lamb for a celebratory drink, everyone accepted. Alf Marshall could not pull the pints quick enough and as fast as his wife made a plate of sandwiches, somebody ate them. And nobody thought of leaving until well into the afternoon.

'Had a nice day?' They were back at the Tor, in the grand sitting-room, alone for the first time. Sam coiled his arms around Hannah's neck and gazed deep into her eyes with the wonder that had claimed him from the first moment he set eyes on her that morning. In muddy jeans and wellingtons he found her beautiful. But in that dress, so soft and feminine, he found her enchanting. It was as if she had become some magical creature of his dreams and he feared he might wake-up at any moment and find her gone. Throughout the reception he had found himself touching her arm, her hand, her shoulder, just to prove she was real.

'It's been a beautiful day,' she confirmed, shaking her head in wonder. The ceremony and the reception had far outreached any dreams she might have had. 'I just wish mum and dad could have been there,' she said. But if her dad had still been alive he would not have let her get near a Bunting. It was a stunning thought. She smiled tightly. 'Why do horrible things have to happen to make nice things happen?'

'What?' he eyed her oddly.

'Oh, nothing.' She smiled into his eyes with a fondness that tugged at his chest. 'I'm glad your dad came,' she said sincerely.

'Yes.' He fingered the diamond and ruby pendant hanging round her neck on a twisted gold chain. Then he pulled the gold hunter pocket-watch from his jacket pocket and stared at it in silence.

Hannah's smile softened. She laid her hand on his wrist but did not speak, knowing he needed to savour the thoughts going through his head. Along with the new will, the pendant and the watch were wedding presents from his father, given to them that very morning only minutes before leaving for the church. They were both very beautiful and very valuable. But it was not their worth that was so precious to Sam. They were family heirlooms, passed down through several generations. It was not just a pocket-watch his father had given to him. It was the acceptance of one Bunting of another. Today Sam had been given his full rights and had been taken into the family that he had been clinging frantically to the edge of for all his earlier life.

When he finally looked up she saw the glisten of tears in his eyes. 'Mr Bunting, I love you!' she said with intense feeling, and wrapped her arms around his neck and planted a kiss at the corner of his mouth. 'And when we've got those cows milked I'll show you just how much,' she whispered suggestively in his ear.

He threw back his head and laughed, and his moment of emotion was thrust aside. 'They always did warn me about flighty milkmaids,' he teased, and laid his forehead against hers and looked deep into her eyes. 'But *you're* not doing any milking today.'

'You're not doing it on your own,' she protested. Whatever the occasion the animals still needed attending to. But it was his wedding day, as well. Besides, she wanted him back as quickly as possible.

'David will help me.' His voice brooked no refusal and he held her away and for several seconds looked her up and down.

'What's the matter?' She frowned at him, puzzled.

'I just want to look at you one last time in that dress. You're the most beautiful thing I've ever seen – do you know that? Rhoda did you proud. We owe her.'

The pleasure in his voice warmed her deep inside and she smiled fondly, just as the door opened and David, as if he had heard his name mentioned, poked his head round. 'Can I come in?'

Hannah had to laugh at the look of uncertainty on his young face. It was obvious his mother had told him to leave them alone, but inquisitiveness had got the better of him. 'Of course you can,' she said, and a smile blossomed on his lips and twinkled from the big brown eyes.

Sam returned her knowing smile and planted a light kiss on the end of her nose. 'Don't go anywhere,' he said, a teasing note of warning in his voice. He turned to David. 'Come on, we've got to get into our scruffs.

You've got to help me milk the cows.' Grabbing hold of the not unwilling youngster, he tossed him over his shoulder. David giggled and shrieked with pleasure, as Sam carried him off. When they reached the door, Sam stopped and turned around. 'I won't be long,' he said meaningfully. Then he hurried from the room with a speed that put a smile on her face.

*　　*　　*

As Hannah slipped out of her wedding dress, she gazed around the large bedroom that had once belonged to George Bunting and his wife. It now belonged to herself and Sam. Hanging up the dress, she put it carefully away in the back of the wardrobe that had once stored all Sam's mother's old clothes. She gave a sigh, remembering the first day she had come to that house, how she had thought her world had come to an end. It was only three years, yet so much had changed.

It was strange how even the most dubious things could turn out to be exactly what you needed, she thought, forcing her mind to leave the sadness of losing her father and her home, and come forward to the time she had met Rhoda at the bus station. That day she had thought she was making the biggest mistake of her life – but it had turned out to be one of her best decisions.

It was a long time since she had worn a skirt. The jeans necessary for working on the farm had become her normal, everyday attire, but today she wanted to look nice for Sam: special and feminine, like the woman she felt herself to be inside. So she took a deep russet-red skirt from the wardrobe and put it on. It was straight and fitted snuggly to her hips and, teamed with a cream silky blouse, made her look and feel very much a woman.

Knowing Sam liked to see her hair hanging loose down her back, she removed the daisies and brushed it out and arranged it round her shoulders. Then she took

386

the packet of contraceptive pills out of the dressing-table drawer. She had just popped a pill into her mouth when she almost spat it out again in shock as she heard the first scream.

Gulping the pill down she froze. The sound of splintering glass was followed by a second scream. Flinging the brush down on the dressing table, she raced for the door. The tight skirt restricted her movement and she pulled it up to her thighs, displaying the tops of her stockings held up by lacy-white suspenders, and flew down the stairs.

She reached the bottom of the stairs as a third scream pierced the air, coming from the kitchen. Giving the hem of her skirt a tug to get it back to a more respectable level, she lunged for the kitchen door. At the same time the office door flew open so violently that it smashed into the wall behind, then swung forward to crack the wheelchair as George Bunting came careering out, cursing his disability in a manner Hannah had not heard for some time.

Snatching at the kitchen door and yanking it open, Hannah came up short. Rhoda was pressed up against the wall between the sink and the corner of the room, a scruffy looking man advancing slowly towards her with a broken milk bottle poised in his hand.

Seeing Hannah at the door, Rhoda tried to make a run for it. Pushing the man's outstretched arm away, she ducked beneath it and attempted to get round him. She failed. Grabbing her arm he swung her violently back against the wall. Her body made contact with the wall with an agonizing thud. Rhoda screamed again. Hannah's hand flew to her mouth and caught the unconscious whimper leaving her lips.

'What the . . . ? Get out of the way!' In his eagerness to get to Rhoda's aid, George Bunting shoved Hannah so roughly aside she almost fell to her knees.

With a gasp she caught her balance on the dresser and wished that Sam would come back. But the parlour was too far away for him to have heard. She tried to recall how long he had been gone and if he might be on his way back. Then, telling herself George Bunting was going to need help, she shook herself back together and grabbed the largest saucepan standing on the shelf. She would have liked to have got a shotgun, but they were kept locked away in a case now that they were not used regularly and would have taken too long to get out.

Then the attacker made a very big mistake and Hannah's assistance was not needed. On seeing the wheelchair the man's surprise turned to a scoffing jeer, which delayed his reactions. In an instant George Bunting had hold of his arm, bringing it crashing down across the wheelchair with such force that the broken bottle dropped from his grasp. As it crashed to the floor and splintered into tiny fragments, the man made to grab George Bunting. His free hand reached out, closing round George Bunting's throat. A great fist came up, crashing squarely into his face. The intruder's head snapped back, his eyes bulging in surprise and his hand lost its grip on his opponent's throat. The next moment George Bunting had grabbed the lapels of the man's scruffy jacket and swung him across the floor, sending him crashing into the table. The cutlery and crockery Rhoda had laid ready for tea, all went crashing to the floor, so did three chairs. The man gave a gasp as the breath was knocked out of his lungs and Rhoda whimpered.

He was up in seconds. Baring his teeth like an enraged animal, he lunged once more for George Bunting's neck. Lifting the saucepan high above her head, Hannah moved in, but not fast enough. Before she could strike, George Bunting had grabbed the man's outstretched hands. Rearing the wheelchair on its back legs he spun around, taking the man with him and sending him flying through the air. The man's back hit the wall with a dull thud, a moment before his head followed, cracking noisily against the plaster before slumping forward to rest unsteadily on his chest.

It took several seconds for George Bunting to bring the revolving wheelchair to a standstill. Hannah still had the saucepan poised above her head. She lowered it slowly, staring frozenly at the motionless figure lying in a heap where it had slipped to the floor, leaving a vivid trail of blood smeared down the cream paintwork of the wall behind.

Suddenly coming back to life, she gave a gasp and the saucepan dropped and clattered noisily to the floor. Then she raced across the room and threw herself on to her knees by the man's side. She grabbed his lifeless-looking wrist but her fingers were trembling too much to find a pulse. Dropping his hand, she placed her flat palm on his chest and gave a great sigh of relief. His chest was moving, rising and falling as he continued to breathe. 'He's all right,' she said, looking from the silently stunned George Bunting, to Rhoda, still pressed tightly against the wall.

'Are you sure?' George Bunting asked, carefully.

Hannah looked at the floppy head and the light brown and grey hair matted with blood. She lifted his chin and looked into his face but there was no response. When she let it go it returned drunkenly to his chest. He was out cold. 'Well, he's alive,' she said, feeling his chest once more, just to make sure. 'I wonder who he is?'

As Hannah asked the question, she suddenly knew the answer. Rhoda gave a sob and threw herself at George Bunting. 'What are we going to do?' she begged, clinging to him as if he was her very life.

'Nothing,' he reassured gently, and Hannah turned back to study the man, knowing it was Rhoda's husband she was looking at. 'He'll be all right. We'll get the doctor to take a look at him, then send him packing.'

Rhoda did not appear convinced. 'He'll come back.'

'Then we will send him packing again.' He stroked a consoling hand over her hair. The French pleat that had looked so smart at the wedding was coming undone and untidy bits stuck out here and there. But her frightened, dishevelled appearance did not diminish the fondness of his gaze.

Hannah felt very moved. She hoped Sam would still be looking at her in the same way when they were that old. The thought reminded her that it was her wedding day.

'Call the doctor.' She looked up, George Bunting's tone making it obvious it had not been the first time he had given the instruction.

Her head slowly nodding in reply, she stood up and went to the telephone, all the time wanting Sam to come back from the milking parlour.

As if in answer to her prayers, as she replaced the telephone receiver the back door opened.

Sam took one look round the kitchen and came up short. No-one spoke. As Hannah opened her mouth to explain, David saved her the trouble. Suddenly letting out a startled wail, he clawed his way up Sam's body and into his arms. There he hid his face in Sam's neck, and sobbed, 'Make him go away! Make him go away!'

Hannah's heart turned inside her chest. The man was unconscious and yet David was still terrified of him.

'It's all right, David. No-one is going to hurt you.' It was George Bunting who spoke.

Sam turned to his father. 'Is that . . . ?'

His father gave a nod. 'Yes . . . that is Tom Spencer.'

'What happened?' Sam's voice was filled with a disbelief that did not lessen as his father related the whole story. When he reached the end Sam silently handed David to his mother. Then he went to Hannah, pulling her into his arms and gazing deep into her eyes, his own eyes shadowed with sadness and regret. He opened his mouth to speak, then closed it again, not knowing what to say to make this, their wedding day, happy again.

She gave him a thin smile. 'Why today?' she asked.

He could only shake his head in despair.

The uninvited visitor began to moan and stir and Sam let Hannah go and went to him. Taking a clean handkerchief from his pocket, he held it to the back of the man's injured head. Hannah stood and watched her new husband. His actions were so gentle and she felt a great resentment to the injured man; to George Bunting for causing the injury; to Rhoda for being the reason for the man's visit. This was her wedding day, she thought bitterly. Sam should be touching *her*, no-one else. And certainly not someone who was in cahoots with Jed and her Aunt Renee. She wondered if that was the reason he had appeared today. If Jed and Renee had found out Sam was marrying her and sent him on purpose, to spoil the occasion. She wouldn't put it past them.

With a feeling of increasing disappointment, she went to the table, pulled up a chair and sank into it. Then she wrapped her arms tightly around herself, feeling in need of protection. She wondered how she could have woken up that morning believing nothing would ever go wrong again. Her own common sense should have told her that life at Bunting's Tor could never run smoothly for very long.

By the time the doctor arrived, Rhoda's husband was fully returned to the land of the living and protesting loudly that he had been set upon. Sam had long given up attempting to minister first aid. After being told in no uncertain terms to keep his hands to himself, he went over to Hannah and pulled a chair up by her side. Then they all sat watching the belligerent man who, despite his protests, seemed to have forgotten how to stand up and remained sitting propped against the wall. Hannah could only conclude he was doing it for effect. So that when the doctor walked in and saw him, he would also see all the blood behind him. Perhaps he thought if he stood up one of them would rush over with a scrubbing brush and clean up the evidence.

As Dr Hallam stitched the large gash on the back of the man's head, he peered suspiciously at George Bunting. 'What happened?' he asked.

'He's a burglar,' he replied bluntly. 'I caught him. Did you expect me to let him get away with it?'

The doctor shook his head in despair. He had seen too many injuries of this type on one or other of the Buntings not to be wise to how they came by them. He thought it had come to an end now that Jed had gone. But it appeared as though George Bunting had found himself another sparring partner.

'I'm no burglar.' Forgetting the doctor was at work, the man's head came up to glare at Rhoda. The needle jabbed into him and he gave a shriek.

'Hold still!' Dr Hallam ordered, grabbing the man's chin and putting it back into the position he wanted. 'If you don't you could find your hair is stitched on to the front of your face – instead of the back of your head.'

'That's my wife,' he stated irritably, refusing to be silent, but making sure he kept his head still.

'*Was* your wife!' George Bunting put in fiercely. 'She lives here now and no amount of bullying is going to get her to leave.'

The man gave a grunt.

Dr Hallam gave a nod of understanding, his expression changing to one that said he wished he had never got out of bed that morning.

Hannah gave a sigh and Sam's hand reached out to her. She forced a thin smile to her lips and received the same in response. She covered his hand with her other. She wanted to reach out and wrap her arms around him and tell him everything would be all right. The chance would come later, she told herself. When the doctor had gone, and Rhoda's husband had gone, hopefully they could be alone. She glanced at her watch. It was only seven o'clock. The evening was still in its infancy.

'Well, that's my son!' The man's hand shot out and jabbed towards David. The boy whimpered and clung more tightly to his mother. Dr Hallam turned and peered over the top of his glasses at the boy's reaction. 'You can't take him from me. I'll have him!' David whimpered louder and hid his head under Rhoda's arm. 'You just wait and see if I don't,' the man added nastily. 'I've got proof here that you attacked me.' He lifted his hand, making exaggerated pointing actions at the back of his head. 'The doctor here's seen it. He knows! And when they see what you did to me they'll not let him stay here.'

Hannah wanted to ask him if he knew his son's name. He had never used it, always referring to 'the boy', or 'him'. It did not seem very fatherly but then she knew he was not very fatherly. But other people didn't and she worried that Rhoda's unmarried relationship with George Bunting might go against her, if her husband did try to take the matter to the courts – she assumed that was who he meant by 'they'.

George Bunting didn't help ease her mind. He rose to the attack like a bull to a red rag. 'You'll have nothing from here,' he declared, fiercely. 'I had to defend myself against a burglar. No-one let you in here,' he spat, cutting off the protest he saw forming on the man's grim lips. 'Now, if you want to go making anything of that, then I'm quite willing. *You* broke into my house and there are two witnesses who saw you attacking Rhoda. *And me in a wheelchair!*' he stressed pointedly. 'I don't think there's much doubt about which side any judge and jury will come down on.'

Hannah wished she could feel the same confidence. Fortunately her worrying did not last long. Dr Hallam glanced a troubled look at David. Then he turned back to the wounded head and jabbed the needle in, rather too brutally, she thought, although Spencer did not complain. 'If you think you've got proof with me, you can think again. As far as I'm concerned you hit your head on a beam in the barn.' He prodded the needle in for the last time and the man's fists clenched but he did not cry out in pain. 'There, you're all done.' The doctor stood back and pushed the errant strand of silver hair up his forehead and began returning his instruments to the old Gladstone bag. 'Now . . .' he added, as he clamped the bag shut, '. . . if you don't have any transport I suggest you let me drop you in the village. Or you've got a long walk!' His grey eyes fixed the man pointedly.

When he finally agreed to go with the doctor, Hannah gave an audible sigh of relief and Sam immediately jumped up to show them out – obviously as eager to get rid of their unwanted guest as she was.

They were at the door before Tom Spencer suddenly stopped and turned round with a nasty grin. 'I almost forgot. Jed sends his congratulations.'

Neither Hannah nor Sam made a reply. The doctor grabbed hold of Tom Spencer's arm and dragged him through the door. And Hannah congratulated herself on not giving in to the urge to sink to the man's own level and fling herself physically at his leering face, which put her so much in mind of Jed's silly smirk.

'I'm sorry.' Rhoda looked bereft, as she turned to Hannah. 'This was your day and it's ruined.'

Hannah pressed her hand to the other woman's shoulder. 'No it isn't,' she assured, feeling a stab of guilt for her earlier unchivalrous thoughts. 'The first bit was wonderful and . . .' She came up short, a pink glow running up her cheeks. She had been about to say the last part will also be wonderful. 'And what more could happen now?' she quickly amended, and prayed she was going to be proved right.

Her prayers were answered. When Sam returned after seeing the doctor's shooting-brake go off down the lane, Rhoda leaped into action and fed both the children.

She seemed to have forgotten all her problems when she woke Jenny, who had slept peacefully through everything in her pram in the hall. The mess was quickly cleared away and David was being ushered upstairs to bed along with Jenny. Within minutes George Bunting had also mysteriously vanished and Hannah had Sam all to herself.

'I think we have been deserted,' she said, as she sat at the table and let her gaze run round the empty kitchen, before settling fondly on his face.

'I'm sorry for what happened.' Sam held his hand out and she slipped her hand into it, and stood up as if being drawn upwards by the intensity of the gaze that washed down on her. 'I could throttle Jed. I'd like to know how he found out about the wedding.'

'Anyone could have told him,' she said. 'It wasn't a state secret.' She would bet her last tanner it had been Jed's drinking pals on market day. But she had no wish to spoil the moment with talk of Jed. 'Well, it could never be said that life on the Tor was dull and boring,' she joked, her voice brightening and making light of the events of the late afternoon.

Sam laughed and pulled her into his arms. 'There are times when I'd prefer to have a bit of the mundane.'

'Not tonight, Sam Bunting,' she said, narrowing her eyes in a teasing rebuke. 'I've waited a long time for this. I'll put up with nothing remotely mundane.'

He laughed again, a full, penetrating laugh that came from way down inside his chest and seemed to reach right inside her own to touch something very special deep within her. Then he swept her up into his arms and, with his eyes pinned to hers every step of the way, carried her up the stairs and into their bedroom for the very first time.

He placed her on the great bed and came down by her side. His lips brushed against her forehead, cheek, the tip of her nose, before coming to rest against her lips in a caress so gentle it had the feel of the fleece of a new born lamb.

'Oh, Sam!' she murmured against his neck. 'I love you so much.' Tears pushed at her eyes. After her father's sudden and violent death she had not thought she could ever be happy again. Now she felt happier than she had ever felt in her life. It seemed unkind to her parents to feel this way. But she comforted herself with the knowledge that her parents would have been as happy as she was, knowing she had found the rare kind of love they, themselves, had shared.

'And I love you, Hannah Bunting.' His eyes seemed to glitter as he spoke the name that tied her to him. 'So much. So very, very much.' He kissed her again, this time with a force that matched the need building inside her. She answered in kind, pushing herself eagerly against him.

When finally he pulled away, there was a smile on his lips which told her better than words that he was sharing her feelings. Pushing himself up he began to unfasten the tiny pearl buttons on her blouse. She looked down at his hands and a smile grew on her face. Both hands worked together, there was no distinction between left and right. Each one handled the small, shiny buttons with equal dexterity, as he slowly and deliberately loosened each one in turn. When the last one was unfastened, he brushed aside her blouse and planted a kiss on the swell of her breast where it protruded from the lacy top of her bra.

She gave a little cry and her fingers tangled in the softness of his hair, and she pulled him closer. He kissed her shoulder, her throat, her ear, then reversed the journey until his lips had found her breast again. Her swelled nipples thrust against the flimsy fabric of her bra and his teeth closed gently on the hardness of one taut bud.

She cried out again, and her hands ran over his shoulders and down his back – covered by his shirt!

In an instant she was tearing at the buttons, wanting, needing to feel him beneath her fingers. He laughed at her clumsiness and took over the job himself, before she did permanent damage to the new shirt.

It was not until they were both naked and his eyes were feasting on all her beauty, that he reached out to touch her breast – and suddenly drew back. It had been the left hand he reached out with and he would have changed it for the right, but she pulled it back.

'No!' she said, staring determinedly into his darkening eyes. 'I want you, Sam . . . all of you!' There were to be no barriers in their love, no walls that should not be scaled.

He shook his head. 'But . . .' he began.

'No!' she insisted, and lifted her free hand to touch his cheek. 'I want this . . .' she said, '. . . and this . . .' her hand ran down his shoulder and to his chest, '. . . and this . . . and this.' Her hand moved, touching different parts of his body each time she spoke. Finally, she said, 'And this!' and she placed his deformed hand against her breast. As she felt its response closing around the fullness and brushing her nipple, she felt the prickle of tears come to her eyes. 'I want every bit of you, Sam.'

As he gazed down into her eyes she could see he was also touched with emotion. 'And I want every bit of you,' he responded, and the emotion she had seen in his eyes was crackling in his voice.

She smiled then, with all the love and fondness that was swelling in her heart, just as her breast swelled in his hand. 'Then take it,' she said simply, holding her arms open to him.

He needed no more prompting. It was only a short time before she felt the uncertain stiffness leave his left hand, as it explored her body. She knew then that the deformity had, at last, been forgotten. Her love for him had broken through the final taboo and the realization made her dizzy with pleasure.

As they joined together in the ultimate blessing of their love, her joy was complete. She had her man, the one she had lain awake endless nights aching for.

Much later, when they lay wrapped in each other's arms, in quiet contentment, listening to the silence of the darkness, she knew that all the waiting and aching had been worthwhile.

PART TWO

A Time for Sowing,
a Time for Reaping

Chapter Twenty-Five

1967

Despite Hannah's wedding day prognosis that life at the Tor never ran smoothly for very long, the next few years were to prove her wrong. The lack of a wedding ring did not stop George Bunting and Rhoda living contentedly as man and wife. Although he still found it necessary to have a shouting match with Hannah or Sam every now and again – just to prove he was still in command, Sam said. But things never got out of hand any more because Rhoda always had the knack of calming everybody down and bringing peace back.

David's love for the farm and the animals increased with his age and George Bunting began to view him as his protégé. They had many conversations together about animal husbandry and how to run a farm. There were even times when he would go out into the yard with the boy to show him the right way to do some job he had never tackled before: although such excursions were only very occasional; he still preferred the inside of the house to the outside world. But the thirteen-year-old could do no wrong. While Jenny, now a lively four-year-old with a mischievous streak, he merely tolerated.

The farm ran like clockwork and Sam even found the time not only to teach Hannah to drive, but also Rhoda as well. George Bunting celebrated this achievement with the purchase of a cream Morris Minor for them both to use.

Rhoda's husband never made a second appearance and they never heard or saw anything of Jed. In fact Jed was so conspicuous by his absence that Hannah began to believe someone must have done them the favour of shoving him in the river, or something equally final. And as time went by, she really did begin to believe they might never see him again.

The summer had been a glorious long and hot one. The type of weather when it is a privilege to work outside in the open air, rather than cooped up in a stuffy office or sweltering factory. Life had seemed perfect to Hannah, but when the weather changed she realized their run of good luck was about to change. It was the bitterly cold and frosty month of November when they heard the news that was far more perturbing than having Jed turn up on the doorstep.

Foot-and-mouth! A term which spread dread throughout the farming community.

There was an outbreak and seventeen cases reported at Oswestry in Shropshire: seventy miles to the west of Derby, but close enough for Derbyshire to become a controlled area. The market was closed down. Stock could not be moved, unless for slaughter. Rigorous precautions were taken, but it was not enough. By the eighth of the month the disease had reached the county.

'Well?' Hannah held her breath the way she always did when Sam had been on the telephone, getting the updated report from the Ministry of Agriculture.

He shook his head, the bleakness in his eyes answering for him.

Hannah pulled a chair from beneath the table and pressed him into it. 'It's bad.' He fell silent for a short time. 'It's all over the county,' he finally said, his voice flat with a mixture of despair and defeat. He arched his back and rubbed tiredly at his neck. 'It can only be a matter of time.'

'Don't say that!' she rebuked sternly. It was a long time since she had seen him in such gloom. It was not like the husband she had fallen more and more in love with as time had gone by. It was more like the Sam of pre-marital days, who had the depressing knack of going out to meet defeat halfway. She pushed his hand away from his neck, laid her own hands on his shoulders and began to massage the knot of muscle at the base of his neck. She knew it would be there, it had been a permanent fixture since the first case had been reported. What she did not know was if the tension caused the depression, or the depression the tension.

'We haven't got it *yet*!' she stressed. '*If* and when we do, will be the time to worry.' She dug her thumbs deep into his flesh in a manner of chastisement. He threw his head back on a groan of pain, then one of pleasure as her fingers gentled once more, cajoling the tension out of him. She fell silent then, listening to his murmurs of pleasure as her fingers continued to work and the muscles yielded and softened. Her hands moved on, across his shoulders and down his chest. 'Do you think they will be long?' she asked, her mouth close to his ear. George Bunting had been like a bear with a sore head for the past week. They had put it down to worry about the foot-and-mouth. Then, yesterday, his face had swollen up and they had learned he was suffering the agonies of toothache. This morning Rhoda had forced him into the car and taken him to the dentist to get it fixed, at the same time taking Jenny for a new pair of shoes. With David at school it was a rare moment for them to have the house all to themselves.

He clutched at her hands as they reached the waistband of his jeans and would have gone lower. 'I don't think we'll see them before lunch time.' He smiled in intimate understanding, as he turned to look up into her eyes, so close to his own. 'So, Mrs Bunting, you could do me a favour.'

'Oh, and what might that be?' she asked, feigning innocence.

'You can show me your girl clothes,' he growled,

twisting round in the chair and pulling her on to his lap. What he called her 'girl clothes' were the skimpy silk and lace items of underwear she had taken to wearing beneath her jeans and baggy sweaters, for him, and also to remind herself that she really was a woman.

'Sam Bunting you're incorrigible.' She swiped at his arm, wriggled free, and was out of the room before he was out of the chair.

He caught her halfway up the stairs and, with much laughter, saw all he wanted of the delicate blue slips of lace, before they were scattered over the stairs along with their heavy jeans and woolly jumpers.

Hannah gave a contented sigh, as they lay with arms and legs entwined beneath the sheets in the great bed, each one knowing they had work to do, but loath to relinquish the final contact. Sam buried his face in the mass of red hair spread across the white pillow. He breathed deeply, savouring the clean, woody smell of fresh pine. He loved her hair and his smile was filled with that love, as he looked up into her face. He lifted his left hand and ran the thickened digit that should have been his forefinger gently up and down her cheek.

Hannah smiled, caught hold of the hand and brought it to her lips. After their first night together he had never allowed his insecurities to return. He touched her freely with both hands, without restraint or doubt. When they were alone he now accepted himself as the man he really was. And the feeling of worth was spreading into the rest of his life, as well. He no longer hid his hand away in his pocket when they were away from the farm; or fumbled to hand over money only with his right hand; or showed any shame if he held out the left hand to take something from someone who shied away. She knew such reactions still hurt him, but not so much that he could no longer handle it.

'What are you thinking about?' he asked, studying her serious expression with suspicion.

She shook her head and let go of his hand. 'Nothing,' she said, and broke into a mischievous smile. 'Except that it is verging on the sinful to be in bed at this hour of the day.' Turning to face him, she pressed her body close to his, her smile broadening as she felt the awakening hardness telling her he was as ready for her again as she was for him. She snuggled closer to him. 'But I can't think of anyone I'd rather be sinful with,' she teased, coiling her arms around his neck and pressing her mouth hotly to his.

They were almost caught out. The sound of the Morris' engine coming into the yard, had Sam leaping out of bed and out of the bedroom to collect their discarded clothes strewn all over the stairs. Fortunately the time it took Rhoda to get the folding wheelchair out of the car and get George Bunting into it, gave them time to dress and reach the kitchen first.

'That will teach you,' Sam scolded playfully, trying to assist in straightening Hannah's tousled hair, while she straightened her jumper.

'Leave it!' She slapped his hand away, but she was smiling. 'They'll be wondering why no-one's gone out to help.'

'Then I will have to tell them it was the wayward milk-maid again.' He glanced her a knowing smile and went to the door. 'Sorry, I didn't hear you arrive,' she heard him lie, and she smiled as she shoved her hair into a rubber band.

'Grandad's had a big needle stuck in his mouth,' Jenny announced importantly, as she came bursting through the door.

'Oh dear!' Hannah bent down to the little girl's height and stared into her eyes, looking duly serious. 'I'll bet that's made him grumpy.'

Jenny gave a nod and screwed her face into a childish grimace. 'Auntie Rhoda said if he didn't stop complaining she'd stop the car and put him out and make him wheel himself home.' She spoke as if imparting a great confidence.

'Did she!' Hannah had to smile, but she had the feeling it might be the last time for a while. The removal of the offending tooth had obviously not been an instant salve to his aggravation.

'Mind the bloody walls!' His father cursed in true style, as Sam carefully manoeuvred him into the kitchen.

'Stop swearing, George!' Rhoda tapped him on the shoulder and flashed him a warning glare. 'Jenny can hear you.'

'I don't care who can bl . . . can hear me,' he amended meekly. Then fell silent, but his expression remained stubbornly belligerent.

This is all we need! Hannah thought, and began helping put away the groceries Rhoda was taking from her bag and putting on the table. She had been successful in making Sam forget the impending danger of foot-and-mouth, for a little while, at least. His earlier tension had gone and he had looked relaxed and happy. Now he had his father in one of his most aggressive moods to contend with and it would all come back.

'I'll make you a cuppa.' She sounded overly cheerful, even to herself. 'It will help your mouth.'

'I can't drink anything,' he snapped. 'I'm all frozen up. Or do you want to see me dribbling like a baby?'

Resting one hand on her hip she turned to him, one hundred and one choice responses flying through her head. But that was what he wanted, would provide fuel for his ammunition, she told herself, and bit her lip and remained silent.

'I want a drink,' Jenny put in. 'The dentist has got a quarium.'

Hannah and Sam frowned at the little girl.

'An aquarium,' Rhoda corrected.

'With fish in it?' Sam asked.

'Yes. Lots of fish. One as big as that.' She held her

406

hands so far apart that they could only imagine a baby shark had been stuffed into the tank.

'Don't be silly. It was no more than three inches long and even you know three inches doesn't stretch that far.'

Jenny's face fell and Hannah and Sam glared at the wheelchair's occupant. But it was Rhoda who got a reply in first. 'George!' she warned. 'The fish was at least six inches long and in some places the water seemed to magnify it.' She glared at him pointedly, her head making tiny, almost imperceptible jerks towards Jenny, when he remained silent.

He finally got the message. Or chose to get it, Hannah thought. He and Rhoda shared an empathy and always seemed to know what the other was thinking, so he would have immediately understood the silent sign-language. 'Perhaps it was that big,' he conceded. 'I was sitting at the other side from you and it looked like a tiddler from there.'

'What's a tiddler?' Jenny asked, immediately placated.

He finished explaining the difference between big fish and little fish, just as the kettle began to boil. 'I'm not hanging round to watch you lot eat and drink,' he said, spinning the wheelchair round and heading for the door. 'I'll be in the office until after dinner. I don't want to be disturbed,' was his final comment before he left the kitchen.

Sam gave a breathy sigh and glanced bleakly at Rhoda. 'Normal service resumed, I see. It must have been a big tooth, he's almost reverted to the days before you were here.'

'Was it that bad – the tooth?' Hannah poured a cup of orange juice for Jenny. 'Did it take a lot of getting out?'

'It isn't just that.' Rhoda slipped out of her coat and dropped it over the back of a chair. Then she rested one hand on the back of the same chair and ran the fingers of the other anxiously through her hair.

'What's happened?' Sam and Hannah spoke a duet, but Rhoda's expression was too serious to make a joke of it.

'Jed,' she said simply.

The room fell silent, as if each one of them was of the opinion if they did not pursue the subject it might go away. Even Jenny joined in, looking at each of the motionless grown-ups in turn, a puzzled frown creasing her tiny button nose and crinkling the big navy blue eyes.

It was Sam who broke the spell. 'What about Jed?' he asked, obvious caution in his voice.

'We met him.' Rhoda lifted her hand, then let it drop to her side as if it had become a ton weight. 'Can you believe that? The first time he has left the farm since your wedding day . . .' her hand swept towards the office and its occupant, '. . . and we have to bump into Jed!'

'What happened?' Hannah asked, hearing her own voice as if coming from far away. But no! Life had been so good. 'He isn't coming up . . . is he?'

Rhoda shook her head and gave a shrug. 'I don't know. I left George in the car while I took Jenny to get the shoes.'

'I got blue ones,' Jenny chirped in.

'Yes, dear,' Rhoda replied gently. 'We'll all see them later.' She smiled affectionately at the little girl and passed a glance over the red tartan dress she was wearing. 'Why don't you go and change into your dungarees before you eat dinner. You don't want to spoil your pretty dress.'

For once, Jenny agreed without argument and went running out of the room, the bag containing her new shoes tucked under her arm.

Rhoda turned back to Sam and Hannah. 'Anyway, we left him alone and when we got back Jed was there. They were having an almighty row.' She bit her lip and stared at the table top with resignation.

'What's new!' Sam glanced at Hannah, and she lifted expressive eyebrows at him. 'What were they arguing about?' He turned his attention back to Rhoda.

Again Rhoda shook her head. 'Your dad wouldn't say much afterwards. And Jed fell silent when he saw us – well, Jenny actually, I think. He looked at her as if she was poison.' Her lips curled in disgust as she spoke the last. 'But I heard Jed saying he was going to finish this place – and that he had the weapon to do it with.' Her voice diminishing at the end, she pulled another chair out and sank on to it, as if her body had become too heavy for her to support.

Hannah stared anxiously at Sam. Jed was back. After four years of peace and tranquillity he had returned, and was instantly plotting against them. 'What will he do now?' She spoke more to herself, as she had not intended voicing the question.

'Nothing,' Sam reassured, coming up behind her and laying his hands on her shoulders. 'He'll do nothing, because that's what he always does – nothing!' He gave her a little shake to stress his words.

She gave a sigh and dropped her head back against his shoulder. 'I wish I could believe you.' He sounded full of confidence, but she was obviously made of weaker stuff and could not find half the same conviction.

'You can,' he insisted. 'He's got nothing planned. How could he have? It was pure coincidence that he happened to be in the right place at the right time. He didn't know dad was going to be there. He just took the opportunity to have a go when it was presented. Whatever he threatened would have come off the top of his head. And that's all it was, harmless threats, to get the old man going.'

She turned into his arms and clung to him, feeling in need of the safety and protection of his closeness. 'But he's so vindictive. He told Rhoda's husband where she was; even sending him up here on our wedding day.'

He shook his head very emphatically. 'No. Renee told Rhoda's husband. Oh, Jed would have egged her on. But it would have been Renee who had to do it. He's my brother remember. I know him of old. He'll hold the gun, but somebody else has to pull the trigger. He hasn't got the guts. The only thing he's ever done on his own is take the old man's car and lose it gambling. I don't think that took much intelligence or guts. Otherwise he just makes a lot of noise about doing nothing.'

What he was saying was correct. Jed tried to cause trouble by saying what he was going to do, but very seldom did he actually get around to doing it. Hannah gave a sigh and pulled away from him. 'I'm being silly, aren't I?'

'*Yes!*' he agreed meaningfully. Then his eyes began to dance. 'And it's almost sinful to be silly when you could be happy instead,' he said teasingly, his smile broadening as his words closely resembled those she had spoken herself, not so very long ago.

The smile that spread across her face was confident enough, but she could not so easily wipe away the unease inside. It was not for herself that she was worried. It was for Sam. He had enough to worry him at the moment without the addition of wondering if his errant brother was about to turn up on the doorstep.

Whatever Sam said to try and reassure her, she knew she would not be able to rest for listening for the sound of an unexpected car engine, heralding the arrival of an unwanted visitor. Now the contact had been renewed Jed would come. It was like a tangible feeling in her bones. He was the last person they needed with the threat of the foot-and-mouth epidemic hanging over their heads – so he would definitely turn up!

Chapter Twenty-Six

The foot-and-mouth epidemic raged through the country like wildfire. The farm became a prison, no-one daring to go outside of its walls unless it was strictly necessary. The cows were brought up from the bottom meadow so that it was easier to keep an eye on them. The sheep were rounded up and taken off the Tor and brought down to the farm: partly in readiness for winter; partly to get them into the confines of a closed shed and away from the Tor where there was a public footpath. The Ministry of Agriculture had asked people not to venture out into the countryside for fear of spreading contamination. But you always got someone who 'knew their rights' and refused to be put off, ignoring the damage they might be doing.

They had not seen anyone actually crossing the Tor. But in case anyone should venture up there, Sam had decided to put up notices asking people to stay on the footpath. Hannah was not sure they would do any good: the type of person who would think of walking up there at the moment was the type of person who would not care enough to take any notice. But, sensing Sam's need to be doing something constructive to fight the threat, she went along with him, holding the homemade signposts upright while he thumped them into the hard ground with a mallet.

There were three posts in all: one for each end of the footpath and one for the middle. Hannah had both hands clamped around the middle one and Sam was belting the top of the post with all his might, when a movement caught her eye. She was so surprised she let the post go, Sam miss-hit and the mallet almost swung into his leg and crushed his knee.

'What the blazes are you doing?'

'There's someone down there!' Her voice was incredulous as she stared down into the field below the craggy cliff face. 'What on earth are they doing?' They had no right to be down there in the fields with the cows at any time. But now . . . with the risk of contamination!

Freezing mist swirled around the lower field, cloaking the identities of the two men as they tramped around the grass with their heads bowed – as if they were looking for something they had lost.

Recognition came to Sam first. 'I'll swing for him!' he suddenly grated, throwing the mallet down with a surge of anger.

Startled by his ferocity, Hannah's gaze pivoted to him. 'It's Jed?' she questioned, the incredulity of her voice lost on a blast of icy wind.

'It's Jed!' he confirmed bitterly. 'Hey!' he shouted angrily. But his voice could not rise above the wind and the two men down below heard nothing. He shouted again. The two men continued to tramp around the field in weird unconforming patterns, seemingly with no purpose.

'What are they doing?' Hannah repeated, holding the stray wisps of hair that had escaped her pony-tail away from her face and frowning at Sam.

'I don't know. But I'm going to find out.'

'Oh Sam!' She grabbed his sleeve and held him back. 'Be careful! There are two of them.'

He shook her off, opened his mouth to speak, then suddenly stopped himself. His head spun back to the field below. 'Oh no!' He shook his head in disbelief. Then wondered why he should think his brother was not capable of it. He turned to Hannah, the horror of his thoughts planted on his face. 'They've been on a farm with it. They're trying to infect our grass. They're trying to bring it here!'

He did not have to state what 'it' was. 'No! No . . . he couldn't.' She looked at him as if he had gone mad. Then she grabbed his arm again, fear for his safety rearing inside her. 'How could they have got on to a contaminated farm. Once it's reported they are closed off. It isn't possible.' She was clutching at straws and she knew it. They could have sneaked into anyone's fields without being seen – just the way they had got into the field down there. If she and Sam hadn't been putting up the posts they would never have known they'd been there.

'Then tell me what they are doing?' The bleakness in his eyes chilled Hannah to the bone and she shivered.

She fell silent. She had no answer and he knew it. The next moment he tore his arm from her grasp and was racing across the Tor. Hannah quickly followed, trying to catch up. But the distance between them increased with every stride, as Sam covered the ground with the speed and determination of a hunting cheetah. Her lungs were bursting and as tiredness increased her feet slipped and slithered on the frosty grass. But she kept on going, her legs spurred by the fear of Sam facing the two men alone.

When Sam reached the farmyard he veered right, going behind the stables and taking the shortest cut to the field. Hannah was about to follow, but at the last minute changed her mind and raced through the farmyard.

'Peg!' she screamed as she ran, catching hold of her scarf as it escaped from the neck of her coat. 'Peg! Derwent! Mack! Dogs! Come on! Here! Here!' Stuffing the scarf back untidily, she raced on.

Having been kept imprisoned in the yard since the first outbreak of foot-and-mouth had been reported, the dogs were only too ready for a taste of freedom. When Hannah reached the five-bar-gate at the bottom of the yard and, not stopping to open it, flung herself over the top, an assortment of black and white and black and tan fur flew over with her. All the dogs had risen to the call and they raced across the hillside at her heels, fortunately too well trained to get in her way and trip her over.

When they reached the field she stopped dead, the dogs all clustering round her legs. Sam was standing facing Jed, his body tensed in a threatening promise. Their voices were raised and, now she was closer, she could see the second man was Tom Spencer, Rhoda's husband.

'Oh no!' she gasped out without thinking. Sensing the tension, Peg gave a whine and began to slink forward to her master's side. 'Heel!' Hannah gave the command, again before thought. All three men were poised angrily, obviously ready for a fight. She stared anxiously at the back of Sam's stiff shoulders, then she turned to Peg. The collie was looking up at her with bewilderment in her big, dark eyes. She could not understand why she should be stopped from protecting her master and Hannah had second thoughts. Perhaps it would be better if one of the dogs was by his side – it might make Jed hesitate from getting physical. 'Go,' she said, and flicked her hand towards Sam.

Peg didn't need telling twice. She ran to Sam, dropping on her belly by his side, ears back, emitting a low growl as she pinned her gaze on Jed, who was the closest threat to Sam.

Jed gave a mocking laugh. 'A cripple and a daft bitch!' he scorned.

'A cripple who'll see you off *his* land!' Sam grated, his emphasis on the ownership causing a dangerous glimmer to spark in his brother's eyes.

'With whose help?' Jed challenged, stepping forward with clenched fists.

Thinking he was about to strike the first blow, Hannah rushed forward. The pack of growling dogs were with her all the way.

Sam's arm came out, holding her back. 'I can handle this,' he assured confidently. 'I was right,' he added, without looking at her. 'He has been on infected land.'

'Oh no!' Hannah could not believe even Jed was so vindictive.

Her distress brought a sarcastic laugh from his sneering lips and Sam's shoulders stiffened.

'No, Sam,' she begged. 'Don't fight him. That's what he wants.' She looked into Tom Spencer's twisted leer. Like Jed he was spoiling for a fight, his fists being the only language he knew. Both of them would set about Sam without any qualms about fairness.

She and Sam had the dogs on their side, she reminded herself. But she was not sure the dogs would understand the command attack. They made a lot of noise and could affect a threatening pose, but when it came down to baring their teeth and getting stuck in, she wasn't sure they would know what to do. They were trained to *protect* the animals, not savage them. They were also trained to obey the commands of certain people – like the family! And they all knew Jed as family. And Jed knew all the commands as well as Sam and herself.

'That's it, listen to the sergeant major!' Jed's lip curled, his gaze flicking over her as if she was a piece of dirt.

Sam's shoulders stiffened further. 'I'll not have anyone insulting my wife!' he ground.

'He isn't insulting me,' Hannah quickly put in, trying to defuse the situation. 'To insult me he would have to mean something to me. Now let's go and call the police and tell them we have prowlers.' Taking hold of Sam's arm, she tried to pull him away. It was a fatal error. Sam tugged his arm away from her. But, in doing so, he turned his head to look at her, only for a moment, but a moment too long.

Grabbing the chance, Jed leapt at them, sending both Sam and Hannah crashing to the floor.

When Hannah regained her senses it was to find herself sitting in the cold, wet grass, Sam and Jed rolling around one on top of the other. Peg was trying to join in, but her advances were obstructed by flailing arms and legs, both

Jed's and Sam's. And Hannah was not sure if the collie was joining in the fight, or joining in the fun. It was then she saw Tom Spencer coming forward, the long shiny blade of a knife poised in his hand.

'No!' she screamed, leaping to her feet. 'Derwent! Mack!' She called on the two largest and strongest dogs. Panic filled her voice, lifting it up to hit the face of the Tor and bounce back and around the surrounding hills, as she put herself between Rhoda's husband and the brawling pair on the ground.

In the next instant any doubts she had harboured that the dogs would not know how to fight were wiped away. Like a true-blue police dog, Derwent leapt at the arm holding the knife and sank his teeth into the man's wrist. Mack was right behind him. He lunged bodily at Tom Spencer, sending him sprawling backwards. As soon as the man was down, the other dogs joined the mêlée.

Hannah hesitated a moment, staring undecidedly at the squirming heap of legs and tails, with an increasing number of grunts and groans coming from beneath. But any consideration that she should call them off was soon pushed aside as being soft and foolish. The dogs had him outnumbered without any assistance from herself and she left them to it and turned to Sam – only to find she wasn't needed there, either.

Peg had finally seen the true meaning of the situation and instead of trying to get into the middle of them, had a very firm hold on Jed's arm. While Sam had his brother's neck securely locked in the crook of his arm.

'Are you all right?'

Sam gave a nod, before jerking his head towards the pack of dogs. 'Get them off,' he said.

'Cease!' she called, running to the dogs and pulling them back. 'Drop the knife!' she warned. 'Or I'll set them on you again!' She did not know if the man still had the knife in his hand, or if he was still capable of using it. But she was taking no chances. 'Stay!' she ordered, as the dogs stood back. They made a circle around the prone man, who still had Mack on top of him.

Hannah bent down to pull Mack away. Her scarf had come loose again and fell in the way. She tossed it back round her neck and reached for Mack again. The dog seemed to have worn himself out and had only half his usual strength. But as Hannah put him down on the ground away from the man, she felt the wet, sticky fur down his side. When she stood up and looked at her hand, it was red with blood. Her gaze pivoted to Tom Spencer. He appeared shocked and dazed and his clothes were torn, but there was no sign of any serious injury that the blood could have come from.

'Mack!' Her voice was little more than a whimper and she dropped to her knees by the collie's side and carefully turned him over. He gave a whine and his big sad eyes looked up into her face, as if pleading for her help. 'Oh Mack!' she cried. A long gaping wound ran across his hip bone and down his thigh. Blood was pouring from it and his coat had turned scarlet. 'He's knifed Mack!' she called to Sam, and grabbed the scarf from her neck. Sam swore and must have tightened his hold on Jed, for Jed let out a groan.

Turning quickly to Derwent, Hannah pointed at the man on the ground. 'Keep!' she ordered, and Derwent lay on his belly, eyes and ears alert and nose pointed at the man, as if he was guarding an errant sheep. But Hannah did not see. She knew Derwent would obey the command and she immediately returned her attention to Mack. Straightening her scarf to use as a bandage, she bound it tightly round Mack's hip and leg and attempted to staunch the bleeding.

'Is it bad?' Sam asked with concern.

'Yes.' She glanced anxiously at him. 'It needs stitching. He's losing too much blood.'

'Right . . . up!' Pushing himself on to his feet he dragged Jed with him.

'What are we going to do?' Hannah looked doubly worried. Mack needed taking for treatment without a moment to lose. But if she took him she would be leaving Sam alone. She knew he would not go and leave her alone.

But before Sam could tell her she had to be the one to go, a shot rang through the air. Hannah's head spun round, the shock of the unexpected, ear-splitting sound widening her eyes. They widened further when she saw Rhoda struggling to get the wheelchair across the field in the bumpy grass. George Bunting, cursing and swearing as he urged her on, had one shotgun in his hands and another lying across his lap.

'What the blazes is going off?' he demanded. His voice blasted through the air with a similar strength to the shotgun blast, even though they were still some way away.

Her screaming race through the yard had brought more than the dogs, Hannah thought. 'Mack is hurt,' she called, and held up her hands, displaying her bloodied palms.

He held his own hand up then, to stop Rhoda's struggle while she still had some breath left in her lungs. 'Come over here!' he demanded, the frustration of inability sharpening his voice. 'Come to me!'

Lifting Mack into her arms, Hannah immediately went to him. It was a struggle. The large dog was sinking fast and he was a dead weight in her arms. Her legs began to buckle and her feet became even more unsteady in the slippery grass. 'I have to get him to the vet,' she said, her voice coming in short gasps, even though she had only carried the dog a short distance.

George Bunting took one look at Mack, then at Hannah. 'You'll not make it,' he said. 'Sam will have to take him. He'll be the fastest.'

'But . . .' Sam began to protest. He had not moved from the spot, or loosened his grip on Jed.

'Let him go,' his father insisted, before Sam could say anything more. 'He's not going anywhere.' Lifting the shotgun he aimed the long barrel at his two sons. 'Not with this about to put an end to his manhood.' Very deliberately he lowered the barrel to the apex of Jed's legs. 'And my sight is not impaired,' he added pointedly. 'I still have the ability to castrate a bull at the other end of the field.'

Jed shifted nervously.

'Keep still!' his father ordered.

Mack gave a plaintive whine and Hannah looked down into the soul-wrenching depths of his sad eyes. 'Sam!' she begged, her own eyes beseeching her husband.

It was enough. Pushing Jed roughly from him so that he fell to the ground on all fours, Sam hurried to her. 'But don't let him go before I get back!' He was speaking to his father as he jabbed his finger hard at the pathetic sight of his brother still down on all fours. 'He reckons he's been on infected land. And he was walking all round our fields!' Not waiting long enough to see the blood drain from his father's face, he turned back to Jed, his finger stabbing at the air once more. 'If any of our stock goes down with it I'll personally wring your neck.' He took Mack from Hannah then. 'Don't let him get away,' he said. She did not know if he did not trust his father to obey his order; or if he considered it would take more than one person to hold Jed.

Although she would not be happy until she saw Jed leaving the Tor, she shook her head. 'I won't,' she promised, yet shivered at the burning hate she could see in her husband's eyes. This was the final straw for him, she thought. Jed had played his last card and, if she could not find a way to calm Sam, there would be no slamming out of the door after raised voices. Jed was going to pay in full this time. The look on Sam's face told her so . . . and it terrified her.

'Be careful with Mack,' she warned. 'And hurry,' she added, as Sam turned away and set off running across the field, Mack cradled securely in his arms.

'Don't worry,' he called, glancing at her over his shoulder.

Hannah smiled tightly. She did not know if he had been telling her not to worry about Mack, or about Jed and everything else. But for that brief moment he had turned to her, the anger had been gone from him and she had been looking into the eyes of the man she loved. It was only a very small thing, but it meant the world to her.

'Let's have you over here!' George Bunting beckoned to Jed with the gun's barrel. 'And get him over here, as well.' He swung the barrel at the figure on the floor, still surrounded by dogs and with Derwent keeping a very close guard.

When Jed tried to move the dogs, they growled and stood their ground.

Hannah smiled. She had misjudged the dogs earlier, thinking they would not know how to be fierce. Well they had proved her wrong and proved themselves worthy in the field of battle – just as worthy as they proved themselves in the peaceful, non-violent way they tended the sheep in the normal run of things.

'Here!' George Bunting called, and emitted a high-pitched whistle. Instantly obeying the call, the dogs raced to the wheelchair and sat down, making two flanks on either side like a very proud guard of honour.

Jed tossed a sneer at his father, before bending down to help his companion to his feet. He was still white and shaken and he clung to Jed's arms as they came forward.

Only then did the identity of the second man become clear to the two newcomers. Rhoda gasped, her hand flying to her throat.

'Birds of a feather.' George Bunting's lip curled contemptuously. 'Well, you're both about to get your wings clipped.' He jabbed the gun at Jed. 'Is it true?' he demanded. 'Have you been with foot-and-mouth?'

Jed gave another sneer. 'Frightened for your precious farm?'

The gun's barrel swung to Tom Spencer. 'Is it true?' George Bunting's voice dropped lower, but was no less threatening for it.

'Go to hell,' the man spat.

Hannah's anxious gaze pivoted to Rhoda, and saw the same anxiety there. She began to wish Sam had not gone.

'Not before my time,' George Bunting replied, confidently adding, 'But you will – unless you start answering my questions.' As his voice died away the gun fired.

Hannah and Rhoda both almost leaped out of their skins. Jed took a step backwards and Tom Spencer hopped around on one foot like a demented hen, and a flock of starlings took to the air in erratic, screeching flight.

'You haven't . . . ?' Hannah's dismayed gaze swung to George Bunting, then to Tom Spencer nursing his foot. The toecap of his boot was shredded by shotgun pellets.

Without much concern, George Bunting handed the empty gun to Rhoda and picked up the one lying on his lap.

'You maniac! You shot my foot!' Tom Spencer cried, as his wife dutifully took the spent cartridges from the used gun, replaced them with new and handed it back.

'No I didn't!' George Bunting countered with complete confidence. 'But I will next time,' he added, and Hannah shuddered and hoped and prayed there was not going to be a next time.

'Put your foot down you idiot!' Jed glared at his companion, obviously irritated by the display. 'He's only trying to frighten you.'

George Bunting let out a roar that startled the starlings all over again. The air darkened as they seemed to fill the sky with their panicked swooping and frantic cries, and when they vanished over the hill and silence returned, Hannah gave a grateful sigh.

'Trying to frighten you,' George Bunting scoffed. 'I think I'm succeeding.' He levelled the shotgun in his hands at the men and swung it from one to the other.

'Now . . . who is going to tell me what I want to know?' The gun's barrel came to rest pointed at Tom Spencer's abdomen. 'Have you been on infected land?' he repeated. When there was no reply his finger moved, tightening on the trigger.

Hannah drew a noisy breath.

'Yes!' Jed arrogantly declared, silencing Tom Spencer as he was about to speak.

'Where?' his father demanded.

Jed stumbled a moment too long. 'Westgate Farm,' he said.

'How did you get on?'

'Easily. We went last night. They haven't got an armed guard on the place.' Jed's mouth twisted in contempt.

'Which fields did you go in?'

What was this – twenty questions? Hannah wondered if it was all necessary.

'The top ones close to the track. Where they keep the Friesians.'

George Bunting dropped back in the chair and let the gun lie on his knee. Then he picked the second gun up and handed it to Hannah. 'You take that.' When she had it in her hands and it was pointing at the two men, he handed the other to Rhoda. 'And you take that one. And if either of these two makes a run for it – use them!' He turned a stony glare on his son. 'You two can push me back,' he ordered.

Hannah was surprised Jed so readily agreed. She could only surmise he saw it as a way to their imminent escape, as he took one side of his father's chair and Tom Spencer took the other. But as she walked along with the gun poised in her hands, feeling like a refugee from the Wild West, she wondered if George Bunting might be reconsidering his decision. They seemed to be able to find every deep hole in the field and it was only the strength of his arms that had stopped him going sprawling across the ground on several occasions.

By the time they reached the farmhouse, George Bunting had gone right through the dictionary of swear words, and back again. But once they were inside, and he felt himself on solid ground again, he calmed down and took charge once more. He told Hannah to stand at the door leading into the hall, the shotgun still in her hand. Then he put himself, along with the second gun, by the back door, so they had all the escape routes cut off.

Rhoda sat at the table with her head in her hands, trying not to look at the man to whom she was legally married. Hannah was not sure who she felt most sorry for: Rhoda or herself. Tom Spencer kept taunting Rhoda with threats of taking David from her and Hannah could feel the other woman's fear filling the kitchen. But she was also in turmoil herself, frantically worrying about what Sam would do when he got back – not to mention her anxieties for Mack's safety. The dog had been so brave in loyally responding to her command. She could not bear it if anything happened to him.

She began to wonder why she had not refused Sam's instruction to make sure Jed stayed there. Things would be a lot easier, and a lot safer, if Jed was gone when Sam got back. But . . . !

Looking over to the back door she could see George Bunting did not share her feelings. He would not let Jed go without a fight. She half wished Jed would make a dash for her door, so she could let him get through by making out he pushed her to the floor. But he did not try to push her aside, or get anywhere near the door. He remained where he was, standing in front of his father, goading him continually.

If he thought jibing at his father was going to aid his escape, he was even more stupid than she had thought, she told herself. But it was not Jed's stupidity that caused her the most concern. It was his father's response. Or lack of it. George Bunting sat silently and calmly, allowing his son's jibes to go right over his head. His attitude was so strange and uncharacteristic that it worried Hannah far more than if they had been at each other with their fists. She could not imagine why his father was not biting back, especially after Jed had admitted he had been deliberately trying to contaminate the land. Her only conclusion was that he was biding his time, waiting for Sam's return so they could reap some horrible revenge.

When finally the Land Rover came sweeping into the yard, Hannah was filled with a mixture of relief and dread; relief that Sam was now here to sort things out; dread over how he would do so.

Fortunately her anxieties were very short-lived. As the Land Rover's engine died away a second engine was heard. She craned her neck to see the Land Rover through the window without moving from her post. Sam was just climbing out. As he closed the door a police car pulled up by his side.

The police! He had brought the police. Relief swept through her so violently that her head began to swim and her vision danced. She lifted a hand, attempting to hold her unsteady head still. Without realizing what she was doing her other hand fell to her side, the gun hanging loosely in her fingers.

'Are you all right?' Hannah heard the words, but was not endowed with enough awareness to know they were being spoken to her. Not until Rhoda grabbed hold of her arms and repeated the question, did she fully comprehend.

'Yes . . . yes . . .' She nodded her head. Not a wise move. A fresh wave of dizziness claimed her reason and she grabbed for the wall for support. The gun clattered noisily to the floor.

She heard George Bunting's voice ordering, 'Get her into a chair.' The next thing she knew she was sitting in the chair, her head and arms were resting on the table and Sam was coming through the door with two great burly policemen right behind him. She lifted her head and sat up, and thankfully her brain stood still in her skull.

'Now then, what have we got here.' It was the first policeman who spoke. He had stripes on his sleeves and a peaked cap instead of a pointed helmet.

Hannah wanted to laugh. He sounded like something out of *Dixon of Dock Green*. But the policeman looked very serious and she had pulled herself together enough to know it was not the right time for a display of amusement.

The policeman gave the gun on the floor a very serious study. Then he gave the one in George Bunting's hands the same. 'Do we need those?' he questioned pointedly.

'Just a deterrent, Sergeant.' George Bunting propped his gun against the wall and made a deliberate gesture of lifting his hands away from it. The sergeant seemed to be happy with that and turned away, giving the second policeman the nod to pick Hannah's gun up from the floor. He did so and laid it on the table.

'Which one of you had the knife?' The sergeant's gaze swung between Jed and Tom Spencer.

'He did.' Sam pointed at the culprit.

'Have you still got it?' The policeman's voice was very stern. It was a far cry from Benny, the village bobby, whose main occupation was cycling round the country lanes and stopping for a chat and cup of tea every now and then.

Tom Spencer shook his head.

Hannah looked questioningly at Rhoda. Rhoda shook her head. She turned to George Bunting but received only a blank expression. She gave a sigh. 'We forgot it,' she said, with an apologetic grimace at the policeman, who she expected to be angry. 'It must be back in the field – if he really hasn't got it!' she added pointedly, having no faith in the man's denial. But then she suddenly turned to Jed. 'Or he could have it,' she said, remembering Jed had been in a position to pick it up

425

and put it in his pocket when he helped the other man get up.

'Have you?' The sergeant's voice hardened. He turned deliberately to Jed, fixing him with a very cold glare. 'If you have got it you'll do yourself more good by handing it over right now.'

A pink tinge ran up Jed's cheeks. For several moments he prevaricated, then finally gave in and pulled the blood-stained knife from his pocket, belligerently slapping the hilt into the policeman's outstretched hand.

'That attitude won't help you, sonny.' The policeman's glare hardened. 'Now, what else have you been doing? Is it true you've been trying to spread foot-and-mouth?'

'No!' It was George Bunting who responded, very loudly, and very clearly. Everybody turned to him in surprise. 'He doesn't even know which farm has got it and which hasn't,' he continued. 'He's already told me he went to Westgate to pick it up. *They are clean!*' He turned to Jed, his gaze condemning him for the fool he was. 'It's Northgate that has got it,' he said simply.

'Are you sure?' Sam and the sergeant spoke together.

'Positive. I got him to tell me which fields he went in. He described Westgate to perfection, including their herd. Friesians, he said. Northgate haven't got any Friesians!'

'Why . . . you . . . !' Sam lunged at Jed, clamping his hands round his neck and shaking him furiously.

'There'll be no need for that!' Sam was dragged back, a policeman on each arm. 'This is our job now.' There was a stern note of rebuke in the sergeant's voice.

'I'd like to throttle him,' Sam grated, his anger increased because the man he was talking about was his brother – his own flesh and blood! He wheeled away and, dragging a chair noisily from beneath the table, threw himself into it.

Hannah reached out and laid her hand over his. 'It will be all right,' she assured, trusting that now the police

426

had been drawn into it Jed would not get away scot-free.

Sam attempted a smile. But it was very small and tight, and she could see the bitterness caused by his vindictive brother still lingering in his eyes.

The policemen began to question Jed on the credibility of his father's statement. 'Is Mack all right?' she whispered to Sam.

He gave a nod. 'He might have a stiff leg but he should come through OK. I can fetch him home tonight.'

She smiled and fell silent, realizing they were missing what was going on.

The questioning had come to an end and Jed and Tom Spencer were going to be taken away. The sergeant turned to George Bunting. 'Will you be able to get down to the station to make a full report? We can send someone up here to do it, if you'd rather.'

'I'll come down,' George Bunting replied, pride putting the insistent edge in his voice that always came to life when his ability was brought into question.

The sergeant never got time to reply. Tom Spencer suddenly threw himself across the room at the table. Seeing his intention, Sam lunged across the table at the gun, but he was not fast enough. The barrel was pointing towards him and before he could get his hands around the cold metal, Tom Spencer had hold of the butt. All in the same instant, he swung the barrel round and pulled the trigger.

The force of the shot lifted Rhoda and her chair up in the air and threw her across the room and crashing against the wall. She let out an agonized scream and sank drunkenly to the floor, a deep red stain growing over her lemon-yellow jumper at her chest.

George Bunting let out an animal-like groan. Everyone turned to him, including Jed, who had a victorious sneer plastered on his face – but only for a moment.

A double shot rang out, followed by a numbing silence. Everyone looked on in horror as Jed fell flat on his back, as if poleaxed. The sneer was gone and would never return.

He no longer had lips to twist, eyes to glimmer, or nose to curl. Where his face had been was reduced to a battered pulp, oozing the life-blood which spattered the wall and floor all around him.

Chapter Twenty-Seven

In the chaotic aftermath of so much violence, Hannah worked like an automaton. She phoned for the ambulance. She fetched towels. She assisted the policeman as he tended to Rhoda. But all of it was done only because the sergeant was telling her to do it. It was as if her senses had been knocked out of her. She could not think, could not do anything of her own accord.

Then when the ambulance finally arrived and she was left with nothing to do, she felt oddly wanting, needing something, anything to take her mind away from what had happened.

With a speed that increased Hannah's anxiety for her friend's condition, Rhoda was put on a stretcher and lifted into the back of the ambulance. One of the ambulance men immediately fitted an oxygen mask over her face, then stuck a needle into her arm and had her fixed up to a drip while Sam was helping his colleague to get Jed also into the ambulance.

There was no mask, no needle for him. Just a thick grey blanket covering what remained of him. He was past human care. She pictured the bloody mess that was now where his handsome face had been and she shuddered. When the driver began to close the door a little sound came from her throat and she lifted her hand and tried to stop him.

Sam held her back. 'You can't go.' He spoke gently, looking into her face with concern. 'I need you here.'

His face was so pale, with lips stretched tautly, but not in a smile. 'Oh Sam!' she gasped, and fell against him, needing him as much as he needed her. 'What will happen to him?'

He shook his head, knowing it was his father she was speaking of, but unable to give an answer. George Bunting had not spoken one word since blasting both barrels of the shotgun into his son's face. He had meekly handed the gun over to the astonished sergeant, then sat staring at Rhoda. His eyes had not left her once, and they had been filled with such pain. Not until they had been carrying her out had he moved. He had lifted his hand and touched her arm as she went past, and for the first time in his life Sam had seen tears glistening in his father's eyes.

When the ambulance was gone they went back into the kitchen, to find him sitting woodenly staring at the bloodstain on the wall where Rhoda had been. He did not once look at the much larger stain on the floor that had been his son's blood.

Tom Spencer was handcuffed to a chair with the policeman hovering over him. The sergeant was busy scribbling in his notebook.

'We'll have to get this cleaned up before the children come home,' Sam said.

Hannah shuddered. She had forgotten David and Jenny. 'Thank God David was at school! And thank God Jenny was playing with a friend!' The horror had been bad enough for them to witness, but she could not imagine what it would have done to the children.

'Thank God!' Sam echoed with feeling. 'But they mustn't see this mess, either.'

Hannah nodded her head and, steeling herself for what had to be done, fetched the scrubbing brush from the cupboard and stuck the bucket under the tap. As she watched the water level slowly rising up the side of the galvanized steel, she prayed that Rhoda would be all right. She did not deserve to die, she said silently, hoping someone with some influence might be listening. Rhoda had done so much for the family: made George Bunting human; turned the house into a home and run it without asking for any assistance; brought David up to forget all the horror and brutality of his first years and so be able to lead a happy life; made Jenny believe she was special because of her hand, that it was something to be proud of. It was because of Rhoda that Jenny wasn't here now. She had gone out of her way to make friends for the child and get her to mix with others of the same age. There were not many days went by without Jenny playing at someone's house, or having a friend come there to play.

'We'll have to take you down to the station,' the sergeant said to George Bunting. He was speaking gently and he looked almost apologetic. Hannah was grateful for that. It meant the policeman understood a little of the reasons why what had happened had happened.

George Bunting did not reply, neither did he look at the man or make any indication that he had heard. The sergeant turned to Sam. 'It will be best if we come back for him,' he said. 'We'll take the other first.' He jerked his head at the scowling Tom Spencer. 'There'll be more room for him if we send a separate car.' He glanced at George Bunting. 'And he isn't going anywhere,' he added.

'No, he isn't going anywhere,' Sam repeated flatly.

Turning off the tap, Hannah turned to Sam. His shoulders were drooped as if he was carrying a ton weight and his arms hung impotently by his side. She gave an inward sigh of despair. No matter how horrific the afternoon had been for her, it had been worse for Sam. He had watched his father gun down his brother and, no matter what had gone by in the past, blood was thicker than water and it was times like these when the good memories surfaced.

Leaving the bucket in the sink she went to his side. 'It will be all right,' she said, taking hold of his hand and giving it a comforting squeeze. She did not know how she could find the words in her head. At that moment she could not see how anything would ever be all right, ever again. But she knew it was what she had to say to him, letting him know he was not totally alone.

He managed a thin smile, but it was as bleak as the icy mist swirling round the house like a shroud. She gave a sigh and looked at the sergeant, as if he might offer some advice. But he was looking at her bucket standing in the sink, then at the blood stains on the wall and floor.

His large chest lifted on a silent sigh. 'I suppose it's all right for you to clean up.'

'We've got to clean up!' Hannah's voice was a wail. Her pleading gaze swung from one policeman to the other. 'The children will be coming home. They can't see this!'

He pursed his lips thoughtfully. 'Aye, all right then,' he finally agreed. 'You can't live with it like this. Clean up. We saw it all, so I don't suppose there'll be any more evidence needed.'

Hannah thought of Rhoda and Jed lying in the ambulance. One dead, one seriously injured. What more evidence did they need?

'Thank you, sergeant,' Sam said, realizing his wife wasn't going to say it.

The policeman gave a nod. 'We'll leave you to get on with it.' He nodded to his colleague to release Tom Spencer from the chair and take him out to the car. 'We'll be back later,' the sergeant informed Sam, as he went through the door.

At first neither Hannah nor Sam moved. They stood staring into space, their hands still clasped tightly together, as if each one was gaining strength from the other.

It was Hannah who came to life first. 'Come on,' she said, 'the sooner we start the sooner we finish.' She moved to pull away, but Sam pulled her back.

'See to him first,' he said, drawing her attention to the still and silent figure in the wheelchair. It was only then that she saw his father's jumper was spattered with blood, so were his hands and there were even a few splashes on his face.

She turned back to Sam with emotion pressing at her eyes. 'Yes,' she said simply, and hurried to his father's room to find a clean jumper.

They both worked feverishly, as if the mess was their only problem and cleaning it up would put everything back to normal again. Of course it did not. But at least it got the kitchen looking like a kitchen once more, instead of a chamber of horrors. It was twenty-minutes-to-four when they put all the dirty towels and cloths they had used to mop up into a sack and hid it behind the stables. They were not sure they should dispose of George Bunting's stained jumper, the police might need it for evidence, so Hannah had put it in a carrier bag and left it in the bottom of his wardrobe – where neither David nor Jenny were likely to see it. 'I'll burn the towels when I come back,' Sam said.

'I'll go,' Hannah offered. It should have been her job to collect David from school and pick Jenny up on the way back. 'Then you can get the bonfire over with before they come home.' Jenny was too young to understand, but she did not like the thought of David watching smoke rising into the sky and having vivid imaginings of what was being burnt.

Sam shook his head. 'I don't want you driving at the moment,' he said, care for her safety uppermost in his mind. 'But perhaps you could get the bonfire over before we come back – if you think it's all right to leave him?' He glanced anxiously at his father, then turned back to her with concern. 'Will you be all right?'

'Of course I will.' She made her voice sound confident, even though being left alone with the silent George Bunting was not exactly what she would have chosen. Not because she was frightened of him. But because she was not sure if she would do or say the right things. He needed help, that was obvious. He needed someone to get him to open up and get rid of all the sorrow he had closed himself in with. But she was not sure she was that person.

As the Land Rover went out of the yard, she turned away to find a congregation of dogs sitting behind her. Their big, soft eyes looked at her as if they understood all that had happened. 'You did well today,' she said, remembering that they had been their saviours – in the beginning, at least. She gave them all a pat on the head and scratched each furry chin to convey her gratitude. 'You did nothing wrong. No-one could have foreseen the outcome.' And if you hadn't stopped Jed and Tom Spencer from running away, it might have been Sam they had just taken away in the ambulance, she thought. 'I'll bring you all a biscuit,' she promised, forcing her mind to happier matters, as she finished petting the last dog. Then she went back inside.

There was a strange chill about the kitchen and the silence was so shattering that her gaze pivoted anxiously to George Bunting. She had the feeling if he was still alive she should have been able to hear his breathing. He was alive – if that was the correct word for the numb stupor that held him. She could see the rise and fall of his chest, but there was no other movement. Feeling the chill of the room sinking into her, she tossed more coal on to the already roaring fire and wrapped her arms around herself in protection.

She turned to George Bunting. 'Everything will be all right.' She spoke the same assurance given to Sam, once again not knowing where it had come from. She went to him and placed her hand over the lifeless ones that lay in his lap. He felt so cold and it took all her strength to not recoil. 'Rhoda is fine now. She's getting the treatment she needs.' She wanted to add: they won't let her die. But she did not have the courage. Too much like famous last words, she told herself.

There was a flicker of life in his dead eyes. But it was gone so quickly that she thought she must have imagined it. She asked him if he wanted a drink – nothing. She suggested he might like to go into the sitting-room and put the television on – nothing.

With a sigh she gave up and went to get the dog biscuits. 'I promised them some,' she said, holding the bag up for him to see. 'They're all waiting in the yard. Then I'm going to burn . . . the . . . er . . .' she hesitated, not wanting to refer to bloody towels and rags. 'I've got some bits and pieces to burn. I won't be long.' A spark of interest returned to his eyes and did not vanish again. She paused, waiting for him to speak. He remained silent. 'I won't be long,' she repeated, and would have walked out then. But as she passed him he suddenly reached out and touched her arm.

'Let me feed them.' He looked at the bag of dog biscuits in her hand, then up into her face.

She smiled. It had been a long time since he had fed the dogs, but she was reminded of the man before the accident – who would never let anyone else get near his beloved collies. 'Of course you can. You hold that and I'll push you out.' She placed the bag of biscuits on his lap and turned the wheelchair round and steered him through the door and out into the farmyard. It was a good sign, she told herself. Maybe the dogs were just what he needed. He might tell them things he would not tell another person.

The dogs eagerly gathered round and Hannah left him in the midst of them, happily content that he was on the mend.

Tipping the bloodied contents of the sack on to the ground, she doused it with petrol and tossed a match on to it. It burnt well, the flames leaping up and adding a touch of pink to her pale cheeks. Within minutes there was nothing left but black ash. She raked it over, making sure there were no hot spots left to start up again – the last thing they needed was a fire on top of everything else. She stared down at the black remnants all spread around.

For some reason she was still doubtful and she fetched a bucket of water and drenched it all, just to make sure.

It was not until she had a sodden mess that had no chance of leaping back into flames, that she realized she was just wasting time. She was putting off the moment when she had to step back inside the kitchen that seemed to have had all the warmth and comfort wrung out of it. And if George Bunting was talking to the dogs she wanted to leave him that way for as long as possible, she thought, comforting herself that she was thinking of him and not only herself.

Pondering on the unwelcome task of shortly having to tell the children what had happened, she finally went back to the house. The dogs were all gathered round something in the middle of the yard but George Bunting was no longer outside. She gave a sigh. The dogs had not held him as long as she had hoped and he had gone back inside on his own.

It was not until she reached the dogs that she saw they were gathered round the bag of biscuits. It was lying on the ground!

The bag would have fallen off his knee as he tried to get back inside over the doorstep. But even as she said the words to herself, she knew that if he had gone inside he would not just have left the bag of biscuits open in the middle of the yard so the dogs could have a free-for-all. He had always been too particular about keeping them fit. Panic clutching at her, she looked around. There was no sign of him anywhere. She raced into the house. The kitchen was empty, so was the bedroom he had shared with Rhoda, the office and sitting-room also. She was halfway up the stairs when reason returned enough to tell her he could not get up them any more. Racing down again she flew out into the yard once more. He had to be out here, she told herself. But where? Crashing into the stables found her nothing, except disdainful snorts from Samson and Delilah who greatly objected to having her coming upon them like a whirling dervish. The milking parlour was deserted and there was no human head amongst the mass of bleating sheep's heads in the biggest shed in the yard.

'Where?' she screamed in frustration, as she raced back up the yard, her feet slipping and sliding on the frosty mud. She flew to the gate. He couldn't have gone off down the lane, she told herself. But when she saw the empty lane stretching out before her she experienced a sinking disappointment. There was no wheelchair trundling down the hill that she could race after; no George Bunting she could grab back and give a piece of her mind for putting her through this.

She spun back to the house. It was then she saw it. A gasp flew from her mouth. She blinked. It wasn't possible! 'How?' she voiced in utter disbelief, too stunned to do anything and for several heartbeats only standing there and staring. 'How could he get up there?' she asked, as Peg came sniffing round her feet. But Hannah did not see the collie's concern for her distress. All she could see was George Bunting's wheelchair perched precariously on the edge of the craggy face of the Tor.

In the next moment she leaped back to life. Almost tripping over Peg, she tore up the path, forcing herself to a speed that tightened her chest and cut her breathing into short, noisy gasps as she fought against the wind and its sudden gusting, backwards thrusts. Along the grassy upward slope, then over the top she ran. All she could think was that she had to get to him.

As she got nearer she could see the wheelchair was perched as precariously close to the edge as it had appeared from the farm. He was sitting staring outwards, not looking at the hills or the sky, but into the void of empty air that swept down to the field below.

'George!' she shouted, the very first time she had ever called him by his first name alone. He did not look round.

She did not know if he was choosing to ignore her or if her voice had been lost on the wind. 'George!' She tried again, stumbling in her haste and almost falling down a hidden hole in the long grass. Again there was no reaction to tell her if he had heard.

'No! No! No!' she began to sob, as the pain in her chest became unbearable and exhaustion made her feet slip and slide more frequently.

She was within ten yards of him, when he suddenly lifted his face to the grey sky. 'Rhoda,' he called, not with pain or anguish, but as if she was there and he was greeting her. Then he gave one mighty shove and launched himself and the wheelchair over the edge.

'No!' Hannah screamed, throwing herself at him. But she was too late. Like a bird he took to the air, his arms reaching out to welcome death. The cursed wheelchair, the bain of his latter years, following behind him.

Hannah lay prostrate, clinging frantically to the grass. Her head and shoulders were suspended over the edge and only then did she realize she could have gone with him. She looked down the sheer face, at the crumpled body lying so very still, the wheelchair smashed into two separate pieces lying close by. The ground suddenly began to move, coming up to meet her then dropping suddenly away again. Tightening her grip on the fragile grass, she closed her eyes. A whimper rose in her throat. 'Sam,' she whispered, not daring to move as shock trembled through her.

She was not sure how long she stayed there. It seemed like an eternity, but could have been seconds. Slowly her reason returned, telling her she had to do something. With eyes tightly closed, she clamped her hands to the hard soil beneath the grass of her first tenuous hold, and using great caution, wriggled backwards, inch by inch, not daring to move too much, or too suddenly. When she first dared open her eyes she thought she must have moved back far enough to be safe – only to find she had moved all of three inches. She quickly closed her eyes and began to wriggle again. This time she did not stop until she felt grass tickling her face. Heaving a sigh of relief, she scrambled on to all fours and crawled to a safer distance.

Her legs were trembling and almost let her down when she first felt herself to be far enough away from the precipitous edge to stand up. She glanced at her watch. It was twenty-five-past-four. The knowledge that Sam would be back by now, returned the strength to her legs and urged them to move and she began to run.

The scene inside the kitchen was not a happy one. As soon as she walked through the door, she knew Sam had already told the children. Jenny sat at the table, looking bewildered and being far too still and silent for the lively little girl she usually was. Sam was standing by the sink, a sobbing David in his arms.

Sam looked up at her with surprise. 'I thought you must have gone down to the station with him,' he said.

She shook her head. He thought the police had come back to collect his father and she had gone with them. 'I . . . I need to talk to you.'

Sam looked down at the distraught boy in his arms, then back to her with an expression that asked: can't it wait.

She shook her head again, just as the telephone began to ring. It startled her and her eyes pivoted to the old, black Bakelite instrument, but it rang several times before she went to it and slowly lifted the receiver. It was as if she already knew the message it would give.

'Hello,' she said cautiously, then stood very still and quiet as she listened. When the message came to an end, she said simply, 'Thank you.' As she put the receiver down, she turned to Sam with a numbness that went beyond despair.

'What . . . ?' he asked. But his tone of voice told her he already knew the answer.

For a moment she stared at David's bent head. Then she looked into Sam's face and nodded her head at the door, telling him she had to speak to him alone.

Prising the boy away from him, he pushed him down on to a chair. 'I won't be long. I want to talk to Hannah,' he said, looking deep into the lad's swollen eyes.

David gave a snuffle and nodded his head.

Sam gave him a reassuring squeeze on the shoulder. 'We'll only be outside. We won't be far away,' he assured, with a gentleness that increased the emotion swelling in Hannah's throat. Then he took her arm and guided her through the door.

The moment they were in the yard and the door closed behind them, Hannah said flatly, 'Rhoda is dead.'

Sam gave a groan.

'She died at nineteen-minutes-past-four,' she sobbed, too stunned to realize the time would mean nothing to him. 'Within seconds,' she continued, not thinking. She did not know exactly what time George Bunting had thrown himself off the Tor, but it must have been very close. She remembered him calling out Rhoda's name – as if he was seeing her.

'What do you mean?'

She looked up into his puzzled eyes and the truth hit her. 'Oh Sam!' She fell against him and began to sob. He did not know his father was dead, and she had to tell him. Taking a firm grip on her own emotion, she told him what had happened, where she had been.

When she began speaking he had not had much colour. When she came to the end he had none. His face looked like paper. 'But how? How? How?' It was all he could utter. The same question she had asked herself as she hurried back across the Tor. How had he got himself up the muddy path and over the grassy Tor? How had the wheelchair not tipped up on the bumpy surface and thrown him out on to the ground? And, most of all, how had he done it so quickly?

440

She dropped her head, burying her face against his chest. 'I should not have left him,' she said, her voice heavy with guilt.

'Hush!' Sam rested his face against the top of her head. 'It wasn't your fault. I'd have done the same.' He spoke with loving concern and held her tightly. 'Oh, Hannah, I'm so glad you're here,' he said with feeling.

'And I'm glad you're here,' she echoed, but as she looked up into the bleakness of his features, she could not help but think that if she had never been there none of this would have happened: his father's accident; Rhoda; even Jed might not have gone so far as to get himself thrown out if she had not been around to irritate him. All because the wind blew a tree down. An ill wind, she thought. Some would call it an act of God. She stared sadly into Sam's darkly shadowed eyes, feeling the emotion in her throat knotting tighter. It had been an act of God that had brought them together, and for that she would always thank the Almighty. But it seemed so unfair that others had to suffer for her happiness. 'Come on.' Standing back she tugged at his hand. 'We have to go and tell David about his mother.' It was not a task she was looking forward to, but at that moment it seemed immensely preferable to wallowing in her own depressing thoughts.

Sam gave a nod. 'We shouldn't leave them alone at a time like this.'

Jenny was still looking bewildered, but now her legs were swinging to and fro and her thumb was stuck in her mouth. David's head was bent low, his arms hanging loosely between his legs. His sobbing had stopped and his silence was twice as shattering.

Hannah went to him. Taking his arms she pulled him to his feet and wrapped her arms around him. A bitter sweet smile came to her lips as he fell against her. He was growing fast and his height had taken some of the weight from him. His lanky thirteen-year-old frame put her in mind of the thin little boy she had first come across at the bus station – it seemed so long ago now. She gave a little gasp as emotion got the better of her.

Sam stepped forward. 'Do you want me . . . ?' he began.

She shook her head. It was her turn now to share the burden. 'David,' she said gently, bringing the boy's distraught face up to hers. 'That telephone call was from the hospital.'

'Is mum getting better?'

It was a moment before she could reply. The tears she had been holding back, welled in her eyes. She shook her head, forcing them back. 'Your mum died, love,' she said simply, not knowing a better way to put it.

He stared woodenly at her face, as if he had not heard. Then his head began to shake from side to side. 'No! No! No!' It was all he could say, his eyes pleading with her to tell him the words she had just spoken were not true.

'It's better than her suffering,' Sam said, coming to them and laying his arm around the boy's shoulders.

For several moments the only sound in the room was the crackling of the fire. Then David began to sob, slowly and hopelessly. His head fell against Hannah and his fingers clenched and turned so tightly in the wool at the back of her jumper, that she had the feeling there would be a hole in it when he had finished.

It was then that a tiny voice said, 'Why has Auntie Rhoda died?' Hannah and Sam both looked up, just as Jenny's bottom lip dithered and a large tear rolled from her big, bewildered eyes.

'Oh, love!' Sam rushed to the little girl, sweeping her up in his arms. Because Rhoda was David's mother they had been more concerned for him, and Jenny's unusual silence had made them forget she was sitting there listening to it all.

'Isn't she coming back?'

Sam shook his head. 'No, love.' His voice was so quiet, as if not speaking too loudly would soften the blow.

Jenny's little arms coiled tightly round his neck and her glistening eyes fastened very seriously on his. 'Who will put me to bed?' she asked.

The despair of the innocently childish enquiry explained so clearly just how much Rhoda was going to be missed. Neither Sam nor Hannah could reply immediately and before they could find words, David's head suddenly came up.

'Where will I go? I've got nowhere to live now,' he gasped, his grief stricken face crumpling all over again.

'Oh, Love!' Hannah pulled him back to her and tightened her arms around him. 'You'll live here! With us! We'd never send you away. We're your family. You're one of us. You belong here!'

As David clung to her and sobbed with an intensity that shook her own limbs, she lifted her gaze above his bent head and found Sam's eye looking back at her. He smiled at her, with a sadness that spoke far greater than words. In the space of a day they had got a family: the children he had not dared to give her. But what a way to get them! It was that ill wind again, she told herself, and returned his smile with moist eyes.

Chapter Twenty-Eight

George Bunting, Rhoda and Jed were all buried the week before Christmas. They had had to wait that long before the inquest was over and the police had satisfied their enquiries. Hannah found it very wearing and irritating. After all, the police had been there, had seen it happening and she really could not understand the necessity of them asking questions to which they already knew the answers. It just delayed everything, when all they wanted to do was put it behind them and get life at the Tor back to normal. To make matters worse, Tom Spencer's trial would not be coming up until the summer. That, Hannah felt, should have had priority. The man was being kept in prison but no sentence had been passed.

'He should get life,' she had told Sam. 'They should throw away the key. I want to know Tom Spencer is going to be kept inside for a very long time – long enough for David to grow into a man and not be afraid of him when he comes out. Oh! why did they do away with the death sentence?'

Sam had wrapped his arm around her shoulders and pulled her close. He tried to comfort her but he knew his words were of little help. As far as he was concerned Tom Spencer should be charged with murder, but he knew it was not so simple as that. He hoped that the man would not get some clever barrister who would try to claim it was a 'crime of passion' and get him off with nothing more than a slap on the wrist. Under the circumstances his defence lawyers could try, and if he did get off lightly he did not know what it would do to David – or to Hannah. Beneath their cloud of depression Christmas was not a happy time. Hannah did her best to try and make it a festive occasion for the children, but the memories were too new and still too strong to obliterate with a few sprigs of holly and shiny balls on a tree.

Jenny seemed to be getting over it the best, her tender years making it easier for her to forget. Unfortunately, it was not so easy for David. Being older, Sam and Hannah had decided he should be told the truth of what had happened. He had taken it very hard and was now throwing himself into work, not giving himself a moment to rest – or to think and remember.

The minute he arrived home from school he would change into working jeans and be off out to the yard. If he was inside for any length of time he would start cleaning the windows, washing down cupboard doors, sweeping the kitchen floor.

Sam tried to reassure Hannah that time would heal, but she could not stop worrying about David. He was working too hard and looking tired. And so was Sam. She was helping him in the yard whenever she could. The house was by no means as spick and span as when Rhoda had been in charge. But just keeping it half-respectable, along with getting all the meals, was taking up more time than she would have liked. Fortunately, Jenny had started school after the Christmas holiday, so she was not around the house all day in need of attention.

Nevertheless, they needed help and were on the look out for a farm-hand. Hannah was sure they would get someone now George Bunting was no longer at the Tor. But with the foot-and-mouth still hanging over their heads it was a difficult time to take on staff. It wasn't for lack of men looking for work. With farms all over the county having to slaughter their herds there were plenty of men being laid off. But Sam was nervous of taking on someone who had come from a place with the disease. And both he and Hannah had discounted the old solution of getting another housekeeper. They both felt it was best for David and Jenny to have someone they knew looking after them. Especially David. It would have been painful for him to see a stranger step into his mother's shoes.

So they battled on, in more ways than one. The new year had come in like a lion, with bitterly cold winds and a lot of snow. The snow plough was fixed to the Land Rover's radiator and every day Sam had to force a path down the lane to get David and Jenny to school. Then they kept their fingers crossed that they would be able to get down in the afternoon to bring them back home.

Hannah was crossing the yard, watching her steps on the crunchy, frozen snow, all the dog bowls balanced precariously in her hands. The wind was at its most vicious, biting through even the thickest clothing, and her head was bent low, so that it was only by chance she noticed Sam. He was perched on an old milk churn standing outside the milking parlour door, with a row of silver icicles hanging from the guttering above his head, like daggers ready to fall. His head was bowed and his hands were clasped tightly together between his knees. He looked as if he was in prayer.

She stopped short and stared at him. The dogs began to bound around her legs, but their noisy demands to be fed did not make him look up. 'Sam!' she called. 'What is it?' There was no response and she rushed to the stables and dropped the food bowls down on the floor to get rid of the nuisance dogs. Then she hurried to him.

'What is it?' she demanded, fear putting a sharpness in her voice that she had not intended.

He looked up slowly, a bleakness in his eyes that was colder than the wind cutting through her bones. 'I didn't think anything else could go wrong,' he said, and gave a bark of bitter laughter that made him sound more like his dead brother than himself. 'I thought we'd had it all for a good long time – that we were safe!' The last was said with irony.

'Safe from what?' she questioned, feeling the breath still in her lungs as she read his mind.

'We've got it,' he said simply.

'Oh no!' She dropped heavily on to the milk churn by his side and almost fell off when it rocked unsteadily.

Sam grabbed her hastily outflung arm. 'Steady on! We don't need any broken arms or legs . . . as well!'

It made her smile, even though she felt like crying. It also brought a smile to Sam's lips, though not to his eyes. He looked up at the grey stone house. 'Do you think this place is cursed?' The words were spoken too seriously to be joking.

She clasped his left hand in both her own and pulled it close to her heart. 'Cursed with love,' she said in earnest. 'Because, Sam Bunting, even when you've got a face fit to turn the cream, I still feel more love for you in here than I do for my own self.'

His smile did reach his eyes then. 'I know that,' he said, with a feeling that warmed her deep inside. 'And I know I'm glad you're here with me.' Echoing the words he had spoken the day of the shootings, he pulled her head down to rest on his shoulder. They remained that way until the icy air began to bite too hard and his chest lifted on a sigh. She looked up into his resigned face, as he said, 'I'd better go and notify the Ministry.' He stood up and pulled her to her feet. Then, hand in hand, they walked slowly across the yard, both knowing it was too late to hurry. Whether they notified the Ministry of Agriculture in five minutes, or fifty, the outcome was going to be the same.

*   *   *

For the following weeks life on the Tor resembled living in a morgue. Heavy oilskins had to be worn around the farm, so they could be doused with disinfectant every time anyone had been round the yard. A bed of disinfected straw was laid at the gates so that any vehicles coming or going had their tyres cleansed on passing. And there were new notices. This time not polite requests not to stray, but definite orders to keep out. They were everywhere. Four were stuck on the gate posts and there were others all around the boundary of the land. Hannah began to feel like a leper, as if she herself was unclean and not fit to associate with the world outside their contaminated kingdom.

The entire herd and flock had to be slaughtered and burned, including the pregnant ewes. For days a thick pall of smoke hung over the Tor, adding to everyone's depression. David was inconsolable. He cried as he had cried on the day his mother died. For several weeks after the last slaughter they were still coming across him, hidden in a stall with one of the horses, or surrounded by a group of puzzled dogs, sobbing quietly.

It was on one such occasion when Hannah was going to feed the hens that she found him huddled in the hay in one of the dutch barns. She stopped short. Peg was with him, her head resting in his lap, her eyes looking up at him with a soft, doe-like concern. They made such a heart-rending picture and Hannah shook her head, wondering what it was going to take to make David forget everything. So much had happened, one event on top of another, and his young shoulders were very fragile and not up to taking the strain.

'We'll get back to normal,' she reassured, moving forward and making her presence known. 'When the epidemic has run its course we'll stock up again. You'll have more animals to look after.' At least she hoped he would. Sam had not spoken of re-stocking. In fact he hadn't spoken of much lately. When the disease had first hit them he had managed it well. But then he had had plenty to do, even if it had been depressing work. Once the animals had gone and the farm had been cleaned and cleaned and cleaned again, he had withdrawn into himself. It was only delayed reaction to the disease on top of the shootings, she had told herself at first. But it was now going on a bit too long for her liking.

David lifted red-rimmed eyes to her and gave a loud snuffle. 'But what if there isn't enough money?'

'Oh love!' She sank to her knees, shocked by the way his young mind worked. Then she smiled and pulled him into her arms, remembering the little boy with half a cup of hot chocolate at the bus station café. The years had not made him forget, either. Her heart ached that such young shoulders could feel such old problems. 'Money is no problem,' she assured. 'And it certainly is not anything you have to think about. Sam and I will deal with all that – and *we're* not worried about it!' George Bunting had left the farm and everything to Sam, without any mention of it then being passed to Jenny. And the amount of money he had left was far more than anyone had expected. Sam had been under the impression that all the money was in the farm account. But his father had possessed a secret personal account that held more money than Hannah had thought possible for one person to own. 'Life might be difficult at the moment . . .' she said, holding David away and looking deep into his eyes, '. . . but money is of no concern at all.'

He managed a smile, but it was very weak.

*　　*　　*

It was the end of March before all the restrictions were lifted and everyone in the farming community breathed a sigh of relief that the epidemic had finally worn itself out. But the good news did not have the expected affect at Bunting's Tor.

Sam continued to brood. In the mornings he took David and Jenny to school and in the afternoons he fetched them home again. In between those times he wandered around the farm, through the empty fields and over the deserted Tor. In the evenings he would close himself off in the office, the way his father used to do. They very rarely made love, and when they did it was as if he was not completely with her, as if a part of him had gone and been lost. But still Hannah bit her lip from complaining, or asking him outright when he was going to start doing some work again and make the effort to return the farm to normal. She still had the feeling he was finding it difficult coming to terms with his father's death – and Jed's. Despite all the hate and bitterness that had passed between them, he was not immune to the horrific way his brother had died.

'It will take a bit of time,' she said to David, when he asked why they had not yet got themselves a new herd and flock. It hurt to say it because she knew the lack of stock was having a bad effect on the boy. He needed the animals to look after and care for to make him forget his loss. She gave a sigh. Sam was not the only one it had affected. They had all been affected in some way, and now *they* were being affected again by *his* present manner. It had to come to an end, she told herself. Sam had to be told. His lack of enthusiasm was not doing David any good . . . and it was getting her down, as well.

But that evening she began to get the stirrings of a headache and went to bed early and had no chance to speak to him. In the middle of the night she was violently sick, an event which continued to happen at regular intervals throughout the rest of the night and for the following two days. After that she was only sick when she ate or drank anything, but now she had diarrhoea as well. Nothing would stay in her increasingly tender stomach.

'If it isn't one thing it's another,' she mumbled, around the thermometer stuck in her mouth.

Dr Hallam's astute eyes frowned at her over the top of his spectacles. 'Shut up and keep it under your tongue,' he ordered.

She clamped her lips together and remained silent until he pulled the thermometer out and studied it carefully.

'It's only the tummy bug that's going around,' he pronounced. 'You've just got a bad dose of it.'

She gave a sigh. 'As I said, if it isn't one thing it's another.' It was not like her to send for the doctor for something so minor, but it had been going on for five days now and she felt so weak and useless.

Dr Hallam peered over his glasses again. 'Yes, well it is probably that attitude that has got you such a bad dose. It isn't like you to just lie there and give in. Start fighting it and you'll be better in a couple of days.' She'd be better in a couple of days anyway, he thought, returning the thermometer to the old Gladstone bag and taking out a bottle of cloudy white medicine. But giving her something to think about wouldn't hurt. She had let herself get run down. It wasn't surprising, what with everything. But it was unusual for her to even pick up a passing cold, and he felt a gentle shove might help speed her recovery along. He scribbled on the bottle's label and put it down on the bedside table. 'That will help settle your stomach. The vomiting should stop today but the diarrhoea will go on a bit longer.'

'I can handle that if you can stop me being sick.' Her stomach felt like a punch-bag and the retching as if she was being torn apart.

'Try and drink. You need plenty of liquid.' Snapping his scruffy bag shut, he picked it up and once more peered over the top of his glasses. 'If the sickness has not stopped by tomorrow morning, let me know.' Pushing his glasses further up his nose, he bid her goodbye and walked out.

The sickness stopped later that afternoon. By the following day she was feeling almost like her old self again and got up and went downstairs for the first time in five days. For the next three days Sam nursed her and cared for her as if she was still sick. While he was being so good to her she had not got the heart to start nagging him about the farm. But when she began to get restless and wanting to be up and doing things for herself, and he still wanted to do everything for her, she began to see his reluctance was more to do with himself. Her illness had forced him back into a working pattern of life, but it was her working pattern: in the house; cleaning; cooking; looking after the children. It was giving him something to do and he had found that having something to do kept his mind away from brooding. But it also meant he was hiding from the farm and from his real work. He was hiding from his real life, Hannah told herself worriedly, and knew she should not have waited so long before making him see he needed to re-stock the farm – for his own well-being.

The following morning when Sam returned after taking David and Jenny to school, Hannah was waiting for him with Samson and Delilah saddled and bridled. She wanted to get him out into the open, into the countryside that meant so much to him. And it was a beautiful day, perfect for taking a slow walk across the Tor while they talked.

'I thought we'd take them out together,' she said, as he stepped out of the Land Rover and frowned at the pair. He looked about to object. 'Come on!' she insisted. 'You can't disappoint the horses now they're ready.' Hoisting herself on to Delilah's back, she tossed Samson's rein to him.

He caught it, but still held back.

'It's just the day for it.' She looked up into the clear blue sky. It was the end of May but it could have been high summer. There was not a cloud to be seen and the only hint of wind was a gentle, warming breeze.

'Are you sure you're up to it?'

He was repeating the same question he asked every time she picked up a tea-towel or a dirty cup. Did he expect her to stay an invalid, just so he did not have to face reality? She gave an inward sigh. 'What else have you got to do?' she asked pointedly.

He gave a grim smile. Then surprised her by saying, 'Absolutely nothing!' She had expected a list of household chores. Then he threw himself on to Samson's saddle and led the way silently out of the yard.

They kept the pace slow at first. But Samson's frustration soon began to show. His head tossed and his irritable eyes rolled, and he strained on the rein.

'He's raring to go,' Hannah said, turning to look at Sam and hoping some of the stallion's enthusiasm might rub off on him and make him rare off – down to the market to re-stock!

'Maybe he's got somewhere to go.' The harshness of his voice startled her and before she could respond he had given Samson his head and the stallion was galloping away.

Hannah urged Delilah forward. But Samson was at full pelt and, as fast as the little mare went, she could not close the gap. Not until they reached the far end of the flat plateau did Sam draw Samson in, pulling him to a stop very close to the spot where his father had pulled the horse to a stop on the fateful day he had raced Hannah across the Tor. But that was in the past and could not be mended and she would not think of anything now, except Sam and the future.

When she brought Delilah up close to Samson's side, Sam was gazing out over the countryside that swept down to the valley bottom way below. Hannah matched him, sitting silently and gazing out over the land, his land. The sun picked out the hoary whiteness of May blossom scattered through the fresh, green hedgerows. Once the view would have pleased her, but the silence and stillness of the empty fields was soul destroying. Even the birds seemed to have deserted the air at that moment.

'Look at it!' Sam finally said, the flatness of defeat in his voice. 'What is it?'

'It's yours,' she stressed meaningfully, her eyes filled with purpose as they turned to him. 'Don't stop loving it.'

He smiled at her then, but with the sadness that had been his constant companion of late. 'It's ours,' he pointed out. He turned back to gaze at the redundant fields and heaved a sigh. 'I'll not stop loving it. But . . .' he paused, '. . . all the work . . . all the care . . . then to watch them all go that way.'

'That's the way of farming.' She stared at him bewilderedly. He had farmed all his life, he knew the outcome well enough: you reared the stock, cared for them, but the end result was always the same. When the stock left the farm you tried not to think too much about their inevitable destination.

'It isn't the way for pregnant ewes!' His sudden burst of anger startled the horses. Both pranced and skittered erratically. When they had been calmed down, he turned to her sadly. 'I don't ever again want to watch any animal I've cared for going up in smoke.' His voice was taut and filled with the pain of anger.

'I know!' Her smile was tight with regret. Moving Delilah up to the big grey's side, she reached out a comforting hand to him. 'You just have to put it all behind you and start again,' she said gently. 'You can now. You've waited long enough.' The Ministry of Agriculture stipulated twenty-eight days had to pass from the last slaughter before new stock could be put back into the fields. They had gone over double that time, plus some. 'It's your livelihood, Sam. You have to make yourself do it!'

He shook his head. 'Not any more. We could live very comfortably for the rest of our days on what dad left.'

'Oh Sam!' she uttered in shock and disbelief. 'You wouldn't be happy without the farm.'

'I might,' he said, with a confidence that stunned her. 'I might be a lot happier doing something else.'

'What else could you do? This place is in your blood. You owe it to yourself, your father and all the generations of Buntings who have loved this land before you, to keep it going. Where would you be now if one of them had given up at the first setback? Do you think it built itself? Don't you think blood, sweat and tears went into every stone?' She fell silent then, waiting for some response.

It took a while. At first he only stared at her, looking as if he wanted to get right down off Samson's back, drag her off Delilah's back and shake her until her teeth rattled. Hannah remained firm, silently pleading for an answer from his tight lips. But when he finally spoke it was not what she wanted to hear.

'But everything has changed,' he said flatly. 'It feels as if somebody is saying now that dad has gone the rest should go. As if it shouldn't really belong to me.'

'Rubbish!' she countered hotly. 'Your father left it to you because he knew you were a good enough farmer to keep it going. That you were the one who could handle a crisis like this. He wouldn't have left it to you if he had thought you were going to give up at the first sign of trouble. He would have sooner set fire to the place and razed it to the ground himself.' When she reached the end she was trembling from fear of failure. She could not fail, she begged, fixing him with a determined glare that brooked no disagreement. It hurt her to be angry with him, but she had to stay firm, for his own sake. If she allowed him to turn his back on the farm she would be as guilty of murder as Tom Spencer, because without the stock to tend and the land to care for Sam would die: he would have nothing left to live for. 'If your dad had still been alive today he would have sent you out to buy a new herd the moment the fields were clear – and you would have done it without question or complaint. So why can't you do it now, for yourself. And if you're not worth doing it for, then you should be doing it for the children.' Her gaze hardened and condemned him on the last. 'Enough has changed for them to cope with in one go.' She hesitated, then, her voice gentling, continued, 'We need to get life back to normal for the children, and for ourselves. David especially. He needs a farm filled with animals to make him forget. We're all they've got now, we can't let them down. If we can't pick ourselves up and start all over again how can we expect them to? They need you Sam, to be just the same as you were before. I need you, Sam.'

He looked up then, his eyes glittering with unshed tears, and she felt a spark of hope even before, his voice thick with emotion, he said, 'And you have me.'

Relief rushed through her. 'I love you, Sam Bunting!' She spoke with great feeling, as she felt her love for him swell inside her chest, happy to have been released from the prison it had been trapped in. And she reached over and took hold of his hand, needing to feel the touch that had been denied her these past weeks.

'And I love you. And I need you just the way we were before.' His smile was full of the love he spoke of and he reached out and curled his hand around her neck and pulled her closer, kissing her lingeringly.

When he let her go, she pulled away just far enough to look deep into his eyes. 'Then don't let's change a thing,' she said. 'Unless it's bringing a new herd and a new flock into the empty fields.'

'You're right,' he agreed, and a sigh of regret lifted his chest. 'I've been selfish.'

'Not selfish,' she assured. 'Just confused,' she added knowledgeably. After all, she knew exactly how he felt, had experienced it all herself. His father and his brother and the life he had known since childhood had been snatched violently away from him. Just as hers had been when the oak tree smashed through her home. 'One good turn deserves another,' she said.

It made him frown and she laughed at him. 'Sam Bunting . . .' she scolded, '. . . you haven't forgotten it was you who took me in and showed me that life was worth living again – when I'd lost everything!' she reminded him, narrowing her eyes in teasing rebuke.

He gave a laugh which softened into a smile of deep affection. 'If I remember right that was more dad's doing than mine.'

'But it was you I stayed here for.' Her voice was soft with emotion, as she recalled the times she had tried to leave, only to change her mind – as if someone, somewhere had been telling her not to. Although she laughed at the improbability of her thoughts, she still said, 'I'm glad I listened. I'm glad *I* took the chance of that new life.'

'And I'm glad you were the only saucy little milkmaid who was not afraid of Bunting's Claw.' Throwing his leg over Samson's back, he dropped to the ground. 'Because . . .' he said, a meaningful light entering his eyes and banishing his earlier sadness, '. . . there isn't anybody in the whole wide world I'd rather have by my side to start all over again with.' He held up his arms and she slid into them.

'And exactly what do you mean by saucy?' she questioned, feigning shock as he let her slowly to the ground. But there was a smile on her face at the joke he had aimed at himself, at Bunting's Claw, the name that had been torture to him.

'Hannah Bunting!' he exclaimed, in the same manner she had previously used on him. 'You haven't forgotten it was you who took me into the stables and showed me that life was worth living?' His dark eyebrows arched in amusement.

'Oh yes!' She cocked her chin at him and narrowed her eyes. 'I was under the impression that you had a hand in that.'

He grimaced. 'And what a hand,' he said. But there was none of the old repugnance in his voice and when he lifted his deformed hand and held it out before him, there was a smile on his face.

'What a hand,' she repeated with feeling, and took his hand and pressed it to her cheek and touched her lips to the thickened digit that should have been his thumb. 'But one of the only two hands that I ever want to feel touching me!'

'Oh Hannah!' he mouthed thickly. Then he drew her into his arms and kissed her with an urgency that matched the early days of their marriage. She responded in kind, moulding herself to the length of him and feeling she had come home. As he lowered her slowly into the long, sun-warmed grass, she knew the wild, beautiful Tor was where they both belonged: Sam with the farm of his ancestors; she with the man she loved.

Chapter Twenty-Nine

'Come on lazy bones,' Sam urged. He was up and dressed and ready to go out of the bedroom. He slanted a gaze at Hannah. 'It's all over now,' he said meaningfully.

She gave a nod of understanding. Yesterday had been Tom Spencer's court case and the man had finally got his just deserts. The judge had shown no pity, had taken no notice of the man's whining excuses that he was driven to it because his wife was 'living over the broom' with another man, and had given him a life sentence. It was what Hannah had prayed for, even with remission he would not be out again until David was a man and well able to deal with him. She gave a sigh. She should be happy. But . . . !

'We've got a farm to run again!' Sam pointed out, when she made no attempt to move herself. Sheep once more roamed the Tor and the bottom pasture was filled with a new herd of pedigree Friesians.

She stared at him blankly. Should she tell him? Indecision rolled around inside her head. No, she finally decided – backing out once again.

'I'm coming,' she said, and forced herself out of bed, pretending the gnawing queasiness inside her stomach did not exist.

Fortunately, once Sam had seen her stirring he was happy and left her alone to pursue the regular exercise of deep breathing needed to keep the contents of her stomach where they were. She sat on the bed, drawing the noisy breaths: in and out, in and out. Up to now they had been sufficient to conceal her condition for the length of time it took to get downstairs and consume the slice of toast that would still the churning. But she could not go on like this for much longer. Sam had to be told – before he found out for himself.

Still taking deep breaths, she stood up and began to dress. She should go and see the doctor and find out for sure before she told Sam, she thought. The zip of her jeans was only halfway up when she stopped short. She was sure! She did not need a doctor to confirm her condition. She dropped heavily on to the bed once more. Letting her head fall forward she closed her eyes tightly, as if the action would be enough to blank out her imagination of Sam's reaction to the news that he was to become a father. She gave a groan, as if in physical pain. She had no doubt that she was pregnant, everything pointed to it. After her first missed period she had told herself it was only because she had been ill. But she had known even then that she was trying to convince herself. Because she knew that the day on the Tor, when Sam had made love to her so gently in the grass, that he had given her a baby. That very evening she knew it could have happened. When she went to bed she found her packet of contraceptive pills in the drawer. The day was Thursday. The last pill to have been taken from the packet was Tuesday, the previous week. Since the beginning of her illness she had forgotten to take them – and it was nine days!

Forcing herself up off the bed she tugged her zip to its full height. She was feeling in need of a bit of brightness to lift her wilting spirits and tugged a royal blue tee shirt over her head. But the bright colour had very little effect on her grey mood, and as she went to the door she suddenly stopped and placed her hands over her stomach. She was carrying Sam's baby and she wanted it and would love it – but what would it do to Sam if it was born with the deformity he had vowed never to pass on?

The kitchen was empty. Sam had gone out to call the cows up and Hannah had heard David in the bathroom as she came past the door. Jenny never appeared until she was called and her breakfast was waiting on the table.

Happy that everything was running as normal and she had time to eat the illicit piece of toast, Hannah popped a slice of bread into the toaster. When it was ready she ate it as slowly as was possible. But she had to swallow the very last bite without chewing it, as she heard David running down the stairs.

'I'm all behind,' she said, frantically throwing bacon into the frying pan as he came through the door.

He went straight to the bread and began slicing it up.

He never had to be asked. He was just like his mother, Hannah thought smiling to herself. Rhoda had always been able to sense when things needed doing, or when they needed leaving alone. It was fortunate he had very little of his father in him, she told herself, and brought herself up short, the thought thrusting her own condition at her. Maybe her baby would be more like her than Sam. She broke an egg into the frying pan and paused. That was not what she wanted. She wanted Sam's baby to be like him: to look like him; be as kind and gentle as he was – but not to have his left hand!

She gave a sigh. She was asking for the moon and stars. She wanted Sam's baby to be perfect so it would prove to him that he was perfect. But if it wasn't . . . The second egg she cracked missed the frying pan and splattered down the side of the oven. 'Oh . . . !' she groaned in frustration.

'What's wrong?' David came to her side, looking anxious.

'Nothing.' She attempted a smile, but knew it was rather lop-sided. 'I got up late and now I can't catch up with myself.'

His eyes watched her steadily, with an understanding far greater than his thirteen years. It made him look even more like his mother and put a tightness in

Hannah's chest. Whatever her problems might be, they were nothing compared to what he had gone through in his short life, she reminded herself. She forced a smile, that this time managed to appear genuine. 'How do you feel about yesterday?' When they had told him the verdict he had nodded his head as if he approved, but he had not spoken, and Sam had said it was best to give him time to consider it before trying to get him to comment.

'I'm glad. I don't want to ever see him again.'

The loathing in his voice put a tight smile on Hannah's lips. 'You won't have to,' she said, and wrapped an arm around his shoulders and gave him a hug. 'But don't let it turn you bitter. Hatred can eat you up and your mum would not have wanted that, she loved you too much. He's gone now, he can't hurt you any more.'

He gave a nod. Then he grimaced. 'You were late to start with, don't you think you should be getting on. The boss will be back in a minute, looking for his breakfast. Then we'll both get the sack.' His joking put a smile on her face, even though she could see he was only changing the subject – it was still too painful for him.

'You go and shout Jenny down and let me get on.' She turned him round and gave him a little shove towards the door, and hoped his pain would finally go and not prove to be the malignant kind. But when she turned back to the sizzling bacon and eggs her mind returned to her own pressing problem. She forked the bacon round the frying pan and gnawed at her bottom lip. It was not only Sam that had to be told the house was going to have a newcomer. David and Jenny also deserved to know the reason for her odd behaviour. Especially David, who might get the wrong impression and think it was something to do with himself. He was naturally very delicate at the moment and could easily leap to the wrong conclusion. She gave a sigh. If she was not careful her tension was going to upset the whole house.

By the time Sam came through the door, David and Jenny were eating their breakfasts and Hannah's mind was made up. After dropping the children at school she would visit Dr Hallam's surgery. Then she would come back and tell Sam.

*   *   *

'Would you like me to come and have a word with Sam?'

Hannah stared blankly at the lock of silver hair hanging over Dr Hallam's forehead. She wondered why she was feeling so shocked. She had known she was pregnant. Yet hearing the professional verdict had stunned her, as if she had been clinging to a slender thread of hope that she could be wrong.

She shook her head. Her voice was lost to her and she dropped her gaze to the deep-red carpet, worn by years of patients' feet seeking solace and reassurance. How many other women had sat in that scuffed brown leather chair and been told they were carrying a child? How many had rejoiced? How many had felt the way she was now feeling: that the earth had been swept from beneath their feet.

'Don't *you* want the baby, Hannah?' The old man's voice was gentle with concern.

'Oh yes!' There was no hesitation, no doubt in her voice. She wanted Sam's baby. It had not been planned and she had never thought herself the maternal type. But now she knew it was there, oh how she wanted it!

When she fell silent the doctor leaned forward, rested his elbows on his brown-check plus-fours, clasped his hands and looked deep into her eyes. 'Because Sam has Lobster Claw Syndrome does not mean any children he has will also be affected.'

'But it doesn't mean they won't either,' she said flatly.

The doctor gave a shrug. 'There is no point in me lying to you, Hannah. You know the chances as well as I do. But until the baby is born I think you should try

463

and believe it will be all right. Worrying will do *you* no good!'

'But even if the baby is not affected it could still pass it on to a child of its own,' she said. It was a statement not a question. She was thinking of Jenny, and Jed's arrogant assumption that he had been perfect.

'Yes. The condition is hereditary. It could go on. Or it could stamp itself out. It has been known.'

The doctor was speaking sense when he said she should hope for the best, she told herself. She was meeting trouble halfway and that was not her usual way of doing things.

'And even if the baby is born with the deformed hand, it isn't the end of the world,' Dr Hallam asserted knowledgeably. 'There are far worse things to be afflicted with. Sam, himself, has got on all right with it – despite having to live with his father's shame. And Jenny never lets it get her down. In fact she is quite proud of it. She's always telling me it was made that way because she is special.'

Hannah smiled thinly. If only Rhoda was still there. Rhoda would have known exactly what to do and say. At least she now had an insight into Rhoda's way of dealing with problems, she told herself. 'Thank you, Dr Hallam,' she said, and stood up ready to leave.

He gave her a smile that was more befitting a favourite niece, than just another patient. 'Your mum and dad would have been thrilled with the news.' He spoke with a feeling that touched her heart.

'Yes,' she said. 'Thank you,' she repeated, trying to swallow back the lump clogging her throat. The doctor had known exactly the right words to say. In all her torment over Sam she had not stopped to think of the other two people who had meant as much to her. Her parents would have been pleased. Especially her dad.

She returned to the farm on a wave of hope, determined to tell Sam the moment she saw him. Unfortunately she drove into the yard to find the vet's cream Land Rover standing there, surrounded by nosy dogs. She had forgotten Col Jennison was due to make a visit to check on the ewes the new tups had serviced.

To make sure the rams were doing their job properly and the ewes were pregnant!

She could have saved herself the journey to the doctor's and got Col to look at her, she thought drily. If the situation had not been so serious, she would have laughed at the irony of it all.

She found them in the kitchen, sitting at the table drinking large mugs of tea. As she walked through the door they both burst out laughing at something Col had just said.

'I take it the tups are in full working order?' She guessed from the joviality that all had gone well – in that direction at least.

Col tossed his blond head and grinned at her. He was the younger partner of the veterinary practice they used. He was not much older than Sam himself and seeing them together always put Hannah in mind of a black and white photograph negative. Col's creamy white hair and the palest blue eyes Hannah had ever seen, were a stark contrast to Sam's black hair and dark eyes. But today they looked even more like opposites. Col had on a white tee shirt with cream cotton slacks, while Sam had a black tee shirt and dark-blue denim jeans. They were almost identical builds and both incredibly handsome, in their own way.

'Of course they are in full working order.' Col affected injured pride. 'You bought those rams on the advice of a very good vet. Nobody is firing duds around here,' he added cheekily.

Both men laughed. Hannah smiled, but had to turn away to hide the blush she felt touching her cheeks. Little did they know, she thought. It was not only the stock that was in full working order. She busied herself with sticking a load of washing in the machine, and wished Col would go and she could get Sam alone and assure him his virility was just as good as his rams'.

She got her wish. It was not many minutes before Col drained his mug and stood up. Then he looked Hannah up and down, taking in her very unusual attire. She was wearing an olive-green, button-through dress with a short, straight skirt and brown cuban-heeled court shoes. He turned to Sam with a mischievous grin. 'It is true then? She has got legs! I was beginning to think it was only a rumour. They don't see daylight very often.'

Sam laughed. 'Oh aye, it's true.'

Hannah slanted an admonishing gaze at Col. 'I don't see you going round mucky farmyards in pinstriped suits.' She knew he was only joking but tension added a spike to her voice that she had not intended. She had deliberately changed into the dress so that she looked and felt her best for when she told Sam their news.

Fortunately, Col took no offence and laughed. 'The bowler hat would frighten the cattle. Not to mention the brolly!'

Realizing she had been out of order, as he passed her on the way to the door, she tossed her head at him and forced herself to match his teasing. 'For your cheek that mug of tea will cost you a bob! You can knock it off your bill,' she added, smiling as he tossed a grin at her before going through the door.

But her smile vanished as soon as the door closed. She watched Sam walk Col to his Land Rover and stand chatting for a few minutes. Then she held her breath as the vehicle drew away and Sam came back to the house.

'He gets worse instead of better,' he said, coming through the door with a smile on his face.

'Yes,' she said, and prayed the smile would still be on his face when she had finished speaking. The only problem was she never got the chance to begin speaking.

Sam stopped just inside the door. 'I'm going over to see Viv Bennett,' he announced. 'Col thinks she might be about to sell up.'

'Oh . . . !' Hannah turned to him, bewildered. 'Does she need help?' she asked. She did not want Sam to go anywhere just at that moment, but her compassion for Viv swelled inside her. The woman owned Northgate Farm. Just over a year ago Viv's husband had died after a long struggle against cancer. Viv had tried to keep the place going after his death but the foot-and-mouth had hit her and that had been the final straw. The last time Hannah had seen her in the village she had guessed the woman had lost heart and was on the verge of giving up.

Sam shook his head. 'Not with any work,' he said, and Hannah frowned. 'Viv hasn't re-stocked. But I was thinking if she was wanting to sell I'd make her an offer.'

'What!' It was the last thing she had imagined he was going to say. Northgate Farm bordered the western side of his land and would be a natural extension to the Tor. But, although it was not of the acreage of the Tor, it was not small. It would mean he owned all the land on that side of the village. 'Why on earth would you want to buy it?' She pulled a chair from beneath the table and sank on to it, the previous problem suddenly forgotten.

He stuck his hands into his pockets and gave a shrug. 'It's got good pasture. We could increase the dairy herd. And when the time comes it will be just right to set David up in.'

She gave an astonished gasp. 'David is only thirteen!'

'I know,' he replied confidently. 'But there will come a day when he wants to cut away from us and be independent. It will be nice to know we've got it there for him.'

'But what . . . ?' She stopped short. She had been about to ask what about this place. She had always looked on David as Sam's heir and she had assumed he had been doing the same. A cold shiver ran down her spine. He could not have guessed she was pregnant – could he? And surely he did not think Jenny was going to become a farmer; the girl possessed as much interest in the animals as her father had shown. No, she told herself, he had not thought any of those things.

'Has Col just told you?' Her voice was sharp with the anger that narrowed her eyes. 'He has, hasn't he?' she insisted. 'You've only just heard about it. You haven't given it any thought at all.' She lifted her arms wide in frustration, then dropped them defeatedly to her sides.

'Col has just told me,' he confirmed, with a lack of concern that made her want to scream at him to stop it. 'But I have thought about extending before now.'

'You never mentioned it!'

'I didn't think there was much chance.' He pulled his hands from his pockets and scratched thoughtfully at his head. 'I don't know. I suppose it must be the inherited Bunting urge to make this place bigger. They've all done it, in the past. Each one could draw a ring round a certain part and say that's my bit.' He hesitated. 'I want to do the same, Hannah.'

She stared at him in amazement. This was a new side of him, one she had never known existed, one she would have preferred never to have seen. It made him more like his father than she wished to believe. And, if he went ahead and bought Northgate, that is how the villagers would view him: just another Bunting trying to lord it over everybody.

She shook her head. 'Does it have to be a place the size of Northgate? What about the smaller ones down the other side of the Tor? One of those might come up for sale.'

Sam did not share her feelings. He shook his head. 'There might never be another chance,' he said. 'Besides, it will help Viv. I can't see there being too many people wanting to buy at the moment. The foot-and-mouth is still too fresh in people's minds.'

Hannah could not dispute that. Viv Bennett was not likely to be overwhelmed with offers. Which also meant that if Sam looked interested the woman would bite his hand off. 'Think about it for a day or two,' she suggested hopefully.

His hands went back inside his pockets. He sucked on his bottom lip and rocked back on his heels a couple of times. Hannah gave an inward sigh, knowing he was not going to see reason. 'It won't hurt to go and find out for certain,' he said, proving her right. 'I don't want to sit and consider it only to find Col was wrong. I'll do as I planned. I'll go and see Viv and find out what's what. Then I'll know if I've got anything to think about or not.'

Hannah could only watch in silence as he walked out. She prayed Col had got it wrong and he had just come upon Viv at a low moment. Because she knew if Northgate was up for sale, Sam was not going to be put off buying it.

Heaving a sigh, she placed her hands over her still-flat stomach. 'This is my bit!' she said bitterly, mimicking his own words. 'And it's his bit, as well. If he only knew it!' It was then it occurred to her that she did have a bit to give him that he could put to the great Bunting empire. It wasn't a lot, only amounting to one field, a garden and an orchard, and the remains of a cottage. But it was something solid for him to add to the deeds of the Tor; something to feed his sudden need to be seen as a true-blue Bunting. She had forgotten the field still, by rights, belonged to her. They already used it as they rotated the herd from one field to another, giving them good pasture while the grass in the field they had been taken from was left to grow and revive.

After scrubbing some potatoes and sticking them in the oven to bake for lunch, she prepared a hotpot for the evening meal. While she worked she practised her speech for when Sam got back. First she would tell him he could have her land for 'his bit'. Then she would tell him he was going to be a father. In theory it was simple, getting it into motion proved to be another matter.

Lunch time came and went and there was no Sam. The baked potatoes had the appearance of burnt offerings when she was forced to take them from the oven. Then she watched them slowly shrivel up like prunes as they stood desolately by the sink. But they did not look half as desolate as Hannah felt when Sam finally returned.

She was at the bottom of the yard and it was past two o'clock when the Land Rover came through the gate. By which time she had prepared the day's meals, fed the dogs, ducks and hens, and carried a large bail of hay to the first field where Samson and Delilah were enjoying the freedom of the summer's day – all done wearing the green dress.

She still felt she needed the Dutch courage of looking her best when she spoke to Sam and she had refused to take the dress off in favour of more suitable working clothes. But when she saw him striding down the yard towards her, shaking his head and smiling all at the same time, she knew keeping the dress on had not been the best decision of the day.

'What do you think you're doing?' He looked her up and down with amusement and pulled a piece of hay from her hair. 'You'll ruin it – if you haven't already.'

She looked down at the dress. It was filthy. Bits of hay were stuck all over her and corn dust was spread down the left side of the skirt from feeding the birds. Her shoes were no better, covered in dusty earth and the colour indistinguishable. She felt a mess and she looked a mess.

'I can wear a dress if I want to,' she snapped, taking her frustration out on him.

'Oh come on! You haven't taken Col's joking to heart.' He cocked his head on one side and peered into her eyes. 'You know what he's like. He doesn't mean anything.'

'Of course it wasn't Col!' Her anger doubled that he thought her stupid enough to be taken in by Col's banter. She glared at him coolly. Despite her temper he still had a

silly grin on his face: like the cat that got the cream. 'And where the devil have you been till now?' she demanded.

His spreading grin increased her irritation. 'Buying a farm,' he quipped.

'What?' She had the feeling all her blood drained into her feet.

'Buying a farm,' he repeated, slowly and deliberately.

'What the devil do you mean? You can't buy a farm in an afternoon.' She pushed him aside and began to hurry up the yard. She had the feeling she did not want to hear anything else he had to say.

'Yes I can.' His confidence stopped her in her tracks.

She turned slowly to face him. 'What do you mean?' Her voice was as flat as the dullness sinking in the pit of her stomach.

'We are now the new owners of Northgate Farm!' He held his arms wide, looking very pleased with himself.

'Sam . . . ! You . . . you can't have?'

He gave a shrug. 'Well, near as damn it.' He moved forward, placed his hands on her shoulders and looked deep into her troubled eyes. 'Nothing is signed and sealed yet. But Viv wants to get out as soon as she can. She's got no stock. Only the two dogs, that she is taking with her. She's got her eye on a little cottage in Lincolnshire, close by her sister. She isn't even taking all the furniture because she won't have the room for it. So I've bought Northgate lock, stock and barrel.'

'What do you mean?' She knew she was repeating herself, but it was all she could say.

'Viv and I have agreed a price. She wanted everything done quickly so she wouldn't miss out on the place near her sister. So we've been together to see a solicitor and got everything in motion.'

'Oh Sam!' She did not know how she stopped herself from crying. 'You could have had my land,' she said sadly. Then her voice hardened. 'But I don't suppose one field and a plot of waste ground was good enough for you!' She threw her arms up, pushing his hands away from her. 'Not for a Bunting! Like chickens pecking in the dust. That was what your father called us!' All the bitterness of the long-forgotten memory swelled in her voice. Her mind's eye filled with an image of George Bunting sitting on Samson's back, looking down his long nose at her father. It was so real she had the feeling she could have reached out and touched the navy-blue jacket, the silver breeches, the shiny boots – everything she had hated about him at that time. She tried to remind herself that the imperious rider on the grey horse had died long before George Bunting met his fate. But as she pivoted her eyes to Sam's face to rid her mind of the memory, it was George Bunting she saw, the man on the horse. The Lord of the Manor!

It had been such a slow process she had not noticed the change in her husband's features and physique. Jed was the one, she tried to insist. It was Jed who had been his father's double! But her eyes told her she was lying. The Sam she was looking at was no longer the thinner, softer version. His body had broadened out and so had his cheeks. Still, the eyes were a shade lighter, blue instead of black, but everything else was George Bunting.

'No!' she screamed, not sure if she was denying what she saw, or what Sam was trying to do by buying Northgate Farm. 'It won't make you any more of a man!' She shook her head, her worried gaze fixing him bleakly. 'Don't you see that? It didn't help your father. It only made him a laughing stock.'

He gave a scorn-filled snort and shook his head in a vehement denial of what she was telling him. 'I've been a laughing stock for long enough. It's time I showed them I'm a force to be reckoned with.' The hardness in his voice made her shudder.

'Oh no! No, Sam!' Her head shook faster. This was not her Sam speaking. It could not be. 'Who's going to work the extra land? How will you manage all of it? It isn't possible!' She was clutching at straws and the panic in her voice increased as she spoke.

'Yes it is.' His voice softened. 'Come on, Hannah. I don't know why you're getting so upset about it?'

'Getting upset!' she repeated hotly. 'I'll tell you why I'm getting upset. *Because I'm pregnant!*' She brought herself up short. It had not been the way she intended to tell him: blurting it out as if she was angry about it; condemning him for it; blaming him for it.

He did not speak. Everything fell under an oppressive silence. Not even a bird sang in the sky. The whole world seemed to have ceased living for the terrible seconds that followed.

It was Hannah who found her voice first. 'I am going to have a baby.' This time it was spoken gently, with no harshness in the words.

Any thought that he might have already guessed at her condition was wiped away. Every drop of blood drained from his face and his shock was too stunning to be anything but the real thing.

'How?' he asked, the word seeming to leave a bitter taste on his lips.

She looked at him blankly, unable to reply.

'How?' He grabbed her arms, as if wanting to shake her.

'I forgot to take my pill,' she said flatly, staring into his angry eyes and wondering how everything she had planned could have gone so horribly wrong in so short a time. They were supposed to be sitting down in the kitchen, discussing this calmly and sensibly.

'You forgot!' he bellowed. He did shake her then. 'How could you have been so stupid?'

'It was when I was ill. I didn't think – I'm sorry,' she gasped, the words spluttering from her lips as the breath was shaken from her lungs.

'Sorry!' He thrust her away from him as if she had suddenly become tainted. 'You'd bring a child into the world with this?' He thrust his left hand into her face, the two thickened digits snapping before her eyes and giving them the true appearance of a lobster's claw. 'And all you can say is sorry!'

She swiped his hand away. 'Yes,' she declared fiercely. '*I am sorry!* But not for myself. Or for the child . . . because *I* will love it! It's you I'm sorry for. You can't let the past go. Deep down you still believe you're the deformed cripple of Bunting's Claw. The joke. Something to be laughed at and mocked. You think buying Northgate and making your realm bigger will make people see you differently. You're blind, Sam. People already see you for what you are. Bunting's Claw died along with your father. Perhaps even before that. Nobody points fingers at Jenny. Nobody shuns her! Because she isn't afraid of what she is. She accepts she is different . . . and makes the most of it. So what if our baby is born with your hand! It is only one hand! Would you prefer it to be born with no legs and have to endure the life your father did in his last years?' It was not a fair comparison. George Bunting's life had been one of imprisonment because he had chosen it to be. But she was too angry to be reasonable. 'Would you? Would you?' On the last she was screaming, and she grabbed his arms and shook him the way he had shaken her.

He immediately retaliated. The fingers of his right hand bit into her flesh, while the pincers of the left felt like a vice attempting to crush right through her bones, as he caught her attacking arms and forced them to be still. Then, slowly, yet with more fury than if he had flung her off, he pushed her away from him. 'You haven't got a clue!' His pale cheeks vibrated as he ground the words through his lips. 'You don't know anything about it, or me . . . or what you have done!'

'*What I've done!*' she blazed, incensed and astonished. 'I think you had a part in it, as well!'

He shook his head, his lips twisting in a bitterness that made him appear even more like his father. 'Oh no!' he snarled. 'Do you think I believe you forgot to take your pills? You did it on purpose. You wanted a baby and you *chose* to feed that selfish need!'

'I did not!' Her hand flew up to hit him. His left hand was quicker, the claw fending her off before her palm could make contact with his cheek.

'I'll never forgive you for this!' His face contorted with a rage that made him almost unrecognizable. She took a step back, the words stinging her more than a physical assault.

For several seconds they glared at each other, their crushing silence thrusting them miles apart, worlds apart. Suddenly they were divided by a gap that no words, no affection, no love, could ever reach across.

Then he wheeled away and stormed out of the yard and took the path on to the Tor . . . and left her standing there.

Chapter Thirty

Sam went ahead with the decision to buy Northgate Farm. He did not consult Hannah about it again. She only knew the purchase had been completed because Viv Bennett moved out and Sam doubled the size of the dairy herd and put the new cows in Northgate fields. He took on two farm-hands to help with the extra work. He had no trouble finding men willing to come to the Tor. One of them was a man from the village, but that did not appear to make him see Hannah had been correct when she said people's feelings had changed towards the farm, and towards him. Neither did it soften his attitude towards her.

When he finally came down from the Tor on the day she had told him he was to become a father, he had gone straight upstairs without speaking. After putting up with his banging around for a full hour, she had had to go up and find out what he was doing. She found he was moving all his things out of their bedroom, and moving back into his old room.

She had received no reply when she asked, 'Why?' So she had left him to it, thinking it was a matter that would sort itself out with time. Despite what he said about her lack of comprehension, she did understand a little of what he was feeling, what he was going through. He had been so adamant that he did not want a child that he now felt trapped and that the baby she was carrying was being forced on him against his wishes. But he would learn to love it, she told herself, with a confidence that, when she looked back on it, she found frighteningly naive.

Unfortunately, the passing of time proved how very wrong Hannah had been. Sam withdrew into himself and grew more distant from her. He spoke only when necessary, and some days not at all. After the first month she had given up trying to talk some reason into him and now the house was once more filled with the aura of emptiness and lack of love that she had found when she first arrived there. She tried to be happy when the children were around and make it appear there was nothing wrong. But she knew both David and Jenny were at a loss to understand the tension that now constantly vibrated between Sam and herself. It worried her greatly that she was not able to sit down and explain things to the two children, but she did not know how to tell them Sam was being the way he was because she was having a baby he did not want. She was frightened it would make them feel that if he did not want that child, then he would not want them, either.

By the time she was into the sixth month of her pregnancy it was all beginning to wear her down. The morning queasiness of the early days had long gone but she was getting large now and found she was tiring easily, and it was becoming more and more difficult to keep a smile plastered on her face for the children's sake.

*   *   *

'Can I stay at Susan's tonight?' Jenny asked.

Hannah stopped stuffing dirty sheets into the washing machine and slowly straightened up, pressing her hands to the back of her hips and arching her spine as she did so. She was only six months, she reminded herself, and wondered how on earth she was going to manage another three. She was grimacing, at herself, as she turned to the little girl, but she soon broke into a smile. Jenny was fastening her coat, and though she was still a couple of months off her sixth birthday the left hand was working just as well as the right and the buttons were proving no problem. She gave an inward sigh and wished Sam would open his eyes and see the same things she did.

'Whose idea is that?' she questioned, slanting suspicious eyes at Jenny. 'Susan's mum's? Or yours!'

'Susan said it was all right.' Her big navy blue eyes widened in hopeful innocence.

'It isn't up to Susan, love.' Hannah crouched down, making herself the same height as the little girl and wrapped an arm around her shoulders. 'You must not go inviting yourself to other people's homes. It isn't very polite. You have to wait to be asked.' The big Bunting eyes filled with tears and Jenny's bottom lip trembled. Hannah hugged the little girl to her. 'I know,' she suggested. 'Why don't we ask Susan to come and stay the night here?'

Unfortunately, the offer did not get the expected response. Jenny began to sob loudly. 'I don't want Susan to come here,' she gasped, burying her head against Hannah's shoulder.

'Why, love?' Hannah frowned, and stroked the thick black curls that ran down to the little girl's shoulder blades. 'What's wrong with Susan coming here?' Having Jenny's friends to stay overnight was not a regular habit. They had done it a few times during the summer but recently Jenny had not asked for anyone to come. Or to come to play for a couple of hours after school! Oh no! she thought. She had been so wrapped up in her own problems that she had failed to notice Jenny seemed suddenly to have become friendless.

Seeing a picture of Sam standing alone in the school playground, she held Jenny away and looked deep into her tear-streaked face. 'What's wrong?' she asked. 'Tell me what it is. Don't be frightened.'

The little girl's head slipped forward, her tears dripping on to the floor. Hannah's heart turned inside her chest.

478

Expecting the worst, she pulled the distraught little figure to her, holding her tight. 'Don't cry, love. Tell me what's wrong?'

'Don't want Susan to see Uncle Sam,' Jenny sobbed. 'He isn't nice any more.'

'Oh love!' Hannah let out a great breath of relief. It was not Jenny being castigated as another generation of Bunting's Claw, it was still Sam's inability to forget the past. He had turned his back not only on herself but also on his little niece; she could only imagine it was because Jenny reminded him too much of himself. It wasn't the same with David. Although he was quiet with the lad in the house, she had seen them together in the yard and the fields, appearing to be getting along as they had always done.

'He doesn't like me any more so I don't like him,' Jenny sobbed, her tiny shoulders continuing to shudder against Hannah's arms.

Hannah shook her head in despair. It had to stop, she told herself. He was destroying all of them along with himself and she could not allow that to happen.

She quickly dried Jenny's eyes and settled her on a chair, still snuffling but no longer sobbing uncontrollably. 'It will be all right,' she assured, and hurried to the telephone and dialled Susan's mother. 'I know this is an imposition but I'm in a bit of a spot. I was wondering if you could have Jenny stay the night with you?'

Susan's mother was happy to oblige and Jenny was smiling all the way to school.

One problem dealt with, Hannah thought, as she watched Jenny run eagerly to the school door. Two more to go, she told herself, and returned to the car to take David to the big school in the next village. It was not until the Morris pulled up at the entrance to David's large, modern school, that she said, 'Are you finding Sam difficult at the moment?'

He gave a shrug. 'He is a bit strange.'

That must be the understatement of the year, Hannah thought.

'But he's all right when we're outside,' he quickly added, leaping to Sam's defence.

Hannah smiled thinly. 'I know,' she said, and gave a little sigh. It was only when David was in the house and she was present that Sam was 'a bit strange' as he had put it. In the yard David found him the same as always, and the two new farm-hands seemed to get on with him all right.

'But . . .' David dropped his head and toyed nervously with his fingers. It was several seconds before he continued. 'I know he's moved into another bedroom.' His voice was flat and sad. 'Mum had to do that when my dad had been hitting her.' He looked up worriedly. 'He hasn't started hitting you . . . has he?'

The concern on his face touched Hannah's heart in the way Jenny's sobbing had: like a knife slicing through her. 'Oh no!' she was quick to reassure, shaking her head vehemently. She placed her hand over both of his, as they lay in his lap with a looseness that spoke of impotency. 'Sam would never do that!' The confidence of her voice put a smile on his face, albeit rather small and weak. 'He's got things on his mind, that's all.' She did not continue the conversation. David was wise beyond his years and she had no wish to add a further burden to his adolescent shoulders. 'Have you got your football kit?' she asked, changing the subject.

He gave a nod and got out of the car.

'See you at the usual time then,' she said. She watched him walk down the length of the long tarmac drive and a heaviness settled in her chest that seemed to match the weight pressing on his shoulders. Fortunately, when he reached the far end and was met by two other boys, his back straightened and he visibly brightened. She gave a sigh of relief and turned the key and started the engine. At least he was not completely like Sam, she thought, as she drove away. He wasn't like Jenny in wanting friends

480

to come back to the farm after school, but when he was at school he was popular and well-liked. She hoped it would be enough to help him forget the insecurities of his early life.

Sam was in the yard when she returned. He was messing around with the engine of an old tractor. Hannah had never seen it before but, like the many pieces of strange equipment that kept turning up in the yard, she assumed it must have come from Northgate.

Climbing out of the car she went straight over to him. 'I want to speak to you!' she said, staring very deliberately at the side of his face.

'I'm busy,' was his short reply.

'So am I!' she shot back. 'But this can't wait!'

He continued to fiddle with the oily piece of engine in his hands. She continued to stare at him, refusing to be put off, to give in. She had given in too long already. She had given him enough time to come to his senses. She would wait no longer. 'I want to speak to you!' she repeated stiffly. 'If you won't come into the kitchen and do it in private, then I'll say what I've got to say right here!'

As if on cue, Phil Hardy, the new farm-hand who came from the village, poked his head round the milking-parlour door. 'Where's the udder cream?' he shouted.

'In the cupboard to the right of the tank,' Sam replied, then returned his attention to the tractor's greasy part.

'Well?' she questioned, settling her hands on where her hips used to be and fixing him with a very determined gaze. 'Do I say it here – where it will be overheard?'

For a short time he glared at her, then finally gave in with a breathy sigh of exasperation. 'It will have to be quick,' he said, making no attempt to conceal his irritation. But he did at least put the tractor part down to follow her across the yard.

'Well,' he demanded, standing just inside the kitchen door so he did not have to take his mucky wellingtons off.

He made a deliberate show of holding his grease-coated hands out where she could see them.

She bit her lip against telling him to get his hands washed. She knew that would only have had him spinning round and storming out again. Pulling her coat off, she tossed it across the table, then turned to face him squarely. 'I've had enough of this, Sam,' she said. 'You're making life miserable for everyone and it's got to stop.'

'*I'm* making life miserable!' His amazement appeared genuine and Hannah gave a grunt of disbelief. 'It wasn't *me* got myself pregnant!'

'It was *you* who got *me* pregnant!' she blazed.

'Not knowingly!' he returned with equal heat. 'You knew how I felt.' He thrust his hand out at her in accusation, then dropped it to hang defeatedly at his side, leaving a large smear on his blue denim jeans.

There was something so desperately unhappy about the action. Hannah's heart curled inside her chest. 'Don't do this!' she implored. She moved towards him, holding her arms out in invitation. 'I love you, Sam. And you love me. Don't let us lose that!'

But as she would have touched him he wheeled away. 'If you loved me you would have got rid of it,' he grated, his back turned to her and cutting her to the core.

Her hand flew up to cover the gasp leaping from her mouth. 'You would have had me murder *our* baby?' Her shock was immense. She recalled him suggesting putting Jenny in the water butt, never thinking he had meant what he was saying. But there was something so coldly final about his voice that she had the feeling he meant every word he had just spoken.

'*Your baby!*' He wheeled back to face her, the bitterness in his eyes slicing right into her own and making her visibly flinch. 'It is *your* baby! *Yours!* I want nothing to do with it.'

She shook her head. She heard every word but she could not believe the man she loved had vanished completely. Her Sam could not mean such horrible things. 'I don't believe you,' she said. 'I know you're hurting and I understand why. I have the same fears. This baby belongs to both of us. We're both responsible for bringing it into the world. And until it's born we don't know what it will be like. It might be . . .' She hesitated, biting the word 'normal' back.

He read her mind. '*Normal!*' he inserted for her.

'Yes, normal!' she blazed, thrusting her chin up and her face into his. 'It might be perfect, without a blemish on its complexion – just like Jed! Now he was normal. Oh yes, he was normal! Is that the type of normal you want for *your* child?'

His lips compressed into a thin line and his cheeks vibrated with the force of his anger. '*Your* child!' he persisted. 'It's yours, Hannah! You chose to bring it into the world, you can take responsibility for it.'

Before she had time to object, he wheeled away again. This time he did not stop until he was out in the yard and the back door had closed noisily behind him.

Hannah turned from the door with a feeling of such total defeat. It seemed to be a tangible thing actually touching her, pressing on her skin and weighing her down far more than the baby in her womb. It was over, she told herself. It was a numbing realization, but one she could not escape. The happiness she had found for a few brief years with Sam was over, gone. She had known his reactions would be intense, had known he would be afraid and anxious. But even at her lowest times, she had not foreseen their baby being an end to everything else they had shared.

With a sigh as heavy as her heart, she pulled out a chair and sank into it. Her back had been aching all morning and now her head had joined it. Feeling too desolate to do anything else, she dropped her elbows on to the table and cradled her chin.

She was not aware of the passing of time. She was not

even aware she was thinking and planning, until she suddenly stood up and went to the drawer where all the spare keys were kept. She rummaged through, passing over the bunch of small Yale keys for the outbuildings, the medium sized bunch that were for all the doors inside the house, several sets of car keys and the monster that unlocked the grand front door. Then she found it. Her hand closed round a large bunch of various sized keys, all tied together on a piece of grubby pink ribbon with a small white card attached. Straightening the crumpled card she stared at the neat italic script in royal blue ink: Northgate Farm!

It was only chance that she knew they were there. Sam had gone off one day with the keys to the Morris in his pocket. She had looked in the drawer, which usually she never touched, to find the spare set because she had to go and collect David and Jenny from school. The Northgate keys had been lying on the top with the label fresh and uncrumpled, as if they had only just been put there.

She pushed the keys into the pocket of her navy blue corduroy trousers and hurried up the stairs. She packed quickly, stuffing all her belongings into two suitcases and an assortment of carrier bags without any consideration for the condition they would be in when they came out at the other end. After her own things, she packed Jenny's. But she was not sure what to do about David. He idolized Sam and the farm was the most important thing in his life. She did not want to deprive the boy of either by pressing him into something against his will. So she packed enough to see him through a couple of nights, in case he wanted to go with her. But the rest of his things stayed behind, should he choose to do the same. He was old enough to make his own choice, she told herself.

When all the bags and packages were downstairs she brought the Morris round to the little-used front door, where she could load it up without being seen from the yard. It was not that she expected Sam to try and stop her, but now she had made the decision she wanted to get away with as little fuss as possible.

While she was packing everything into the car, she was too busy to think. Not until the boot was stuffed solid and the back seat lost to view, did she pause and look up at the large imposing house she was leaving. The last time, she thought, and as she stared at the grey stone walls Rhoda's face flashed past her eyes, and George Bunting's, and Jed's. Eight years! Was that really all it was? So much had happened since she had first come there, frightened and alone. It seemed several lifetimes had been lived, not just eight years. The faces of the past suddenly vanished, to be replaced by Sam's. The Sam she used to know, not angry or bitter, but smiling down at her, loving her.

Tears misted her eyes and she jumped quickly into the car and drove away.

*   *   *

The empty yard at Northgate exuded an air of neglect. There was no tractor, no dogs or hens pecking around, just a lot of mud washed down from the hill behind during the several days of rain they had just had. As Hannah climbed out of the car, she felt the first spots falling from the grey clouds that had been gathering since her early morning journey down to school.

She heaved a sigh, her gaze passing over the desolate yard and deserted outbuildings. The double-fronted stone cottage, with ivy climbing all round the door and windows, would have looked pretty in sunshine. But with her mood comparing favourably to the grey day, Hannah found nothing welcoming in the isolated building. She wasn't sure why she thought of it as isolated. It stood alone, but was much closer to the village than the Tor had been. Yet she had never felt isolated at the Tor.

Because Sam had been there, she reminded herself. Then quickly pushed him from her mind, pulled the keys from her pocket and crossed the yard to the door. As she turned the key in the lock she hoped the furniture was still going to be there. Viv could have changed her mind and taken it with her. Or Sam could have thrown it out. He wouldn't have told her if he had.

The door swung open on to an empty room. Hannah's heart sank. She stepped inside and looked bleakly round. The walls were covered in a garish scarlet, rose-patterned paper. At the windows hung curtains of a similar pattern but in a deep cerise pink. A carpet with vivid slashes of the same cerise combined with a lighter pink covered most of the floor.

She took a deep breath and reminded herself she was not looking for a palace. Gaudy or not, at least she had a carpet and curtains.

There was a door on the back wall and two on the left. She went to the nearest. It squeaked murderously on its old, rusty hinges, as she swung it open. She smiled. It was a smaller room than the first one, but it was fully furnished. There was an old, battered, black leather *chaise longue* pushed against the wall and two pink moquette fireside chairs that appeared to be almost new, one on each side of a tiny, brick, arch fireplace. A folding table stood beneath the window, which was blessed with the same bright curtains as the other room, and there was an old oak dresser with a pink glass vase and an assortment of pot dogs standing on it. The carpet square was old and worn, but showed signs of at one time being grey and blue.

Obviously bought before Viv's pink period, Hannah thought, finding a little humour inside herself now she found she had at least one room to live in.

The second door led to the first floor, up a narrow, winding staircase very much like the one of her old childhood home. She peeped up it but did not go up just then. She wanted to know how much of a kitchen she had got, so went first to the third door.

Again she smiled and said a silent thank-you. There

was a table and four chairs and the old gas stove, though vintage, was still working. There was even a box of matches lying by the side and she struck one and touched it to the jet. It immediately popped to life. She switched it off and looked around. There were several cupboards, all empty, and a strange wooden box shape running along the wall by the sink. Her smile broadened when she pulled it away to reveal a large cast-iron bath standing on clawed feet. That will be much better than having to lug a tub in front of the fire, she thought, and went to inspect the bedrooms with a smile still on her face.

There were three bedrooms. Like downstairs, one was completely empty. But the other two were both furnished with a bed, dressing-table, wardrobe and a small bedside cabinet.

Feeling tired, but happier inside now she felt she had a proper home, Hannah began to unpack the Morris. She dumped all the bags in the empty downstairs room. The clothes could wait until later. She wanted to get the beds made ready and the kitchen workable before she had to go and pick David up from school. And, if she could find some coal, a fire laid. The place had only been standing empty for a couple of months, but it could have been years, from the damp coldness clinging to the walls.

She found the coal house, a brick built lean-to, at the back of the cottage. There was not a lot of coal in it but she managed to scrape enough together to last a couple of days, which would give her time to get a load delivered. Then she got the fire going and had enough time to call at the village shop and stock up with groceries before she had to pick David up. She had not taken any food from the Tor. It was easy enough for her to get her own and she had wanted to leave Sam with a good stock of provisions.

They were at the turning of the narrow lane that led to Northgate, when she stopped the car. 'I've got something to tell you,' she said, turning to look into David's puzzled face. 'I have left the Tor. I have left Sam.' She spoke bluntly: it was too late for excuses and cover-ups. David's mouth dropped open. 'You know Sam and I haven't been getting on very well lately,' she continued. 'So I've decided it's best if we live apart.'

'Where are you going to?' David asked, his crestfallen expression turning her heart.

'It's all right,' she reached across to him and laid her hand on his arm. 'I'm not going far. I've moved in here.' She nodded up the lane. 'Into Northgate.' She watched him carefully, as she added, 'Jenny will come with me. You can come, too . . . if that is what you want?' she quickly put in, seeing an objection being bitten back at his lips and adding to the confusion in his eyes.

Hannah smiled fondly. He was torn with indecision, not wanting to hurt either her or Sam. 'It doesn't matter if you don't want to come.' Her voice was gentle with understanding and she gave his arm a reassuring squeeze. 'If you would rather stay with Sam I'll take you up there and come and pick you up in the morning for school, just as normal. It's your choice, David.'

He dropped his head and toyed with his fingers.

'I won't mind if you choose Sam,' she said, trying to ease the burden of his guilt. She could see he wanted to go to Sam and the farm, but was afraid to hurt her by saying so.

He looked up slowly, tears in his eyes. 'I'll come to Northgate with you, if you need me to.'

'Oh love!' She pulled him into her arms and held him tight. 'What I need is not important. It's what *you* need that matters.' She held him away and peered into the watery depths of his brown eyes, just as the tears began to run freely down his cheeks. 'You want to go to the Tor, don't you?'

It was several seconds before he slowly nodded his head.

A tight, affectionate smile pulled at her lips. 'Then that

is fine by me.' She hugged him to her again. 'You can come to Northgate whenever you please. And it will be better that Sam has someone with him,' she said. He sobbed against her shoulder and she felt the pressure of tears come to her own eyes and for several minutes they clung to each other and cried.

The rest of the journey was conducted in silence. Hannah stopped the car outside the large stone gateposts of the Tor. There was no-one in the yard but she still felt she could not go inside. It was part of her past now and too painful to return to.

David turned to her. 'Will you and Jenny be all right at Northgate on your own?'

She smiled at the concern on his face. 'We'll be fine,' she said confidently, knowing if she sounded anything less he would have changed his mind and insisted on coming back with her . . . to be the man of the house.

He gave a nod and moved to get out, then hesitated. 'Don't you love Sam any more?' he asked.

Such a simple question but so unexpected. Her stomach lurched and the effect sent the baby squirming in her womb. With a little gasp her hands dropped to where a tiny limb was thrusting against her abdomen. She had the feeling the baby was trying to say: 'Stop! Let me get out. I want to stay here!'

'Are you all right?' David's concern turned to anxiety.

'Yes,' she quickly replied, and took a deep breath. 'Yes, yes I'm fine.' She returned her hands to the steering wheel and clutched it tightly. 'And in answer to the previous question.' She levelled her gaze at him. 'Yes, I still love Sam. But, sometimes, that is not enough.'

It was obvious from his bewildered expression that he did not understand, but he got out of the car.

'Take this.' She handed him the plastic carrier which held the pair of pyjamas, shirt and underwear in case he had chosen to go with her. 'I'll pick you up here in the morning.' She jabbed her finger downwards, making it

489

quite clear she would be waiting outside the gates expecting him to come to her.

He gave a nod. Then he stood and watched as she turned the car around, the plastic bag clutched tightly in both hands.

He looked like a homeless orphan with all his belongings clutched to him, Hannah thought, as she shunted the car first one way then the other. The lane was so narrow she had to perform something like a ten-point turn before getting the car pointing in the right direction, and it gave her plenty of time to look at the tall, thin figure standing sadly at the gate. He reminded her so much of the frightened and uncertain little boy she had first met with his mother at the bus station. Tears filled her eyes as she shoved the gear roughly into first. They began to pour down her cheeks and her vision was anything but clear when she roared off down the lane, grateful she knew the way like the back of her hand.

* * *

For the next weeks life fell into a pattern for Hannah. During the week she would drive each morning to the gates of the Tor and collect David. He was always standing waiting for her – and so was Sam. Not by the gate with David, about twenty feet inside the yard. He never spoke, never inclined his head in acknowledgement. He just stood there, hands stuffed into his pockets, stiff and silent as a statue. The afternoons were the same. When she dropped David off Sam would be waiting, in the same place and the same position, as if he had not moved since morning.

'Why don't you come and talk to him?' David asked, on the last day of term before the Christmas holiday. 'He'd speak if you came in – I know he would.'

And I'd speak if he came out, she thought. She shook her head. Sam had to make the first move. He had to show her he was willing to accept both her and the baby. Until he could do that, there was nothing she would, or could do. Unfortunately, she doubted he would ever be able to accept either the baby – or herself – again.

By the end of January, the silently watching figure outside the large stone gateposts each time she arrived was beginning to get on her nerves. She could not comprehend why he did it, what satisfaction he got from making her feel uncomfortable. Unless he was trying to make her feel guilty for deserting him.

Uh! he had a nerve, she thought irritably. Then snapped at Jenny when the little girl knocked a bag of apples off the back seat and they rolled all round the floor of the car. One went beneath the accelerator. Hannah stamped on the brake, frantic to get the car stopped before the apple moved over to the brake pedal and stopped it functioning properly. Grumbling to herself, she tried to pick the apple up, but her great hulk of a stomach got in the way and her hands got nowhere near the wretched fruit. She had to get out, she realized, frustration exploding into anger. Getting in and out of the car was not the easiest of movements for her at the moment. 'Why can't you leave things alone?' she snapped, as she struggled to her feet, then struggled into a crouching position to reach across the car to get the offending apple. 'You always have to interfere. Poking your nose into things that don't concern you.' She continued to chastize Jenny until, with a sigh of relief, her hand closed around the apple.

The others were not so inaccessible but it still took several minutes to round them all up and get them back into the bag. By which time Jenny's hands were covering her face and she had begun to wail loudly.

'You can shut up! It's me that should be crying!' Hannah snapped, as she braced herself against the seat to get herself standing up once more. But as she hauled her heavy body upright, a sharp pain stabbed down her side. With a groan she clutched at her side and fell panting against the car. She stood very still, taking deep breaths until the pain had gone. Then she lowered herself carefully into the driver's seat.

Fortunately, Jenny continued to sob with her face buried in her hands and saw nothing. For that Hannah was grateful. She did not want fear to be added to the child's distress. 'All right, love,' she said gently. 'It's all right.' She wanted to turn and comfort the little girl, but dare not do anything so drastic as twisting round. The pain had gone now, but she had a funny feeling in one side of her stomach. 'I'm sorry,' she said. 'Stop crying, love. I didn't mean to snap your head off.' Her frustration was being taken out on the wrong person, she told herself. It wasn't Jenny she was angry with. It was that blessed, immobile figure persistently standing in the farmyard.

The sobbing eventually came to an end and Hannah started the car, although she did not drive home. She went straight to Dr Hallam's surgery.

'You really should be taking it more easy!' the doctor scolded firmly, as his hands moved gently over the mound of Hannah's stomach. 'You're not doing yourself any good . . . or the baby!' On the last he slanted a pointed gaze at her.

'I'm not doing that much,' she protested feebly. Northgate didn't give her half the work she had been doing at the Tor. And even if she had wanted to exert herself in her new home, the tiredness that overtook her so suddenly was making sure she found it impossible.

'Well, you've got to do even less.' He concluded his inspection and pulled her baggy jumper down for her. Then he helped her up into a sitting position on the couch. 'If you don't listen to me I will have you in hospital,' he warned, as he went to his desk and sat down.

'I'll listen,' she was quick to reply, and eased herself off the couch and pulled her trousers up. She could not be in hospital for too long because of Jenny.

Dr Hallam began to scribble on her notes. 'I don't suppose you've mended your differences with Sam?' he asked, slanting a gaze at her over the top of the glasses perched on the end of his nose.

'No,' she replied simply.

He shook his head. 'It isn't good for you to be on your own.'

'I've got Jenny.'

He did not immediately reply, but made a pyramid with his hands and took on an expression of deep thought. 'Where will she go when you go into hospital?' he finally asked, and swept a hand out to instruct her to sit down in the chair by the side of his desk.

She gave an inward sigh. Now he had taken a look at her and pronounced everything all right, she wanted to be gone. Nevertheless, she sat down. 'I've got a few weeks to sort that out,' she said, edging away from the real reply: she had no idea.

'Not that long. You're rather larger than I would have expected. Are you sure you've got your dates right?'

'Yes,' she replied, with a surprising confidence for the flatness of her voice. The doctor eyed her oddly. I could tell you to the minute, she silently informed him, sadness expanding within her as she recalled a warm spring day on the Tor.

Dr Hallam stared at her notes for several long seconds. 'I want to see you every week from now on,' he finally said. 'Unless you feel there is any need to come sooner.' He slanted his eyes once more over the top of his glasses. 'If you think there is anything to worry about I want to see you back here immediately. Do you understand?'

She gave a nod.

'And the next time I see you I want to hear you've got someone to take Jenny off your hands when the time arises.' He spoke with strict, fatherly concern.

* * *

'I wish we had a television,' Jenny suddenly said, interrupting Hannah mid-sentence. They were sitting in the pink moquette chairs in front of a blazing fire and Hannah was reading to her.

'We will have . . . one day.' She smiled fondly at the little girl. Jenny had been quiet all evening. Since the sharp telling-off in the car, she realized guiltily.

'Tomorrow . . . can we go and get one tomorrow?' Jenny's sombre face suddenly brightened.

Hannah shook her head. 'No, love. Not tomorrow,' she said, and the little girl's gloom returned. She had not gone out of her way to get anything new for the cottage, had not even bothered to have a telephone installed – which, she kept telling herself, should be the first thing to get. With a sigh she leaned back in the chair and wondered why she had not tried to make their lives more comfortable. Was she secretly clinging to the idea that Sam would one day come riding over the fields on Samson's back, like a knight on his charger to sweep her up and take her home?

This is your home! she reminded herself, angry that she could still think of the Tor as 'home'. There would be no knights and no chargers coming her way.

'They've got a television at the Tor,' Jenny put in.

Hannah stared at the little girl in surprise, taken aback by the suggestion in the petulant statement. Jenny had shown no hesitation over the move to Northgate. There had been none of David's doubts or tears. She had clapped her hands with glee and declared, 'Good! I don't want to live with Uncle Sam any more.' But, from the look on her face at that moment, Hannah had the awful feeling she had changed her mind.

'Do you want to go back and live there?' she asked carefully.

'Yes,' Jenny replied without hesitation. 'I want to watch *Blue Peter*.'

For several moments Hannah did not know what to say. She would miss Jenny, but if she really wanted to go back to the Tor then she would not make her stay away. She did not know if Sam would welcome the little girl back. It would be difficult for him to give her the attention she needed. She was a long way off being David's age and having any independence.

'Sam might not be able to look after you,' she finally said, keeping her voice gentle and praying she was not going to upset the child further. 'He really doesn't have the time to look after you and do the work on the farm.'

'You can come and look after me!' It was spoken with the tone of someone who could not believe the other person could be so stupid.

'I can't, Jenny. If you want to go back I can ask Sam. But I can't promise that he will be able to let you. And I definitely can't come with you.'

'Don't want to go then!' Jenny curled herself into an unapproachable ball in the corner of the chair and hid her face. 'I'm not going without you!' Her shoulders began to shake and noisy sobs were muffled against the pink moquette.

Hannah flopped back in her chair with a sigh. She stared at the distraught little bundle in the chair opposite, and gave another sigh. 'When I go into hospital to have the baby you will have to go and stay at the Tor, with David and Sam.' It wasn't the best time, she knew, but she decided it was best to get all the tears over in one go.

'No! Won't go!'

'You have to go!' Tension once more got the better of Hannah and she spoke far more sharply than intended.

The muffled sobbing rose in strength and speed.

'Oh love!' Hannah was immediately filled with remorse. 'Come here.' She pulled Jenny out of the chair and on to her knee. Jenny buried her head against her shoulder and refused to look at her, but the sobbing ended. 'It will

495

only be for a day or two,' she assured. 'You can't stay here on your own. Someone has to look after you.'

'Can't I come with you?'

'No, poppet.' She stroked her hand over the shiny black curls and wondered if her own baby would be endowed with the Bunting locks. She hoped so. She wanted it to be a boy, with a face the image of his father and grandfather. A true Bunting, in the hope that the family need to keep the breed going would prove too much for Sam.

Tears misted her eyes and she rested her chin on the top of Jenny's head and began to cry softly. She was wishing in the wind. The need to build and enlarge the Bunting domain was already in Sam, had made him buy Northgate. Yet he still could not find it necessary to fetch her back, to have her and his child with him . . . where they belonged.

Jenny looked up then, her childish confusion making Hannah's tears run faster. 'Don't cry,' she said, and lifted her tiny clawed hand and brushed the tears from Hannah's face. 'I'll be good.'

Hannah hugged the little girl tightly to her. 'You are good, love. It's just me. I'll be better when the baby is here. Carrying this lump about is making me grumpy.' She patted her stomach and attempted a reassuring smile. 'It won't be long now.' She knew she was trying to comfort herself as much as Jenny. It was not just lugging the extra weight around that was getting her down, it was the waiting, the not knowing if her baby was going to be born with the deformity or not.

For all her denials that it was of no concern, it did matter to her. She wanted the baby to be born with two good hands, to be, as Sam had put it, normal. Because she wanted to be able to go up to the Tor and show Sam his perfect son – in the hope that he might then accept his child, and taking it into his home, also take her back into his home.

Chapter Thirty-One

The month of February was not a kind one. The temperature dropped very low and, if it was not snowing, it was raining. The ground became icy and treacherous underfoot and the little Morris struggled to get up the lanes, despite them being cleared.

Each morning Sam sent one of the hands down the lane in the Land Rover, clearing a path from the Tor to the village, and also clearing the side lane leading to Northgate Farm. He also stopped Hannah making the journey up the steeper part of the hill to the Tor. At the beginning of the bad weather David had told her not to fetch him any more. He was relaying a message from Sam, that he would do the daily journey while the roads were bad. He had also offered to pick Jenny up and take her, as well. But the little girl had become very clinging and so Hannah had declined the offer. She was concerned about doing anything that would make Jenny begin feeling jealousy towards the baby even before it was born, and she felt it best to give her all her attention while it was still possible.

It was a particularly bad morning. Icicles hung from the gutters and the frosty walls glittered as if encrusted with diamonds. Everything was frozen solid and it took several attempts before the little Morris' engine finally coughed and spluttered to life. As usual, the lane had been cleared of the night-time's fall of snow in time for Hannah to take Jenny to school. But the air was so cold that the newly revealed surface had immediately turned into a skating-rink and the car was reduced to crawling all the way into the village.

They pulled up outside the school just as Jenny's friend, Susan, and her mother were picking their way carefully across the slippery road. Jean Bridges shook her head at Hannah and came over to the car. 'Don't you go getting out in this!' she warned, bending her head to the window as Hannah rolled it down. 'You've got no business being out in it at all!'

'I'm all right in the car.' It was a lame excuse for her stupidity. All the way down the lane she had been calling herself a fool for not taking up Sam's offer.

As if to confirm Hannah's theory, Jenny jumped out of the car and slipped on to her bottom.

Hannah's head spun round. 'Are you all right?' she asked anxiously. But a duet of giggles, as Susan grabbed her friend's arm and helped to haul her back to her feet, told her there was nothing broken. It took several attempts and a lot more giggling before Jenny was actually upright again, as each time they pulled against each other their feet went in different directions on the icy snow.

Jean had to take a hand to get both little girls standing on their own two feet again. 'I've got wet knickers,' Jenny pronounced, pulling a face and very carefully feeling the back of her pants, where she had sat on the snow. Susan went into another paroxysm of giggles.

'You'll have to go and stand next to a radiator,' Jean suggested. 'They'll soon dry.' She turned back to the car and slanted a pointed gaze at Hannah. 'It's lethal,' she said. 'And *you'll* get more than wet knickers!' she added meaningfully.

Hannah gave a nod. 'I know. But . . . !' She gave a sigh, realizing she had to go cap in hand to Sam. She was wondering how she could get a message to him without having to go all the way up to the Tor, when Jean took the problem from her hands.

'Get yourself back home and don't come out again,' she said. 'I'll pick Jenny up with Susan and she can come home with us. Then Barry will bring her up when he gets

498

in.' She bent her head again and studied Hannah closely. 'Never mind the snow, you look as if you could do with the rest anyway.'

Hannah gave another nod. 'I'm not sleeping much at the moment. Can't get comfortable.' Jean gave a nod of understanding. 'But I'd be grateful . . .' She suddenly stopped herself and turned to Jenny. 'Do you want to go home with Susan?' she asked. At one time she knew the answer would have been a definite yes. But recently all Jenny wanted to do after school was get home and be with her, not even wanting to bring any friends along.

Jenny's face fell and she looked very uncertain.

'Of course you do!' Jean urged. 'Susan would like you to come and play with her.'

'Come and play! Come and play!' Susan put in eagerly.

It still took several seconds for Jenny to agree.

'Thank you,' Hannah mouthed meaningfully to Jean.

Jean gave her a wink, then a sharp reprimand to take it easy, before taking a little girl in each hand and escorting them safely inside the school door.

* * *

The snow began to fall just after four o'clock: large flakes that floated slowly and serenely to the ground like autumn leaves. From the little sitting-room window Hannah watched it laying a gentle blanket over the snow-plough's tracks. She gave a sigh and arched her spine, attempting to relieve the annoying ache that had been in the small of her back since late morning, and now seemed to be moving round her sides. She turned back to the fire and sat down in one of the pink moquette chairs. It was what she had been doing all day. Up and down. Up and down. She could sit for a while but then she became restless and had to move. She found it very irritating: having the chance to put her feet up and rest and not being able to.

By five o'clock she was back at the window and there was nothing serene about the weather. The snow was falling thick and fast, making blinding zigzags against the background of darkness as the wind hurled it first one way then the other. She could see the beginning of a drift climbing up the cow-shed wall and she began to get nervous about Jenny. Barry Bridges would not get home till after six on a normal evening. In this weather there was no telling how late he would be and if it didn't abate he would not get his car up the lane to get Jenny home.

If only she had been sensible and had a telephone put in, she thought, her anxiety increasing with the addition of anger that was aimed inward at her own stupidity. If she had a phone she could have called Sam and asked him to clear the lane. But she could not get in touch with him and he would not think to do it himself because he would assume Jenny was now safely at home.

What did it matter? she asked herself, rubbing impatiently at the small of her back. Jenny was safe with Susan and her parents. Telling herself to stop worrying about something she could do nothing about, and which did not need anything doing about it anyway, she returned to the chair. But she could not stop herself continually glancing at the window and watching the dense flurry of snow falling in the pale beam of the single farmyard light.

Restlessness once more overtaking her, she got up again and went to the kitchen. Cutting a slice of bread she spread it with lemon curd and made a pot of tea. Pouring herself a cup she took it back to the sitting-room, but the bread and lemon curd was left in the kitchen, untouched.

What was the matter with her? she asked herself. She had been on edge all day, even before she had anything to worry about. Now she had a real problem she felt so keyed up she might burst.

Forcing herself to sip slowly on the tea, she stared into the fire. As she watched the flames dance and frolic in the grate with far too much gaiety for her unsettled thoughts, she wished the night away.

Six o'clock came and went, then seven, eight, nine. Hauling her heavy weight out of the chair she went to the window yet again. The snow had finally eased, and so had the wind. The flakes were no longer being flung angrily at the ground, but fell in gentler gusts like cherry blossom in a sharp May wind. The yard was covered in a thick white blanket, clean and unspoiled by foot-prints or tyre tracks. The sight emphasized her solitude. She suddenly felt very alone.

Jenny would not be coming home tonight, she told herself, turning away from the window with a shiver. She glanced bleakly at the fire she had allowed to burn dangerously low. Her dirty cup and saucer was standing in the hearth.

She went to the coal scuttle, only to find it empty. It was not too much of a problem, she had a bucket of coal stored in the kitchen so she never had to find her way to the coal-house in the dark. She turned to go to the kitchen and get the coal, then remembered the dirty cup and saucer. Resting her hand on the arm of one of the chairs, she bent and picked up the cup and saucer. It was as she heaved herself upright again that the pain came: a slashing stabbing pain that seemed to enter her body in the region of her lower back and come all round her sides to finish in her stomach.

She gasped, dropped the cup and saucer and clutched her stomach. Then she felt she was fainting and grabbed for the chair again. Bent over double she took quick, short breaths. Slowly the pain subsided. She straightened up. No, she thought, begged, pleaded. Not now! Please not now!

She stood for a time clinging to the chair and breathing deeply, and telling herself she was wrong; she was not going into labour. It began slowly, she knew it did. Then what was that, she asked herself? And realized she would prefer to think she was going into labour than that something was going very wrong.

She looked around the room as if she expected some miracle to have happened and to find she was no longer alone. Another pain came, not as violent as the first, but still with the strength to make her gasp and dig her fingers into the chair's arm.

'Sam!' she called. 'Sam! Sam!'

The pain subsided. She gathered herself together enough to know she had to get help. Using the furniture and the walls for support she made her way slowly to the front door. But when she opened it she was confronted by a drift of snow that came up her hips.

'Oh no! No!' she groaned, closing the door firmly against the snow and sinking back on its support as another pain clawed at her body. This time when it subsided she knew she had no choice. She was on her own and she had to deal with it herself. Her baby was on its way and, if the strength of the contractions were anything to go by, it was coming very quickly.

Dropping on to all fours she crawled up the stairs. She had to stop once halfway up, then again at the top, as fresh pains made movement impossible. At least Jenny was not there. She preferred to be alone than have the little girl terrified out of her wits.

The bed looked very welcoming when she finally made it into the bedroom, but she forced herself first to the dressing-table. The bottom drawer was filled with baby clothes, soft white towels and sheets. Everything was new and still packed in bags. Still kneeling on the floor, she took a pack of towels and tore the Cellophane wrapping away. The pain came again. She bent double, clutching the towels to her stomach. The pains were coming faster. She glanced at the clock. Twenty-five-minutes-to-ten. It had taken her almost ten minutes to get up the stairs. She looked longingly at the bed. In her agony it appeared to be miles away. Clutching the towels in one arm and using

502

the other hand to crawl, she slowly dragged herself across the floor. As she reached the bed her waters broke, but she had no concern for the mess. The baby was all that mattered: her baby and Sam's baby. She had to get herself as comfortable as possible and prepare for the birth.

Tossing the covers back she rolled on to the bed, experiencing a moment's exultation that she had reached her goal. The next moment another contraction sliced through her body and she was thrust once more into agony. When it had passed she just lay there, feeling a great exhaustion overwhelming her. She could not be worn out yet, she told herself. It had only just begun.

After a few moments she gathered the strength to reach over and put the clean white towels on the bedside cabinet, ready to wrap the baby in. Then she struggled out of her trousers and pants and pulled the bed covers over to keep herself warm. Telling herself that birth was a completely natural process that she had assisted many a cow and a ewe with, she attempted to relax and calmly wait each new contraction – each time glancing at the clock to make sure the time span between was decreasing. Six minutes . . . six minutes . . . Five minutes . . . five minutes . . .

Then suddenly her body was being torn apart after only two minutes. 'Sam!' she screamed, taken by surprise. But there was no Sam to answer. There was no-one. The silence of the cottage was numbing. She had never felt so alone in all her life. Suddenly she was very, very frightened.

The pains increased, sharper and more severe. Perspiration ran down her temples, soaked her whole body. She threw the bed covers back needing air. The sweat immediately froze on her skin and she pulled the bed covers back over her again. Only to boil up and toss them away again. She no longer looked at the clock. Her brain was too busy trying to break through the miasma of pain to know what she was actually doing.

'Sam! Sam! Sam!' She called his name over and over again, needing him more than she had ever needed him before. A moment's coherence made her recall the wall of snow outside and realize that, even had he known what was happening, he would not have been able to get to her.

She began to pray. 'Please let the baby be safe,' she begged, throwing herself on the mercy of the God whose presence she had previously doubted. 'Let it live.' She was only half-aware of what she was doing and had no recollection of what she was saying, as she thrashed around the bed begging for Sam to be given his son.

It was then that she began to hear voices.

'Hannah! Hannah! Hannah!'

She was back in the ruins of the cottage and George Bunting was calling her. 'Here,' she whispered, just as she had whispered on that long ago day.

'Hannah! Hannah!' The voice continued. It was getting closer. He was coming, coming to rescue her, coming to take her away. But . . . ! He was dead! George Bunting was dead. She must be dying. He was coming to take her to where he was, so she must be dying. There was no fear in the thought, just an overwhelming relief to be freed from the pain.

'Here I am,' she said, lifting her arms towards a fallen oak tree and waiting to see him crawl up it. She could hear his footsteps pounding the trunk as he raced up. Raced! Running! He could not . . .

The bedroom door flew open, crashing back against the wall with such violence that the plaster behind cracked and fell to the floor.

The noise startled Hannah back to sensibility.

'Sam!' She was not sure if it was only in her mind, or if she actually uttered his name.

He paused, catching his breath and taking in the scene of the half-naked body wrapped in a tangle of sheets and blankets, a mess of damp red hair half held together by a loose rubber band, the other half spread in a tangle across the pillow and over her face.

'Sam!' she said, this time knowing she had spoken and knowing he was really there, even if he did look like the abominable snowman. Snow caked his wellingtons, clung to his clothes and hair and eyebrows. His face was all pink and red and chapped where the sweat of exertion had frozen on his skin.

'You bloody little fool!'

The intensity of the oath confused her. Was it really Sam? It sounded more like his father. The pain took her again, lifting her away from the bed, the room, and anyone who might be there.

Sam rushed forward, snatching his gloves off and flinging them to the floor. His coat followed. 'Hannah! Hannah! It's all right. I'm here.' Falling to his knees by the bed, he grasped her hand and clutched it tightly in both of his own. 'You're not alone, love!'

Not alone! Love! She returned to the moment, opening her eyes to see her hand in his. He was there. She could hear his voice, feel his touch. But none of her senses were as wonderful as the sight of his left hand: the claw-like digits coiled tightly round her own hand, proving he really was the only man in the world she wanted to be by her side at that moment.

'Oh Sam!' she said, emotion cracking her voice as she gazed into his eyes with fear and wonder. 'I was so frightened.'

'Hush.' He brushed the tangled hair away from her face. 'You're all right now. I'm here. Everything will be fine.' He forced himself to sound confident and in command of the situation. He knew the last thing she wanted to know was that he was just as terrified as she was.

Her fears evaporated in the soothing balm of his voice. She smiled her gratitude into his eyes and, when the next contraction came, the pain seemed far less intense and much more manageable with his hand to cling on to.

She had two more contractions. By the third it seemed the baby realized its father had arrived and it was now time for it to come into the world.

Sam immediately leapt to his feet. Then, with the calmness and knowledge learnt over the years of lambing and calving, he brought his child safely into the world.

'What . . . what is it?' Hannah asked breathlessly, struggling on to her elbows to look down between her raised knees and see the bundle Sam was holding so reverently in his hands.

He did not speak, but only shook his head.

'What . . . !' she demanded, feeling herself go cold with apprehension.

His head was still shaking as he looked up to her. But when she saw the glisten of tears in his eyes she knew it was shaking in wonder, not denial. 'It's all right,' he said, the same wonder filling his voice, just as the baby gave a loud, robust cry. 'It's got two perfect hands.'

'*But what is it?*' She began to laugh and cry at the same time. In that moment she felt tired yet exultant, and more in love with her husband than she had ever felt before. She shook her head at him, seeing he was still too joyously overwhelmed by the baby's perfection to realize what she was asking. 'Trust a Bunting to miss the important bit,' she said.

He looked at her dumbly, then suddenly broke into a smile. 'You have a fine son, Mrs *Bunting*!' he stressed pointedly, making it quite clear she was one of the family she was maligning. He lay his precious bundle on her stomach and pulled the covers over to keep both him and his mother warm. 'And so have I,' he said, his tears beginning to run freely down his face. 'If his mother will still have me?'

Taking hold of her son, she gazed wonderingly at the perfect little body; the cap of black Bunting hair on top of the face that had all the hallmarks of being a replica of his father's; the long legs that indicated he would have the Bunting height; the two perfect little hands that were his father's pride and joy. Then she looked up at the father. 'There's nobody else I'll have,' she said, smiling through her tears and lifting a hand to him. 'I love you, Sam Bunting. And so does your son.'

He took her hand and fell to his knees, pressing it to his lips. 'And I love you. Both of you.' He laid his free hand on his son and dropped his head close to hers. 'Can you ever forgive me? I was such a fool. Everyday I stood and waited, wanting to come out and get you back. But I'd said some terrible things.' His eyes dropped to his son and she knew he was referring to his suggestion of an abortion. 'I thought you must hate me for that. I hated myself for it. And I dare not come to you, because I thought you would never be able to forgive me.'

'I'll forgive you . . . if you do something for us?'

'Anything,' he said, looking deep into her eyes and loving what he saw there.

'We both want to come home!' she expressed meaningfully.

'Of course . . .' He stopped short, glancing a grimace at the window. Then he broke into a smile. 'The impossible I can cope with,' he said, gazing proudly at the son he had brought into the world. 'But miracles will take a bit longer.' He dropped his forehead on to hers and they laughed together, as relief mingled with their love.

'I don't know what made you come, but I'm glad you did. I don't know what would have happened . . .' Her voice broke and tears misted the gaze that fell on her son. She recalled the moment she realized he was making that final push into the world, how she had thought he had been waiting for his father to arrive before being born. Well, she did not know about the baby, but she had the feeling that she had been waiting, holding back until Sam was there, not wanting their baby to be born into a fatherless state.

'Jean Bridges telephoned me. She was getting herself into a bit of a panic about not being able to let you know she was keeping Jenny overnight. She was worried about you getting anxious. She said you looked terrible first thing.'

Hannah grimaced. 'I don't think I looked that bad,' she said, but was only mildly offended as she realized how much she had to thank Jean for. She smiled. 'Thank you, Jean,' she said with feeling, then looked up into Sam's eyes with emotion spilling from her own. 'And thank you for battling the Land Rover through it all.'

He gave a grunt. 'The Land Rover got stuck less than halfway here. I had to do the rest on foot.'

'Oh Sam!' she gasped, imagining, with horror, the difficult journey he had undertaken . . . just for her. 'I love . . .' she began, then suddenly her body was once more clasped in pain and all she could do was cry out.

Sam grabbed the baby from her. 'What is it?' His voice was filled with panic and he had to ask the question, even though he could see she was in no position to reply. But it only took a few seconds for him to grasp what was happening. 'Twins!' he gasped. 'There's another!'

'Yes . . . yes,' she stammered, grabbing her thoughts together when tranquillity returned. 'The towels!' She pointed frantically at the clean white towels. 'Wrap him in one and get a drawer empty and put him in it. Hurry,' she insisted, when Sam hesitated uncertainly. She was very much aware she was going to need him again, and quickly, and the baby had to be put somewhere safe and warm before he could do anything for her.

Seven minutes later and exactly seventeen minutes after the first, the second baby Bunting came into the world.

This time Hannah was not kept waiting. She did not even have to ask the question. With fresh tears glistening in his eyes, Sam held his second perfect son up for her to see. 'Like peas in a pod,' he said.

*   *   *

Hannah awoke to the brightness of daylight enhanced by the whiteness of the snow-covered countryside. She turned her head to see Sam sitting in one of the pink moquette chairs. She smiled, recalling the sound of him struggling to get it up the narrow staircase late last night. He had refused to go into Jenny's room and leave her alone.

He returned her smile. 'How are you feeling?' he asked, coming over to the bed.

'Fine,' she said, feeling the warm glow of fulfilment deep inside. 'How are they?' She lifted her head to peer at the two drawers standing side by side, each supported by two kitchen chairs. 'Not a very auspicious start to life.'

Sam's face clouded. 'No,' he agreed, and glanced bleakly around the rather tatty room. 'If I hadn't been stupid enough to buy this place you wouldn't have had anywhere to run to,' he said, regret spilling from his voice and from the gaze he fastened to her face. 'If only I'd listened to you.'

'Hush!' She reached for his left hand and, as he sat down on the bed, pulled it close to her chest. 'You got this place for David and . . .' she glanced meaningfully at the two drawers, '. . . how things have turned out, it is going to be needed.'

'Oh no!' He shook his head insistently. 'Don't start me on the Bunting craze for heirs and continuing the line and the need to expand. I've learned my lesson there. From now on I shall just be very grateful for all that I've got. Besides . . .' he glanced over his shoulder at his sleeping sons, '. . . they might not take to farming.'

Hannah smiled at him fondly. She had not thought it possible for her love for him to grow and increase, but it had, just then, when she saw she had got her old Sam back. The man who had gone out and purchased Northgate Farm for no other reason than that it was up for sale, had gone. 'They might not,' she agreed, also glancing at her two identical sons. But she doubted it.

They were from good farming stock on both sides of their ancestors. It was in their blood, just as it was in hers and in Sam's. But she did not point that out to him. It would make him remember there might also be something else in their blood. Their sons could be like Jed, carrying the deformity without it showing, and now was not the time to remind him of that.

Lifting her arms, she pulled him down on to the bed to lie by her side. 'Do you know something, Sam Bunting? I know somebody who would be a very proud man today.'

He looked at her oddly, then smiled in slow understanding. 'Yes,' he said, emotion sparkling in his eyes and giving his voice a breathy quality.

She dropped her head on to his chest and tightened her arms around him. She did not know if the deformity would return in further generations, and she did not care. Because today Bunting's Claw had been wiped away for ever and ever. Future generations might have a deformed hand, but it would never again be mocked, never again be looked on as the devil's curse. Sam had not one, but two perfect little specimens to show the world that inside he was no different from any other man.

A smile pulled at her lips, as she listened to her husband's strong and steady heartbeat thumping beneath her ear, and considered the irony of it all. For George Bunting, the man whose arrogance had brought about the name of Bunting's Claw, would be the one who was strutting about with the proudest expression . . . if he had still been alive today.

THE END

RACHEL'S DAUGHTER
by Janet Haslam

Rachel Cooper's father kept his family in a state of terrified subservience. When he died – apoplectic with rage at
having been crossed, at last, by his son – Rachel was left
to care for her helpless mother and difficult young sister.
Raped by a local youth whose love she thought she had
gained, she gave birth in secret to a daughter who had
to be given away for adoption.

Hating and mistrusting all men, Rachel's only friend was
Polly, the local wise woman whose support and counsel
was to bring her through the worst of times. She managed
to develop a successful career and to win the love of a
good, kindly man, but her sufferings were not yet over.
At last, with courage and the will to survive, Rachel found
true fulfilment and a reconciliation with the daughter she
thought she had lost forever.

0 552 13976 9

A SELECTED LIST OF FINE NOVELS AVAILABLE
FROM CORGI BOOKS

THE PRICES SHOWN BELOW WERE CORRECT AT THE TIME OF GOING TO
PRESS. HOWEVER TRANSWORLD PUBLISHERS RESERVE THE RIGHT TO SHOW
NEW RETAIL PRICES ON COVERS WHICH MAY DIFFER FROM THOSE PREVIOUSLY
ADVERTISED IN THE TEXT OR ELSEWHERE.

❐	13933 5	THE LEAVING OF LIVERPOOL	Lyn Andrews	£3.99
❐	13718 9	LIVERPOOL LOU	Lyn Andrews	£3.99
❐	13829 0	THE SMOKE SCREEN	Louise Brindley	£3.99
❐	13255 1	GARDEN OF LIES	Eileen Goudge	£4.99
❐	13686 7	THE SHOEMAKER'S DAUGHTER	Iris Gower	£4.99
❐	13688 3	THE OYSTER CATCHERS	Iris Gower	£4.99
❐	13384 1	A WHISPER TO THE LIVING	Ruth Hamilton	£4.99
❐	13977 7	SPINNING JENNY	Ruth Hamilton	£4.99
❐	13872 X	LEGACY OF LOVE	Caroline Harvey	£4.99
❐	13917 3	A SECOND LEGACY	Caroline Harvey	£4.99
❐	13976 9	RACHEL'S DAUGHTER	Janet Haslam	£4.99
❐	14104 6	LOVE OVER GOLD	Susannah James	£3.99
❐	13758 8	PHANTOM	Susan Kay	£4.99
❐	13708 1	OUT TO LUNCH	Tania Kindersley	£3.99
❐	13706 5	THE GOLDEN TULIP	Rosalind Laker	£4.99
❐	13880 0	THE VENETIAN MASK	Rosalind Laker	£4.99
❐	13910 6	BLUEBIRDS	Margaret Mayhew	£4.99
❐	12641 1	THE SUMMER OF THE BARSHINKEYS	Diane Pearson	£4.99
❐	13904 1	VOICES OF SUMMER	Diane Pearson	£4.99
❐	13969 6	AN EMBARRASSMENT OF RICHES	Margaret Pemberton	£4.99
❐	13093 1	WHITE CHRISTMAS IN SAIGON	Margaret Pemberton	£4.99
❐	13921 1	ALICE DAVENPORT	Audrey Reimann	£4.99
❐	12803 1	RUTH APPLEBY	Elvi Rhodes	£4.99
❐	13636 0	CARA'S LAND	Elvi Rhodes	£4.99
❐	13346 9	SUMMER VISITORS	Susan Sallis	£4.99
❐	13545 3	BY SUN AND CANDLELIGHT	Susan Sallis	£4.99
❐	14106 2	THE TRAP	Mary Jane Staples	£4.99
❐	13888 6	A ROSE FOR EVERY MONTH	Sally Stewart	£4.99
❐	13834 7	THE DARKNESS OF CORN	Caroline Stickland	£3.99
❐	14118 6	THE HUNGRY TIDE	Valerie Wood	£4.99

All Corgi/Bantam Books are available at your bookshop or newsagent, or can be ordered
from the following address:
Corgi/Bantam Books
Cash Sales Department
P.O. Box 11, Falmouth, Cornwall TR10 9EN

UK and B.F.P.O. customers please send a cheque or postal order (no currency) and
allow £1.00 for postage and packing for the first book plus 50p for the second book
and 30p for each additional book to a maximum charge of £3.00 (7 books plus).

Overseas customers, including Eire, please allow £2.00 for postage and packing for the
first book plus £1.00 for the second book and 50p for each subsequent title ordered.

NAME (Block letters) ....

ADDRESS ....